FIREFLIES

LISE GOLD

To Karen,
My pen pal :)

Being deeply loved by someone gives you strength,
while loving someone deeply gives you courage.

— Lao Tzu

LONDON, UK

A film of condensed steam settled on the glass divider of the shower when Mia turned on the hot tap in her small bathroom. She stepped into the tub and scrubbed herself with a sponge, making sure to keep her head away from the running water so her hair wouldn't get wet. The extra half hour in bed had left her little time for a coffee and a blow-dry before she headed to the airport. Mia consciously checked her mood; she felt restless today. *Nothing new there.* Staying home for longer than a day never did her any good, and she was looking forward to the flight and seeing some of her favourite colleagues again after three very long days at home. But she'd made it through her weekend by reorganizing her walk-in closet, playing with the neighbours' cat, who kept on letting himself in through her balcony door, studying for her *'Arabic for beginners'* course, and by doing a bit of food shopping. It was hard to sleep at night when she wasn't exhausted, and last night had been no different, with only a meagre four hours of rest. Today was a new day though, and every morning felt like a small victory, especially now that she was over the eight-month mark of sobriety.

"You're doing well, Mia," she mumbled to herself. Relieved at the prospect of going back to work, she raised her index finger against the steamed-up glass and wrote: 'Day 248'.

"HURRY UP, Mia. We're five minutes behind."

Mia collected her paperwork, grabbed her case and followed her colleague towards cabin crew security at Heathrow Airport.

"Relax, Lynn. We've got plenty of time." She handed Lynn her clipboard. Over the course of thirteen years, Mia had done this thousands of times before and she knew exactly how long it would take to get to the briefing room. She unzipped her case, took her laptop out and put it in a tray, next to her liquids, before greeting her colleagues at the security gate. "Besides, I'm the one in charge so no one's going to lock the door on us."

Lynn sighed. "Yeah, you're right. Thank God for that." She giggled. "It's never a bad thing to be friends with your boss."

"I guess it isn't." Mia quickly scrolled through her phone, checking for her cabin crew members' birthdays, before she tossed it in the tray with her laptop. There were none today, so she wouldn't have to congratulate anyone in the briefing. "Who's the new captain? Do you know him?"

Lynn glanced over the time-sheet and frowned. "Captain Alfarsi. Never heard of him. You?"

"No," Mia said absent-mindedly. "I've never flown with him before." She had more important things to think about than the captain. "I'm glad we'll have some time in Dubai.

At least I'll be able to fit in a trip to the hairdresser." She rubbed her temples and closed her eyes for a brief moment, slightly worried about the growing headache just before a long-haul flight. "I couldn't get out of bed this morning, so I haven't even washed my hair and it's getting too long to handle without conditioner now."

"You can fit in six hairdressing appointments tomorrow if you want," Lynn replied cheerfully. "We're not flying back until after midnight." She held up a finger. "But just so you know, I'm not coming with you this time. Getting up at the crack of dawn this morning wasn't easy for me either, and I'm seriously looking forward to a lie-in." She adjusted her navy hat over her flaming red hair, making sure it balanced just a little to the left.

"Oh yeah? Heavy weekend?" Mia gave her favourite colleague a wry smile.

"Kind of." Lynn took out her laptop too and put it in a tray before placing the clipboard and her handbag in another. "Hey, you should come out with us next week. We've got a three night lay-over in New York and we're planning a big one." She made a drinking gesture and laughed.

"Going out isn't my thing, as you well know." Mia raised both arms as she walked through the body scanner. She picked up her belongings on the other side and zipped up her case. "In fact, it's probably my worst nightmare. I prefer to curl up with a good book and wake up fresh."

"Oh, come on. You always say that." Lynn lowered her arms and straightened her jacket as she joined Mia on the other side of the security gate. "I'm not going to keep asking you forever."

"No need to." Mia helped Lynn gather her things and led the way towards the staff quarters. "I'm not really a drinker."

"Boring." Lynn rolled her eyes. "You're my favourite

colleague and I can't even get drunk with you." She lowered her voice as they approached the briefing room. "Besides, you'll never get laid if you don't go out and meet new people."

Mia chuckled. "I'm quite happy by myself, thank you," she said, keeping her voice down. "And even if I wanted to meet someone, there are plenty of apps for that nowadays." She turned to Lynn with a sarcastic smile. "But so far, women have been nothing but trouble for me, so I think I might be better off alone." She swiped her card to open briefing room twenty-eight and walked to the front of the room before addressing the group of cabin crew members waiting for her.

"Hi everyone, sorry we're a little late. My name is Mia Donoghue and I'm the Sr. Purser today, in charge of cabin crew and passengers for flight number CY3044 to Dubai." She gave them a smile and a wave. "I know most of you already know myself and each other, but we have a couple of new faces here, so it would be nice if we could all introduce ourselves first."

The thirteen cabin crew members, including Lynn, called out their names and positions, one at a time. Mia knew most of them quite well by now, but the airline's recent expansion to three new destinations had meant that there were usually one or two new crew members she hadn't met before. After the introductions, she passed on and discussed information regarding the flight, the passenger list, special diets or allergies, VIP passengers and disgruntled or risk-list passengers. Then she distributed the workload and the tasks to the cabin crew members and spent fifteen minutes discussing safety and first aid scenarios, testing them on their knowledge.

"Okay, is everything clear? Are there any questions?" she asked, after all topics had been discussed. "Nothing?" She looked around the room. "Excellent, we've got a little bit of time left, so help yourselves to a coffee before we board."

2

LONDON, UK

Ava made her way to her assigned crew room for the tech crew briefing with her two senior officers. Only three weeks into her new job, she still had to get used to being in charge. Although she liked being number one, having men reporting into her, who were often much older, could be challenging. She took a deep breath as she gave herself an internal pep-talk. *You've got this, Ava. Isn't this what you thrive on? Being in control?*

"Morning, Captain," her first officer Jack Weldon, said. Jack and her second officer Frank Fletcher-Hunt were already sitting at the table, both sipping coffee from take-away cups. She felt a stir of unease as she walked up to the two men who, judging from the expression on their faces, had just been talking about her. She'd already flown with Jack and knew he wasn't going to cause any problems for now. He considered himself too funny and good-looking to feel threatened by a woman, and his borderline offensive jokes were harmless. Frank was more reserved. He looked like he was in his late-forties, which was older than usual for a second officer. His physique was skinny, his eyes hollow and tired, and his combed back dark hair was just starting to turn grey.

"Hi Jack, nice to be flying with you again. And Frank, great to meet you. I'm Captain Ava Alfarsi. Please call me Ava." She shook their hands before glancing at her watch. "Am I late?"

"Nope." Jack shook his head. "We're just early. Frank's missus dropped us off. She works here, at the airport."

"Oh yeah? What does she do?" Ava asked.

"Ground control." Frank's answer was short, as if he had no intention of making small talk with her.

Ava pretended she hadn't noticed. It would get better, she knew it would. Jack had already loosened up around her, and so would Frank, eventually. "Okay, great. I'll have time to get myself one of those, then," she said, pointing to their coffee cups. She walked over to the coffee machine, made herself an espresso and winced when she took a sip. The watery substance tasted nothing like espresso. "What the hell is this?"

"Yeah, about that..." Frank said, pointing at her cup. "Someone should have warned you about that machine. I haven't been near it in years." He held up his own artisan coffee, which smelled delicious, his eyes narrowing as he curiously observed Ava.

Ava had seen that look many times in the past weeks. They all thought she was too young for the job when they first met her. Her age, her looks, and the fact that she was a woman, didn't help gain respect from the people she flew with. Their first reaction was always to look her up and down in surprise, as if they'd expected her to be on the cover of some Middle-Eastern fashion magazine rather than in the cockpit. It wasn't right, but it was something she would have to get used to.

"Alright, let's get to it then," she said as she sat down, pushing her coffee cup away. "Dubai."

"Yep." Jack grinned. "Dubai is good. We always stay at the same hotel as the cabin crew when we're there."

Frank chuckled too, but he didn't say anything.

"Okay." Ava arched an eyebrow, ignoring the sexual implication of Jack's comment. "That's great. It will give me the opportunity to get to know some of them." She knew it wasn't common for captains to know all crew members personally, but she'd always preferred getting to know the people she flew with. It was nice to have the option to spend time with people other than her tech crew, who, in her experience, often had no interest in mingling with the cabin crew unless they thought they might get laid, which was clearly the case with Jack. She opened her leather binder containing the flight file, and turned towards her colleagues.

"I assume you two know each other, considering you're carpooling?" Both men nodded. "Okay. So, we can skip the formalities. Frank, we haven't flown together before. As I said, feel free to call me Ava. If we're out there and either of you notice something unusual, confusing, or something that seems incorrect, please bring it to my attention straight away so we can handle the situation. If you disagree with any of my decisions or actions, let me know immediately. Is that clear?"

"All clear," Jack said.

"Clear." Frank nodded.

"Great." Ava gave them both a nod. "Jack, are you okay to do take-off? I'll do the landing." She knew Jack was eager to step up, just like she had been when she was in his shoes.

"Absolutely," Jack said, trying to hide his excitement.

"Alright. You'll be doing take-off then." She made notes on the front page of the logbook as they went through their breaks schedules and divided the tasks they would perform during the flight. "Frank, can you please update us on the weather?"

"I sure can, Captain." Frank handed them both a printout and gave them an update on the weather forecast, which included the estimated wind speed and directions for each anticipated runway. They reviewed their route and discussed alternate routes in case of adverse weather conditions. Then they went through the aircraft performance, assessed its weight and balance, checking for any last-minute changes before deciding on how much fuel to take. Ava could tell both officers had flown the route before. They were confident in their answers and seemed relaxed about their upcoming flight.

Ava flipped a page and talked them through several company messages in the trip report. There was one wheelchair passenger and two babies, both in economy. "We also have five stand-by passengers on the list," she said. "I'm happy to take them all, if you are." Although she had the final say, she involved her officers in all the decision-making in the hope of establishing a good working relationship. So far, her efforts seemed to be appreciated, and she noticed that Frank's attitude towards her was slowly thawing. *Good. Maybe I'm getting somewhere with this one.*

3

LONDON, UK

"So, to continue our dating conversation," Lynn said as they made their way on to the aircraft, "have you ever considered going out with a man again?" She gave Mia a playful nudge. "I can most definitely recommend it. Last week I went out with a first officer from Falcon Air and he spent all night..."

"Gross. Spare me the details," Mia interrupted her. She held up a hand and grimaced as they entered the A380, greeting the cleaning crew, who were just about to leave. "I don't want to hear anything about your sex life, Lynn. It's disturbing. And as far as men are concerned, that chapter in my life closed a long time ago. Sixteen years ago, to be precise." She looked around the spacious aircraft and waved at one of the pilots she'd flown with many times before. "Hey Jack. You okay?"

Jack gave her a nod as he typed in the code to open the cockpit door. "All good," he said. "Just waiting for the new captain. She had to use the ladies room." Jack articulated the word *ladies* with a grin.

"Are you saying Captain Alfarsi is a woman?" Mia asked.

Then she shook her head. "Who cares? Good for her. And you should take it easy on the sarcasm, Jack. She's your boss, which means she's a better pilot than you are." Mia threw him a bottle of water and opened one for herself as she followed Lynn throughout the aircraft, checking the fire extinguishers, the first-aid box contents, the portable oxygen units and the crew rest area. Everything was fine, but then it usually was. She was glad to finally work for a quality airline. Mia had landed herself the job of senior purser just over a year ago, which meant that she now only worked in first class during most flights, taking care of her staff and the VIP passengers. With only twelve to twenty pax max, and therefore fewer call bells, it was a delight compared to the overfull economy cabins, filled with crying children and demanding passengers, who were, of course, always right. Besides the standard qualifications required for cabin crew, she'd been through a rigid training programme, including management training, paediatric and emergency first aid, fire marshal training, a wine course, a barista course, silver service training, etiquette training, and even a course on how to style her hair and apply her make-up in a certain way. The latter, she didn't care for normally, but the standards of first class demanded that all cabin crew looked pristine and fresh-faced at all times.

"Here." Lynn handed her one of the crew tablets, which stored all the information on their passengers and VIP's, including their likes and dislikes, diets or allergies, preferred choices in beverages and the purpose of their trip.

"Only one trouble-maker today," Mia said, thinking out loud as she scrolled through the list of passengers once more. She recognized the name on seat 3b immediately. "I'll take Lord McIver, I know how to handle him."

"Thanks." Lynn looked sideways, distracted by something at the front. "Oh my, look at that. Maybe you should take care of the tech crew too." She winked playfully, gesturing to the front of the aircraft.

Mia remained focussed on her tablet. "The tech-crew? I thought that was your thing? Bagging yourself a pilot so you can retire early?" She laughed at her own joke.

"Just look, Mia."

Mia reluctantly turned her head towards the front, where their new captain was lingering by the stairs leading up to the cockpit, looking at her phone. Mia's attention spiked when she caught a glimpse of the woman's face as she lifted her head and greeted some of the cabin crew members. She looked nervous, Mia thought. Or maybe she was just imagining that. Mia had met the occasional female captain before, but there hadn't been many. Even from afar, she could see that this woman was beyond stunning. She was tall, a bit taller than herself, Mia guessed, and had a slender figure. The hair underneath her cap was jet-black, pulled back into a long ponytail, and she had a cute smile. Mia tried to make eye-contact, so she could give her a welcome wave, but the captain didn't notice her. Instead, she walked up the short flight of stairs, opened the door to the flight-deck and disappeared inside.

Lynn turned back to Mia. "Holy shit, she's gorgeous," she whispered. "Don't you think?"

Mia didn't answer and turned back to her tablet, pretending to memorize her passengers' names.

"Come on, Mia. You have to serve her today. We hardly ever get female captains," Lynn said with a mischievous grin. "And although she's sizzling hot, that still won't do it for me, I'm afraid."

"Right." Mia rolled her eyes. "Just because you're a perv doesn't mean I am, and anyway, it's pretty dumb of you to assume that all female pilots are gay, don't you think?" She walked over to the bar to check if all the cabinets were stocked and put the bottles of champagne into the blast cooler. "Also, it's kind of offensive of you to imply that I'm so desperate that I'll launch myself onto any lesbian I come across."

Lynn ignored her friend's sneer, helping herself to a chocolate truffle from one of the fridges. "Whatever," she continued with a mouthful. "I still think you should look after the flight crew today. I'll go and see if the other crew members are ready for boarding."

4

LONDON, UK

"Cabin crew, take your positions." The captain's voice was soft, but confident.

Mia, Lynn, and their colleague Farik lined up at the first-class entrance to greet their passengers. After take-off, Farik would tend the bar whilst Mia and Lynn served dinner. Farik was a master in small-talk and cocktail making. After years of experience in five-star hotels and Michelin restaurants, he knew exactly what first-class passengers expected, and Mia was grateful not to have to mingle with the 'social drinkers' amongst them today. People always got way too drunk on flights.

"All set." Lynn checked her make-up in her hand mirror and straightened Farik's tie before she opened the curtain. Their first passenger was escorted in through the jet bridge that directly connected the airport lounge to the aircraft.

"Welcome Mrs. Huntington, it's great to have you back." Mia smiled at the elderly lady she'd had on her flights many times before.

"It's nice to see you too, Mia." Mrs. Huntington's escort handed Mia her hand luggage to put in the storage by her seat before she sat down in the spacious private cabin that included a small desk with stationery, a stocked mini bar, a touch-screen and a vanity locker with a toiletry bag, hair products and an extractable mirror. Upon request, the seat would be folded down after take-off, and topped with a memory foam mattress, two fluffy pillows, a down duvet and a sleep suit while the passenger had a shower or a drink at the bar. Mia switched on the screen for her passenger and pulled out the drinks table from the front cabin wall.

"Can I get you a mimosa? Or would you prefer something else today?"

"A mimosa would be wonderful, thank you."

Mia adjusted the pillow behind Mrs. Huntington's back and the old lady sighed as she sunk back into her chair.

"Thank you, Mia. That's very comfortable."

Mia nodded and smiled again. The constant smiling was challenging sometimes, but never with Mrs. Huntington. She had told Mia on one of her previous flights, that she was COO of her family business, with offices in London, New York, Hong Kong and Dubai. She was always in a good mood and a pleasure to have on the flight.

Today's flight was only seven hours, which meant their passengers would be less restless and demanding than on the long-haul flights. They would also be less likely to want their beds made, and that would save the cabin crew a lot of time. Mia made the mimosa and served it on a tray with a linen napkin and a selection of finger foods. She then turned to her more challenging passenger - Lord Calum McIver – who generally did not like anything about the service, yet he kept returning to their airline over and over again.

"Good morning Lord McIver. What can I do for you today?" Mia decided not to give him suggestions on beverages this time as he always found a way of laughing them off, even though he'd ordered the exact same thing before. He nodded briefly, then looked at her through his beady little eyes.

"Hello Mia. It's you again. Thank Christ, I was starting to worry I'd have to make do with the lazy one in the back." He didn't bother to lower his voice when Lynn passed his cabin. Mia ignored his sneer towards her friend and stretched her mouth into a dazzling smile instead.

"Can I get you a drink? And would you like to have your bed made after take-off?" Lord McIver let out a sarcastic chuckle and shook his head.

"My bed made? Did you really think I've come this far by sleeping all day?"

"I wouldn't think so," Mia answered politely, "but everyone needs some sleep every now and then." She handed him a leather binder with the drinks selection. Although it was only eight in the morning, she was certain about one thing: Lord McIver was always in the mood for a stiff drink. "We have a new Scotch, a twelve-year old double cask."

He took the binder and glanced over the list. "Very well. I shall try that one. I'll have a double."

Mia poured him a double, plus another generous slug of the fine Scotch, then walked over to the control panel and adjusted the temperature of his seat just enough to make him feel cosy and sleepy after his drink. It always worked. In seven hours' time he would wake up with his laptop open in front of him, asking her why she hadn't made his bed, but at least he wouldn't bother her with ridiculous demands throughout the day.

"I'M GOING to bring Jack his lunch," Mia said to Lynn after everyone had been served. "And I'll check if they want anything else."

"Ha! I knew you couldn't resist it. So, you *are* interested?" Lynn was on to her, she always was. Mia couldn't stand the way she seemed to know exactly what she was thinking, and she never held back when it came to verbalizing her thoughts.

"Not in the least," Mia retorted without sounding too convincing. "Thought I'd relieve you of one of your duties for once. You should be grateful."

Without thinking, she went into the crew toilet to check her hair and make-up. She still looked presentable, although she never liked seeing the excessive eyeliner and red lipstick in the mirror. It made her feel like a clown from time to time, but the airline had strict policies, and she'd gotten used to them now. Her long, dark brown hair was done up in a braided knot, topped off with a navy and gold scrunchie that matched her fitted navy skirt, white shirt and navy blazer. Thankfully, she didn't have to wear her heels and hat during service, but after landing, she'd have to put the painful pumps back on her swollen feet, before thanking the passengers for their custom on their way out. Mia stared back at her brown eyes in the middle of her heart-shaped face and gave herself a smile. She was only thirty-three, but the make-up made her look older and that was a good thing. Passengers tended to put more trust in the more mature looking flight attendants, especially in first class. She washed her hands, feeling slightly nervous before she made her way to the cockpit.

LONDON, UK TO DUBAI, UAE

"It's Mia here. I have your lunch, Jack." Mia spoke loud and clear through the intercom. She took a step aside for the intercom camera to register there was no one behind her and typed in the code to open the door to the cockpit when the light turned green. The captain was the first to turn around when she entered.

"Hi Captain. It's nice to meet you." Mia handed Jack his tray and held out her hand to formally greet her.

The captain studied her name tag and shook her hand. "Mia, of course. You're the senior purser. It's a pleasure to meet you. I'm Ava Alfarsi. Please call me Ava."

Mia noticed that the captain looked relaxed, now that she was safely tucked away in her cockpit. She felt an unusual flutter in her belly when their eyes locked.

"Okay, Ava. I'll be back in an hour with Frank's lunch, and in two hours with yours. Is that okay?" Food for the tech crew was never served at the same time, to prevent a food-poisoning outbreak, so the cabin crew had a strict schedule to adhere to when it came to flight deck service.

Ava held her gaze before retracting her hand. It was an

elegant hand, like the hand of a piano player, or an artist, with long fingers, short polished nails and a slender wrist.

"That's great, thank you," she said. "Could I have an extra water too, please? Sparkling, if possible."

"Sure." Mia smiled as she looked into Ava's green eyes. They were so light, they seemed almost otherworldly. For a moment, she forgot what she was there for. Ava's hair was shimmering under the light above her, and she looked much more approachable now, without the formal uniform cap she was wearing earlier. Her skin was unusually pale compared to her jet dark hair, with only a small natural blush on her high cheekbones. She looked like she was of Middle Eastern descent, Mia thought. *Wow. She really is gorgeous.*

"I'm sorry." Mia shook her head and turned to the senior officers. "Frank? Can I get you anything else? Jack?"

"Water for me too." Frank held up a hand. "Sparkling with lemon, a dash of elderflower cordial and two ice-cubes."

Ava turned to him, raised an eyebrow and let out a sarcastic laugh. "Leave the damn lemon and elderflower, Frank. I'm sure Mia's got better things to do than to prepare your girlie drinks." She regretted the words as soon as they were out – the half joke would do her no favours with Frank, but she didn't like his tone when he was talking to Mia. She looked up at Mia again, her eyes fixed on her face, as if she was trying to read her mind. Mia stood nailed to the ground, unable to look away. There was something about the captain's intense stare that scared her and intrigued her at the same time.

"Yes, of course. I'm sorry. Just water is fine," Frank said with a sour face, interrupting their moment.

"Don't be sorry." Mia stepped away from them and

turned at the cabin door. "It's not a problem. I'll be back in an hour."

"And another black coffee for me!" Jack said, as he tried to wave her back. But Mia was gone and had forgotten he was even there.

MIA SLIPPED into the toilet and leaned against the wall, taking a deep breath. *Fuck. What was that?* She turned on the tap and splashed some cold water over her face, then remembered too late that she was covered in make-up. *Okay Mia, get yourself together. She might be the sexiest woman you've ever seen but that doesn't mean she's gay, or even remotely interested in you.* "Calm," she said to her reflection as she carefully dabbed her face dry. "Just stay calm and do your job. You're in charge today."

"So, what's the new captain like?" Lynn asked, walking past Mia with a trolley full of Arabic coffee, stuffed dates and fresh baklava.

Mia looked down at her shaking hands as she tried to pour sparkling water into a glass with elderflower cordial, lemon and ice. "She's okay. Nice."

Lynn stopped, walked two steps back and studied her face. "Just nice, huh?" She shot Mia a cheeky grin before she walked on to serve coffee to a couple in the back row.

LONDON, UK TO DUBAI, UAE

Ava settled back in her seat, relaxing a little after a couple of hours in cruise mode.

"Is this your first Dubai trip?" Jack asked. His take-off had been flawless, and he was in a great mood. By now, Ava was even warming to him a little. Frank was still a bit grumpy but didn't seem too bad either. He'd finally started talking after boredom had gotten the better of him.

"No, I've done Dubai a couple of times, but not often. It's my first flight there with this airline, though." She smiled. "But don't worry guys, I think I remember where it is."

Both Jack and Frank laughed.

"You'd better." Jack nodded towards the cabin. "Have you met any of the cabin crew members yet?" he asked. "A couple of us are meeting up in New York next week for a night out. I saw you were on the schedule too, you should join us." He winked. "No flying for forty-eight hours, you know what that means."

"Thanks for the invite." Ava smiled as she performed her navigation checks and updated her notes. "I'd love to take you up on that, but I think I might be busy."

"Ah!" Jack wiggled his eyebrows. "So, you're going on a date? Any Tinders lined up?" When Frank nudged him, he suddenly realised he was being too nosey and, although Ava wasn't in the least offended, it was, after all, his captain he was speaking to. "I'm sorry," he said. "Are you married? Or seeing someone?" He shook his head. "I'm, sorry, I didn't mean to..."

"No, it's fine," Ava interrupted him. "I'm single. And I'm not on any dating apps either, just meeting a friend, maybe." She kept her tone as friendly as possible, without giving too much away. It wasn't any of his business, but she didn't blame him for asking. They were going to be spending a lot of time together after all, and it would become very boring without small talk. The buzzer zoomed as the senior purser made her presence known and entered the cockpit again. Ava turned to take another good look at the attractive woman with the dark hair and big, brown eyes. That was one of the perks of her job, she had to admit. Eye-candy. Not that many of the cabin crew were gay, and even if they were, she didn't date on the job. Hell, she didn't date much in general. She smiled and took the dinner tray that Mia handed her, studying her face. *Is she okay?* Mia's eyes were wide, staring at her as if she'd just seen a ghost. It was the kind of look Ava had seen before, but it always surprised her. Ava never considered herself to be good-looking, although she was told she was on a regular basis. She didn't dedicate much time to her appearance, as opposed to the cabin crew, and she didn't look in the mirror very often either. She was a pilot after all, behind the scenes and out of sight.

"Here's your dinner, Captain. I mean, Ava."

Ava took the tray and placed it on the folding table in her armrest. The sight of Mia made her heart skip a beat for the third time that day. She seemed a bit nervous, coming into the cockpit, and she'd repeatedly forgotten their orders and had brought Frank, who was a vegetarian, a sirloin steak only an hour ago. There was a moment, Ava was sure of that, in which they seemed to communicate on a whole different level, trying to work each other out with nothing more than a fleeting look. She smiled. *This is weird.* Ava continued to stare up at Mia, wondering why she was unable to take her eyes off of her. Mia was a bit shorter than herself and had a great figure. Her skin was tanned, and she had a nice glow to her cheeks. *Or was she perhaps blushing?* Her eyes were a dark hazel colour, almost hidden by her dilated pupils, and there was a small scar right underneath her hairline on the left side of her forehead, barely visible underneath her make-up. Ava swallowed hard and pulled herself together.

"Thank you, Mia. This looks great. I guess I'll see you in Dubai."

DUBAI, UAE

va watched Mia walk in front of her towards the minibus that would take them to their hotel, just a short drive from the airport. Usually, the tech crew and the cabin crew stayed in separate hotels, but Dubai was an exception, as the hotel they would stay at was owned by the airline's mother company. *Good God, she's sexy. I hope I get to speak to her.* Ava noticed the slight wiggle in her hips as she rolled her small suitcase alongside her. Mia's reaction when they'd met in the cockpit hadn't gone unnoticed, and the strangest thing was that Ava couldn't help but feel a little shaken up herself. It was very unusual for her to feel an instant attraction, but there was clearly some weird pull between them, as she couldn't seem to stop herself from staring at Mia's behind. It was hard to gauge Mia's sexuality. She was in uniform and looked like most other flight attendants on their airline. But something about the look in Mia's eyes had told her the interest was mutual. Ava shook her head and rolled her eyes, cursing herself for lusting after one of the cabin crew members, only three weeks into her job. *Jesus, where did this come from?*

It was like the mere sight of Mia had awoken a rush of excitement in her, and she was dying to know more about the dark-haired purser. She watched Mia laugh as she got on the bus with her colleagues. Her laugh was loud and genuine, as she shared in the fun with the red-headed purser.

Ava took her hat off for a moment, ran a hand through her hair and put it back on. After check-in, she'd finally be able to rid herself of her uniform, which was way too warm for the Emirati heat. That was one of the strict airline rules; wearing the uniform was mandatory until you reached your hotel. They weren't allowed to take off their jackets, their hats, or even their badges until they reached the privacy of their rooms. Ava was looking forward to a swim, an early night, and maybe a couple of hours of sightseeing tomorrow to celebrate her first flight to Dubai in her brand-new job.

"Captain?"

Ava looked up and realised she was standing in front of the minibus, lost in her own thoughts. The driver was trying to get her attention, his hand reaching out to take her suitcase.

"Sorry," she said, smiling at him gratefully as she handed him her luggage. "I think I'm tired."

"That's quite alright." The driver stacked her case on top of the others in the luggage compartment and turned to the crew in the bus. "All aboard people? I'm off the clock in half an hour so anyone who's still in the toilets will have to hitch hike." There was a mumble from the crew, and the bus driver laughed at his own joke as he drove away from Dubai airport, towards their hotel.

"Who's up for going to a belly dancing performance tonight?" Lynn shouted through the bus. "Omar's Palace does late-night dinner and a show on Thursdays."

The crew didn't look too excited, most of them too wiped out to speak.

"I am", Farik shouted back. "I do love me some belly dancing." He stood up and shook his hips. "I took some classes in my teens. Is there a competition?"

"No competition." Lynn rolled her eyes. "You're supposed to watch, not steal the limelight. Besides, I don't think they'll appreciate male belly dancers here."

"Don't be so dramatic, negative Nancy," Farik sneered. "The locals are a lot less homophobic than you think. Believe me, I know."

"Will you please sit down, sir?" the driver asked over the microphone. "And put your seatbelt on, thank you. You're not in the club yet, with all due respect."

Farik sighed and sat back down, securing his seat belt.

"I'M IN," Mia said, turning to Lynn. She felt tired too but knew she wouldn't be able to sleep straight away. Besides, Dubai nights were never crazy nights. The only places that sold alcohol were the swanky hotels, nightclubs and bars in Jumeirah, and a night out there came with a hefty price tag that most of the cabin crew couldn't afford. Omar's Palace sounded safe.

"We're in too," Sammy, their newest cabin crew member yelled from the back of the bus, referring to herself and her colleague sitting next to her.

"Great." Lynn handed Sammy her phone. "I'll send you the details later if you give me your number." She leaned over the edge of the seat in front of her and tapped Jack's shoulder. "Do you guys want to come? Frank? Jack? Captain?"

"Sure," Ava heard herself say. "Why not?" Although

socializing was the last thing she felt like doing right now, she told herself that she needed to get to know the crew a little better. The fact that the beautiful brunette would be there too was a bonus, of course.

"I'll come," Jack followed.

"Me too," Frank said. That was no surprise to Mia. Frank usually followed Jack around, and Jack in turn, tended to follow around any captain who would let him.

"Fantastic." Lynn smiled. "I'll text you, Jack. Can you pass the message on when the booking's been confirmed, please?"

Suddenly, there seemed to be more interest in the enterprise, as if people were scared of missing out on a dinner with the new captain. Hands were raised, and there was mumbling back and forth between crew members.

"Okay." Lynn laughed, after double-checking the list of names, just before they arrived at their hotel. "We've got sixteen people for dinner now. That's more than we've ever had in one room after service hours, so I'll try my best to get a table. If not, I'll see you all at reception at nine and we'll figure something out then." She sat back again, put the list in her handbag and turned to Mia, lowering her voice. "Looks like you might get some time with the captain tonight."

DUBAI, UAE

Mia took off her hat, dropped her case on the floor and fell onto the bed. She felt exhausted but couldn't help but wonder if the pool was still open. She looked at her watch. It was almost eight o'clock, and a refreshing swim was exactly what she needed right now to wake herself up before dinner. She got up again, opened the curtains and stepped out onto her balcony, facing the pool. It was quiet, but the gates were still open. Just as she was about to turn around to put on her swimsuit, she caught a glimpse of someone diving in. *Is that...?* Mia leaned over the railing to get a better look at the woman who was now swimming right underneath her. *Oh God, it's her. It's the captain.* The simple black swimsuit she was wearing had a surprisingly sexy back, cut out entirely and only held in place by two thin straps, crossing just below her shoulder blades.

Ava swam fast, with long strokes and excellent technique, Mia noticed. Just like her sister, who was an avid swimmer, Mia had been on the school swimming team herself, but she'd never be able to keep up with this one. Ava made a flip-turn under water and pushed herself off the wall of the pool, keeping her body in a perfectly straight line as she raced through the water in the opposite direction. Mia sat down in one of the balcony chairs and watched her as she swam, indulging in Ava's impressive strokes and her even more impressive body. *Should I join her in the pool? She'll probably think I'm stalking her after all that awkwardness today.* Mia cursed herself once more for coming across as a nervy newbie. She'd returned to the cockpit twice, forgetting Frank's coffee on both occasions, and she'd messed up the orders, serving him a steak while he was actually a vegetarian. Finally, she was so embarrassed that she'd had to send Lynn in to deal with Frank's lunch.

Why do I care what she thinks of me? Anyway, her guess was that Ava had a pretty wife sitting at home, waiting for her. Or husband. That was a possibility, of course. But somehow, Mia had the feeling that Ava was on her team. Maybe it was the look she had given her when she'd introduced herself. It wasn't flirtatious, but it wasn't like the way straight women looked at her either.

Ava had apparently decided she'd had enough. She swam towards the steps and got out in one fluid motion, directing her gaze up to the balconies facing the pool. Mia lowered her head and dove below the balcony railing, remembering too late that the balcony wall was made of glass.

"Fuck!" she whispered, turning her face down to the floor. She crawled backwards, into the safety of her room, trying to avoid showing her face. Not that there could have been any mistake about her identity. She still had her purser jacket on, and the only other female who had the same one was Lynn, who had fiery red hair. Mia leaned back against her bed and buried her face in her hands. *Maybe she didn't see me. Maybe I got away with it...* Why hadn't she just waved at Ava like any other normal person would? Why had she crawled backwards, into her room like a...? Like a what? Not even other species did that. It wasn't like she was socially awkward or had something to hide. She carefully approached the balcony again, making sure to stay behind the curtain this time and saw that Ava was now lying down on one of the sun loungers, catching her breath.

Feeling annoyed with herself, Mia stood up and walked over to the bathroom, where she got into the shower instead. There was no way she was going down there now.

DUBAI, UAE

"Hi guys," Jack shouted over the music, stealing a seat next to Sammy, the new girl.

Mia jumped at the sound of his voice, looking over her shoulder to see if he'd brought Ava along. She gave Jack a quick wave, then curiously glanced around the restaurant. She didn't recognize Ava immediately, although she certainly stood out in the crowd. Despite her casual attire, consisting of jeans and a white t-shirt, Ava was by far the most stunning woman in the room. Mia cursed herself for not making more of an effort, but she'd been too mortified to think straight. After her faux-pas on the balcony, she'd had a quick shower during which she'd avoided getting her hair wet because blow-drying it would simply take too much time. She'd forgotten to take out the topknot and she realised she was still wearing the heavy layer of make-up that made her whole appearance look way too dressy when combined with her simple black dress.

"Hey." Mia tried to sound casual as she waved Ava over, she wasn't even convincing herself. Had she forgotten how to use her voice?

"Hey yourself." Ava squeezed in next to Mia on the bench behind the group table. "Are you having a good time? How's the food?"

"It's fun," Mia said, surprised that Ava seemed determined to sit down next to her. "The food is mediocre, I suspect we might be in a tourist trap, but the atmosphere is great." Mia offered Ava a plate of falafel on a bed of houmous and salad. "The performance hasn't started yet, so you're just in time. They'll bring more food out in a minute."

"Great. I like belly dancing. If they're good," Ava added, putting some falafel on one of the spare plates.

"Sounds like you know your belly dancing," Mia said, trying to avoid Ava's gaze. It made her nervous, looking into those green eyes, and she didn't want to come across as an overly keen puppy, because that was bound to happen if she looked into them for too long.

"I dabble." Ava laughed. "Just kidding. I don't belly dance, but I used to watch it a lot when I was a kid, and I can tell a good performance from a bad one." She looked at her watch. "I'm sorry we're late. We had trouble getting a cab. There must be some conference in town, there's so much traffic." She smiled, making Mia go weak in all sorts of places. "I'm glad you guys invited us out tonight. I'm not sure if I could have coped with just Jack and Frank. As educated men go, those two are quite basic in their conversational skills, if you know what I mean." She held up a hand. "No offence to either of them of course, I mean, they're great guys and..."

"No need to explain," Mia interrupted her. "I know what they're like. All I can say is that I don't envy you, having to put up with those two and the likes of them twenty-four-seven. I don't think anyone here would actually be interested in them, apart from maybe..." She cocked her head and tried to gauge the progress of Jack's attempt to wrap Sammy around his little finger. He was going all out, leaning in on his elbows opposite her, showing off his inherited Rolex Submariner. He was flexing his muscles while he pretended to listen and acted an 'I find you hilarious' laugh. Sammy seemed bored. Mia looked from Jack to Ava and back, making sure Ava had spotted the failed attempt too. "Actually, I think even Sammy's sick of him already. Wow." She sat back, processing the scene. "I have to say, I didn't see that one coming. Jack usually gets his way when it comes to women."

Ava laughed. "You're funny, Mia." Her eyes wandered to the stage, where a dancer had just appeared, shimmying to the staccato beats under a warm spotlight. She moved forward with her arms spread out, shaking her shoulders when she reached the edge of the stage. The audience clapped and cheered for the dancer, who was scantily clad in a red and gold skirt and a beaded choli top. "She's good."

"How can you tell?" Mia asked as she looked at the beautiful woman with hair hanging down to her thighs. The dancer lowered her arms and reached for the sheer red veil on her skirt before spinning around at the exact moment the tambourines and flutes started to play. "I mean, I think she's great, but then I think all of them are great. The way they move, it's beautiful to watch."

"Look at her hips." Ava moved a little closer, so Mia could hear her over the loud music. "Can you see that nothing is moving, apart from her hips?" The belly dancer was shimmying again, with her back to the audience. "It's really hard to isolate your movements like that."

Mia wiggled in her seat in an attempt to test the theory and laughed. "Never mind. It might be better if I try this in my hotel room tonight. But yeah..." she studied the graceful movements of the dancer, now swaying her hips, following the shape of an eight as her arms and fingers all moved independently. "I can see where you're coming from, it looks very technical, actually."

"It's really hard, and one of the oldest art forms." Ava put an arm around Mia's back and placed both hands on her waist. "It's a great way to train your core, especially these muscles, right here." A warm glow spread between Mia's thighs when Ava gave her abdominals a quick squeeze. She tensed and turned her head to look at Ava. Their faces were close as her gaze dropped down to Ava's mouth for a split second. *Fuck.* Mia realised she wanted to kiss her.

"Right," she mumbled, picking up her tea glass. It was empty, and she hoped Ava hadn't noticed. "I might have to sign up for some classes then."

Ava settled back in her seat and watched the show as if nothing had happened. "You don't look like you need the exercise, Mia. But I've got the feeling you might be good at it. You've got a natural sway in your hips when you walk."

Mia raised her eyebrows, even more perplexed now. "Do I?" *Jesus, if that wasn't flirting...* Although she was a bit out of practice, she was pretty sure that it was.

"Yes. You do." Ava smiled. "It's cute."

Mia's heart was beating fast as she felt heat creep up her neck towards her face. She heard Jack and Frank clapping and cheering along with the rest of the crew. Despite the absence of alcohol in the venue, the crowd were getting rowdy now, as two more dancers dressed in red came on to the stage. Mia dug deep to think of a witty reply, anything to keep their conversation going.

"Where are you from?" she asked, annoyed with herself for not being able to come up with anything better. Ava's presence had turned her brain to mush, and right now, it was the only thing she could think of.

"Cambridge," Ava said, watching the show. "But I live in London."

"I mean your heritage." Mia tried to relax, but she was so self-conscious, sitting next to the hot captain who had just touched her intimately and flirted with her, that her voice sounded rather shaky when she spoke. "You don't look English."

"My parents are from Jordan." Ava looked at her briefly, before turning back to the stage. "They live in the UK though."

"Do you speak Arabic?" Mia watched the three dancers in red swirl around, moving in unison.

"Yeah. I'm not fluent, but I do. My parents made me take classes, so I wouldn't lose my conversational skills as I grew older and only hung out with English kids. I'm glad they did now. It's useful, especially in my job, with all the traveling. I can't write in Arabic script but I can read a little." Ava leaned in to her slightly, and Mia did the same, almost melting into her seat the moment their arms touched. She didn't move back, and neither did Ava.

"My turn to ask questions now," Ava said with a cheeky grin, clapping when the first performance was over. "Do you live in London?"

"Yeah." Mia didn't dare look at her now. Not now that they were sitting so close. She was afraid she'd lose her ability to speak if her eyes met Ava's again. Those amazing green eyes that sucked her in and captivated her. "But I grew up in a small village just outside..."

"Hey, Captain!" Jack interrupted their conversation from the other end of the table. "I mean, Ava," he corrected himself. "Have you met Sammy yet?" He waved for Ava to come over. "Her brother is a pilot too, for Bizz Air. I think you might have flown with him, a couple of years ago."

Ava let out a soft sigh, too subtle for anyone to notice, apart from Mia.

"I've got to go and mingle. Sorry." She put a hand on Mia's arm. "But I'm sure I'll speak to you later. I'd like to know more about you."

"Sure." Mia managed to hide her disappointment and smiled when Lynn swapped places with Ava. "We'll speak later."

THE REST of the night passed in a haze. Mia tried to focus on the dancers and Lynn's rattling next to her, but her eyes kept wandering back to Ava, who was sitting at the end of the table talking to Jack, Sammy and some other cabin crew members. Occasionally, Ava would cast her a fleeting glance too, as if she was looking for an opportunity to get her old seat back.

"I think I'm going to head back to the hotel," Mia finally said to Lynn. "I can barely keep my eyes open. Are you going back with the others or do you want to share a cab?"

Lynn yawned, just as Mia did the same. "I'm coming with you. I'm exhausted too." She looked around the table. Everyone was starting to look tired now. "Come on, let's get out of here before they make me arrange taxis for everyone."

10

DUBAI, UAE

Dubai was hot and sunny, but that was nothing new. Mia pulled her baseball cap further over her forehead as she walked along the waterfront in Bur Dubai, the old part of town. Her long-sleeved white top and white linen trousers were her go-to outfit every time she came here. They covered enough skin to be considered decent and the fabric kept her as cool as she could possibly be in the desert heat. Because of her long, brown hair, people always assumed she was a local, and so she managed to avoid the overtures of the rowdy salesmen once again as she passed through the souk. She found her way through the maze-like streets of Al Bastakiya, the oldest residential neighbourhood of Dubai, without any trouble. The houses were built close to one another on zig-zagged streets, ensuring shade in the hot summer months. Mia strolled through the whitewashed alleyways, passed mud-bricked houses topped with wind towers, and tranquil private court-yards with feature fountains, until she reached her favourite local teahouse. It was located outside on a street corner, shaded by a roof that was covered with purple bougainvillea. The low couches were comfortable, the teas and sweets to die for, and the staff were friendly and polite. Mia loved coming here, and she smiled as she greeted the waiter, who recognized her from previous visits.

Lynn was already waiting for her on a corner couch and waved when she saw her.

"Your hair looks nice." Lynn stood up, removed Mia's cap and ran her hand through her newly styled hair. "Wow, sharp cut. They seem to do a decent job here." She looked regretful as she tugged at her own red locks. "Maybe I should have come along after all."

Mia laughed and put her cap back on. "As if anything apart from food or cocktails could ever get you out of bed."

"You're right." Lynn grinned. "I did have an amazing ten hours of beauty sleep. It's the hotel beds here. They're just so lush, it's like sleeping on a cloud." She picked up the menu and bit her lip in concentration as she tried to work out what was what. "So, last night was fun, right?"

"Yeah. It was great." Mia looked at the menu too. "I think everyone had a good time."

"I know. I can't believe I managed to get almost everyone together." Lynn flipped the menu to the next page, where she pointed out the mint tea with honey to the waiter. "Tea?" she asked, turning to Mia.

"Yes. For me too please. And some baklava if they have it."

"Oh, and some kunafa please," Lynn added, turning to the waiter.

The waiter nodded as he wrote down their order. "Great choice, Madam." He placed a small silver tray on the low table in front of them with teaspoons, a pot of runny honey and a bowl of dates.

"So, about the captain... Eva Alfresi?" Lynn raised an

eyebrow while giving Mia a mocking stare. "You spoke to her last night, didn't you? How come you never told me about your conversation on our way back?"

"You were sleeping," Mia replied dryly.

Lynn held up a hand. "Okay, fair enough." She paused, narrowing her eyes. "So? What's she like? Is she nice? Was I right? Is she gay?"

Mia laughed. "Yes, I spoke to her and yes, she's nice. Just nice though, that's all there is to it," she lied. "And her name is Ava, actually. Ava Alfarsi."

"I know, I'm just messing with you." Lynn took the generous glass of mint tea from the waiter and stirred in some honey. "Sexy name though. Sounds mysterious, don't you think?" A smile tugged at the corners of her mouth.

"Stop teasing me, Lynn." Mia took her own tea, thanking the waiter in Arabic. "I only spoke to her for about five minutes."

"And?"

Mia looked up to the sky in despair when she realised Lynn had no intention of giving up her interrogation. "Okay, she's hot. Is that what you want me to say? Sure, I'll say it. Ava is smoking hot. You were right, she's so my type. But come on, Lynn. You don't really think she's gay, single and interested in me, all at the same time, do you? That would be too good to be true and I'm not that lucky. Besides, purser-pilot romances never end well; we've both seen our fair share of those."

"Never stopped me from trying." Lynn grinned. "Hey, I'm just saying, it's hard to meet people outside our industry when we're always away. Captain Alfarsi is going to be on our flight back, and now we've established that you like her...." She pointed a finger at Mia. "I suggest you take the burden of serving the flight crew again and try to talk to her some more." Lynn sighed when Mia didn't answer. "Please, Mia. What if she *is* gay? I kind of get that feeling with her. And what if she does like you? It's clear that you more than like *her*. You get all fidgety when we talk about her."

Mia immediately stopped folding her napkin over and over again and gave Lynn a warning look. "Okay Lynn, point taken. I'll try to make an effort with her. Now, can we please talk about something else? The weather? Your latest obsession with Captain whomever it is this time? Anything but my love life, okay?"

11

DUBAI, UAE

"Hey, you."

Mia immediately recognised the warm voice behind her and turned around. Ava was wearing jersey shorts and a grey t-shirt. The sweat marks covering the entire front of her shirt indicated that she'd been running for some time. A jolt of joy shot through Mia's core when their eyes met.

"Ava. I didn't expect you here."

Ava laughed. "You mean here, on the hotel grounds, where half of the crew goes running? I was kind of hoping I'd bump into you." She cocked her head, studying Mia. "You look different today."

"If you mean that I'm all sweaty and blotchy from my run then yes, I suppose I look different." Mia chuckled.

"No, you look nice different." Ava shook her head. "Sorry, I didn't mean to imply that you didn't look nice yesterday, it's just that your face... it's so pretty without make-up."

"Oh that." Mia blushed. "Thank you, I suppose." She

gave her a nervous smile and bent forward to stretch, avoiding Ava's eyes that were looking her up and down. She suddenly regretted wearing nothing but a crop top with her three-quarter length running tights, especially now that she was standing next to Ava. "Are you done with your run yet?" she asked, trying to sound casual.

"Yeah." Ava stretched along with her. "But I'll do another round if you'll run with me."

Mia was still trying to catch her breath from her own run that had been longer than usual. She wasn't sure if she could do another minute because her legs felt like they were about to give way underneath her.

"Sure," she heard herself say. "If you think you can keep up with me."

That brought a smile to Ava's face. "Okay, let's go."

Mia had to admit that Ava seemed much more athletic than herself, but there was no way she was going to give in. She sprinted ahead of her and laughed when Ava immediately speeded up too, passing her as she jumped over a low bench.

"I NEED TO SIT DOWN." Mia gasped as she collapsed on the lawn. "You won," she panted. "I should have known you would."

Ava lay down next to her in the grass, equally out of breath. "That was probably my personal record," she said, laughing. "Believe me, I don't normally run this much. I was just trying to impr..." She shook her head, swallowing her words. "I mean I happen to like a bit of healthy competition."

Mia steadied herself on her elbows and looked sideways

at her gorgeous colleague. *Was she just about to say that she was trying to impress me?*

"I've noticed." She chuckled. "And apparently, you don't like to lose." Mia stole a glance at Ava's chest that was heaving up and down. Her sports bra was showing through the thin fabric of her t-shirt, and she couldn't help but wonder what she would look like without it.

"You're right." Ava grinned. "But now I'm so tired, I think I could fall asleep right here and now." She opened one eye while she shielded her face from the sun. "Do you run every day?"

"No, only when I feel like it, but I had way too many sweets with my tea earlier today so wanted to burn off some calories. That and I was starting to feel sleepy, so I thought it might help." Mia stretched her arms out above her head. "But you seem quite the sporty type. Running, swimming..." She realised she'd given herself away as soon as the word had left her mouth. "I mean, I saw you swimming last night. You're good," she quickly added.

"I knew you were watching me swim. I saw you too." Ava gave her a teasing smile. She paused for a moment, then said: "So, do you have any plans for the rest of the afternoon? You're not flying back until late, right?"

Mia's heart skipped a beat. *Is she trying to ask me out? Oh God, she's asking me out.* She paused to think before answering. "Depends on what your plans are," she said with a slight hesitation in her voice.

"Oh, I didn't mean..." Ava sat straight up, crossed her legs and gave her an apologetic smile, waving her hand. "I mean, I would, of course, but I'm flying back at six. We're not on the same flight anymore." She sighed, annoyed with how clumsy she sounded. "I've been called in for another flight instead, so I'm leaving in an hour. One of the captains had a family emergency."

"Oh, I'm sorry, I..." Mia's cheeks went bright red. "This is so embarrassing. I thought you were hinting at doing something together. Please forget I ever said that." She cringed, wishing she could make it unsaid. She wanted to sink into the ground and disappear.

"No, it's fine." Ava moved a little closer and put a reassuring hand on Mia's. "I was just making small talk, but I would love to go for dinner or do something next time we're flying together. I just can't today."

"Where are you flying to?" Mia asked in an attempt to divert the subject away from her own stupidity.

"I'm doing a flight to Kuala Lumpur with a forty-eight-hour layover before returning to the UK."

Mia managed a smile, not feeling any less embarrassed. "Nice. I love going there but for some reason they hardly ever schedule me in for Malaysia."

"I seem to be in luck then." Ava stood up. "Or maybe not. Who knows? I might be missing out." She smiled and walked back to the hotel, leaving Mia sitting on the lawn, staring up at her.

"ALL ABOARD, peeps! We're off to terminal one in five minutes!" The bus driver waved from the lobby entrance. "And remember, stay safe and don't forget to call me when you're home."

Mia was lingering by the reception desk in a long summer dress, waiting for Lynn, when Ava joined the Kuala Lumpur flight crew. Mia observed her as she handed the driver her suitcase. She was in uniform and looked smoking hot in her sharp-cut blazer and her pilot's cap.

"What about you, Mia?" The driver looked Mia up and down. "Where's your uniform? And where's your hair bun? It didn't fly away, did it?"

"No, Henry." Mia managed a chuckle at one of his many mediocre jokes. "I'm on the late flight tonight. Midnight pick-up. Is that yours too, or will you be home by then?"

Henry shook his head. "Midnight is bedtime for me. Don't do nightshifts, never have. It gives me constipation." He patted his belly.

Mia laughed, genuinely this time. She had no idea what to say to that.

"You two must be close if he's discussing his bowel movements with you," Ava whispered as she brushed past her.

Mia tried to keep a straight face as she looked at Ava, who was now standing beside her, handing her key card to the receptionist.

"Well, I've done Dubai more times than I can count, and Henry has been here from day one, so we go way back," she said, surprised that Ava hadn't lost interest in her after their embarrassing misunderstanding. "But we don't make a habit of discussing his stool."

"That's reassuring," Ava said with a bemused look, only taking her eyes off Mia to sign her hotel bill. She turned to face her, leaning on the counter. "Hey, about earlier... I don't want it to be awkward between us after that little misunderstanding."

Mia felt her cheeks flush. "Yeah, I'm sorry about that."

"No," Ava said. "I'm sorry." She hesitated, glancing over at her colleagues who were getting on the bus. "Do you want to go for a coffee next time?"

There was a silence, in which Mia nodded a little too eagerly for her own liking. "Sure. Anytime. Just hit me up on the minibus next time we're on the same flight." *Shit. Did I just say that? Hit me up? Really?*

"Great. I'll hit you up." Ava laughed at Mia's mortified expression. "But it might be a couple of weeks before we're both on the same flight again so until that time..." She grabbed her purse and winked. "Stay safe and don't forget to call me when you're home."

12

CAMBRIDGE, UK

"Ava, baby. You look exhausted." The tall, elegant woman who opened the door pulled Ava into a tender embrace.

Ava hugged her mother back in the door opening.

"Hey Mum. It's good to see you." Her mother looked immaculate as always. With her pristinely plucked eyebrows, her sharp cut black bob and her silk white blouse, worn over black trousers, she looked more like a fashion editor than a university professor. "You look good." Ava ran a hand through her mother's hair and planted a kiss on her cheek before heading inside the small but charming townhouse in the centre of Cambridge. It had been a hectic couple of weeks, and she hadn't realised how tired she was until she slumped down on her parents' couch in the living room. The newness of her job, combined with her crazy schedule that came with constant jet-lags, had sucked the energy out of her. Then there was the sudden change of route from Dubai that had drained her even more. Ava liked to be prepared for the week ahead at all times, and she liked to know exactly what was going to happen. Changes in her schedule didn't come up very often, but when they did, she found herself feeling uncomfortable, and unable to sleep.

But now, life was predictable again, and she was looking forward to some nice, relaxed family time, and especially her mother's Jordanian home cooking. She took a deep breath and closed her eyes.

"Mmm... Ava sniffed the air. Are you making galayet bandora?" she asked, referring to her favourite lamb and tomato dish.

"Of course, darling. I know how much you love it. I've also made mujadara and lots of yummy, healthy side dishes." She walked around the room, fluffing up the many pillows on the couch and on the other chairs. "I had the afternoon off and it's not often that we have the whole family together."

After thirty years in the UK, there was only a slight hint of an accent left in her mother's speech, and there wasn't much reference to her heritage in her appearance either. When entering the house, however, there was no escaping her Jordanian background. The smell of food, the colourful tapestries and abundance of pillows, the imported dining table with fabric- covered benches, the built-in shelves, the lanterns and the deep red accents that warmed the room. It always fascinated Ava how a typical English house could look so different on the inside. Sometimes it felt like entering another world, but it was her world, and Ava loved coming home.

"Your father is picking up your brother and Natasha from the train station, they'll be here any minute."

Ava smiled as she took the glass of tea her mother handed her. "I would have come earlier to help you if I'd have known you were going to make a fuss."

"Nonsense. By the looks of it, you needed to catch up on sleep. How has your new job been so far?"

"It's been good." Ava took a sip of the tea, then squeezed some extra honey in. "Hectic, but good. It will get better once I get used to the new policies and airports, at the moment I have to think about every single thing I do. Also, the leadership part of it is stressing me out a bit, but the briefings are getting easier each time." She shook her head and laughed. "I can't believe both my parents are lecturers, and my brother is a motivational speaker, while I can't even be in charge of more than one person without getting nervous."

"It will get better." Her mother put down a tray of Middle Eastern sweets. "And your colleagues? Are they nice? What about your co-pilots?"

"I've only met five senior officers," Ava said through a mouthful. "But yeah. So far, everyone has been supportive and nice. I've met some of the cabin crew too when we all went out for dinner last week. I think we'll get on."

"Good. That's good." Her mother's smile was genuine. "And I'm glad you're getting the chance to eat some of your favourite foods, now that you're doing lots of Emirati flights, so I don't have to worry about your unhealthy eating habits."

The front door opened, and Ava heard the shuffling of umbrellas, coats and bags in the hallway.

"This bloody weather," her father sighed. "Always the same." His eyes lit up when he saw Ava, and he spread out his arms as he walked towards her. "Ava. You're home. I was wondering when we'd finally get to see you again." He hugged his daughter, squeezing her shoulders a little too hard, as always. Then he turned to their other guest. "This is Natasha, Zaid's girlfriend."

"Hi Ava, I've heard a lot about you."

"Likewise. I'm glad to finally meet you." Ava shook the pretty, blonde girl's hand and smiled before turning to her brother to hug him. "Zaid. You're looking more handsome every time I see you." She looked from Zaid to Natasha and back. "And I see you've been lucky, meeting this beautiful woman. Good for you."

Ava was glad Natasha had already visited the week before, while she was on call. It would make the awkward first meeting a lot easier, now that the rest of the family already knew her. Ava wasn't at her most comfortable around new people, never had been. Perhaps shy wasn't the way she would describe herself, but she wouldn't be one to start a conversation either. Which was why she couldn't help but wonder how it had been so easy when she'd spent time with Mia. She had run up to her without thinking. She had approached her twice in one day, talked to her, and even flirted a little. It was a strange development, but it felt good, and she couldn't seem to stop thinking about the attractive brunette. She hadn't seen Mia in ten days, since she'd left the hotel in Dubai, and the fact that she'd been counting those days was very out of character for her.

"Ava?" Zaid's voice sounded far away.

"What? Sorry, I was..."

"I asked if you were dating anyone?" Zaid cocked his head. "I was just telling Natasha that you're a big, fat lezzer and she has a friend who's also..."

Ava gave him a playful push, shutting him up. "I'm not dating," she replied dryly. "And I don't have time for it either, so save yourself the energy." She gave Natasha a smile. "Sorry, no offence to your friend but I have no interest in being set up."

"Okay, noted." Natasha laughed. "But that's what I said

when my friend tried to set me up with your brother, and look at me now, having dinner with his family." She followed Zaid over to the dining table, where they sat down next to each other, holding hands under the table. Ava grinned at the cheesy display, but it was heart-warming, seeing her brother in love. She tried to recall the last time she'd been in love, but she couldn't remember. Was it Lisbeth in high school? Maybe. The memory was too vague to be sure. Was it Annabel, who had left her for someone else when she was twenty-eight, leaving her to sulk and drink for days on end? Ava didn't think so. That had just bruised her ego. She dug deeper, but there was no one there, apart from Danielle, the footballer's wife she'd had a brief affair with, three years ago. But that wasn't love either. That was lust, and besides, Ava was the one who had ended it, when she'd got tired of Danielle's indecisiveness. Ava never fought for her. Sometimes, Danielle was available, and sometimes, Ava wouldn't hear from her for weeks on end. Danielle had always been torn between her comfortable life with an even more comfortable bank account, and her sexuality, which was absurd because Danielle was clearly gayer than a rainbow unicorn. That was what had drawn Ava towards her, the day they'd met at a polo event they'd both been invited to. The look of pure lust in Danielle's eyes when they were introduced. She'd recognized Ava for what she was straight away: a very single lady who loved the ladies. The fact that Danielle needed her to feed her sexual desires had been a turn-on, but also a curse. Ava had wasted so many nights listening to her rants about her life and her sad, heterosexual marriage that she got nothing out of, apart from fame and money, knowing all too well that she would never leave her husband. No. Love was not something Ava was familiar with. Not the sweet, innocent kind that her brother and Natasha seemed to share. She sat down opposite Zaid and smiled when her mother filled the table with all her favourite foods. Her father sat down too, chattering away with Natasha. Ava was grateful for her parents, for letting her be who she was. If only her parents' family in Jordan knew that one of their children was gay, and the other one dating a Russian glamour model... She chuckled at that thought.

"Eat!" her mother exclaimed. "You're looking too skinny, Ava. Must be all the junk food you're eating at the airports." She put a jug of ice-water on the table and sat down at the head, opposite Ava's father.

Ava laughed. "Last time I checked, Mum, junk food makes you put on weight. I'm actually quite healthy, I just run a lot. I need the exercise because I'm sitting for hours on end, so I need to let out some steam a couple of times a week."

"Running is bad for your knees. I read it in a study last week." Her mother held up a finger. "Apparently, yoga is the best way to stay active. I tried it for the first time last week, at the gym." She winced as she rolled her shoulders. "I'm still suffering, but it feels good, like I've breathed new life into my body."

"Good for you, Noor," Ava's father said, grinning. "Two classes a week keeps her off my back for a little while, so I'm nothing but supportive." He turned to Ava and winked. "Stops her from talking about moving back to Jordan when she's retired."

"Are you really thinking of moving back there?" Ava was surprised, as the subject had never been mentioned, ever. She just assumed that her parents were happy in the UK and wanted to spend the rest of their days there.

"I've thought about it, sure." Her mother shrugged. "It's

becoming more and more appealing, especially with my retirement lurking around the corner. My sister is still there, and your grandmother." She turned to Ava and Zaid. "They're not getting any younger and we aren't either. I'd like to spend some time with them while I still can, and two weeks of holiday a year just isn't the same. I'd like to go for two years, maybe three. Not forever. I mean, I couldn't possibly leave my babies behind for longer than that. We'd buy you both tickets of course, to come and visit." She paused. "So yes, I've thought about it a lot. But your father doesn't want to hear anything about it. He's too attached to the pub and his brass band now."

"Why don't you plan a couple of months first?" Zaid said. "See how that works out?"

"She wants to sell the house." Their father sighed. "And she's right, we could buy both a small place in Jordan and a flat outside Cambridge with the money we'll make on it. We bought this house twenty-five years ago for peanuts, and the market here is booming now. But... I like Cambridge. That's all I can say. I don't really want to leave."

"I don't want you both to leave either," Zaid said. "Who's going to cook for us when you're not here, Mum? And who's going to wash my football gear after my games on Saturdays? It's certainly not going to be Natasha," he joked.

"You're certainly right about that," Natasha said, poking him in the ribs.

"I think you're old enough to do your own laundry by now, Zaid." Their mother was having none of his emotional blackmail. "If you're old enough to earn a PhD in Psychology, write a best-selling book and give motivational speeches to crowds of people, I'm sure you'll manage a simple white wash."

"Whatever," Zaid grunted. "Just think about it, okay?

And think about Dad. Look at his poor little face. He doesn't want to leave his friends and his trombone club or whatever it is he does on his Sunday afternoons in that club house for old people."

"Brass band," their father corrected him. "It's a brass band and stop making it sound like I'm going to some seniors' social club. If any of you ever bothered to come and see us perform, you'd know that we're actually really good."

"Alright Dad, I'm sorry. No disrespect to your tambourine skills," Zaid teased.

"Trumpet, Zaid. I play the trumpet. There are no tambourines involved, ever."

Ava noticed her father was getting worked up and kicked Zaid under the table.

He nodded. "Sorry, Dad, I'm only messing with you. Hey, I have an idea. How about we do a little group sesh? A bit of family therapy? We could all talk about this crazy idea of Mum's, express how we're feeling. I'll mediate."

"No," Ava said. "Gross, please no. I've had just about enough of your therapy theatre. And if you as much as attempt to throw one more motivational slogan or dish out advice on how to find love through positivity at me..." She pointed at the piece of lamb on his plate. "You'll be leaving this table with that lamb bone up your ass." She laughed as she held up a hand. "Who's with me?" Without hesitation, Natasha was the first to raise her hand, followed by their mother and at last, their father, who gave Zaid an apologetic shrug.

"Sorry Zaid. You're on your own."

13

ISLAMABAD, PAKISTAN

"Hi Mum. Happy birthday!" Mia tried hard to put on a cheerful tone when she called her parents from her hotel room in Islamabad. She was exhausted, nodding off behind her desk where she was checking her emails, but had remembered it was her mother's birthday just in time.

"Thank you, sweetie." Her mother sounded chirpy. "It's a shame you can't be here. We're all celebrating with cheese and wine tonight. We've got your sister over, she's got a few days off from Uni, and the neighbours, and some friends from Bingo. Oh, and also a couple we met on holiday in Benidorm last year. They're coming all the way here from Brighton and they're staying in a hotel in town. Isn't that nice?"

"That sounds like it's going to be a great evening," Mia said. "I got you a gift in Dubai last week, I'll bring it over next time I visit."

"You shouldn't have, sweetie. Just your presence, that's all we want. Your father and I haven't seen you in months, and Ami... well it must have been almost a year since you were both here." She paused to think. "Or has it been longer than that? I hope you two keep in touch now and then?"

Mia winced at her sister's name. "Yeah, we do," she lied. "Not very often, but I do speak to her."

"Good." Her mother was easily reassured. "Then she must have told you that she's up for selection for the national swimming team?"

"No, I didn't know that." Mia was stunned. "I knew she was a good swimmer, but the national team? Wow, that's a big deal, Mum."

"Yes, it's exciting, isn't it? Considering everything that happened, it's..." Her mother broke off her sentence, suddenly remembering the long list of no-go topics. "Anyway, we're very proud of her. On her way to becoming a physiotherapist and now this?"

"I'm glad to hear Ami's doing so well, Mum."

"And we're very proud of you too, of course," her mother added. "Jet-setting around the world, working in first class and hanging out with celebrities."

"I don't hang out with celebrities." Mia couldn't help but laugh through the guilt that built up inside her each time Ami's name was mentioned. "I serve them food and drinks once in a while, that's about it. But please congratulate Ami for me, that's fantastic news. I know how much she loves swimming and I hope she gets through. Imagine, having an athlete in the family."

"Yes, imagine that." Her mother sighed. "And where are you right now?"

"Pakistan." Mia clenched the phone between her ear and her shoulder while she filled up the kettle with bottled water to make herself a cup of tea before going to sleep. "But not for long, I'm flying back tomorrow."

"Isn't it dangerous there? I hope you're careful."

"Don't worry. I'm at the airport hotel and I'm too tired to venture outside." Mia found a cup in the desk drawer and searched for a tea bag in her luggage. "Anyway, I'm going to sleep now, I've got an early flight. Have a great birthday, Mum. Give everyone a kiss from me, will you?"

"Okay, Mia. I will. And be careful out there."

MIA SIPPED HER TEA, zapping through the channels on the monstrosity of a TV that could almost be considered retro by now. She was wide awake, after her conversation with her mother. Most of the channels showed dramatic soap operas, involving weddings or family betrayal. Despite the language barrier, it wasn't hard to figure out what was going on. The exaggerated facial expressions said it all, and so did the near fist fights between brothers or cousins, every ten minutes or so. She'd tried watching a movie on her laptop earlier, but as always, the websites she used for streaming were blocked by the Pakistani firewall. She flicked to the next channel and smiled in amusement at a music video, showcasing a man who was driving his flashy red convertible in typical Bollywood style. His white shirt was blowing in the wind as the camera zoomed in on his gold watch. There was another close-up of a woman, ogling him longingly for an awkwardly long time while shaking her hips to the loud music playing from his speakers when he came to a halt before a traffic light. The driver cast the woman a flirty look and sang something Mia couldn't understand. It was too cheesy for words. Mia giggled and turned up the volume. *At least it's entertaining.* The traffic light turned green and the man sped off again, in search of more beautiful women to impress with his driving, bobbing his head to the beat of the music. He drove faster and faster, towards the next traffic light that had just switched from green to orange and ran a hand through his hair as he stepped on the gas in an attempt to beat the red light to it. Mia winced when another car suddenly came from the right, crashing into him. The scene switched to slow motion, and she averted her gaze at the sound of colliding metal and splintering glass. For a moment, it felt like her heart had stopped beating. Memories came flooding back, and she couldn't move, couldn't breathe. *Her little sister Ami. A gruesome cry. Panic. A tree.* And then everything turned black. Mia held on to her chest, lowering herself onto the floor, gasping for air. Her heart pounded so fast that she could feel it thumping in her throat. She curled up and pulled her knees towards her, like she always did when she had a panic attack, exhaling through her mouth, making a whooshing sound. She inhaled again through her nose, counting to four, held it for another three counts and exhaled again. *Breathe. Slowly. Ami's okay now. You're okay.*

14

LONDON, UK TO NEW YORK, USA

"Mia. It's a pleasure to be flying with you again." Ava sounded out of breath.

Mia was surprised to see that Ava had caught up with her, leaving her flight crew behind, and as soon as she smiled, Mia went weak in her knees.

"Ava. Nice to see you too." She swallowed hard, unprepared for the effect Ava had on her, once again. She'd been anticipating this moment and practising small talk in her head but now that she was face to face with Ava, she had no idea what to say. "New York?" she finally managed with forced casualness, as if she hadn't been cross checking their schedules for days.

"Yep." Ava winked. "Just like you and everyone else here."

Mia rolled her eyes. "Of course." Something stirred deep down when their eyes met for a brief moment. Ava's intense green eyes seemed to lift her off the ground. There was curiosity in them, as if she was trying to gauge Mia.

Ava sighed when she heard Jack call her name behind them. "I have to go. See you later?"

"Sure. I'll bring in your lunch." Mia's heart was still racing from their encounter when Lynn and Farik both hooked an arm through hers.

"She practically asked for your number," Lynn whispered.

Mia shook her head, releasing herself from their grip. "Stop it, guys. She was just being polite. It's nothing."

"I know a nothing when I see one," Farik said. "And that wasn't a nothing. That was more of a..." He paused and lowered his voice for dramatic effect. "A something."

Mia decided to ignore him as she pulled out her swipe card, opening the staff gate to airline security. Once they were through, an airport cart was waiting to take them to their gate, as the gate number had changed last-minute.

"I love Heathrow Airport, especially when I don't have to walk." Farik stuffed the last of his salmon bagel into his mouth and continued mumbling through a mouthful. "Great food and free magazines." He snatched one of the airport glossies from a shelf as they drove past, resulting in an annoyed look from their driver.

"Keep your hands inside the vehicle," he warned. "I told you last time already."

"Sorry. Won't happen again," Farik shouted, knowing all too well that he would do it the next time and the time after that until finally, he would get thrown off the cart before they reached their gate.

Mia shook her head and laughed. Farik was something else. He was like a chameleon; camp, loud and unapologetic off duty, but as soon as he boarded the plane, he was polite, poised and softly spoken, swapping his Brummie accent for a very convincing Queen's English. Their passengers loved him. Mia watched him wipe the grin off his face and straighten his back when they neared the gate while she painted on her own smile, greeting the early birds in economy class who were waiting to board.

"MIA. TECH CREW?" Lynn nudged Mia with a grin, nodding towards the cockpit. "They've requested coffee before take-off. Apparently, the machine in the briefing room was broken." She reached for her trolley and handed Mia a tray with three takeaway cups.

"Eh, sure. I'll do it." She didn't bother protesting, there was no fooling Lynn anymore. Mia made her way through the narrow corridor leading to the cockpit and followed the security procedure before letting herself in.

"Hey guys. I have your coffees." Mia looked from Ava to Jack and his colleague Raf, and back, resting her eyes on Ava.

"Here's yours," she said to Ava. "Strong and black. Double shot." She handed Raf, today's second officer, his coffee. "And here's yours. Latte, two sugars."

Jack took his own cup off the tray. "And a flat white for me."

"Any other drinks to go with your lunch later?" Mia tried to be as to the point as she could. The tech crew didn't like to be disturbed, especially not right before take-off, and she needed Ava to know that she wasn't normally as clumsy and forgetful as she was the last time she served them.

"Another bottle of sparkling water would be great," Ava handed Mia her empty bottle, holding on to it for just a little longer than necessary as their fingertips touched.

"A hot chocolate for me please," Raf said.

Jack looked up at her. "I'll have a beer." He grinned. "Just kidding, I'm fine."

"Okay." Mia slipped the tray under her arm, fighting to

ignore the butterflies in her belly. "Anything else to keep your energy going?"

Ava opened her mouth to speak, then decided against it. "No thanks. You're the best, Mia." She smiled before she turned back to the control panel for the final procedures.

LYNN LAUGHED when Mia came back into first class. "You look like you could do with some fresh air, woman." She patted Mia on her rosy cheeks. "Is it warm in here or did the captain just make your temperature rise?"

Mia laughed too. "Shut up, Lynn. Just doing my job." She turned towards the drinks cabinet, finally allowing herself to smile freely. She wasn't sure how Ava had managed to get her on cloud nine with nothing more than a flirty smile, but it sure made her job a whole lot more interesting.

MIA WAS HANDING out drinks and finger food after take-off, making sure everyone was comfortable before dinner would be served, when Ava's warm voice sounded through the speakers, sending shivers down her spine.

"Ladies and Gentlemen, welcome aboard flight CN6555 to John F Kennedy Airport, New York. This is your captain speaking. First, I'd like to welcome you all aboard. We are currently cruising at an altitude of 30000 feet at an airspeed of 390 miles per hour. The time is 4.04 PM and with the tail-wind, we're expecting to land in New York at 7 PM, fifteen minutes ahead of schedule. The weather forecast is sunny, and the temperature is expected to be around twenty-eight degrees. I'll keep in touch until we reach our destination but for now, please sit back, relax, and let our wonderful cabin crew take care of you while you enjoy your flight."

God, I love her voice. Mia shook her head when she realised she was swooning over Ava's announcement. Lynn had noticed, and she gave her a teasing grin.

"I bet you wonder what she sounds like in bed," she whispered. "Oh, Mia! Do that again." She lowered her voice even more, making sure the passengers couldn't hear her. "Oh Mia, yes..."

Mia elbowed her as she walked past, ignoring Lynn's smirk. She desperately tried to focus on anything but the fact that Ava was right there, behind that door. *Get your shit together, woman. You've got people to take care of.*

"GOOD AFTERNOON, Ms. Marigold. How are you today?" Mia bent down before her favourite passenger. Although Ms. Marigold was in the aft galley today, and in the capable hands of Lynn, Mia always liked to say hello to her frequent flyers. Ms. Marigold was slumped in her seat, looking skinnier and more fragile than ever, and her bony hands trembled as she took a sip of her Champagne. The sweet old lady was a regular on the flight, flying first class back and forth from London to New York at least once a week. Mia had seen her health deteriorate over the past months but had never enquired about it. She put an extra blanket over the lady's legs, just the way she liked it, and adjusted the angle of her screen. Ms. Marigold liked to watch comedies, giggling throughout the flight. She never slept. "Is there anything else we can do for you?"

"No thank you, dear. I'm quite alright. Although I'm feeling a bit achy today, I can't complain. I'm almost eighty-nine years old, you know."

"Eighty-nine?" Mia shot her a surprised look. "Well you

don't look it, Ms. Marigold." She winked. "Must be all those comedies you're watching."

Ms. Marigold took Mia's wrist. "Laughing never hurt anyone, dear." She pulled Mia in closer. "I'll tell you a little secret if you'll let me. There's no business involved this time. I'm on my way to see my sweetheart."

"Really? That's lovely," Mia said. "Have you known each other for long?"

Ms. Marigold shook her head. "No. We only met recently, about half a year ago, just before I retired as chairman of my company. You know, I never had time for relationships, and was always too busy with work but now, I'm spending all my hard-earned money on comfortable flights and nice hotels, and so is he." Pure joy was shining through her eyes.

"And does this charming new love interest have a name?" Mia asked.

"Alfred." Ms. Marigold's eyes lit up at the mention of his name. "He's only five years younger than me, in case you're wondering if I have a toy boy." She laughed. "He's a perfect gentleman and he's taking me to Bamontes for lunch tomorrow."

"Oh, fancy." Mia let Lynn pass behind her. She didn't usually spend so much time talking to passengers, but it was rude to cut Ms. Marigold off now that she was opening up, and besides, Mia was truly interested in the old woman's story. Ms. Marigold was always immaculately dressed in exclusive designer clothes and understated jewellery, and she was never anything but polite and friendly. "I've always wanted to go there. Maybe I'll be so lucky that someone will take me there one day."

"You're not married?" Ms. Marigold looked up at her in surprise. "But you're such a beautiful and kind young woman in the prime of your life. Surely men would be lining up to date you?"

"It's not that simple," Mia said, keeping a genuine smile. "Especially not with this job. I'm away a lot so it's hard for me to make time for people." She shook her head. "But that's okay. I'm happy on my own, just like I assume you were when your job was your number one love in your life. I love to travel. That's my passion, and maybe love will come first one day but for now, I'm happy."

"Quite rightly so." Ms Marigold finished her Champagne and handed Mia the glass before settling back in her chair. "I was an early feminist myself, never needed a man, and I'm sure you won't be the last. But I finally know how nice it is to have someone special and I wish I'd met Alfred fifty years ago." She pointed a finger at Mia. "So, don't let the same thing happen to you my dear, because life will fly by and before you know it, you'll be very old and achy." She laughed and put on her headphones, that seemed way too big for her fragile head. Mia gave her a pat on the shoulder and walked on. "I appreciate the advice. I'll remember that."

LYNN'S EYES were filled with panic as she grabbed Mia's shoulder and pulled her aside. They were cruising over the North Atlantic, four hours into the flight.

"Wait, Lynn." Mia shot her an annoyed look. "I've got drinks here, careful."

"No, it can't wait." Lynn lowered her voice. "You know that old lady you were talking to earlier? Ms. Marigold?"

Mia nodded. "Yeah. What about her?"

"Well..." Lynn continued. "I just touched her hand to check if she wanted anything and I thought it was strange that she was sleeping, because she never sleeps on the flights…" She hesitated. "She didn't wake up, and she felt… different." Lynn's eyes were wide as she swallowed hard. "She was colder than she should be, and her face looked… well, it looked like it was drooping to one side. Then I checked her pulse and there was nothing. I swear, I checked it three times, Mia."

"Fuck," Mia hissed, pulling Lynn further around the corner, towards the cockpit. She was about to ask someone for advice when she realised she was the one in charge of the cabin. "Alright," she said, trying to keep calm. Her heart was racing. "Have any of the passengers noticed?"

"No, I don't think so."

Mia nodded. "Okay, that's good. Let me think for a second. There are no doctors on our passengers list, right?"

"No." Lynn shook her head and frowned. "But I do think we have a vet on board." She took the passenger list and scrolled through the information of the people who had filled in their occupation. People in a medical profession always filled it in, in case of an emergency. Her eyes narrowed as she focussed on a passenger in economy plus. "There's a veterinarian upstairs. Seat 8d. I'll go and get him."

"No." Mia stopped her. "It's my responsibility." She paused for a moment, trying not to let the news upset her. "Poor Ms. Marigold." She looked at Lynn, collecting herself. "Can you please brief the cabin crew? Both floors. I'll talk to the Captain after the veterinarian has checked on her." Mia took a deep breath and headed towards Ms Marigold first, to double check her pulse.

THE VETERINARIAN NODDED after he stood up. By now, some of the passengers had started to notice something was going on. "She's been dead for at least half an hour," he said, lowering his voice. "She looks like she's sleeping, even I was fooled for a moment. I think it might have been a stroke, but the coroner will have to verify that." He put a hand on Mia's arm. "Hey, whatever you do, don't blame yourself. There was nothing you could have done."

"Is she dead?" A woman in the row next to Ms Marigold whispered.

Mia tried to keep her breathing under control as she pressed the button to raise the privacy wall around the cabin. Thank God Ms Marigold wasn't in economy. They'd have to move her body and cover her up in the crew bunk, as the economy deck was full and there'd be nowhere else to hide her.

"I'm afraid so," she said, turning to the lady. "I'd really appreciate it if we could keep this between ourselves, in order to prevent panic breaking out."

"Of course." The woman nodded. Mia could see her brain working overtime, trying to come up with a polite way to blackmail her. She was just one of those people who always complained, in the hope of getting an upgrade. She'd managed today, and there was no doubt that she would use the death of a poor old woman as bargaining power for her next three upgrades at least. Mia wanted to punch her in the face, but instead, she kneeled down next to the woman, trying to remember her name.

"I understand this may be uncomfortable for you, Ms Priestly. Perhaps we could have a chat later to see how we can make it up to you on your next flight with us?"

The woman had victory written all over her face, although she tried to hide it as best as she could. One upgrade would not be enough, Mia was sure of that. "I have to deal with the protocol right now," Mia continued, "but I'll be back shortly." She followed the veterinarian back to his wife on the upper deck and offered them the last two seats in first class.

"Can I come in?" Mia asked through the intercom.

"Are you alone?" Raf asked, switching on the camera so he could see what was happening outside the cockpit.

"Yes, it's just me." Mia took a step aside and gave them a wave. She punched in the code with a shaking hand.

"What's up, Mia?" Jack asked. Ava and Raf turned too, curious as to why Mia let herself in at this point in their flight. It was unheard of, unless there was an emergency.

Mia locked the door behind her. "One of my passengers has just been pronounced dead," she said, pausing for a moment. "Ms Marigold, row 3a, eighty-eight years of age. A veterinarian from economy plus checked her. He thinks it might have been a stroke."

Ava took a deep breath, letting the information sink in. "Thank you, Mia." She rubbed her temple, going through the procedure in her head. "Has she been covered?"

Mia nodded. "She already had a blanket over her, and I put up the cabin wall. No signs of panic so far, and the only woman who saw Ms Marigold's deceased body is willing to keep it quiet." She shrugged. "She will want something in return, I suppose, but I'll get onto that now. Lynn has briefed the rest of the cabin crew."

"Okay." Ava's face was pale. She didn't seem to panic, but Mia could sense that she was very uncomfortable. "You did well. There's no point moving her to the crew bunk, it will only raise more attention to her death. I'll check with the company and ground control to see if we have to divert, but as we're already over half way, I expect they'll want us to continue to New York. I'll let you know in five minutes if you can come back."

AVA TOOK steady breaths as she waited for the company to reply to her message. She'd discussed alternative routes with Jack and Raf, anticipating the unlikely event of them having to turn and fly back to London. Both her officers were busy, noting down coordinates whilst checking the weather behind them. She couldn't let them know that she was shaken by the news Mia had just told them, but it was hard to keep her hands from trembling. For the first time in her career, someone had died on her flight, and although it wasn't her fault, she felt responsible for the wellbeing of her passengers. Besides that, it was the uncertainty that made her nervous too. She'd covered the current situation in her training, and was aware of the procedures, but wasn't comfortable with a potential sudden change in her flight schedule. Not knowing whether they would have to go back or not, unprepared for the conditions they hadn't gone through in their thorough briefing before they took off, was something she dreaded. The decisions were out of her hands, and the control she held on to at all times, could not help her cope now. It was hard to think straight with the anxiety that kept poking at her, threatening to take over. She loosened her tie and opened the top button of her shirt in an attempt to get some air.

Stay calm, Ava. Everything's going to be fine.

"Are you okay, Captain?" Raf noticed she was pulling at her collar.

"I'm fine, Raf. It's just a bit warm in here, that's all."

15

NEW YORK, USA

"I was impressed by how calm you were," Ava said, while she and Mia were waiting for ground medical staff to remove the body. The passengers had been let out first, the crew had left, and now they were the only ones there besides the JFK medical staff, performing tests on Ms Marigold's body before carefully putting her in a body bag and removing her from the plane.

Mia fought back the tears. "I was only just coping," she said. "It's so sad. Just so sad. Ms. Marigold was one of our regulars. She was on her way to see the love of her life. He was going to take her out for lunch at Bamontes tomorrow." She shook her head and sniffed. "I'm sorry, I'm really trying not to cry. I'm not usually this emotional. I guess I'm just a bit shaken up."

"Hey. It's okay to cry, don't apologize." Ava rubbed her shoulder. "What you just had to deal with was hard, Mia. The decision making, a dead body, which you may have never seen before. You're allowed to be upset about it."

Mia nodded, looking down at her shoes. "Has someone ever died on one of your flights?"

"Never," Ava said. "I'm not going to lie, it was a bit of a shock for me too. But I know there was nothing I could have done, and you have to remember that there was nothing *you* could have done. These things happen, although very rarely, and you were the unlucky one to be in charge this time."

"That's easy to say, but I did notice she looked poorly, even though she was in good spirits. I should have kept an eye on her."

"You couldn't have kept an eye on her." Ava took both her shoulders now, forcing Mia to look up at her. "I know how busy you all are, it's unlikely you could have saved her."

"I need to let her partner know," Mia said. "He'll be waiting for her at arrivals."

Ava shook her head. "It's not your responsibility. The company will take care of that."

"But what if they don't? And what if Ms. Marigold's family don't even know she was dating him? Then he might not find out until after the funeral and..."

"Hey. It's going to be okay. He'll enquire with the company when he realises she's not there. You need to go back to the hotel and get some rest. I'll do the same, it's been a long day. The crew bus will have left by now, so we can share a taxi. I'll drop you off at your hotel, it's not far from mine."

"You're right." Mia took a deep breath and collected herself. The touch of Ava's hands had calmed her down, but it also made her feel things she wasn't supposed to feel in this moment. Not so soon after a death on her flight. She pulled her gaze away from the beautiful woman in front of her and left to get her suitcase from the crew locker.

"I bet your hotel is a lot nicer, huh?" Mia said, looking at her booking reference. She was feeling slightly better after they'd had a coffee at the airport before hailing a cab. They hadn't talked much, but now that they were sitting in the back of the cab together, she was praying for a traffic jam, so they'd have some more time to get to know each other a little.

Ava winced. "Yeah, I suppose it is." She took her own booking sheet out of her bag and handed it to Mia. "It's strange, isn't it? How policies have changed over the past ten years? I know there's the whole food poisoning risk, but still, I can't help but wonder if that's an excuse made up by a bunch of cocky pilots who are looking to get the better end of the deal. I mean, we wouldn't be able to fly if we didn't have cabin crew either, right?" She took Mia's sheet and studied the address. "But at least your location is great. Nice and central."

"Oh, so you know New York well then?" Mia looked up at Ava, surprised that she recognized the address.

"As a matter of fact, I do." Ava smiled. "I lived here for three years. I love the city, especially in the summer, when everything is hot and steamy and..." She stopped right there.

Mia's heart raced when their eyes locked. A small smile played around Ava's mouth, as if she could sense Mia's nervousness. *God, she's so in control, it's ridiculous.* Mia tried to keep her cool while Ava leaned in closer, draping her arm over the edge of the backseat. Her hand touched the back of Mia's neck for a brief moment, making her melt into her seat, before she moved it further up, away from her.

"Anyway, I could show you around if you want?" Ava continued as if nothing had happened. "Although you probably know your way around pretty well yourself."

"No." Mia shook her head. "I mean, yes I do," she stam-

mered. "But I'd love an insider's view. If you don't mind?" She managed a smile. "Are you free tonight?"

"I can't tonight, I'm afraid." Ava said when they stopped in front of the hotel where the cabin crew was booked in. "But I'm free tomorrow. I could meet you at your hotel after breakfast and go from there? We could talk about what happened today? It might make you feel better."

"That would be nice." Mia realised she was still sitting in the car instead of getting out and fetching her suitcase. "Well, this is me, I'd better get my bag."

The cab driver opened the trunk, but Mia closed it again by accident. She cursed, fiddling with the lock. *Why do I make a fool out of myself every single time she's near?* She waved at the driver. "Excuse me, could you open it again, please?"

Ava got out and walked around the back to lift the case out for her. "I'm sorry. I almost forgot my manners, I apologize." She smiled as she handed it over to Mia. "You seem to be quite a distraction. It's a good thing you're not my first officer." Mia watched Ava get back into the cab. She rolled down the window and stuck her head out. "I'll see you tomorrow at ten, Mia."

16

NEW YORK, USA

Mia looked around her uninspiring bedroom in Manhattan, wondering what to do with herself. She was still feeling shaken up, but she knew she wouldn't be able to sleep. The stores would be closed by now, so she couldn't go shopping, and she didn't want to join the crew at the bar either. They were planning a big night out, and for someone who didn't drink it was no fun being around people who could hardly walk, let alone talk by the end of the night. She switched on the TV, got bored of flicking through the channels and got into the shower instead. Mia thought of Ava, as she let the hot water wash over her. She closed her eyes, trying to picture her face. On the surface, Ava seemed no different from most other captains Mia had met throughout her career. She was charming, confident and flirtatious. But she was also nice and caring. No other captain Mia had worked with would have taken care of her the way Ava had, today. *She's probably got a date tonight.* Mia imagined Ava having beautiful women on call in every city of the world, waiting for her to visit. Because she was definitely into women, Mia was sure of that now. The looks she'd given her, the little touches, the not so subtle flirting and the comment about her being a distraction... *It doesn't make me special though.* Ava was clearly a flirt and she probably treated all women like that. But a little fun wouldn't hurt, right? Mia hadn't been intimate with anyone since she'd broken up with her ex eight months ago, and if Ava came on to her, there was no way she would say no to a sexy pilot with light green feline eyes and a breathtaking smile. She felt excited at the prospect of spending some time with Ava, even if it was just a coffee and a walk in the morning. It would take her thoughts off Ms Marigold and the sad way her life had ended, just before the date she was so looking forward to.

Showered and changed into jeans and a grey sweatshirt, Mia opened the mini-bar in search of a bottle of water. She always had one with her, in order to avoid minibars altogether, but she'd forgotten it on the plane after the chaos of Ms Marigold's death. Her eyes rested on the whisky for a split second. She closed them and could almost feel the warm liquid burning her throat, calming her down after the stressful shift she'd had. The bittersweet taste, the delightful haziness numbing her senses, the soothing pleasure of being confident and funny... If any day, today she could give herself an excuse to drink. She deserved it today. Her finger traced the neck of the bottle. One small sip couldn't hurt, right? *Don't do it. Seriously, Mia. Don't.* But then other thoughts surfaced, other memories. She got down on her knees and took a couple of deep breaths before grabbing the water and slamming the door shut. She sat there for a couple of minutes on the floor, trying to come up with a distraction plan while she pressed the cool bottle against her forehead. *I need to get out of here.* Her iPad was charging in the socket next to her. She picked it up and googled the only place that could help her right now.

"HEY, where do you think you're going?" Lynn called Mia from the hotel bar as she tried to sneak out unnoticed.

"Yeah, come back here," another cabin crew member, whose name she couldn't remember, shouted.

Mia sighed and made her way over to the bar where she was greeted with great enthusiasm by all the people she'd seen only a couple of hours ago. Lynn leaned into her, already tipsy from her third cocktail, Mia guessed.

"Come on, have a drink with us. Just one. It's not a crime. It will be out of our system way before we go back, and you know you need it after what you've been through. Hell, I need it." Lynn gave Mia a pleading look. "Please Mia. Don't be such a good girl all the time, it makes me look bad." She held up her Manhattan in front of Mia's face. "Here, try it, it's really yummy."

Mia took a step back. "Lynn, I told you I don't drink. Alcohol doesn't agree with me so stop pushing me." She sighed, instinctively rubbing the scar on her forehead. In a way it was a blessing, a reminder of why she didn't drink anymore. "Look, I'm sorry to be boring but I'm meeting someone in town for a late dinner."

"Oh yeah? Who are you meeting? The sexy captain? Because she's not here either, even though the rest of the tech crew is." Everyone at the bar laughed.

Mia was starting to lose her temper, but she managed to laugh it off. "No, just someone I used to go to school with. You don't know her."

Lynn looked her up and down. "I'm not sure if I believe you, but I'll let you off the hook." She leaned in and lowered her voice. "I've got my eye on Stewart, the new economy purser, so don't expect me to go shopping with you tomorrow."

"Don't worry. I won't disturb your little rendezvous." Mia forced herself to give her friend a hug and a kiss on the cheek before heading out into the hot New York summers' night. God, she wanted to punch Lynn sometimes. One drink was all it took to make her blurt things out before she'd thought them through. That was why, despite loving Lynn very much, she knew she couldn't trust her with her secrets. *Sexy captain? Really? How dare she say that in front of everyone?*

"Brooklyn please," Mia said to the cab driver, showing him the address on her phone. She'd never been to Cobble Hill before, but at least she wouldn't run into anyone she knew there.

17

NEW YORK, USA

A va used her phone to navigate through the dark streets of New York after walking for a good twenty minutes from the Brooklyn Bridge. Although she knew the city, and even the area, pretty well, she was unfamiliar with the address she was heading for. She'd done it hundreds of times before in at least twenty different cities. Hiding and slightly on edge, imagining voices of people she knew behind her. It was who she was, who she always would be. After walking up and down the same street twice, she finally found the entrance to the local community centre through a dark alleyway. It was worn down, just like she'd expected; the paint was chipping off the door and a couple of windows had been thrown in and boarded up with cardboard and recycled wood. The good old smell of bitter filter coffee comforted her, and she let herself into the community centre where the familiar semi-circle of cheap plastic folding chairs was set up right by the door. She was late, but they'd forgive her, whoever they were. Better late than never, they used to say. Today, most of the group members were male and in their late fifties or sixties, some of them looking like they were way beyond repair. Ava could always tell them apart. There were the lawyers, the doctors and other respectable members of society, whose friends and colleagues didn't know they were here. Just like her, their jobs carried too much responsibility for anyone to know they weren't as stable as they made out to be. Then there were the blue-collar drinkers, who often drank and gambled away their wages, and the wife-beaters, sometimes sitting next to women who had clearly been the victims of the likes of them. Whether they were Christians, Muslims, Jews, Hindus or atheists, straight or gay, male or female, it was the only place where most of them felt safe to speak their mind. Outside the room, they came from different worlds, and outside the room, they wouldn't have exchanged as much as a glance. But in here, they all had something in common, and there was no judgement. The meeting had already started so Ava grabbed a coffee and a chair and gave everyone a quick wave as a matter of greeting.

A strange sense of recognition hit her when she sat down, as if she'd just spotted someone familiar. She scanned the group again in an attempt to assure herself that she was just being paranoid. Her heart skipped a beat when she saw the woman on the far left, opposite her in the half circle. *It can't be...* She hardly recognised her in jeans and a sweatshirt, her hair still wet from a recent shower, but she was even more beautiful now.

"Hello," the woman said. "My name is Mia and..." Mia looked around the circle before resting her eyes on Ava. She closed them for a split second but continued loud enough for everyone to hear. "And I'm an alcoholic. I've been sober for eight months and nineteen days." Although Mia seemed mutually shocked by Ava's presence, she looked right at her as she spoke the words.

The group mumbled their welcome.

"Thank you for coming, Mia," the appointed Chair said. "Anything you'd like to share with us before we move on?" Mia hesitated while she chewed her cheek, still staring at Ava. The group waited for her to speak but when she fell silent, Ava cleared her throat and introduced herself.

"Hi everyone. I'm Ava and I'm an alcoholic. I've been sober for six years and seven months now." There was some more mumbling, and Ava gave Mia a small smile when their eyes met again. Mia looked guarded, caught out even as she gave her a short a nod. Mia was the last person she'd expected to see here. The woman wearing jeans, trainers and a sweatshirt looked nothing like the heavily made up purser she'd spoken to only a couple of hours ago. Her hair was hanging loosely around her shoulders and she sat slouched in her chair, her legs stretched out and crossed in front of her. *Wow.* Suddenly, the meeting had taken a whole different turn, and Ava almost forgot why she was there. There was a blissful moment, in which she realised that she had more in common with her beautiful colleague than she could ever hope. It didn't last long though before panic struck. Mia worked with her. *What if she tells someone? What if my colleagues find out?* She broke out in a cold sweat, glancing at the door. Her hands started to shake. *It's too late. Why leave now?*

"Ava?"

Ava turned and looked at the Chair, a chubby, strawberry blonde man in his early thirties. "I'm sorry. What did you say?"

"I asked if there's anything you'd like to share today."

"No." She shook her head. "I'm good."

"Okay," the Chair said. "In that case, would you be so kind as to read out the twelve steps?"

Ava took the book he handed her and glanced up at Mia one last time before she started reading.

"We admitted we were powerless over alcohol – that our lives had become unmanageable. We came to believe that a Power greater than ourselves could restore us to sanity..."

"Wait, Mia." Ava tried to catch Mia's attention an hour later, after they'd tidied up the room. She rushed after her, just as Mia tried to slip out quietly. She closed the door behind her, leaving them both in the dark alleyway. "Sorry, I can see you're not in the mood to talk, but it's just a bit of a surprise seeing you here." Mia slowed down hesitantly, then turned around and leaned against the wall.

"Likewise." She looked down at her feet, biting her lip. "Listen, Ava. No one knows this about me. You can't tell anyone. Promise me you won't." It was true. Nobody knew, not even her parents. "It could ruin my career if the airline finds out."

"*Your* career?" Ava huffed. "What about my career? I'm the one who's flying the damn aircraft." She paused. "And even though I'd never dream of flying under the influence- I've never done that by the way- my staff might start talking if they knew. A captain with a drinking problem is not exactly someone our airline would keep in their employ, don't you think?" There was a pause. "I need to know that I can trust you too. That's why we need to talk, so I won't get paranoid every time I come into work after tonight."

Mia studied Ava. Her first impulse was to walk off, pretend that they'd never met tonight, that she'd never been there. She was so used to keeping things to herself that the thought of someone else knowing about her drinking problem felt close to unbearable. But they were both here, and she saw the same panic in Ava's eyes that she'd felt ever since she saw Ava walk in.

"You can trust me," she finally said. "You're right, we both have a lot to lose. Can I trust you?"

Ava nodded. She still looked apprehensive, but there was a slight hint of relief in her eyes. "Yes, you can trust me. You don't have to worry about that. Come on, you know that's the first rule here. Confidentiality?" She lifted Mia's chin to face her, painting a faint smile on her lips. "Now, wouldn't it be a bit awkward if we went our separate ways right now, after meeting here?"

"I suppose so." Mia looked down at her trainers. "It would be awkward if we didn't, but also if we did." She chewed the inside of her cheek again, trying to decide on what to say. "I feel like I've done something really bad, and I've been caught out."

"Me too," Ava said. "I take it from your reaction that you'll keep this to yourself?" Mia didn't answer, so she continued. "No one outside the program knows this about me either, and I mean no one, apart from you right now. We're in the same boat here."

"Okay." Mia nodded, carefully weighing her options. Ava could tell that she was just as much on edge as she was, perhaps even more so. "I need you to know that I've never had a drink before or during a shift," she blurted out of nowhere, feeling a sudden need to defend herself.

"I don't doubt that." Ava put a hand on her shoulder. "I'm not judging you, Mia. We're both here for the same reason." She shrugged. "Hey, do you want to go for a walk or something? We don't have to talk about any of this. Just a walk would be great."

Mia let out a quiet sigh, her shoulders relaxing a little. "Okay. A walk would be nice." She pointed towards the direction of the Brooklyn Bridge. "How about that way?"

"Sure." Ava walked next to her, silent at first, trying to think of something to say. Mia's nervousness made her forget about her own unease, but she was determined to do everything in her power to lighten the mood a little. "What a day, huh? Are you feeling a bit better?"

"A little bit." Mia managed a smile. "It's the stressful situations that bring back the cravings," she said. "And sometimes that makes it harder, because then I have two things to worry about. The incident *and* my cravings."

"Yeah. I know how that feels." Ava buried her hands in her back pockets and took a deep breath, dissecting the familiar smells of New York; some good and some bad. The scent of freshly baked bagels, hotdogs and garbage seemed a lot sweeter tonight, mixed with the perfume that Mia was wearing.

They walked through the laid-back streets of Cobble Hill, along peaceful blocks of brownstones. "I love this neighbourhood," Ava said. "I loved the small-town vibe when I first came here nine years ago, for my second job. I looked for a rental around here and ended up sharing an apartment with another co-pilot, because the prices were already ridiculous back then. Can't imagine what it would cost now."

"Great choice of location though." Mia looked at the curated bookstores and hip coffee shops, scattered in between boutiques, local grocery stores and bakeries that were closed for the night. "I like it here too. It's got a warm feel to it." She hesitated. "Were you a couple? You and the other pilot?"

"No." Ava laughed. "No, Pedro was a man, and men

aren't really my type." She paused, making sure her point had come across. She saw Mia's mouth pull into a small smile. "Our airline offered the opportunity to work out here for a couple of years, and we both applied. I felt the need to start over back then. I'd just had a relapse, after being sober for three years, and although I got my shit together again within days, the drinking culture within the first airline I worked for wasn't a healthy environment for me. When I moved to New York I told everyone, including Pedro whom I lived with, that I didn't drink for religious reasons, and it was much easier that way. I didn't have to explain myself or make excuses. Everyone just respected the fact that I didn't drink. So back then, starting afresh was the best thing I could do to get back on my feet." She looked at Mia. "Call it running, call it cheating, I don't care. It worked. I'm sure you know what I mean."

"Yeah. I used to move a lot. Just within London, but still... it gave me something to do, something to focus on when I was home. And every time felt like a new start, like it got a little easier, you know?" Mia noticed she was calmer now. She had panicked the moment she'd seen Ava in the meeting. Her greatest fear, someone finding out about her secret, had become reality. Which was why she was surprised to find that she felt something pretty close to comfortable now, strolling through New York with Ava. "Do you have a sponsor?" she asked.

"I used to, when I lived here. But I haven't spoken to her in years now, so I suppose she's not my sponsor anymore." Ava frowned. "It's funny. I haven't thought of her in a long time, until you asked, just now. I kind of miss her." She turned to Mia. "Do you have a sponsor?"

"No." Mia shook her head. "I've never had one. I guess I like to do things on my own. I rarely go to meetings in

London, for fear of bumping into someone I know, like tonight, and I'm not close to anyone I've met in the meetings either. Not even in Chatham, where I try to go once a week. I know most of the program members by name, and they're nice people, but I don't socialize with them outside AA."

"Chatham? Why there?"

"No reason. I just jumped on the train one day, because there happened to be a meeting there and I really felt like I needed to go. It was in an old church. I'm not religious, but it felt appropriate somehow, to find strength in a place like that, as opposed to a worn-down community centre or a sterile hospital room. I went back the week after, and now it's my home group."

"That's nice." Ava stopped at the metro entrance and shuffled on the spot. Now that they had started talking, she felt a lot safer, and she wanted to spend more time with Mia. "I only go to meetings about twice a month nowadays, but today was difficult."

"It was." Mia shook her head. "I still can't believe she's gone. On my watch."

"Hey, you're not a nurse, Mia."

"I know." Mia noticed herself opening up to Ava. It felt good to talk to someone, as if a weight was slowly being lifted off her shoulders. "I don't want to go back to the hotel yet," she heard herself say. "The crew might still be at the bar, and Lynn always tries to rope me into joining in. Would you like to get some food? I know a great Mexican restaurant if you're hungry, and they don't serve alcohol in case you're trying to avoid those places..." She looked up at Ava. "They don't have a license, which is rare for Mexican restaurants."

"Mexican sounds good," Ava said. "So, it's you showing me around instead now? I like that."

"Don't expect too much. It's my go-to place when I'm in New York, but apart from that, I've got no other local intel."

"I'm not too sure about that." Ava cocked her head. "Are you talking about *Bonito*?"

Mia's eyes widened. "Yes. *Bonito y Barato*. Delicious and cheap. Have you been there?"

"Yep. It happens to be one of my favourite places too." Ava grinned. "This night might not turn out to be so bad after all."

"No." Mia laughed. "I suppose you're right." She hesitated as they walked. "So... before I saw you in AA, I assumed you were on a date tonight."

"A date?" Ava shook her head in amusement. "I haven't been on one of those in ages. Wait... did you really think I'd go out with another woman tonight and then take you out tomorrow morning? Is that how you see me?"

"So, it was going to be a date tomorrow? Is that what you're saying?" Mia asked, trying to supress a giggle.

Ava seemed taken aback by Mia's sudden directness. "Uhm... I'm sorry. Maybe I was drawing the wrong conclusions. I had the feeling you were fishing for a date, when we spoke in Dubai. But I'm actually not even sure if you're..."

"No, you were right," Mia interrupted her. "I was hinting at that in my own clumsy way. And I am gay." She looked up at Ava. "Have been for a very long time in case you were wondering. A lot of women mistake me for a straight girl who's desperate to experiment." She laughed. "It can get a bit awkward sometimes. I think it's the flight attendant look. It doesn't do me any favours on that front."

"I agree the uniform can be a bit confusing." Ava laughed too. "Well, I'm glad we're both here now, even if it's through the strangest of circumstances. At least we've delved straight into the 'getting-to-know-each-other's-darkest-secrets'-stage," she joked. Ava didn't want to ask about Mia's drinking history. It wasn't any of her business, unless Mia decided to share, and she didn't feel like talking about her own issues either, so she left it at that. Tonight, she needed a light-hearted conversation and a good meal. She felt her belly rumble.

"So, Mia, how do you like being a senior purser?" Ava rolled her eyes at the lame question which, apparently, was the only thing she could come up with. *Come on Ava. You can do better than that.*

"I like it just fine." Mia put on her most charming fake flight-attendant smile and batted her eyelashes. "No, all joking aside, I love it. I get to travel, I get some time to myself and I love the people I work with. My career is going pretty well. It's fun to be a purser but sometimes I just want to be away from people, you know? Sometimes I wish I was in the cockpit like you, protected by that sacred door that people can't get through." She shrugged. "But all in all, I like my job. So, how do you like being a captain? You seem quite young to be one, if you don't mind me saying."

Ava's face lit up when Mia mentioned the word. "Oh God, I love it. Getting my commercial pilot's licence was the best decision ever. My parents wouldn't hear of it at first but I kept on nagging them until they finally gave in. Now they're the ones begging me for ticket discounts and bragging to the neighbours about my career." She laughed. "And yes, I'm one of the youngest captains our airline has ever employed. I'm thirty-seven now, but I've worked hard for it. I know I'm competent and I've done my fair share of hours in the air so there's no reason why I shouldn't be a captain at this point in my life."

"Your parents must be proud." Mia shot her a glance.

"It's quite something, being responsible for hundreds of people's safety whilst up in the air."

"It is. That's why I still go to AA. Even after six years. I can't afford to slip up, or to make mistakes." She looked at Mia. "And neither can you."

"I know." Mia sighed. "So far, I'm managing just fine."

18

NEW YORK, USA

"Lemon or lime?" Mia held up both to squeeze over Ava's ceviche. The quirky little restaurant was busy tonight, but they'd managed to get a small table for two by the window. Mariachi music was playing in the background of the dark dining room filled with cacti, Mexican props and other kitschy decorations, bathing in the red light from the fairy strings in the ceiling. Fake red flower arrangements filled the entire length of the windowsill next to them, matching their red tablecloth with white polka dots.

"Lemon for me, anytime."

"Lemon?" Mia shot Ava an amused look. "That's an interesting choice. Do you mind if I ask why?"

"You're asking me to justify my preference of citrus?" Ava asked, equally playful.

"Yep." Mia put the lemon wedges down next to Ava's plate and squeezed lime over her own dish. "Lime has got so much more depth. It's a crime in my eyes to put lemon on any good quality raw fish, apart from salmon."

"Okay, cool it, you lemon bigot." Ava laughed. "I shall explain myself in depth. Lemons are sweeter and juicier, and they don't have the bitter after taste that limes do. The colour of the peel against the colour of the leaves is one of the most vibrant colour combinations found in nature, and they don't get brown spots like limes. The taste reminds me of my childhood. I'm not a great cook myself, but coming from Jordan, my mother puts lemons in almost every single dish she makes, sweet or savoury. They're anti-bacterial, great for the skin and can help cure acne. Where I come from, we even use them to bleach ankles and knees. Or, you could mix the juice with baking soda and you have teeth bleach." She picked up a lemon wedge and squeezed it over her fish. "See? Tasty, pretty and versatile."

"Wow. You're certainly passionate about your lemons." Mia laughed. "Is that why your teeth are so amazing?" She giggled nervously as she realised she was flirting.

Ava cocked her head and smiled. "You like my teeth?"

"Uhuh." Mia couldn't look at her anymore for fear of turning bright red, so she concentrated on her food instead. "You told me your parents are from Jordan," she said, trying to change the subject. "Did you grow up there?"

Ava shook her head. "No, we moved to England when I was six. My parents, myself, and my younger brother. I grew up in Cambridge. My father was a senior lecturer in Modern Middle Eastern History at the university there and my mother is a professor in archaeology, also at Cambridge. She still works, my father is retired."

"Impressive." Mia looked up, finally meeting Ava's eyes. "Academic family. Are you close to them?"

Ava thought for a moment before she nodded. "Yeah. I'd say so. We've had our difficulties, sure. They're pretty liberal, but it was still a lot for them to process when I came out to them. Apart from that, they always wanted me to go into academia, told me I was too smart to spend my life ferrying people around, which I'm pretty sure I'm not. I could never do what they do." She laughed. "But we're in a good place now. I have dinner with them once a week, unless I'm away."

"That's nice." Mia twirled some salad around her fork. "Although I strongly disagree with them. I think your job is admirable and empowering. It must be amazing to be able to fly this big plane to the other side of the world. I thought about being a pilot, when I was younger. I guess being senior purser is the next best thing, so that's good enough for me."

"Have you ever thought about pilot school?" Ava asked.

"I can't. I have a hearing problem on my left side. Traumatic injury, thirteen years ago. It's nothing I can't live with, but the physical tests are really strict. I'd never pass."

"I'm sorry about that."

"Don't be. It was all my own fault and I've learned to live with it. I always make sure my head is turned to the right when people talk to me, and I lip read when the aircraft engines are roaring. So far, I've been okay."

"Is that how you got that scar?" Ava asked, pointing at Mia's forehead.

Mia ran a finger over it, shifting her eyes to her plate. "Yeah."

Ava decided not to dig any further. She had a feeling it was a touchy subject. "Are you close to your family?"

Mia hesitated, unsure how to answer the question. "Yeah. We're good, I suppose. Not great, but we're okay. I don't see them very much. I have a sister, she's fifteen years younger than me. She studies physiotherapy and she's an accomplished swimmer, she's won some regional championships and is now up for selection for the national team. My mother's a nurse and my father's a postman. Pretty standard English family, I'd say." Mia laughed. "Very standard, actually. You know, two kids, a cat and a car, roast dinner on Sundays, Bingo nights, village fairs, supportive of the local football team, friendly with the neighbours, holidays to Spain, all-inclusive, of course..."

Ava's eyes widened as she laughed. "Wow. You've just summed up everything I dreamed of as a kid. Well, apart from the car, we had two of those."

"I can say the same about you." Mia handed her empty plate back to the waiter and thanked him. "I always craved more exotic things, always felt the need to escape, to explore. Believe me, when you're sixteen and you live in a village where every single day is the same, you'll jump at anything that's different."

"And so, you decided to go into aviation," Ava concluded.

"I did." Mia moved back so the waiter could put down the condiments for their mains. The staff was running here, rather than walking, and health and safety rules didn't seem to apply as they sped in and out of the kitchen with some-times as much as six plates balancing on their hands and arms.

"So, tell me about your sister," Ava said.

"Ami." Mia laughed. Her name is Ami with an 'i'. It's an anagram for Mia, as you've probably worked out. My mother thought it was really clever for some reason, but I never got the novelty of it. The only thing that came from it was a whole lot of confusion as to who was called what from any family member over the age of seventy. Our grandpar-ents always got it wrong when they were still alive. I'm sure if my parents had another child, they would have called him or her Aim, or Mai.

Ava laughed. "Or Iam."

"Yes, or that." Mia laughed too. "Anyway, there's not much to tell about Ami with an 'i'. We're not close, and I hardly ever see her. What about your brother?" she asked, changing the subject. "Are you close?"

"Yeah, we're good," Ava said. His name is Zaid. "Apparently, he's very clever, but I've never witnessed it first-hand."

"What does he do?" Mia asked.

Ava cocked her head. "Does the name Zaid Alfarsi ring a bell?"

"Of course." Mia's eyes widened when it suddenly clicked. "Isn't he the motivator guy? Don't look back, you're not going that way? That one?"

Ava laughed. "Yep. That's my little brother. I say little, but he's only three years younger than me."

"I can't believe it." Mia was stunned to find out that the most successful mass psychologist and motivator in the UK was Ava's brother. She'd seen him on TV a couple of times, getting people all worked up on stage. Apparently, he was quite the talent, hired by highbrow business people and celebrities when he wasn't doing his tours. "Does he do that to you too?" she asked. "The motivational thing, I mean?"

"He'd better not," Ava joked. "He tries, but I'm always on to him. I don't want anything to do with that crap, but I respect him for doing so well for himself. He's a great guy when he doesn't try to make my life miserable with his practical jokes. And he's got many, believe me."

"Oh yeah? Like what?"

Ava rolled her eyes. "Just childlike stuff. When he's at home, it's like he never grew up. Last week, when we were having dinner at our parents' place, he put my house keys in the rose jelly as it was setting in the fridge, and before I left, I spent twenty minutes separating my trainers. They'd been laced together with the most complicated knots I've ever seen, and of course -I should have known- there was the same jelly inside my shoes when I finally put them on. It's not even funny."

"Sounds entertaining to me.' Mia held up a hand. "I'm sorry" She looked at the plate of steaming food that was put down in front of her. "Wow, these tacos look amazing."

Ava groaned as she took the first bite. "Oh my God. They taste amazing too." She closed her eyes and savoured the flavour. "Don't you think food tastes so much better without alcohol?"

Mia laughed at her enthusiasm. "Yes, I suppose you're right. I've never thought of it like that."

"I mean, not all foods of course," Ava continued. "A steak will never be the same without red wine, so I simply stopped eating that. But anything else... mmm." She held up her lemon water and toasted with Mia's glass. "And you know what? It's not the only thing that's better without alcohol."

"Oh yeah? What else?" Mia studied Ava's eyes. They held a certain naughtiness she hadn't seen up till now.

"Kissing." There was a silence.

Mia laughed nervously but Ava didn't seem to regret her provocative statement.

"Really?"

"Yeah. Don't you agree? It's so much more intense when you're sober. You've got nothing to hide behind, no excuses. Just pure, raw lust. The memory is more vivid too, so you can relive it over and over again." Ava smiled and gave her an intense stare with her light green cat eyes. "It's honest."

Mia could hear herself swallow. A jolt of heat shot through her core and she held her breath for what seemed like an eternity, thinking of a reply.

"Right," was all she could manage to say. "I guess when you put it like that..." She allowed herself to indulge in Ava's eyes for a moment. "I haven't had that spark in a while, though. I haven't really met someone I've wanted to kiss so badly that I..." She shook her head. "I go on dates sometimes, but it's hard, when you don't drink. Kissing someone who's just had a margarita is kind of distracting and ordering water on a date doesn't exactly scream 'here's an exciting, exotic, wild and fun person." She chuckled. "It's usually a red flag. People take you for being dull, prim and boring."

"I get that." Ava still had a smirk on her face, clearly enjoying herself. She scooped a spoonful of guacamole onto her other taco and dressed it before eating it with her hands, licking her fingers. "I've had the same problem a couple of times. And the sobriety thing is not something you bring up on a first date either. In a way it's weird if you do, like you're oversharing, but it's also wrong if you don't, because your date deserves to know what she's getting herself into, right?"

Mia nodded. "Oh God, it's so nice to finally talk to someone who gets it. I've thought of dating people in the AA, just to make life easier, but there's really not much choice if you count out the men, the straight women, the people with anger management issues, permanent brain damage from drinking, or anyone over, let's say forty-five or fifty."

Ava laughed. "Well said. I'm with you on that one. So, you're not dating anyone at the moment?"

"No. And I assume you're not either, from what you said earlier?"

"No, I'm not." Ava winked. "Apart from the fact that I'm sitting here with you right now." She asked a passing waiter to light the two candles in between them. The light streaming through the holes in the brightly painted skull-shaped candle holders cast a cosy light over their table. "It kind of feels like a date, doesn't it?"

Mia giggled. "Yeah it does." She put a scoop of salsa on her taco and topped it up with guacamole and cheese. "It would have been a great date, if it was. I'm enjoying myself."

"Does that mean you're staying for dessert?"

Mia had the feeling Ava wasn't referring to the food, but she picked up the menu next to her anyway and studied it while eating her taco.

"I might. If there's anything here that I like," she said after swallowing. She smiled when she felt Ava's eyes on her. "Stop looking at me like that. You're making me nervous."

"I'm sorry." Ava laughed. "I can't seem to help myself tonight. I'd tell you that I'm not normally this full on and that conversation with new people doesn't come easy to me, but you probably wouldn't believe me. Still... please allow me to say that I think you're absolutely stunning." Her eyes met Mia's. "I love that long, dark hair and the dark eyes... It's kind of exotic."

"Well I'll have to disappoint you," Mia said, glowing from the compliment. "I'm all English. As far as I'm aware, anyway." She felt her cheeks go rosy. "For the record, I think you're one of the most attractive women I've ever met too. Your eyes... they're like cat eyes, and the colour is extraordinary. Are all women this gorgeous in Jordan? Because if they are, I might consider moving there." To Mia's great satisfaction, it was Ava's turn to blush.

"The light eyes are not uncommon." Ava refilled their glasses with lemon water. "But I wouldn't recommend moving there if you're looking to score. Homosexuality isn't illegal in Jordan, but it's certainly not celebrated, or even tolerated by most people." She put down her taco and leaned back in her chair. "But other than that, the country is beautiful. I've been back a couple of times over the years, and Petra, my native city, never fails to amaze me. It's so rich in history and natural treasures. They call it the rose-red city because the city's structures are carved out of the red rock of the mountains. It looks otherworldly at night, when it's lit up."

"Do you still have family there?" Mia asked.

"Yeah. My aunt and uncle, who I stay with when I'm there, live in a village just outside Petra, where they run their own textile business. My grandma lives around the corner from them. There's this smell there that always reminds me of my childhood." Ava paused, searching for words. "It smells of dust or sand, I guess." She laughed. "But the good kind. Mixed in with the smell of cigarettes, shisha and everything being too hot, and there's always a faint aroma of food too, wherever you are." Ava laughed. "I'm probably not selling it, but it's definitely worth a trip, if for the food alone."

"I might be so lucky to do that someday, if the airline decides to expand their destinations to Jordan." Mia shivered at the tension between them. It was so obvious, so strong. She had felt it the moment they met, but now she knew that Ava felt the same, the night was starting to get pretty exciting. She let her eyes linger on Ava's mouth for a split second, and subconsciously licked her lips. Her stomach was doing strange things, so she put down her half-eaten taco, unable to finish it. All she wanted was Ava's lips on hers.

Ava noticed her stare. "Are you okay?" Her voice was low and hoarse.

"Hmm. Yeah." Mia mumbled, fighting to tear her gaze away from Ava's mouth. "I'm not so hungry anymore."

"Would you like to share a dessert?"

Mia picked up the menu again. "Lime pie? They don't have lemon pie, I'm afraid." She smiled behind the leather binder.

"I'll go with the lime, just for tonight." Ava said with a grin. "If that makes you happy, Mia."

19

NEW YORK, USA

Ava got out of the taxi in front of Mia's hotel and gave the cab driver a generous tip.

"Thank you. Never mind the other stop, I think I'm good here, actually."

"Are you coming in?" Mia asked. "I can't let you walk all the way back right away."

"It's only five blocks. I like to walk." Ava grinned. "But I do want to make sure you get up to your room safely first."

Mia felt her insides flutter. "That's probably a good idea. Who knows what could happen in the brightly lit and secure corridors of a four-star hotel?"

"So true." Ava followed her in. "Who knows what could happen?"

THEY STOOD in the hallway in front of Mia's room, facing each other as they were about to part ways. Mia was the first to speak.

"Do you want to come in? Just to make sure I get in safely?" she joked.

"No, I have to get back. I..." Ava hesitated, staring at Mia's mouth.

"That's okay," Mia interrupted her when she noticed that Ava was looking for an excuse. "Thanks for tonight. I had a really nice time."

"Me too." Ava brushed a finger against the back of Mia's hand. It was the lightest of touches, yet it felt so loaded. The hairs on Mia's arms rose when Ava looked into her eyes.

"Do you kiss on a first date?"

Mia smiled. "Sometimes. Do you?"

"Yes." Ava lowered her voice. "If I like someone." She took a step forward, closing the distance between them, and took hold of Mia's waist with one hand, while she ran the other through Mia's hair, waiting for permission.

Holy shit. Mia's body was burning, and her heart started pounding in her throat. If there had ever been a time she had been this turned on, she couldn't remember. When she didn't oppose, Ava pushed her back against the door and leaned in. Mia looked up at her, parting her lips. The hunger in Ava's eyes was obvious, and the internal reaction she felt to her hand around her waist was alarmingly intense. Ava's fingers were playing with the hem of her sweater, and she slid a finger underneath in, stroking Mia's bare skin. She softly brushed her lips against Mia's, taking her time. Mia only realised she'd been holding her breath until she exhaled deep, shivering at the sensation. She put her hand around Ava's neck and pulled her in as she kissed her, sinking into the warmth of Ava's mouth. It felt like an explosion. She moaned softly, drowning in the sensation of Ava's tongue playing with hers as Ava pressed herself harder against her. Mia allowed her hands to strum the top of Ava's waistband, and moved them up underneath her t-shirt, tracing her spine. Ava's skin felt warm and soft, and the passionate make-out session had made her go wet within seconds, craving more.

They both jumped back and took a step away from one another when the sound of a bell indicated that the elevator door was about to open. A very drunk Farik stumbled into the hallway with a young man on his arm, laughing at one of his own jokes, as usual. He didn't even see Mia and Ava, too busy to get the man to his hotel room as fast as he could.

Ava sighed when they disappeared out of sight. "I'd better get to my hotel," she said, still flushed from their kiss. She looked down at Mia's lips again, hesitating, then up at her eyes and shook her head, smiling. "Before I lose all control."

"Me too." Mia took her hand, not ready to say goodbye. She was buzzing, still on a high from Ava's grip and the steamy kiss they'd just shared. She wanted Ava in her bed, but it was clear that she wasn't going to go there tonight. "I'll see you tomorrow, then?"

"Yeah. I'll see you in the morning." Ava retracted her hand and blew her a kiss before turning and heading towards the lift.

20

NEW YORK, USA

Mia lay awake, staring up at the ceiling. *Wow. Just wow.* Ava was an exceptionally good kisser, and she felt so turned on that she didn't know what to do with herself. *Is it warm in here?* She got up from the bed and turned on the air con, in desperately trying to cool herself down.

Seeing Ava at the AA meeting had been nothing short of shocking. Mia never expected to come across anyone she knew at the meetings, simply because she never had, in all those years she'd been going. She'd become skilful at lying and avoiding meetings in places her family or friends might be. Seeing someone from the tech crew was the last thing she'd expected, especially the captain. The fact that Ava knew about her drinking problem didn't bother her that much anymore. Ava would never tell a soul, she had too much to lose herself. And even if that weren't the case, Mia had the feeling she could trust her, even though she barely knew her. She felt the silent calmness of relief relax her body and her mind. For years, she'd kept her secret to herself, carrying the burden on her own. It was a whole new experience to be able to share it with someone who understood. Her parents didn't know, her sister didn't know, and her friends didn't know. No one but Ava knew. For years, she'd been dodging questions, planning the occasional visits to her parents on weekdays, because they only drank on Saturdays and Sundays. She didn't want them to know that she still struggled. That she hadn't learnt her lesson, even after what had happened many, many years ago. She didn't want them to know her problem went much deeper than that accident, that her urges would always be a part of her, no matter how many years had passed. She'd hurt their family enough, and no good would come from them knowing she was a recovering alcoholic for no other reason than that she needed to drink to feel good. Mia had experienced no childhood traumas. That, she was certain of. Her parents had supported and accepted her through difficult teenager, and they hadn't made a big deal out of it when she told them she was in love with her first girlfriend. Nothing about her upbringing had been traumatic, and there were no excuses to hide behind. She had never, in all those years of soul searching, been able to find a single trigger for her behaviour and had finally accepted that it was just there. It wasn't trauma, it wasn't genetic, and it certainly wasn't learned behaviour. Mia didn't have many friends, apart from Lynn. She occasionally had coffee with her cousin, who lived a couple of blocks away, and she hung out with her colleagues when they had a layover, but she'd never let people get close enough to share her secret. Even Lynn, whom she'd known for many years, was oblivious to her drinking problem. But things had changed tonight, when she saw Ava. The panic of being found out had turned into a strange sense of comfort. Staying sober would always be a struggle, but tonight, she hadn't felt entirely alone.

Ava. God, she was sexy. She had that mysteriously beautiful Middle-Eastern look that so many people would kill for. *Those eyes...* Mia crawled back into the king-size hotel bed, closed her eyes and tried to picture her, sliding a hand inside her briefs. *And those lips...* She gasped as she touched herself, replaying their kiss over and over again. If only Ava was here now. She craved her. What was her problem? Why couldn't they just have a night of amazing sex, skip all the formalities and the getting-to-know each other better? They could do all that later, but right now, Mia needed to feel Ava's weight on top of her. She had to have her. Each time she thought of their moment in the hotel corridor, her body went weak and the pulsating throb between her legs became too strong to ignore. She rubbed her clit with her fingers, buckling on the mattress as she stimulated herself towards release. Sooner than she expected, the familiar delight of an upcoming orgasm grew inside her, spreading out from her core down to her toes and up to her head, fogging her brain with blissful pleasure. She moaned as she came, closing her eyes in delight. *Ava.*

21

NEW YORK, USA

Ava closed the door behind her, leaned back against it and let out a deep sigh. If she had any willpower left in her, it would have melted after ten more seconds with Mia. And now she was alone in a room, only five blocks away. She'd gotten away just in time. Or had she just made the biggest mistake of her life? Because she seriously regretted leaving. *Why didn't I take her up on her invitation to come in? Why did I run?* Ava had no idea. She could have been draped over Mia by now, feasting on her body, pleasuring her for hours until they were both too exhausted to move. But instead, she'd left. Was she being courteous or just stupid? She couldn't remember anything from her walk back to her hotel. Walking through Manhattan at night was something she loved doing, but everything had passed her in a haze, as if she'd been looking through gauze. *Was I scared? Maybe I was.* Apart from her family, Ava didn't let people close, and discussing personal things was not something she was used to doing. Even her ex-girlfriends always complained that she wouldn't let them in, and they were right, of course. Ava had never told them about her drinking problem. Not even Pedro, who had been her best friend for years. Ava often wondered if she would have told him eventually, had they still been friends. She tried to shake off the loss of that wonderful, simple friendship. Despite the stressful day, tonight had been great, and she wasn't going to let the past ruin that. She'd talked to Mia all night, and she felt different now, hopeful, as if she was writing a new chapter on her life and anything was possible.

Ava pushed herself away from the door, went into the bathroom and turned on the shower before undressing in front of the mirror. Her body looked good since she'd started running more, and the fact that she was getting closer to forty didn't bother her that much. Ava was proud of the muscle definition in her shoulders she'd gained through swimming regularly, and her abs and legs looked great too, after challenging herself to do at least one half-marathon a year. Her breasts were small, but they had a nice shape to them and gravity hadn't won the battle yet. It was nice to be in total control of her body again. She was definitely in a better shape than when she was in her early twenties. The drinking had taken its toll on her body back then, never leaving her with any energy for exercise in the mornings. Now, she was toned, she felt strong, and really enjoyed a good meal. Tonight's dinner had been fabulous, although she was pretty sure it wasn't Bonito's famous tacos that had made her feel the way she did.

Ava stepped into the bathtub and closed her eyes as the hot water trickled down her face. *Mia.* She intrigued her like no one else ever had. Mia had been guarded at first, but as the evening had carried on, she'd loosened up and had been great company. *I wonder what her story is.* Ava was glad she hadn't asked, because it was too soon. Besides that, Mia had not given her any indication that she wanted to talk about her struggles outside AA, and although they now shared something incredibly private, that didn't mean they would start sharing everything. She wanted to know more about her though. Mia's smile made Ava smile too and her laugh was loud and honest. Her dark eyes swallowed her whole and her kiss... well, that kiss was something she wouldn't easily forget. Ava hadn't felt like this around anyone for years. It was scary how much they had in common, how much easier it was to talk to someone who'd battled the same demons. But even without all that, even without the unexpected meeting at AA, there had been an instant attraction to Mia in the cockpit when they first met. That electrifying moment, when Mia had first shaken her hand was still a vivid memory. She'd never believed in instant chemistry, but she couldn't deny she'd felt it with Mia. Ava held her hand under the soap dispenser and pumped a generous amount into her palm, before rubbing the foamy substance all over her body, paying extra attention to her belly and her breasts. She felt sensual tonight.

22

NEW YORK, USA

"**M**orning." Ava put her coffee down and joined the few cabin crew members at their breakfast table. "How's everyone feeling today?" Four pairs of glassy eyes stared at her.

"What are you doing here, Captain?" one of them asked.

"Please, call me Ava." Ava smiled. "Well, I heard the coffee was better here, so I thought I'd come and see for myself."

Lynn looked at her suspiciously, taking a sip of her coffee. "It's honestly not that good, Ava. In fact, I think the machine might need a deep clean."

"Ew," Ava winced after she'd tasted the dark brew. "You're right. This is atrocious." She chuckled. "Okay, I'm not here for the coffee. I'm picking up Mia. Thought it might be good to talk about what happened yesterday." It wasn't really a lie, and it wasn't unheard of for a captain and a senior purser to spend time together.

"Yeah. That was awful. I've never seen, let alone felt, a dead person before." Lynn shook her head. "I also know Mia was fond of that woman."

"Well, for what it's worth, you guys did a great job." Ava turned to Farik. "You look like death warmed up." She burst out laughing.

"Yeah, I'm not great to be honest with you." Farik groaned. "I only dragged myself out of bed because I needed something solid in my stomach. I'm going straight back to my room after I've wolfed down these eggs."

"Me too," Sammy said. "I've been vomming all night. What a great start of my first week, huh?"

"So, you guys had a good night, then? I assume the others are sleeping?" Ava asked.

Sammy nodded, taking a bite of her bacon. "Guess so," she mumbled between mouthfuls. "Either that or they never made it back, who knows?"

"We went clubbing." Farik said in a shaky voice. "And we had shots. Lots of shots. There's a guy in my bed and I don't even remember his name. He's still sleeping." He stared down at the piece of omelette on his fork and gagged before leaving the table with a hand in front of his mouth.

Ava watched him disappear around the corner, towards the restrooms.

"Right. I think I've heard enough." She poured milk into her coffee in an attempt to make it more drinkable.

"Hey."

Ava looked up at Mia, who was standing at the end of the table. Her heart jumped at the sight of her tanned legs underneath the crisp, white shirtdress. She wore white tennis shoes too, as if she'd somehow managed to see into Ava's ultimate fantasies.

"Oh hey. Morning." Ava moved over to Farik's seat, making space for Mia. "I don't think Farik's coming back," she said, pushing his plate away.

Mia looked around the table, trying not to laugh at the

miserable faces. She put down her tea and a big bowl of yoghurt and fruit.

"How are you? You're early. Did you sleep well?" she asked, turning to Ava. "I didn't expect you here, at breakfast."

"Yeah, I slept... eventually," Ava said in a teasing tone. She wasn't worried their colleagues would notice anything in their zombie-like state. "You?"

Mia laughed. "Same here. It took a while." It wasn't awkward, seeing Ava, but she wasn't entirely at ease either. How did people behave around each other when they'd made out the night before? And why was Ava sitting here, with her colleagues? It was challenging to say the least, having to act casual around Ava when she was looking the way she did. She wore running tights that showed off her well-defined thighs and a casual deep V-neck sweater. She looked fresh-faced and free of make-up with her ponytail pulled through the back of her black baseball cap as she smiled at Mia, sipping her coffee.

"Are you still up for a walk?" she asked.

Mia smiled back and nodded. "Absolutely." She cast a fleeting glance at her colleagues, wondering if she should invite them along. She didn't want to, but she didn't want them to get suspicious either. Thankfully, Ava beat her to it.

"I'd ask you guys to come too," she said to the crew, "but you all look like you'd struggle to even make it to the lobby."

"Yuk. Thanks for the invite but I'd rather spend the day on my toilet floor than venture out into the world today," Lynn said. "You two have fun." The rest mumbled their agreement before staring back vacantly into nowhere.

"Alright then." Ava turned to Mia. "I guess it's just us." She winked, and Mia felt her insides flutter. It was barely noticeable, but she did wink. And it was sexy as hell. The flirtatious start to the day was a good sign, Mia thought. They were both still very much on the same wavelength.

"I KNOW it's not as mysterious or adventurous as you might have expected, but if you've never been to Central Park, that's a must for today," Ava said as they slipped into the chaos of Manhattan. "Besides that, the sun is shining, so that makes it even more of a must."

"That sounds like a great idea." Mia gestured to a coffee shop. "But a good coffee in the morning is also a must, and I can't drink that stuff they claim to be coffee in the hotel, so let's get a takeaway first." She cocked her head. "Let me guess... double expresso? Or do you have other preferences outside the cockpit?"

Ava laughed. "You know me so well already. I'll get them though. Now let me guess. You're having a tall latte, no sugar?"

"Nah." Mia shook her head. "I take my coffee order day by day and today, right now, I'm feeling sweet. I'll have a cappuccino. One sugar and chocolate sprinkles on top."

Ava looked at her with a flirty smile as she opened the door to the coffee shop for her. "There's no denying you are sweet, Mia."

SIPPING ON THEIR COFFEES, they passed skyscrapers, hotels, stores, food stands, delis and restaurants as they made their way through the crowds of commuters and early tourists on Times Square. Ava stayed close to Mia, and although she wanted to, she didn't dare take her hand. The chemistry between them was still there, if not stronger now. Each time Mia looked at her, she saw the same desire she'd seen the previous night, and each time they touched, Ava felt a stir, deep down in her stomach.

"I hope you didn't mind me being early," she said when they'd gained a bit of personal space. "It might sound cheesy but I'm just going to say it. I couldn't wait to see you again."

Mia giggled, surprised at Ava's honesty. "Not at all. I was really looking forward to seeing you too." She leaned in slightly, so their arms touched as they walked. "Did you go for a run this morning?"

"No." Ava rolled her shoulders. "I went for a swim instead. There's a rooftop pool in my hotel. The only downside was that Jack was there too." She laughed. "With some girl he picked up last night, so that was slightly uncomfortable."

Mia groaned. "Oh God, don't tell me they were all over each other in the pool while you were there? That's wrong. You're his boss."

"I know." Ava let out a chuckle. "I think he was still drunk. Either that, or he was trying to impress her, primate style. He was loud and obnoxious and wanted to race me."

"Jesus." Mia rolled her eyes. "Did you?"

Ava took off her sweater and tied it around her waist. "Yeah. I won."

"Of course you did." Mia stole a quick glance at the grey tank top Ava wore underneath. It hugged her tight around her waist and her breasts and didn't leave much to the imagination. "I'm glad you taught him a lesson. Jack can be a bit too full of himself for his own good."

"He's not that bad," Ava said. "I've worked with worse. At least he's not resentful of me, like some."

"Really? Who's causing you trouble?" Mia asked.

"No one's causing me trouble." Ava pulled her cap further down, shielding her eyes from the sun. "But I sense that some of the male officers don't like to report to a woman who also happens to be a lot younger. There's a couple of them, I won't mention any names."

"I'm not surprised." Mia huffed. "They're not all bad, but there's no denying that some of them are narcissistic assholes, elbowing their way to the top. It must be hard for them to stomach having someone like you in charge."

Ava shrugged. "They'll come around. I try to give them as much autonomy in their jobs as I can, and that helps, I think. I always hated it when my supervisors tried to micro manage me when I was second officer. It's hard to let go, though. I really like to be in control at all times, so it's some-thing I'm learning to deal with."

"So, you're one of those control freaks," Mia joked.

"Something like that." Ava laughed. "It started when I first joined the program. Control what you can control, I suppose. Taking back control of my life and fighting my urges day in and day out meant that there was little space to let go, in any way. I'm trying to find a balance now, so I don't drive people around me crazy with my rigid habits and detailed planning." She looked at Mia. "That night I joined you guys for dinner in Dubai, that was very out of character for me."

"Because it wasn't planned?"

"Yeah. A change of plans is fine, as long as I'm by myself, and it's my decision. But going somewhere spontaneously with people I don't know, the uncertainty of what's going to happen, not knowing if people will be drinking... that's not something I normally do."

"So why did you go?" Mia asked.

"I'm not sure. Besides the fact that I wanted to get to know the crew, I think you were the main reason I went. I was kind of intrigued by you."

Mia couldn't stop smiling now. "I was intrigued by you too. I still am."

"Even now, after I've just confessed that I'm really boring and predictable?" Ava grinned.

"Even now." Mia squeezed her arm for a brief moment. "Especially now."

THE CHAOS SUBSIDED ONCE they entered Central Park. They talked while walking the winding side paths, where classical musicians were playing on the lawn. Mia bought a bag of nuts to feed the squirrels and cried with laughter once they started climbing up against her legs in an attempt to steal the whole bag. They passed the large lawn of Sheep Meadow, where thousands of people were relaxing, socializing, playing games or enjoying a picnic against the iconic skyscraper backdrop, and they stopped at the Mosaic Memorial in Strawberry Fields, with its abundance of colourful flowers, left behind by John Lennon fans. Street musicians were singing Beatles songs under the shade of the trees that stretched around the lake. Loved-up couples and tourists in rowing boats moved lazily across the lake, as if the heat of a typical New York summer had put life here into slow motion. And that was what it felt like to Mia. Slow motion. She was so aware of every move, every gesture Ava made, and so aware of her own body. She felt calm and at ease and was thoroughly enjoying exploring a part of New York she'd never taken the time to visit, even though it was a regular destination.

They sat down on a bench, resting after their long, casual stroll.

"I really like it here," Mia said, leaning back against Ava's arm over the back of a long stone bench. She shivered when she felt Ava's hand against her jawline, slowly tracing her neck down to her shoulder, where it stayed. Mia closed her eyes, enjoying the intimate moment, while she covered Ava's hand with her own. She could feel the heat of Ava's body, almost touching hers, and she wondered if she'd ever longed for someone as much as she longed for Ava right now. She moved a little closer, leaning into the crook of her arm. "Strange that I've been in New York so many times, but I've never visited Central Park," she said in an attempt to make small talk. "It's always been so full-on, I've never taken the time to relax."

"But you're here now." Ava turned to her and looked into her eyes, making Mia melt into a helpless mess of all wonderful kinds of feelings. Her face was dangerously close. "I loved coming here on my days off when I lived in New York," she continued, almost whispering. "I'd take a thermos and a book and lie by the water for hours, reading and watching people. It's fascinating. You get people here from all walks of life, congregating on this patch of green in the middle of one of the most exciting cities in the world."

"Did you always want to live here?" Mia blushed at their closeness.

"No. It never crossed my mind until the opportunity presented itself. It was good timing." Ava paused. "I wanted to be alone for a while, start over. But there was also this job here that offered me generous amounts of flying hours, enabling me to work my way up to become 1st officer much faster than I would have in the UK. I was really ambitious when I was younger."

"And now?"

Ava shrugged. "Now I'm thirty-seven and I'm happy. I'm where I want to be. I'm in control of the biggest aircraft currently in the sky and no one treats me like I'm incapable just because I'm a woman and they expect me to suck at this." She grinned. "As you well know, most captains are total assholes, treating their first and second officers like shit, not to mention the cabin crew."

"I know." Mia laughed. "I've met my fair share of them throughout my career. My friend Lynn doesn't care. She's still on a mission to bag herself a captain. God, what is it with cabin crew and pilots?" Her eyes widened as soon as the words were out, and she laughed. "Okay, never mind. I might not be in a position to say that anymore."

"Yeah, what is it with cabin crew and pilots?" Ava grinned, her eyes still locked on Mia's.

Mia felt flushed from the full-on flirting. "What I'm trying to say," she giggled, "is that it's refreshing to have someone nice and normal in charge for a change."

"Thank you, that's kind of you to say." Unlike Mia, Ava seemed completely as ease with their flirtation. Her legs were stretched out in front of her and both arms were now resting over the back of the bench, owning the space. She patted the stone surface next to her. "Did you know this is called Shakespeare's bench?"

"Really?"

"Yes. We're in Shakespeare's Garden." Ava pointed to a tree. "That mulberry tree over there is said to have been grown from a graft of a tree planted by Shakespeare himself, and the plants here, like rosemary, pansies and thistle, refer to some of his plays."

"I'm not very familiar with Shakespeare's plays, I'm afraid." Mia moved a little closer to Ava. "Watching Romeo and Juliet in the cinema is as far as my literary education went. But I bet you had quite the cultural upbringing, with two academic parents?"

"Not really. But my father made me read a lot, so I..." Ava

stopped in the middle of her sentence and frowned as she turned towards a group of Chinese tourists. "Are they really doing what I think they're doing?"

Mia laughed when she noticed several people were taking pictures of them. "Are we supposed to smile for the camera?"

Ava laughed too. "I think it might be the bench they're after." She was about to stand up, when one of the group members gestured for her to stay there.

"Don't go. Nice picture!" the girl yelled from behind her big camera.

"Oh, you want us in the picture?" Ava shot her a confused look, pointing to the bench.

"Yes, nice picture," the girl repeated. "Smile."

Ava sat back down, smiling through her teeth next to Mia while the camera's clicked away.

"This is awkward," Mia said, bemused by the absurdity of the situation.

"Oh, but they're going to love this even more." Ava got off the bench and pointed to the armrest on the far side of the long bench that stretched into a half-circle around the courtyard. "This bench is special," she said to the girl with the big camera. "If you whisper something in this side of the armrest, you can hear it on the other side." She beckoned Mia to walk over to the other side and put her ear against it. Mia chuckled as she did so. The words that whispered in her ear sounded like Ava was right next to her.

"You look so fucking sexy in those tennis shoes."

Mia's eyes widened as she looked up at Ava, who gave her a casual shrug. *She wants me.* Her temperature rose at the thought of more to come. More kissing, more touching, more flirting, more of that delicious mouth and body... She wanted to say something back, but one of the men in the group had already jumped in front of her, resting his ear where Mia's had just been. The other group members lined up on the other side, chattering away as they tested the theory.

"Let's go." Ava held out her hand, feeling slightly braver now. Mia took it without hesitation. Heat spread through her body as she felt Ava's hand in hers. The reaction was astonishing, but she tried not to show how affected she was by the simple gesture. She hadn't held anyone's hand in years, but as she shifted her grip, entwining her fingers with Ava's, it felt like the most natural thing in the world.

They exited the park, passing the American Museum of Natural History and zig-zagged through the leafy residential streets of the Upper Westside, where families with prams, and people walking their dogs, seemed to be in no rush in comparison to the crowded Times Square. Ava stopped in front of a small restaurant with only two tables outside, shaded by sunny, yellow parasols.

"It's nice and quiet here, and the food is very good," she said. "Do you mind sitting outside?"

"Not at all, that would be lovely." Mia giggled when Ava pulled out a chair for her. There was a first time for everything.

"Are you feeling better today? Would you like to talk about what happened on the flight?" Ava asked after they'd ordered, stabbing a toothpick into an olive.

"I don't know. I think I'm good." Mia smiled. It was true. She felt amazing. "I really enjoyed last night, Ava. Spending time with you cheered me up, I honestly couldn't have wished for a better turn of events. You know, I was feeling pretty miserable when I went to the AA meeting."

"Me too." Ava crossed her arms on the table and leaned

in. "But I had a great time too. Especially at the end." She shot Mia a flirty glance, arching an eyebrow.

"Yeah. The end was exceptionally good." Mia took off her shades and put them down on the terrace table. She didn't want anything to obstruct the gorgeous view of Ava opposite her. "I wouldn't mind doing that again."

Ava bit her lip, staring right at her. "I think that can be arranged." She took a sip of her sparkling water, keeping her eyes fixed on Mia. "We're still here until five am tomorrow morning." She looked at her watch. "That gives us sixteen hours and thirty minutes of opportunity to do that again."

Mia was blushing now, her cheeks rosy as she looked down at her folded hands. "You certainly know how to keep them keen, Captain."

"I wasn't toying with you, Mia. That wasn't my intention," Ava said. "In all honesty, I don't know why I went back to my hotel last night. I think we both knew what we wanted, and I regretted it as soon as I was alone."

"Yeah. I was wondering about that..." Mia fell silent.

"I'm still not sure, but I think it scared me," Ava continued. "How much I wanted you." She shook her head. "I haven't met someone I really liked in a long time. Before I stopped drinking, I was unbearable to be around, and after that, well, I suppose I was too scared to be judged. Don't get me wrong, it's not that I don't enjoy the odd fling here and there, but they're always women I know I'll never see again. It makes it easier that way."

Mia nodded. "I understand. I've been in relationships over the years, but nothing has worked out. My last one ended after I relapsed on holiday. My ex and I were in Greece for two weeks and I thought one drink wouldn't hurt. In fact, it was Marsha's idea. I'd been sober for years, and she was convinced I had it under control by then. She called me boring and ordered me a small, innocent glass of wine, unfortunately that one glass turned out to be not so innocent after all. It was my own fault though, my decision. It wasn't like she forced it down my throat. Then one small glass turned into a bigger glass. It was still one glass, after all, I told myself, and only the second one. Before I knew it, I was back in my permanently drunk, selfish, nasty state. Marsha left after five days and I checked myself into a yoga resort, sticking to green juice for the rest of my lonesome holiday." She sighed. "I begged her to take me back once I got home, but she'd already packed her bags."

"Do you still miss her?" Ava asked. "Do you think you'll ever get back together?"

"No. Never. It's completely over, we broke off all contact. Besides, someone who calls me boring, and orders me wine knowing that I'm an alcoholic, might not be the best match for me." She paused. "It's funny that I didn't see that until now, until I said it out loud."

Ava made space on the table when the waiter brought their food.

"Yeah. It's strange, isn't it, how distance can change your perspective on things." She tucked into her spring greens and goat's cheese salad. "Everything is clearer from a distance."

"Do you have any experience with that?" Mia asked.

"Doesn't everyone, at some point in their life? When my parents discovered I was hanging out with the wrong crowd and was drinking and smoking weed at seventeen, they sent me to Jordan to live with my uncle and aunt for three months. I was furious at first, contemplating running away, but what could I do? It wasn't my country anymore, I didn't know anyone apart from my cousin, who was a good girl and already engaged at my age. I didn't have any money or the means to go back, so I gave in eventually. I worked in my aunt's textile shop and helped with household chores on my days off. I cooked, cleaned and cut fabric for hours on end until my hands were bleeding, and even accused them of slavery at one point. Turns out, it wasn't that bad after all. My life was so boring there compared to my life at home in London, that I had a lot of time to reflect. That's when my childhood dream of becoming a pilot didn't seem impossible anymore. After two months, I went to an internet café in town, the only one back then, and researched pilot licence programs. I signed up for the recruitment day, and by the time I got home, there was an invitation to the selection in my parents' mailbox, including the breakdown of the costs of the course. It was eighty thousand pounds." She laughed. "I was so stupid and selfish back then, it hadn't even crossed my mind that the enrolment fee would be a lot of money to my parents. Needless to say, we had words about that, for weeks on end. They wanted me to go to university, I wanted to fly. I told them I'd raise the money myself somehow, and in the end, we met somewhere in the middle and they allowed me to go. I vowed to work my ass off on the weekends, which I did. My parents took a loan out and I also managed to get a loan from the airline I trained with."

"Well done you." Mia smiled. She blew on a spoonful of broccoli soup. "So, you used to be a bit of a bad girl, huh? What did you do? Apart from underage drinking and getting stoned."

"I did a little dealing." Ava winced. "I never got caught. I looked young and innocent, so no one ever suspected me. It was just pot, but still...."

"Sounds like you were lucky to get out in time." Mia said.

"I was. I wouldn't be who I am now, if I had a record."
She glanced at Mia nervously.

Mia cocked her head. "Hey, I'm not judging you, if that's
what you're worried about. It was a long time ago and I've
done things too that I'm not proud of." She smiled. "And for
the record, you still look young and innocent."

Ava laughed, relieved she was able to be entirely honest
with Mia. "Why thank you, Mia. But I'm not so sure you'll
still find me innocent once I get you into my bed."

Mia's eyes darkened. "I'll guess I'll just have to find out
for myself."

AFTER LUNCH, they walked past theatres, street musicians,
living statues, preachers and dancers on the first strip of
Broadway. They dodged a half-naked cowboy with a guitar,
who was desperate to serenade them, and watched a street
dance performance. The theatres around her always made
Ava feel like she was home, even though she'd only lived in
New York for a couple of years. She had her arm around
Mia's waist and they were both getting more tactile by the
minute. When they finally reached a quieter street, Mia
couldn't take it anymore. She took Ava's hand and pulled
her into an alleyway.

"Wow, easy tiger," Ava joked. "There are people here,
you know."

"I don't see anyone." Mia gave her a flirtatious look as
she removed Ava's cap and brushed a lock of hair away from
her face. "Come here. No one is going to see us and even if
they do, they're not going to call the police because two
women are making out." She traced Ava's face down to her
neck. "I've been lusting after you all day and now is the
moment you kiss me."

"Is that an order?" Ava moved closer until she had Mia against the wall. She smiled as she took hold of Mia's neck, and then her hair, pulling her head back as she claimed Mia's mouth with her own. Mia moaned, and Ava could feel her getting excited by the way she moved against her. A primal lust rushed through her, almost blinding her with desire. God, how she wanted her. Ava deepened the kiss, pressing her thigh hard between Mia's legs. She slipped a hand underneath Mia's dress and squeezed her ass over the lace briefs, drawing another loud moan from her mouth. She heard a chuckle behind them and Mia immediately pulled out of the kiss. Two teenage girls disappeared around the corner when Ava turned their way.

"Fuck." Mia covered her face with Ava's cap.

Ava laughed. "Relax Mia. As you said, they're not going to call the police, are they?"

"Yeah well, my bad. I suppose I've been raised better than to make out in public, I just couldn't wait anymore." She looked up at Ava and let her eyes rest on her mouth. "Can we go back to the hotel please?" She lowered her voice. "If you want to, I mean. I..."

"Come on," Ava interrupted her, taking her hand. "Let's take a cab. Your hotel or mine?"

"Mine," Mia said matter-of-factly. "It's closer."

THE TAXI RIDE back was filled with sexual tension. There was silence, some clearing of throats and some hungry glances being exchanged. Ava played with Mia's hand in between them and traced her arm up and down. Mia looked down at Ava's hand, then up at her mouth, wanting to kiss her so badly that she could barely control herself.

"I haven't been with anyone in a long time," she whispered.

"Don't worry." Ava leaned in and whispered back in her ear. "I'll take care of you." She took a hold of Mia's wrist. "I want you so badly, Mia. I'm going to do all the things to you that you're thinking of, right now, and I'm going to make you come all night long."

Mia held her breath at the words and put a shaking hand on Ava's thigh. She traced it upwards, until Ava shifted in her seat.

"I want you too."

23

NEW YORK, USA

Back at the hotel, an unwelcome surprise awaited them. Lynn was pacing furiously around the hotel lobby with her arms crossed, looking worried.

"There you are!" she shrieked, walking up to Mia. "I've been trying to get hold of you for the past three hours! Do you not have your phone on you?"

Mia searched for her phone in her bag and saw the dozens of missed calls from Lynn. There were several text messages too, telling her to come back immediately.

"Fuck!" Mia placed a hand in front of her mouth as she scrolled through them. "I'm sorry, I didn't look at my phone and it was on silent."

Lynn shrugged. "Yeah well, you've got five minutes to get ready and pack, we've been called in to cover a sick shift and you're the senior purser. Apparently, one of the cabin crew members on today's flight to London picked up a virus from a passenger and has passed it on to the rest of his crew."

"Okay." Mia nodded slowly, letting this disappointing information sink in. "But you've been drinking..."

"Yeah well, that was last night, and it's almost three

o'clock now. I'm sure they'll make an exception since they've got no one else." Lynn waved her hand impatiently. "The others aren't senior enough to cover the shift, so it's not like we've got a choice."

Ava checked her phone too and sighed in relief when she saw she hadn't been called in. As a captain, she was supposed to be at the ready, but she'd been carried away, so distracted by Mia that she hadn't even thought of looking at her phone all day. Her gaze met Mia's for a split second as they both awkwardly waited for the other to say goodbye in front of Lynn.

Lynn groaned and rolled her eyes. "Okay Mia, why don't you let the captain help you with that heavy bag of yours, I'll give you ten minutes instead. We can share a cab to the airport, I'll let the crew know we'll be there soon." She gave Mia a warning look. "But hurry, up will you?"

"Thanks," Mia said, looking at Lynn gratefully. "I'll be quick."

Ava followed her to the elevator. "There goes our plan." She leaned back against the elevator wall and looked up at the ceiling.

"This is the worst timing ever." Mia leaned in towards her, but the doors opened again, letting others in. She laughed when they walked out.

"I don't think this is meant to be today."

"Yeah. I think the universe is punishing me for walking away from you last night." Ava hesitated. "Do you need help with your suitcase?"

Mia opened the door to her room and pointed at the small case. "I think I can manage that, don't you?" She chuckled. "But if you wouldn't mind waiting two minutes..."

Ava watched from the doorway as Mia put on her tights. Then she removed her shirtdress, leaving her in a thin white lace bra and matching briefs, before putting on her uniform blouse and her skirt. A couple of seconds of Mia's exposed skin was enough to send Ava's body into a craving she didn't know she was capable of. *So close and yet so far.* Mia would fly back, and it could take weeks before their schedules crossed again. *Damn it.*

"I'm sorry I have to leave," Mia said, buttoning up her blouse.

"Don't be. We both know this job is unpredictable, it's not your fault." Ava walked to the bed, picked up Mia's scarf and carefully folded it under the collar of her blouse. She tugged at it gently, bringing Mia's mouth close to her own.

Mia closed her eyes when she felt Ava's breath on her lips. A warm tingle spread between her legs, her body screaming out for Ava to take her. Then, she felt a tongue slide over her bottom lip, before Ava's mouth crashed into hers possessively. She moaned when her tongue found Ava's and she sank into the kiss as Ava grabbed her ass and pulled her in tight. Mia dug her nails into Ava's back, wanting more, needing more. But there was no time. She reluctantly pulled out of the kiss and took a step back, feeling dizzy and out of breath.

"I really have to go now," she stammered with a bewildered look on her face. Her scarf was dangling down her neck, loose, and her hair was messy. She ran into the bathroom, shoved her hairbrush and make-up bag into her handbag and pulled out the handle on her case. "I'll make myself look presentable in the cab."

Ava took the key card Mia handed her. "I'll check you out. Just go." She planted a fleeting kiss on Mia's forehead. "Go."

"Okay. I'll see you soon, hopefully."

"I'll see you soon."

"JESUS, WHAT HAPPENED TO YOU?" Lynn studied Mia's appearance with a disapproving frown when they finally got in the cab and sped off towards the airport. Then her mouth pulled into a smile. "You two are getting it on, aren't you?"

Mia didn't answer. She was busy combing her hair before securing it into a topknot.

"Come on, Mia. Spit it out, girl. I can tell by your face that you've just been smooching her." Lynn searched for Mia's make-up in her handbag and started applying the airline's signature eyeliner above Mia's eyelids, swearing each time the cab drove over a bump. "Well, did you?" she asked.

Mia closed her eyes, allowing Lynn to help her. "Did I what?"

"Did you smooch her? Duh." Lynn shook her head in a dramatic manner at another silence. "Okay, I think you need a strong coffee, Mia. Seems to me like you're still caught up in some daydream." She smiled. "But I'll tell you one thing. You two look sizzling together."

24

NEW YORK, USA

va watched Mia walk out of the room. *There she goes.* What the hell did she do to deserve this today? She was still shaking from their kiss, longing for another, longing for more. She was about to drop off Mia's room key at reception, when she changed her mind and walked back into the room. She closed the door behind her, let herself fall down on Mia's bed and inhaled her scent from the only pillow that had been used. There was a tiny hint of vanilla from her perfume and then there was the smell of Mia. This was where she'd slept. When she was completely stripped of make-up and all the crap she had to wear in her day to day job. It was just Mia, and she smelled amazing. Ava knew she was being pathetic. There was nothing grown-up about burying her face in someone else's pillow, and if her officers could see her now, she wouldn't hear the end of it, ever. Still, she stayed there a little longer, reliving their kiss and the recent memory of Mia's face, just before she'd left. *Enough, Ava. You're thirty-seven for Christ's sake.* Mia had done this to her. Mia had made her this way. She'd had a taste of her, and there was no going back now. It was new territory for Ava, to feel that she needed someone, wanted someone as badly as she wanted Mia. It was physical, sure. The throbbing between her legs still hadn't subsided. But there was more than that. There was the way Mia made her feel when she was with her; alive and happy, and most of all, calm. Not once, after their encounter at AA, had she thought about drinking, not even for a split second. The thought of drinking was usually in the back of her mind, and Ava wasn't sure if that was because some part of her was self-destructive, or because it was something physical that she craved. Anything could trigger the cravings: a whisky advert on a billboard, a song, certain foods she used to enjoy a drink with, stress, or a social event. She tried to stay away from hotel rooms with stocked minibars as much as possible, and she never went to a pub. The smell of beer-soaked carpets and the sight of people knocking back pints like it was nothing made being there almost unbearable. Although Ava was very good at keeping her cravings under control, not one day of her sober life had passed without her longing for a drink. Apart from today. Ava smiled. Today had been a very good day.

She got up, went downstairs and handed over Mia's key card. Then she embarked on another long walk heading to Brooklyn.

"Ava! What in the name of sweet Jesus are you doing here?" The voluptuous black barista, and owner of Ava's favourite coffee place, came tearing around the counter to greet her. She picked her up and spun her around several times as if she weighed nothing, before finally letting go. "Oh my God, it's really you. I thought I'd never see you again. I mean, I heard you weren't at your best before you left, and I just thought..."

"Yeah, yeah. Spare me the painful details, I was there too." Ava gave Imani a hug. "I'm sorry I haven't been in touch, I guess it was just easier that way." She looked her in the eyes. "But I'm sorry. I should have called you, at least."

Imani didn't seem to begrudge the fact that Ava hadn't called her in years. "Don't worry about it, babe. You're here now and it's so good to see you. How about a coffee, huh? It's on the house." Imani called her colleague over. "Hey Bart, will you make us two double espresso and take over from me, please? I've got to catch up with this lady here."

"I'm glad to see that your place is doing so well," Ava said, observing the crowded café. The high stools under the bar, that ran along the windows facing the two corners of the street, were all taken by people working on their laptops, reading or simply catching up over a coffee. The lower tables in the middle of the café were mainly occupied by parents with pushchairs and tourists.

"Can't complain." Imani gestured towards a table and took a seat opposite her. "So, what brings you back here? Are you still flying?"

"Yes." Ava smiled. "I made captain. I'm working for an Emirati airline, based in London, so I'm back home."

"Good for you." Imani rubbed her shoulder. "Are you still going to the meetings?"

"Yeah." Ava nodded. "I went last night, actually. It was around here, in Brooklyn. Do you still go?"

"Now and then." Imani thanked her colleague and handed one of the double espressos to Ava. "But I'm not a regular anymore." She leaned in over the table and took Ava's hands. "I miss being your sponsor though."

"I miss my favourite sponsor too." Ava smiled at her

warmly. "Look I have to say this," she continued. "I'm sorry I just left without saying goodbye. I relapsed... you might have heard from people at the meetings. And I couldn't face you. You were always the one who had faith in me, the one who kept me on the straight and narrow. I couldn't stomach the fact that I'd disappointed you. I've regretted it for years, yet I've never picked up the phone and I don't expect you to forgive me for that. I just came to say that I'm sorry for leaving that way."

"It's okay, babe." Imani gave her a quick squeeze. "We all have our demons to battle, hell I know I do. But running away is never a solution. You can't outrun yourself, girl." She sat back and took a sip from her coffee. "So why now? You must have flown New York many times since you left. Why today?"

"I don't know. I've avoided Brooklyn every time I've come here but last night I was desperate to go to a meeting and the only place open was about ten blocks from this place." She smiled. "It was nice to be back here, and it turned out to be a good night. It made the whole memory a little less painful, I suppose. So, I had some free time this afternoon and I thought of you."

"I'm glad you came. Have you spoken to Pedro since?"

Ava shook her head. "No. I don't think he wants to speak to me. What I did was unforgiveable."

"I'm not too sure about that," Imani said. "Besides, it wasn't just you. It always takes two to tango, it's not like his girlfriend was innocent." She shrugged. "Just saying."

"But he was my friend and I wasn't even in love with her. It was just one of those stupid, selfish things I did when I was drunk, only thinking of myself." Ava looked up, wincing at her old friend. "Does he still live around here? Does he still come here?"

"At least twice a week. When he's not in a hurry, he always sits at that corner table over there where you two used to sit together. Sometimes he's alone, and sometimes he brings a pretty brunette." Imani straightened herself. "Look. You had a knock back, you slipped. You behaved badly and thank God you were off duty. It could happen to anyone. What matters most is that you picked yourself up again and started over, sober. And that's all you, and it's great." She hesitated. "What you didn't do however, is face the consequences of your actions and ask your best friend for forgiveness. Now that's a step of the program you clearly failed to acknowledge."

"He hated me for what I did. And I deserved it." Ava thought back to the night she'd blocked from her memory for years. She was second officer back then, invited to the captain's birthday party in a swanky New York restaurant together with Pedro, who was first officer. Pedro's girlfriend was there too. Ava couldn't even remember her name. *Was it Phoebe? Yes, it was. Phoebe Markinson.* Phoebe used to flirt with her, whenever Pedro wasn't looking. Ava always had the feeling Phoebe was bi-curious, desperate to explore her attraction to women, but she'd never told Pedro about her theory. He was so in awe of her, so in love. She remembered Phoebe touching her whenever the opportunity presented itself. Her hand on Ava's, a kiss to her cheek, running her hands through her hair. Ava never attempted to discourage her. Phoebe was one of those people who would laugh it off and claim she was just being friendly if she'd tried to bring up the subject, and if Ava was entirely honest with herself, she kind of liked the attention. That night, at the captain's birthday dinner, Ava was seated next to Phoebe. Although she wasn't Ava's type, she looked great that night. She wore a body-hugging black dress and black stiletto heels, and her long, blonde hair fell in thick curls around her shoulders. After Ava turned down a glass of wine, Phoebe had insisted she have a sip of hers.

"Come on, sweetie. You really need to loosen up. Who else am I going to have fun with tonight?" she'd said. And Ava had taken a sip. Just one. Just like Mia had, on holiday. And that one sip had turned into a glass, which then turned into a bottle and later, into shots of vodka and who knew what else. She couldn't remember. What she did remember, was kissing Phoebe on the dancefloor at the end of the night. Right in front of Pedro. When Pedro got angry and confronted her, she'd hit him. Hard. Ava had resigned the day after and packed her things when Pedro was out, leaving only a stupid note, saying 'I'm so sorry'. She'd never seen him or spoken to him since.

"I'm so sorry for what I did," she said out loud. "But I'm not sure if I can face him."

"Well I'm not here to preach." Imani crossed her arms. "I can't tell you what to do but I can tell you it will make you feel better if you do *something*." She smiled. "Hey, why don't you come over for dinner tonight? Meet my family? We don't need to talk about this. Just enjoy good company, nice food and a bit of fun with some wonderful little people."

"You've got kids?" Ava was taken aback. "Wow, that idea hadn't even crossed my mind. How old are they?"

"Four and six. Don Junior and Tiffany." Imani was glowing, saying their names out loud. "I found out I was pregnant just before you left. I never got the chance to tell you."

Ava felt another stitch of guilt. "And you're still with Don, your husband?"

"Still together." Imani sighed. "Everything's hunky-dory, apart from the fact that my mother-in-law lives with us. She looks after the kids when I'm at work and makes my life miserable when I'm home." She laughed. "But she's a great cook."

"I'd love to meet your kids," Ava said, genuinely delighted at the prospect of spending the evening with Imani and her family.

"Great." Imani pulled her phone out of her pocket. "Give me a minute. I'll let the big, bad wolf know we have a guest for dinner."

25

LONDON, UK

Mia walked home with a bounce in her step. She rarely enjoyed her walk back home from the tube, especially during rush hour. The never-ending crowd of commuters pouring out of Ealing Common station, blocking her path, always put her in a bad mood, especially when she was tired. But today, she had her earphones in and was humming along to the music. She had three days off and was looking forward to a hot bath, reading a book on her balcony, and maybe a long run. The English summer was kind today, and the sun was out, making everything look just a little bit nicer. The pavements were full of people having dinner at the many restaurants along Ealing Green. Others were rushing home with their briefcases or groceries, on a mission to catch the last bit of sun. Mia spotted a new coffee shop she'd never noticed before, and a hair salon on the corner of her street that looked like it had just been opened. The deep padded chairs in front of the sinks looked inviting, and she decided she'd treat herself to a head massage before returning to work. *I should really try to spend more time at home.*

"Hi Wally. How are you?"

"Oh, hey Mia." The owner of the deli underneath her flat looked up in surprise. "You're looking chirpy."

"Aren't I always?" Mia browsed the dishes behind the counter and suddenly felt hungry. "What have you got today?"

"What do you feel like?" Wally tucked a loose strand of long, grey hair behind his ear and gave her a big smile.

Mia shrugged. "I've got a couple of days off and I don't want to waste my time cooking or shopping, I want to enjoy this weather. So, I need dinner for tonight, and lunch and dinner for tomorrow."

"Okay, let's see." Wally produced three takeaway boxes from underneath the counter and opened the first one. "How about gnocchi with a mushroom sauce for tonight? I've used fresh morels in the sauce so it's absolutely delicious."

"That sounds great. I'll have that." Mia said, her mouth watering already. Wally's deli was an institution around the neighbourhood, and a night in with his food was something she always looked forward to. Out of habit, she kept her gaze fixed on him, avoiding looking at the extensive wine selection behind him. Mia was always a bit anxious, coming in here early evening, or late at night, with the crisp Chablis lurking in the background, calling to her. She noticed she was fine, though. In fact, it was one of the few times where the thought of buying a bottle didn't seem appealing at all.

Wally scooped the pasta into the box and closed the lid. "One minute in the microwave, one and a half max." He wrote the instructions on the box. It always amused Mia how much he worried that people would destroy his food by overheating it. "Now for tomorrow's lunch, I think you might like this pumpkin soup with green pesto and homemade croutons. I'll seal them in a bag for you, so they don't go stale." He didn't wait for an answer before filling the box and bagging the condiments separately. Mia always went with his suggestions. "And rosemary and garlic lamb chops with polenta and glazed carrots." He carefully stacked the boxes into a paper bag. "I'll throw in a mixed salad for free. I know you like your greens."

"Thanks, Wally. You're a sweetheart." Mia paid him and put the change in the tip pot on the counter.

"You're welcome." Wally looked at her over his thick, black rimmed glasses. "What happened to you? You look so... I don't know... happy?" He grinned. "Have you met someone?"

Mia's eyes widened. "What do you mean? No, I mean, I'm just in a good mood and..."

"Never mind, not my business," he said. "You have a good night, Mia. And enjoy your free time."

As soon as she came in, Mia opened all the windows, curtains and the balcony doors, letting a breeze in. She wiped the make-up from her face, had a quick shower and put on a pair of tracksuit bottoms and a tank top. It felt wonderful, walking barefoot again, and she sighed as she let her toes sink into her thick living room carpet. She wasn't anxious to be back home by herself, and she wasn't anxious to have time on her hands, like she would normally be. The sun streamed in through the balcony doors, lighting up her kitchen. It smelled of cleaning products, mixed in with the overripe fruit in the big bowl on her breakfast bar. She picked out the brown apples and threw them away. Mia's flat was always pristine. She had a cleaner once a week, but there was never much to actually clean. The modern, white kitchen that opened up into the living room had been untouched for weeks now, and her bed was rarely slept in. She usually fell asleep on the couch, too comfortable to make it to the bedroom. The place could do with a bit of TLC, though. A fresh lick of paint, maybe some flowers and a few hints of colour here and there. She imagined having Ava over for dinner, sitting right there at the dinner table. She imagined Ava in her bed, afterwards. Mia grinned to herself as she heated up her dinner and walked out on to the small balcony, where she unfolded her lounge chair and sat back with her plate on her lap.

"Oh hi, Rosie," she said in a sweet voice when the neighbour's cat jumped over the railing. She stroked the morbidly obese ginger cat, who had been spending an awful lot of time with her lately. Rosie was actually a boy, Mia had been told. Apparently, the volunteers in the cat shelter were convinced he was a girl initially. By the time his balls started to grow, he was already listening to the name Rosie, and so Tuesday, Mia's extravagant next-door neighbour, had stuck with it. Rosie jumped on her lap, curiously sniffing the contents of her plate.

"That's not what you're after, is it Rosie? Vegetarian pasta?" Mia shook her head dramatically, smiling at the cat. "I promised your mummy not to feed you anymore because the vet said you need to go on a diet." Rosie looked at her and let out a heart-rending cry.

"Is he begging for food again?" Tuesday stuck her head around the balcony partition wall and laughed, shaking her shoulder length, blue hair. She looked like she was sunbathing, dressed in an iridescent mermaid bikini and matching sarong, but you could never be quite sure with

Tuesday. An impressive collection of diamanté piercings decorated her face, and her nails were long, the bright shade of blue matching her hair.

"I don't mind," Mia said, smiling up at her neighbour. "I'd give him something, but I know he's on a diet." She winced. "It's probably my fault that he's put so much weight on, I'm really sorry about that."

"Don't worry about it. I'm just glad you're nice to him. Wait, let me get you something." Tuesday ran inside and came back with a bowl of finely chopped chicken breast. "Here, give him this. I know he prefers to eat at yours and he hasn't had his dinner yet."

"Thanks." Mia stood up, took the bowl and put it on the floor next to her chair. Rosie attacked the food as if he hadn't eaten in weeks, stuffing the chicken into his mouth with his paws, like he always did. The way he attempted to eat like a human still made Mia laugh every single time.

"Been to Wally's?" Tuesday asked, pointing to Mia's plate.

Mia nodded. "He's great, isn't he?"

"He sure is." Tuesday leaned in over the railing and inhaled. "Garlic. I fucking love the smell of garlic."

"Why don't you join me? I've got more than enough food," Mia said, surprising herself. Inviting Tuesday over had never crossed her mind before. But then she never invited people over, especially not people she didn't know very well. *Fuck. What have I done?*

Tuesday straightened her back and yawned. "Really? I'm not going to say no to that." She chuckled. "I've been dozing in the sun for hours and I was just starting to feel hungry when that delicious smell reached me."

Mia chewed her cheek, suddenly panicking. "I have to warn you though, there's no wine here. I don't drink."

"That's okay." Tuesday cocked her head and looked Mia up and down as if seeing her for the first time. "I don't drink either."

"THANK you for letting me share your cat," Mia said when they were having dinner at her small balcony table. Rosie was rubbing up against her leg, begging for a bite. "I love Rosie."

Tuesday wiggled her eyebrows. "What can I say? He's a charmer." She laughed. "He took an interest in you from the first day you moved in. I was a bit jealous at first, I have to admit. But then I realised he doesn't have a garden, or any friends to play with, and I felt bad for wanting him to spend all his time with me. And it's not like we've got anything interesting to discuss."

Mia chuckled. "Don't worry. I'm not planning on getting a cat-flap, but I can't deny that I like the company. I'm away so often that I couldn't possibly have a pet." She smiled at Tuesday and realised she knew absolutely nothing about her friendly neighbour, whom she so often had fleeting conversations with. The heavily made-up woman could have been in her early forties or in her late fifties, it was hard to guess. "Where are you from?" she asked. "You have a slight accent. I couldn't really tell at first, but now that we're sitting here, chatting, I've just noticed."

Tuesday shrugged. "Forty years in the UK and I still haven't been able to shed it completely. I'm from Romania originally. I came here when I was eleven."

"It's charming," Mia said. "I love accents. Is your family in London then?"

"No, I was an orphan. I was finally adopted when I was eleven, but I'm not in contact with my adoptive parents either." Tuesday's expression indicated she'd rather not talk about it.

"Oh, I'm so sorry to hear that."

"That's okay, darling." Tuesday patted Mia's hand. "It was a long time ago and I'm fine now, so there's no point fretting over the past. What about you? Are you from London?"

"No, my parents live in Grazeley, just outside Reading." Mia laughed. "I moved out when I went to university and don't go back that often anymore."

"I see." Tuesday paused. "I take it you're a flight attendant? I always see you coming home in that cute little outfit."

Mia was grateful that Tuesday didn't ask any further questions about her family, as if she could sense that it was better not to go there. "Yes, I am. I'm a senior purser. I've been flying for a long time now, but I'm not bored of it yet."

"I'm not surprised. It must be exciting to go to all those exotic places." Tuesday put her fork down and leaned back in her chair. "I always dreamt of travelling when I was a little girl, but I ended up in accountancy."

"You're an accountant?" Mia couldn't have been more surprised. "You don't look like an accountant." She laughed. "Sorry, no offence. I think you look amazing, but it's not exactly what I expected from you."

"I get that all the time." Tuesday laughed too. "But hey, it pays the bills. I work from home, mostly, so that's nice." Her face pulled into a mischievous grin. "My specialty is creative accountancy. I have a couple of big, private clients." She hesitated before she decided to share more. "Two years in prison didn't teach me a lesson. I just love the thrill of it."

"Prison?" Mia was shocked, and yet she was dying to

know more. The evening was turning out to be a hell of a lot more interesting than she'd expected it to be. She leaned in and lowered her voice as she smiled. "So tell me, please. What was it like doing time?"

26

LONDON, UK

Back in her own bed in London, the alarm clock went off at seven am, but Ava had no problem getting up. She still had five hours before she was expected at Heathrow Airport, and she liked to be sharp and wide awake before going into the briefing. She double-checked the schedule next to her bed. *Cairo. That's right.* It wasn't one of her favourite destinations, but it was only for one night. The gap through the curtains let the early sunlight through, painting her shadow on the wall as she got up. Her bedroom was the only room in the house she was happy with, so far. She'd painted it white, put up some book shelves and artwork, bought grey and white striped curtains and matching sets of bedsheets for her chrome framed double bed. Apart from that, there was only a small grey sofa with a sheepskin throw draped over it, and a Japanese paper lamp in the corner of the room. A reading light was clipped to her bed frame, next to a pair of hand-cuffs she'd lost the keys to, the only reminder of Danielle. It annoyed her she couldn't get them off, but then she hadn't had anyone in her room for at least a year. It was the room where she spent most of her time, so she always kept it tidy. There were no clothes, no shoes and no clutter. Most of her stuff was in the spare bedroom, which she used as a walk-in closet. She went in there, put on a pair of tights, a t-shirt and running shoes, ready to venture into the world.

AVA RAN the same route every day when she was home. Down her street, following the leafy blocks ahead towards Turnham Green Terrace, where the pram-pushers and yoga mat carriers were already out and about. She ran around Chiswick Common, following the paths along neatly trimmed fields where the dog walkers were gathered with their takeaway coffees. She liked this time of day, before the commuters were out, and before the park was full of cyclists. Ava preferred the early sounds of London to her music and she usually left her phone at home. She heard birds singing, dogs barking and music playing from the coffee shops, where the staff were carrying tables and chairs outside while catching up on gossip. She ran around the common twice today, feeling less tired than she normally would, even though she hadn't slept much. She thought of her pleasant night at Imani's house. It had been so great to spend time with her again, and to meet Don and her kids. Even Imani's overbearing mother-in-law had made Ava laugh with her controlling behaviour. It was nice to have Imani back in her life again and she wished she'd contacted her sooner. And then there was Mia. She'd been thinking of Mia for most of the night, fantasizing about what would have happened if she hadn't been called in to fly back. But the lack of sleep didn't seem to affect her mood. In fact, she felt energised and something that came pretty close to happy. She'd already cross checked their schedules and was looking forward to their next flight together. God, she couldn't wait. She wondered if Mia was thinking of her too. Ava still felt a sensation of arousal, each time she thought of their last kiss, which was pretty much constantly.

WHEN SHE GOT HOME, Ava had a long shower, washed her hair and wrapped herself in the fluffy white robe her parents had given her for Christmas. She made scrambled eggs and put a capsule into her Nespresso machine, staring up at the maroon coloured wall as she waited for her cup to fill. It was really about time that she did something about it. Although the flat was tidy and presentable – her cleaner made sure of that – she couldn't stand the colour. *What would Mia think of it?* Danielle had offered her decorator's services many times, but Ava had declined. Having Danielle do up her home was a little bit too close to something serious for her. Besides that, she'd never cared what Danielle thought of her flat, as long as she was handcuffed to her bed once a week, after telling her husband she was going to yoga class. But with Mia, things felt different, and she cared about what Mia thought of her. "White," she said out loud. "White and grey." She liked it in her bedroom, so why not carry it on through the rest of the house?

Ava headed up to her roof terrace where she sat down to eat her breakfast, whilst scrolling through a list of local decorators on her iPad. The luxurious set of black rattan garden furniture with white pillows, consisting of a corner couch, a chair and a large table, covered almost her entire roof, leaving little space for anything else. Ava didn't need more though. Plants needed to be taken care of, and she didn't want to ask her neighbours for help with watering while she was away over the summer months. People always assumed you were friends after calling on a favour and she had no desire to invite them over for dinner to thank them. She was always polite when she met one of them on the staircase but had managed to avoid small talk so far and didn't even know their names. She soaked up the last buttery left-overs with a piece of bread, brought her plate down to the kitchen and made herself another coffee, still working down the list on the iPad while she made her way back up the steep staircase, leading outside. After that, she would do what she always did. Read the newspaper for two hours over her second coffee, ending with the daily Sudoku. Since she'd stopped drinking, her 'waking up regime' had given her something to do before work, whether she had a late or an early shift. It relaxed her and mentally prepared her for a long-haul flight. But there was also an element of control to her regime, one that she'd set up to help her support her sober life. She'd never felt the need to be in control when she was younger. In fact, she was quite reckless back then. But now, it was the one thing that protected her from a relapse. As long as she stayed on top of things and made sure she stuck to her schedule, she'd be fine.

Becoming a captain had been important to Ava. She liked being the one making the decisions and being in charge meant that no one could make her life miserable at work, triggering old habits. She walked the same route to the tube station each time on her way to work, avoiding certain pubs and the off-license and she never accepted social invitations from people she met in London. It was safer that way. Apart from her weekly family dinner and the occasional get-together during lay-overs, Ava was happy with her own company and had been for a very long time.

But as comfortable as it was, keeping her life strictly regimented, with all its components the same, her flat wasn't going to look any nicer by doing nothing about it. She dialled the number for the decorator with the best reviews, ignoring the higher than average fees. It was time to make a positive change.

27

LONDON, UK

"Hey, Mia!" Ava waved at her from the opposite gate as Mia was about to board the aircraft.

Mia turned around at the familiar voice, a jolt of pure joy shooting through her core. *Oh God, there she is.* Seeing Ava again was more than a welcome surprise. Just a glimpse of her was enough to make Mia's day, especially when she called her name. Mia ran her tongue over her teeth, making sure they weren't stained with lipstick, smiled and waved back. For a moment, she thought of running over to her, but she couldn't leave the gate unattended. Shouting was frowned upon too, and so she made a steering wheel gesture and spread her arms out, tilting them from one side to the other.

Ava nodded, amused by her charades. She pointed at her watch, indicating that she didn't have time to come over and talk. Then, she held her arms in the shape of a triangle.

Mia frowned, trying to figure out what she was trying to say. She shrugged helplessly.

Ava changed her tactics. She struck a pose with both

arms up, bending her hands in a ninety-degree angle, both pointing the same way.

"Ah!" Mia shouted, putting a hand in front of her mouth when she realised she was being too loud. "Egypt," she articulated.

Ava gave her a thumbs-up and laughed, then pointed at Mia. Mia thought for a moment, then took her pashmina out of her bag and wrapped it around her head.

"Abu Dhabi?" Ava articulated.

Mia nodded and gave her a thumbs-up too. Then she felt brave and held her fist against her ear, spreading out her pinkie and her thumb, mimicking a phone call. Ava's smile broadened as she nodded. She took a card out of her pocket and gave it to one of the ground staff, pointing at Mia, before rushing over the jet bridge. The ground staff member looked disgruntled, but walked over to Mia anyway, handing her the card.

"I really don't have time for this, you know," she said, giving Mia a warning look.

"I know." Mia cast her a grateful smile. "Thank you, I really appreciate it." She grinned when she looked down at the card with Ava's number in her hands.

28

LONDON, UK TO ABU DHABI, UAE

"Abu Dhabi, here we come," Lynn said with very little enthusiasm.

"What's your problem with Abu Dhabi?" Mia asked. "You always moan when we have a layover there. I actually like it."

"It's never longer than a night though," Lynn said. "I don't have a problem with Abu Dhabi per se, but the arrangement sucks. An eighteen-hour layover means that I can't have a drink, therefore I can't go out, both resulting in zero time for checking out the local Tinder pool."

"Can't you just go on a coffee date? Or a dinner date?" Mia asked. "I mean, if you must. And why are you so obsessed with dating all of a sudden?"

Lynn sat down in between Mia and Farik and fastened her seatbelt. "It's Farik." She stretched out her leg and kicked him sideways while she shot him a dirty look.

"What have I done now?" Farik's eyes widened while he fastened his seatbelt too.

"He told me I'm getting 'of age'," Lynn said, ignoring him.

"Of age? What does that even mean?" Mia looked at them both.

"It means that I'm thirty-four now, and if I want to succeed in my plan of finding a wealthy husband, I'm almost past my sell-by date. According to Farik, millionaires only date women under thirty-five."

Mia laughed. "That's bullshit."

"No, it's not bullshit. It's true." Farik held up one of the free airport magazines. "According to this article, Lynn has seven months left to get married." He lowered his voice. "Scientific research never lies."

Mia smiled sympathetically. "Don't listen to him, Lynn. He's just winding you up. Anyway, why does it have to be a millionaire? Why not date some nice guy who likes you for who you are? Someone who's around your own age maybe? It's not helping that you keep serial-dating these older guys who are just looking for a bit of fun after their divorce. You're too good for that."

Lynn rolled her eyes. "But they have to be able to provide for me. And most older guys tend to have better jobs. I'm not going to do this forever, am I?" Lynn frowned. "Are you?"

"I don't know. I've never thought about it." Mia sat back and tried to relax as they started the descent. It was true. She had no plans for the future. Not long-term anyway. She lived day by day, counting her weeks, months and sometimes even years of sobriety. Occasionally she'd relapse, and she'd have to start counting all over again. That was how she perceived time. But Mia also loved her job, and that made everything a hell of a lot easier. Her job was her life, and it kept her away from the loneliness of her flat and the dark memories that often haunted her when she was by herself. Even when in a relationship, she'd always felt alone as soon as she came home. Apart from this weekend, because this weekend had been good. She'd finally been able to appreciate her free time, daydreaming mostly, and felt rested and full of energy. And she needed that, because it was going to be a busy week. In her thirteen years with the airline, she'd never turned down a shift. She'd worked hard, never complained, and was now one of the youngest cabin crew members to have been promoted to senior purser.

"You don't want to be doing this until you're sixty-five, Mia." Lynn was on a roll. "Believe me. Pushing a trolley with swollen ankles and the lipstick seeping into the wrinkles around your mouth? Not a good look. Anyway, you'll never last that long, even if you wanted to. They'll get rid of us as soon as our boobs start to droop, you just wait and see."

"I bet your boobs are already drooping," Farik said with a smirk. "And if they aren't now, they will be in seven months." He cupped both his hands in front of his chest and let them fall down in his lap, laughing.

"Not talking to you anymore, Farik." Lynn turned to Mia, pretending he wasn't there.

"Have you never thought of what your life will look like in twenty years' time? Don't you want a real home and someone to share it with?"

"Sounds like you just want to share a bank account," Mia teased. "But joking aside, of course I would love to have that. It's just hard to meet someone and especially, to keep someone with this job." She thought of Ava and the number in her pocket. Had Ava been thinking of her? Because she'd certainly been thinking of Ava. In fact, she knew her schedule by heart now. Dubai would be their next flight together. *Only five days to go.*

"Mia?" Mia turned to Lynn.

"Yes?"

"Jesus, Mia, where's your head been lately?" Lynn gave her a slap on her knee. "I was asking if you want to go for lunch tomorrow." She looked at her watch. "I mean today, whatever. When we arrive, anyway. You always know the best restaurants."

"Sure." Mia smiled, trying to focus on their conversation, rather than fantasizing about Ava. "I know a place." She leaned forward, and looked sideways, meeting Farik's eyes. "Are you coming too?"

Farik shook his head. "No. I'm spending the day at my boyfriend's penthouse."

"Your boyfriend?" Lynn arched an eyebrow. "I didn't know you had a boyfriend."

"Not boyfriend-boyfriend," Farik explained. "As in committed relationship." He grinned. "My Abu Dhabi boyfriend."

"Ah. That explains it." Lynn looked at Mia and chuckled. "And have you met this boyfriend before, or have you sold yourself online to the highest bidder?"

"Fuck you, Lynn." Farik rolled his eyes. "I met him in London. He works in the oil business and he's invited me to stay at his five-bedroom penthouse with rooftop swimming pool and a view over the Gulf. So, while you two low-lives are strutting around in the heat, trying to find a place to stuff yourselves with falafel, I'll be sipping Champagne and eating caviar, literally looking down on you from the forty-second floor."

"Okay." Mia laughed. "Is he picking you up from the airport? Are we going to meet him at some point?"

"Nah. I think I'll keep him to myself. Lynn might throw herself at him, the way she's been acting lately." Farik propped his head back against the wall and closed his eyes, pretending to go to sleep.

29

ABU DHABI, UAE

"Come on, Lynn. Cover up. Show some respect."

"Yeah, yeah." Lynn adjusted her scarf over her shoulders as she followed Mia though a crowded market in TCA, home to one of the oldest residential areas in Abu Dhabi. "Anyway, where are you taking me?"

"Lunch." Mia turned to her and frowned. "You said you were hungry?"

Lynn sighed. "I said I was hungry, sure. I didn't say I wanted to be squashed to death." She changed her tactics and started walking sideways in an attempt to get through the masses that were gathered around one of the more popular market stalls selling bread. "I've never had to fight my way through anywhere in this city, it's always reasonably quiet. How did you even manage to find this place?"

"Here. Take my hand, we're almost there." Mia held her hand out for Lynn and pulled her through the last throngs of the crowd, into a courtyard.

"Thank the good Lord." Lynn steadied herself and took a deep breath. "I've never considered myself claustrophobic, but I think I might need therapy now."

They took off their shoes by the restaurant entrance and stepped onto the red and gold carpets that were laid out across the busy room.

"So...," Lynn started, dipping a piece of flatbread into the houmous. "The captain."

"What captain?" Mia tried to keep a straight face. She hadn't told Lynn anything about her evening with Ava and they hadn't discussed their day out in New York the day after either.

Lynn looked up at the ceiling and rolled her eyes in a dramatic manner. "You know who I'm talking about, Mia. Don't play dumb. The hot captain. You guys spent the day together in New York, remember? You looked a bit... let's say flushed when you finally got into the cab with me. Or have you forgotten about that?"

"Ava." Mia smiled, saying her name out loud.

"Yeah, yeah. I know her name." Lynn leaned in and lowered her voice. "So? Are you going to tell me what happened?"

"There's not much to tell. It was nice," Mia said, now grinning from ear to ear. "I really like her."

"And?" Lynn was whispering now. "Any action?"

"Maybe a little." Mia hesitated. "We kissed. A couple of times."

"Aaah... So, you did smooch her." Lynn nodded slowly, looking Mia up and down with a fascinated stare. "I knew I was right when I sent you into the cockpit that day." She waved her hands in excitement. "It's like I knew you guys were a good match. So, she's gay?"

"Yeah, she is." Mia broke off a piece of flatbread and

scooped it through the baba ganoush. "And an exceptionally good kisser."

Lynn laughed. "Fuck me, I'm not surprised. That woman looks like sex on wheels. Hell, even I've fantasized about her once or twice." Her eyes widened. "Oh my God. Did I ruin your little rendezvous in the hotel? I mean, were you about to..." She pointed a finger at Mia, who shrugged.

"It's okay. I'm sure our paths will cross again soon." Mia was unable to supress a grin. "Okay, I checked her schedule. She's on my next call to Dubai in five days' time. I can't wait to see her again."

"Oh my God, just look at your little face." Lynn rubbed Mia's shoulder and squeezed her cheek. "Mia Donoghue, I think you've got a big, fat crush and I don't remember the last time you had one. You never looked this happy when you were with that skanky piece of work who dumped you on holiday for no reason, that's for sure."

Mia laughed. Lynn had zero tact, at least outside the cabin. She'd never told her friend the real reason for her break-up with Marsha, and she didn't intend to.

"Please keep it to yourself, though. I don't want anyone to know. People talk too much, and I don't want either of us to get into trouble."

"Sure." Lynn crossed her middle and index finger. "You know I'd never tell a soul. You're my friend, Mia."

"Thank you." Mia gave her a grateful smile. "So, what about you?" she asked, changing the topic. "Any dates lined up this month?"

Lynn grinned. "Well... I didn't want Farik to know, so I didn't mention it earlier, but I might have my own captain soon."

"Really? Who's that then?" Mia had a hard time keeping

up with Lynn's love life. She seemed to be on a carousel of dates lately.

Lynn looked at her and paused for dramatic effect. "I'll give you a hint. He's tall, grey, good-looking, older, lives in London, drinks ginger beer when he's flying, and he really likes those little nutty chocolates that our first-class passengers get with their coffee." She paused. "I keep them aside for him and he's always very grateful."

"That's more like ten hints." Mia laughed. "But anyway... ginger beer huh? It's not Captain Slender, is it?" Mia winced as she tried to picture Lynn with the older captain, whom they flew with regularly. The age-gap made it hard to imagine them together. "Isn't he old enough to be your father?"

"Yep. Captain Bob Slender," Lynn repeated, swooning over his name. "The devilishly handsome silver fox who just signed his divorce papers last week. He asked me out as soon as the ink was dry. I bet he's been dying to take me out for months." She said it with such enthusiasm that Mia didn't have the heart to question Captain Slender's intentions out loud.

"That's nice," she said instead. "I'm sure you'll have fun together."

"I'm sure we will." Lynn helped herself to the grilled fish that had just been served. "I can't wait to rub it in Farik's face if this works out. Every. Single. Fucking. Day."

30

ABU DHABI, UAE

Mia sat on her hotel room balcony on Yas Island in Abu Dhabi, overlooking the garden and the Arabian Gulf with the skyline of the city behind it. It was in moments like this, that she felt blessed with her job. She was too tired to go into town with Lynn again, or to have dinner at the hotel restaurant with the rest of the crew, but too restless to go to sleep, and so she'd been sitting there for almost two hours, watching the sun go down while she gave herself a manicure. Mia didn't care much for her nails, but her hands were expected to be pristine on the job and she'd finally gotten used to the process of cleaning, filing and polishing. And tonight, it even felt therapeutic. Although it was dark now, the dry heat was still hanging around her like a thick blanket and she inhaled deep each time a hint of the sea breeze managed to reach her, high up on the twenty-ninth floor. The hotel room was small and fairly basic, but the location was one of her favourites. She always appreciated a good view.

In front of her was Ava's number, her card weighed

down with a vase so the wind wouldn't blow it away. *The holy grail.* Not that she hadn't saved the number in her phone already, because that was the first thing she'd done when she had a spare moment on the flight. But she liked to look at the card and read her name over and over again. Mia knew that was probably bordering on creepy, but she didn't care. She picked up her phone and took a sip of her mint tea, still pondering over what to send. The flight had been hectic, coming in, and there had been no time whatsoever to daydream about Ava. Thankfully, she had all the time in the world now. She missed Ava. She missed talking to her, and she missed the only person who knew her best-kept secret, the only person she could truly be herself with.

'Hi Ava   . How's Egypt? I saw on the schedule that we'll be flying to Dubai together next week. Please let me take you out for dinner.'

Was that too impersonal? Boring? She decided to add something.

'I'm really looking forward to seeing you again. X Mia'

There. That was better. She opened a box containing the pecan and honey tart she'd bought at the airport and moaned as she bit into the delicious sweet and flaky pastry. Her phone beeped, and she jumped up in surprise. *Wow. That was quick.*

'Hey Mia. I'd love to go for dinner. Layovers are boring without you.'

Mia smiled as she read it and did a little dance in her seat. She was going on another date with the sexiest captain in the universe. Her phone beeped again.

'Can't wait to see you. How's Abu Dhabi?'

Mia didn't care if she seemed too eager by sending a prompt reply. It felt so good to be in contact and clearly Ava wasn't done talking yet.

'*Boring without you too.*' She hesitated. '*Keep thinking of our kiss.*' Her thumb pressed send before she had the time to change her mind, and she got a reply only seconds later.

'*Same here, gorgeous. I wouldn't mind finally finishing what we started.*'

Wow. Ava was getting all sexy on her now. Mia bit her lip as she typed, the arousal stirring inside her.

'*Promise me you will. I want you so badly, I'm unable to think of anything else.*'

"Fuck," she said out loud. Maybe that was a bit much. She didn't know Ava that well, after all. There was another message.

'*I promise, and I'll be counting down the days. What are you wearing?*'

Mia smiled.

'*Not much, just the hotel robe. What are you wearing?*'

'*Nothing. It's really warm here and I don't like air con.*' Mia closed her eyes and tried to picture Ava naked like she had so many times in the past weeks. A couple of seconds passed before Ava messaged her again. '*I want you to lie down on your bed.*'

'*Why?*' Mia replied. She knew very well why Ava wanted her on the bed, but she liked teasing her.

'*Because I say so.*'

'*Yes, Captain.*' Mia giggled as she walked into her room and lay down on top of her sheets. '*I'm on the bed.*'

'*Open your robe.*' Ava's messages were short and demanding now, and it aroused Mia to the point that she could barely keep her hands off her own body. She opened her robe and took a selfie on the bed, showing her face and her breasts, and sent it.

'*Fuck. Do you have any idea how sexy you look?*'

Mia smiled, shifting on the bed. '*Send me a picture of you, so I have something to look at too.'* She stared at her phone for what seemed like an eternity. Ava sure was taking her time. *Is she teasing me?* When her phone beeped again, there was no picture, only a short reply.

'*No, Mia. I'm in charge now.'* Mia felt another stir of arousal at Ava's domineering tone. A couple of seconds passed again, leaving her waiting in anticipation. *'I want you to touch yourself.'*

'*I am,'* Mia answered, as she slid a trembling finger through her wetness. She gasped when a flash of heat spread between her legs and thought of Ava as she made slow circles with her fingers, trying to keep her gaze fixed on her phone.

'*How does it feel? Are you wet?'*

'*It feels fucking amazing... and yes. I'm so wet.'* Mia attempted to type another message but failed when she got distracted by the feeling of intense pleasure as she accelerated the pace of her fingers, rubbing her clit.

'*Are you close?'* The message Ava sent only minutes after came too late, when Mia was already balancing on the verge of an orgasm. She ignored her phone and let go, holding her breath as the heavenly sensation spread through her, covering her in a warm blanket of ecstasy. She closed her eyes, revelling in a moment of pure bliss as her hips bucked on the mattress. She took a couple of deep breaths and sighed in relief, taking a moment before she picked her phone up again.

'*Too late,'* she typed. *'Just the thought of you...'*

'*I like that .'*

Mia giggled, staring at her phone. She felt incredibly relaxed as she let her head fall back into the pillows. *Jesus, what was that?* Just as she was about to think of a reply, there was another message.

'*Glad I have your number now. Sweet dreams, Mia. XXX*'
'*Sweet dreams, Ava . XXX*'

31

LONDON, UK

"Are you guys okay to lock the door behind you?" Ava cast another glance over the living room and the kitchen. It looked nice and clean and white. "Great work by the way," she added.

"No problem. We're almost done," one of the decorators said, pointing to the only patch of maroon left. Even the light blue farmhouse kitchen looked good, now that it didn't clash with the rest of the dining area and living room. There were big plants in ceramic pots in the corners – low maintenance ones the shopkeeper had assured her – and new curtains and lighting that already made a world of difference. Ava smiled and decided she liked it now.

"Thanks guys. Help yourself to coffee. You know where everything is." She still couldn't believe she'd finally done something about her flat, getting it to look the way she wanted. She'd been home for two full days, and that was just enough time for the three decorators to repaint everything, including the hallway and the bathroom. She'd helped them strip off the nineties wallpaper in the spare bedroom, and had been shopping for artwork, plants, curtains, lamps and pillows to spruce up the place. Her mother had forgiven her for cancelling dinner; she was too excited that Ava was getting rid of the maroon at last. She put on her pilot's cap and closed the door behind her, feeling accomplished and slightly nervous. Mia would be on her flight today.

A NOVEL SENSATION stirred inside her, just at the thought of seeing Mia again. Ava wondered what Mia's life was like, and where she lived, as she entered Turnham tube station. Their exchange of messages had been far from informative and so asking her where she lived, the day after their steamy back and forth, had seemed out of place somehow. She hadn't contacted Mia, and Mia hadn't contacted her. Ava wasn't sure if she'd gone too far with her demanding texts at first, but Mia had seemed more than happy to play along, and so she had let it go eventually. In the end, she was who she was, and there was no point hiding her sexual desires if they were going to end up in bed together.

For the first time since she'd moved into the neighbourhood, Ava looked around the platform instead of staring straight ahead, avoiding eye contact. She knew that most crew members lived somewhere near a tube line that was directly connected to the airport, just like herself. *Maybe she's on the same train?* Ava knew that was wishful thinking. It was unlikely Mia would be on the same train; they came and went every five minutes and even if they were, it would be even more unlikely she'd spot her in one of the overfull compartments. Still, she'd had a longer shower than usual and taken extra care with her hair, straightening her long, black locks. She felt good about herself and smiled as she adjusted her tie in the reflection of the train window when it came to a halt in front of her. She was in luck today; there were several free seats, and she was grateful to be able to sit down during her journey to the airport. The woman opposite Ava was trying hard to get her attention. She kept looking up at her from her book seductively, trying to make contact. She was blonde and attractive and possibly a fair bit younger than Ava. Dressed in a black tracksuit and carrying a fitness bag, she looked like a personal trainer, or maybe even an athlete. People flirting on the tube was nothing new. It happened all the time during the long, boring commutes. Ava ignored her and concentrated on her newspaper instead. Any other day, she would have flirted with the woman, maybe even asked for her number. But today, Mia was the only one on her mind.

32

LONDON, UK TO DUBAI, UAE

"What are you guys laughing about? Shouldn't you be serving drinks?" Mia approached Lynn and Farik, who seemed to be having a blast by the toilets. Lynn jumped up and turned around, wiping the smirk off her face when Farik nudged her.

"Oh, hey, Mia. Would you mind taking care of the Cosby's in 6A and 6B please? I don't think his girlfriend likes me. I suspect she feels threatened by my good looks," she joked. "Please, Mia? You're so good with people."

Mia looked her up and down suspiciously. "Sure. So, what's going on exactly?"

"Nothing," Farik said. "The Crosby's are just being weird to Lynn and we were laughing about something the woman said. Be careful with her, she's got a sharp tongue on her."

"Okay..." Mia hesitated as she walked away, mildly irritated by the ongoing giggling behind her. *Are they messing with me? They'd better not be...*

MIA HAD BEEN busy dealing with last-minute menu changes

when the boarding had started, so she hadn't met any of the passengers yet. Mr. Crosby was a first-time flyer with the airline, and there was nothing on file about his preferences, or how he liked to be treated. Mia double checked the flight log again. Mrs. Crosby wasn't on there, as Mr. Crosby had booked a double cabin under his own name. It happened sometimes, usually with people who wanted complete privacy or more space to themselves, but the fact that his wife's name wasn't on the system was a problem. They'd have to contact the company now and speak to the captain about holding the flight, which meant a delay because of her negligence. *That's impossible. How could I have missed it?* She decided to check on the Crosby's first, so see if there might have been a mistake. Perhaps one of the other passengers had sat down in the wrong seat, and confused Lynn.

Mr. Crosby looked like many men did in their late sixties. Grey hair, chubby physique, friendly face and blotchy skin. If his shirt and his watch reflected his bank account, he was sure to be wealthy, but you could never be certain these days. Some people saved up for years for a watch or, perhaps in his case, as there was no upgrade on the system, he had paid for two first class airline tickets at full price. His wife was much younger, early twenties Mia, guessed, and very pretty. Mia approached them with caution.

"Welcome Mr. Crosby. My name is Mia and I'm the senior purser. We're glad to have you on board. I'll be taking over from here. Is there anything I can get for you? A glass of Champagne perhaps?"

"Thank you." He studied the menu. "It's too early for alcohol. I'll have a coffee please. Black, one sugar."

"Okay, I'll get that for you right now." Mia turned to the woman next to him. "And for you, Mrs. Crosby? Would you like a..." She stopped abruptly, as she realised that Mrs. Crosby was a life-sized doll. At first, she thought the woman was resting, but her eyes were wide open. *Jesus. That's why they were laughing. His wife? Is this guy serious? What do I do?* Mr. Crosby had secured the safety belt over the doll's lap, she noticed. Mia scrolled through the passenger information again, frantically looking for an explanation, but found none. Mr. Crosby had booked two seats, so there was no reason to put the doll away. Being the shape of a human, the doll wouldn't be a safety hazard either, as a suitcase would. Mia cursed Lynn and Farik for pulling a stunt like this on her, although she had to admit, it was pretty good. What was the deal here? She'd heard of people who had relationships with dolls, but she'd never actually encountered a couple where the other half was made of rubber.

"Is there a problem?" Mr. Crosby's expression hardened. "This is Mandy, my wife. Are you not going to take her order..." he looked at Mia's name badge. "...Mia?"

Mia looked from Mr. Crosby to the doll next to him and back. Was this a joke? *Better not treat it as a joke, just to be on the safe side.*

"Of course I will," she said, not sounding too convincing. She turned to the doll, trying to keep a straight face when Lynn walked past, tapping the back of her hand. "I was just checking her name as there's no mention of it here on my schedule. But that's okay, we can make it work. Would you like a drink, Mandy?" The surrounding passengers were listening in on the conversation, fascinated by the absurdity of the situation. Some were quietly giggling or whispering among themselves. A young man was filming on his phone, over the edge of his cabin. She couldn't blame them. She would have done the same.

"Don't talk to her like she's a child, she's a mature

woman for God's sake." Mia took a moment to process what he'd just said, but she didn't flinch. She straightened her back and took a confident stance, knowing all too well she was the centre of attention now.

"You're right, Mr. Crosby, I do apologize. Can I get you a drink, Mandy?" She asked, in a less patronising tone this time. Mandy didn't answer. Her eyes were focussed on the ceiling, as if she was silently praying to be removed from the man next to her, claiming to be her husband. Mia never thought the day would come that she'd feel sorry for a doll, but that day had come nonetheless, against all logic and expectation.

"Mandy would like a glass of Champagne," Mr. Crosby said, without consulting Mandy.

"No problem, I'll get her a glass of Champagne." Mia didn't care anymore. They hadn't covered any of this in her training. It was just too absurd. But since Mr. Crosby had paid a hefty six thousand pounds for his flight and another six thousand for Mandy's, she'd go along with whatever his delusional fantasy was, as long as it didn't involve her. The customer was always right, after all. And what the hell, she might as well have a bit of fun with it.

"Would you like something to eat with that, Mandy?" She looked at the doll intently, showcasing her warmest smile. "Is she shy?" A woman behind Mia burst out into laughter, spilling her Champagne in her lap.

Mr. Crosby shook his head, ignoring the woman, who now had tears running down her cheeks. "Not normally. She's just tired, I think. We got up at five this morning."

"Very well," Mia said. "Let me know if she wants me to make her bed. I've got a feeling she might be more comfortable talking to you."

"Good call." Mr. Crosby gave her an understanding nod

before switching on Mandy's screen and placing the head-phones on her head.

"YOU ARE SO GOING to pay for this," Mia said a little later when she was sitting next to Lynn during a stretch of turbu-lence. She laughed, shaking her head. "And you won't see it coming. That was one nasty trick you pulled on me." She shifted her gaze towards Farik and gave him a warning look. "And you too, glam boy." Farik's eyeliner had bled down onto his cheeks from all the tears he'd shed during his ten-minute laughing fit in the toilet. "You'd better clean up those panda eyes before you go back into the cabin, it's not a good look."

"Talking about looks," Farik said. "You should have seen your face when you..." He burst into laughter again and covered his face as he shook, unable to speak.

Mia ignored him and closed her eyes for a brief moment, listening to the voice that she'd been longing to hear all week.

"Ladies and gentlemen, this is the captain speaking..."

33

DUBAI, UAE

"I heard we had an interesting passenger on board," Ava said with a smirk. She was lingering on the jet bridge with her leather duffel over her shoulder, drinking a can of Coke. Her co-pilots had already disappeared, both desperate for a cigarette.

Mia laughed as she caught up with her. "Were you waiting for me, Captain?" Her tone was flirtatious. "I assume they've told you all about it? I don't think I'm ever going to hear the end of this." She followed Ava out across the bridge.

"Yeah. Farik told me as I was on my way to the toilet. He was bright-red and could barely speak." Ava grinned. "And yes, I was waiting for you. It was nice to finally be on a flight with you again, Mia. I really appreciated those cute little chocolates you brought with my coffee." She hesitated. "Are we still on for dinner tonight?"

Mia's heart started racing. "I'm glad you remembered." She smiled as their eyes met. Ava stood right next to her in her uniform, and the potential prospect of another steamy make-out session, and quite possibly much more, was almost too much to handle.

"How could I forget?" Ava searched for her passport as they lined up before customs. She seemed nervous, Mia thought. "I'm glad you're picking the restaurant, since you know your way around here." She gave Mia's hand a quick squeeze. "Shall we meet in the lobby at seven? That is, if you haven't changed your mind. If you have, no hard feelings."

Mia shivered at the touch, smiling from ear to ear. "I think you can tell by my face that there's no way I'm going to cancel tonight." She winked as she stepped forward, presenting her passport to the customs officer.

"READY?" Ava looked Mia up and down thoroughly as she stood up from the couch in the lobby. *Damn, she's hot.* "You look great." Mia was wearing a simple blue and white striped dress that was modest enough for wandering through the streets of Dubai but seductive enough to make Ava's heart skip a beat. Her long, dark hair was straightened and tucked behind her ears, and she wore small pearl earrings.

"You don't look so bad yourself." Mia couldn't stop smiling at the sight of Ava's tight jeans, which were hanging low on her hips. *And those eyes...* She laughed, when she realised she was staring. "Okay," she said, pulling herself together. "I know a nice little place by the harbour. We can walk there, if you like? It's in a conservative area, so we can't be obvious about the fact that we're on a date, if you know what I mean?"

"I'm not sure if I'll be able to control myself." Ava gave her a mischievous smile. "But I'll do my best."

THEY ENTERED the labyrinth alleys of the Al Bastakiya neighbourhood, full of museums and cafés, and walked in the direction of Dubai Creek, passing traditional Emirati tea houses, restored wind tower houses, mosques and stunning courtyards. The quiet streets became more crowded as they neared the textile souk, where the day had only just started, and merchandise was being displayed for the busy night ahead. Mia would have walked through as fast as she could without her cap, in an attempt to avoid the pushy salesmen, but Ava seemed more than comfortable to take a look at what they were selling as she started haggling over a set of pillow-cases like it was second nature to her, engaging in their friendly banter.

"For my mother," she explained when they exited the souk. "She's obsessed with pillows and tapestry, you should see her house."

"Oh yeah? Is it very traditional?"

"You could say that. It looks like a textile shop, basically." Ava laughed. "But hey, if it makes her happy, I'll keep on buying them."

"What about you?" Mia asked. "Where do you live when you're not flying?"

"I've got a flat in Turnham Green. It's on the tube line to Heathrow, so it was more for convenience, but I really like the area now. I'm not there very often though." She shrugged. "I've lived there for five years now, and only got around to having it redecorated yesterday."

"I know what you mean." Mia stopped to buy a box of sweets. "I'm still living in a tiny one-bedroom flat in Ealing Common," she said, paying the stall holder. "I know I should upgrade, really. But I'm not home often enough to want to make the commitment. And when I am there for several days in a row, I don't know what to do with myself, because I'm so used to being away."

"Do you ever think you'll settle down with someone?" Ava asked.

"Maybe. If I found the right person." Mia blushed at the question. "You?" She opened the box of Turkish delight and held it up for Ava to pick one.

"Same. It's not out of the question. But I haven't been in a relationship with anyone for so long, that I've stopped thinking of it as an option." She chose a pink jelly from the box. "You like sweet things, don't you, Mia?"

"I sure do." Mia grinned as she chewed and swallowed. "That's why I like *you*. Sweet and sexy." Her eyes lingered on Ava's. She was enjoying the fact that for once, she didn't have a prompt reply.

Ava laughed. "You're pretty sweet and sexy yourself. If only I could grab your ass and kiss you right now. I..." She shook her head in frustration.

"Say no more," Mia interrupted her. "I might jump you if you do." By now, she was so turned on that she had a hard time controlling herself. She nodded towards the waterfront. "Come on, we'll take an abra to the other side of the creek. I need to cool down." Mia beckoned Ava to follow her as she paid the man who was holding the walking plank in place.

"This is cool." Ava sat down next to Mia in the back, making sure she was close enough for their arms to touch. She held onto the edge of the long, narrow, wooden boat as they took off while the last passengers were still jumping on board, making it rock from side to side. "I like it when people take me somewhere new." She looked over to the other side of the creek, where more souks and traditional shops awaited them. "It's actually really charming here. I always thought Dubai was all about swanky hotels and jet-set parties, but this is quite the opposite."

"Well, there is that too." Mia nodded in the general direction of Jumeirah, the strip of man-made beach. "Not far from the hotel we're staying at are the world's biggest shopping malls, white man-made beaches and luxurious hotels, just like you see in magazines. And that's fun too, don't get me wrong..." She hesitated. "But I like the old town. The locals are friendly, as opposed to the rich businessmen in the hotels in Jumeirah, who are determined to find a date for the night and think they can buy anyone." She rolled her eyes. "You have no idea how annoying it is when you're minding your own business, walking along the poolside and some pervert starts commenting on your ass."

Ava laughed. "I'm not surprised. You have a nice ass." She kept her voice down. "Or am I being the pervert now?"

"No." Mia giggled and shifted on the bench. "You can comment on my ass anytime, Captain."

"That's good to know." Ava shifted a little closer, leaning into her. "Because I've got plenty more things to comment on, but I don't think this is the right place for it, so I'll save that for later tonight."

Mia felt a twinge in her belly and took a deep breath, avoiding Ava's stare. Her green eyes were so intense that she couldn't handle more than a couple of seconds before she completely lost herself. *Tonight.* She wasn't sure what to say.

"Okay," she finally whispered. "I'll be looking forward to that."

They jumped off once they reached the other side of the creek and passed through the Gold Souk, where the narrow stalls were hung with golden jewellery in every form and size possible. The opulence and the richness of the market never failed to amaze Mia. Spotlights, that were fixed underneath the jewellery that was draped along the walls, creating a golden glow throughout the covered market.

"Thank you for the tour." Ava said. "I love it here. It reminds me of Jordan. It's nice."

"Well, there's the Perfume Souk and the Spice Souk as well, but I bet you're hungry by now so maybe we could save that for another..." Mia hesitated and smiled. "Date?"

"Yeah." Ava smiled too. "The next date."

Mia led them to an establishment by Deira Creek, serving traditional Yemeni food. They were welcomed and sent upstairs through the back, to the women's section of the restaurant, where they sat down on the floor by a window that gave them a breath-taking view over Dubai Creek and the city. The restaurant's interior was bare, but the abundance of people feasting, and the copious amounts of food on their tables, made it charming and intriguing.

"You're going to love this," Mia said as their server put down mutton soup and salad to graze on while they browsed the menu.

"I know I will." Ava tasted the soup and smiled. "This tastes quite similar to my mother's home cooking." She paused. "Actually, it might even be a bit better. Great choice, Mia."

"Of course, you're familiar with the cuisine. I didn't think about that." Mia put down her menu. "Then you won't mind ordering, will you?" She shifted and re-folded her legs underneath her. "I like anything so don't worry about me."

"Sure." Ava gestured for their server to come back and discussed the dishes with her in Arabic. Then she handed her the menus and continued for another minute or so, with what seemed like small talk. "I think I might have over-ordered," she said. "But I think we should try most of it."

Charcoal grilled fish, grilled vegetables, fragrant rice

with pomegranate, flatbread and salads were spread out over the table a little later.

"I can never quite figure out how to eat with my hands," Mia said, laughing as she cleaned her fingers on a napkin. "What's the right way to do it?"

"I'm no expert. We eat with a knife and fork at home and so do most people in Jordan. But I know it's important to eat with your right hand only," Ava said. "Then you can use your other hand to offer drinks, wipe your mouth or pass the trays to others." She nodded to the large tray in front of them. "It's only us now, so it doesn't matter all that much, but if you're with a group, make sure you scoop up the food from the section right in front of you and eat around the spot you started from. This tray it called a sidr, and as you gather around it, it's common to take a seat next to either someone of your own sex or your spouse. I can only tell you what the etiquette is in Jordan, it might be slightly different here. Other than that, it's common to move back a bit after you've finished and say: 'Al Hamdu Li Lah.' It means Praise to God."

"But you're not religious, right?" Mia asked, folding her flatbread over a piece of fish.

"No, I'm not. My parents aren't either, but we still all say it when we eat together. It's more of a cultural habit." She refilled Mia's tea cup. "You blend in well with the Middle-Eastern lifestyle. I mean, you obviously know where to find the best food, and you always dress appropriately." Ava laughed. "You even know some basic sentences and you're a natural at eating with your hands."

Mia smiled. "It's funny how life can take weird turns somehow." She sandwiched a piece of fish between her bread and scooped it through the yoghurt dip. "I started working for this airline because of its destinations. With me being a recovering alcoholic and all, I thought it might be easier to work for a Middle-Eastern airline. Less temptation, for obvious reasons. I mean, we do fly to other destinations as well, of course, but seventy percent of the flights go to countries where I don't feel like an outsider for not drinking in social situations and where my mini bar isn't stocked to the brim with brandy and vodka. I like that. And now, after years of staying here, I feel at home here. I've come to appreciate the food, the culture and the people, and I know my way around like a local."

"Makes sense." Ava nodded. "Would you ever consider moving to Dubai or Abu-Dhabi? It would be fairly easy for you to get a transfer."

Mia thought about it for a moment. "I don't think so." She paused. "I guess I would, if it wasn't for the fact that I'm gay and I couldn't be open about my sexuality. The head-office here would most likely fire me if they found out and I don't like the idea of stepping back into the closet."

"Yeah. There's that minor detail," Ava said, letting out a sarcastic huff. "Exactly my thoughts." She made a pocket of bread, filled it with salad and topped it off with lemon juice. "I'm so grateful for the fact that my parents are open-minded and for moving us to London. I would have never become a pilot if we'd stayed in Jordan."

"I'm not so sure about that." Mia cocked her head and shot Ava a curious glance. "I've got a feeling you would have found a way. You seem pretty determined to me."

Ava held her gaze, a small smile playing around her mouth. "Maybe. I usually get what I want."

34

DUBAI, UAE

"That was a fun night." Mia lingered in front of her room. She'd been fantasizing about kissing Ava all night, lusting over her mouth during dinner. But two women caught kissing in a hotel corridor in Dubai, where even heterosexual affection was frowned upon, was a recipe for disaster, and she wasn't willing to risk getting thrown out of the hotel. "Do you want to come in?" she asked.

Ava smiled. "Yeah. I do want to come in." She placed her hand over Mia's on the door handle and leaned in towards her ear, making the hairs on Mia's arm stand up.

"I've been thinking about kissing you. A lot."

Mia took in a quick breath as she opened the door. "Same here." She switched on the lights, before turning to Ava as she closed the door behind them. Finally, she allowed herself to drown in those green eyes that were oozing with desire. She traced Ava's cheek and pulled a loose strand of hair back, securing it behind her ear. "Then please kiss me again, like you did last time."

Ava moved closer, staring at Mia's mouth. She leaned in and traced Mia's upper lip with her tongue, before pressing her mouth against it while sliding a hand behind Mia's neck, pulling her in. She moaned, closing her eyes. Her stomach was doing crazy things, and the tingle between her legs left her in agony as she hiked up Mia's dress with her other hand and placed it on her firm bottom. Ava hadn't wanted to kiss anyone this badly in a very long time, and she could tell by the way Mia pressed herself against her that she felt the same. The soft moans escaping Mia's mouth made her want her even more. She parted her lips, allowing herself to sink into the kiss.

Mia let out a sigh when Ava pulled out of the kiss. Her eyes were full of need, looking down at Mia as she tried to catch her breath. Mia leaned in again, drawn towards Ava's lips. They were moist and soft and so inviting. She wrapped her arms around Ava's neck and kissed her, harder this time, more persistent. Ava took hold of her ass with both hands now and squeezed it before lifting her up on to the dressing table. Mia spread her legs and pulled Ava in between them without breaking the kiss. A cry escaped her mouth when she felt Ava's thigh pressing against her centre and her hand on her back, hiking up her dress even more.

"Wait." Mia leaned back and pulled her dress over her head, tossing it aside on the floor. She wanted Ava to know that it was okay to touch her, to take her. And most of all, she wanted Ava out of her clothes too. She started unbuttoning Ava's shirt with shaking hands. Ava let her gaze wander over Mia's half-naked body, only covered by black lace briefs and a matching bra, a sight that left little to the imagination. She looked sexy as hell, sitting there with that look of carnal desire in her eyes. The bra was sheer, her hard nipples clearly visible underneath the delicate fabric. Ava slid the bra straps off her shoulders and unhooked the back in one fluid motion. Her lips parted at the sight of Mia's breasts. They were full, soft and inviting, begging for her mouth. She lowered herself to kiss Mia's breasts, then softly bit down on a nipple. Mia moaned, leaned back and arched her back for Ava to devour her breasts, moaning louder when she felt Ava's tongue slide over her other nipple.

"You're so God damn sexy." Ava's voice was low and hoarse. "I want you so badly, Mia."

Mia stood up so Ava could slide down her briefs. A shiver went down her spine at the realisation that she was completely naked in front of the only woman she wanted. She pulled Ava's shirt off and started unbuttoning her jeans, taking in her athletic body. Her mouth watered at the sight of Ava's abs. Ava was sexier than she'd ever imagined close up, but the best perhaps, was the look on Ava's face that told her that she wanted her more than anything. Mia glanced over at the bed, sliding a hand into the back of Ava's jeans. "Can you take these off please?"

Ava shook her head, a small smile playing around her mouth. "Turn around, Mia."

Mia bit her lip at the words. She cocked her head, taking in Ava's face. She seemed serious. Mia swallowed as a shot of heat went straight to her core, settling between her legs. She turned around, coming face to face with her own reflection in the mirror. Ava was behind her, reaching around her as she kissed her neck and bit into her earlobe. *Holy fuck.* It turned her on like nothing else, seeing Ava's delicate hands massaging her breasts while she scraped her teeth over her neck.

"That feels so good." She sighed and took a deep breath when Ava's hands travelled down towards her belly, until her right hand reached between her legs, cupping her centre and squeezing it harder than she'd expected. "Fuck!" she exclaimed in a mixture of surprise and delight. Mia's legs started to tremble at the impact Ava's skilled hands were having on her and she threw her head back against Ava's shoulder as she caressed her clit. She could feel Ava's breath in her ear, faster now, as she slid two fingers through her folds, tracing her upwards. Mia started squirming in her tight grip, losing the last bit of reserve she had been clinging on to before pushing her ass back against Ava's thighs. Seeing herself being taken by Ava, watching her smile each time a moan escaped her mouth was mesmerizing. Ava lowered her hand again, moving further down between her legs this time, entering her with a finger.

"You're so wet," she whispered. "You feel so good, Mia"

Mia's eyelids fluttered when she felt Ava inside her, and she spread her legs further apart. "Fuck me, Ava," she begged. "I need this."

Ava retracted her hand and moved it around to the back, resting it on Mia's bottom. Her mouth was pressed against Mia's ear, still holding her close with her other arm.

"Bend over," she whispered between ragged breaths.

Mia bent forward, resting her palms on the dressing table as she watched Ava place a trail of kisses down her spine. Ava traced Mia's bottom, and slipped her hand between her legs from behind, drawing a loud moan from Mia when she entered her with two fingers.

"Yes, like that." Mia groaned, pushing back against Ava's hand to feel her deeper inside of her. The primal lust that took over her body and mind was like nothing she'd ever experienced. She'd pictured herself and Ava over and over in her fantasies, but it hadn't even come close to how aroused she felt now. Ava's eyes turned darker as they locked with Mia's in the mirror. She moved in and out of her faster, rocking her hips against Mia's ass until Mia started to lose her breath, pounding back against her hand. Ava knew she was close, and so she reached down with her other hand, cupping Mia's centre again, until she cried out and stiffened in her grip. She watched Mia's face in the mirror, her eyes closed tight, her mouth open, letting out one last ecstatic moan as she contracted around her fingers. Her hair was hanging down in front of her, framing her face, almost reaching her breasts. A trickle of sweat made its way from her forehead down to her nose and fell on to the dressing table. Ava sighed in delight. Seeing Mia like this was beautiful and it had turned her on so much, that she was close to climaxing herself. She lifted Mia's face up and pulled her against her chest while she was still inside her.

"You're amazing, Mia," she said, kissing her cheek down to her neck.

Mia let out another deep sigh and chuckled. "I think it's safe to say that you're the one who's amazing." She turned to face Ava, gasping as she felt her fingers slip out of her. She put her arms around Ava's neck and stared deep into her eyes before she kissed her slowly and deeply. "But now it's my turn." She tugged at Ava's sports bra in an attempt to take it off, but Ava clamped a hand around her wrist, stopping her from going any further.

"What's wrong?" Mia freed herself from Ava's grip. She glanced at the small breasts and the erect nipples that showed through Ava's bra in front of her and felt herself getting wet again as she reached out to trace Ava's toned upper body, from her well-defined shoulders to her breasts and down to her waistline.

"Nothing's wrong," Ava said, almost whispering. She caught Mia's hands again, just as they were about to slip under her waistband. She held them as she brought her mouth close to Mia's ear. "I just don't like to be told what to do." She walked them over to the bed and gestured for Mia to lie down.

"Not even by me?" Mia lay down and patted the space on the mattress next to her. Ava cast Mia a curious look as she got onto the bed. If Mia was trying to drive her crazy, she was certainly succeeding. "Because I'm pretty sure I can make you change your mind." Mia continued, climbing on top of Ava and straddling her. She skimmed her stomach down to the open buttons of her jeans again.

Ava looked up at Mia, and let her eyes wander over her full breasts, her amazing body and the seductive look on her face. She wasn't used to this, wasn't used to being seduced, or even pleasured, and for a moment, she was okay with that.

"Wait." She said, suddenly changing her mind. She took hold of Mia's hips, pushed her off her and turned them around so she was on top. "No. I don't like being told what to do. Not even by you, Mia."

Mia stared up at her, a smile playing around her mouth. "You sure like to be in control, don't you, Captain? I didn't think you were this... aaah." She stopped talking when Ava thrusted her fingers back into her. It felt so good. "Yes, oh God, yes."

Ava took both of Mia's wrists with her other hand and pinned them down over her head while she kissed her hard and deep, lowering herself on top of her.

Mia was too turned on to even think about what was happening, and every second passed in a delightful haze. Ava's green eyes boring into hers, the streaks of dark hair tickling her face, the soft, warm skin covering her body and the hard nipples pressing against her own breasts through the fabric of Ava's bra. She felt the weight of Ava on top of her and her thigh between her legs, spreading her further apart as she pushed into her.

"Oh God, that feels good." Mia moaned and cupped Ava's neck, tugging her down into another kiss. It was the sexiest encounter she'd ever experienced, and Mia knew she'd remember it forever.

Ava pulled out of Mia and looked down at her with longing eyes. "You have no idea how much I've wanted you." She traced her wet fingers down over Mia's breasts and her stomach until she reached between her legs again. She watched Mia as she cried out, buckling underneath her when she slid a lazy finger through her folds.

"Yes. Oh God, yes!"

"I can feel how much you want this again and it's driving me wild," Ava whispered, teasing Mia with slow strokes. Mia's thighs were trembling and so were her hands when Ava took them back into a tight grip with her other hand, placing them above her head on the pillow again. She slid two fingers back inside Mia, moaning at the wetness she felt.

"Oh yes. Don't stop Ava, please." Mia threw her head back, holding her breath as Ava pushed deeper into her. She found a slow and sensual rhythm, moving into her with her fingers and her body. She moved her thumb to Mia's clit and stimulated her evenly, slowly. She watched Mia's eyelashes flutter and listened to her ragged breathing that became faster and faster until she felt Mia tighten around her fingers. Ava loved the sight of her, engulfed in pleasure. She loved being the one who was making Mia feel like this.

"Yes, Ava. Right there. Don't stop." Ava kissed her deeply while she climaxed again. She felt it with every sense in her body as Mia came underneath her, completely at her mercy. Mia opened her eyes to look at her, still trembling.

"You're fucking amazing, Mia." Ava pulled out of her slowly, drawing a final moan from Mia's mouth.

35

DUBAI, UAE

Ava ran a fingertip up over Mia's cheek, resting it on the small scar on her forehead. Their arms and legs were entangled in each other, and in the sheets. Mia was naked, and Ava had removed her jeans. The balcony door was open, blowing a soft breeze through the hotel room. She turned on her side to face Mia, leaning on her elbow.

"What happened?"

Mia sighed, pulling Ava's hand away from the scar. "I uhm..." She paused.

"It's okay. You don't need to tell me." Ava's voice was soft and gentle.

"No." Mia said, her expression turning more serious. "I want you to know." She lay still and looked up at the ceiling, seemingly miles away as she thought back of the day she'd had the biggest wake-up call of her life. Before that, everything was fine. Perhaps not perfect, but fine. Mia went through life as a drinker, and she had other problems too, but that hadn't seemed like a big deal at the time. She'd told herself she would deal with it when the time was right. But the time was never quite right.

"My drinking problem started out really innocently at first," Mia said, keeping her voice down. "I was never very adventurous, but I started drinking in university, like most people, just to fit in I guess. Moving away from the security of my little town and my friends was a big step for me, perhaps I wasn't mature enough to handle it. I didn't know anyone when I moved to London. I shared a flat with three other girls who were so much cooler than me. They already knew each other and were looking for a fourth flatmate to lower their monthly rent. I was terrified they would see through me at first and was worried what they would think of me if they knew I was into girls. I wanted to fit in so badly." She was silent for a moment while she chewed her cheek. "I'd had a glass of wine or two before that, but never used it as a means to deal with life. When they offered me some strong concoction of cheap liquor in my first week, I was so happy that they wanted to hang out with me. I noticed I got braver after each drink, less timid and chattier. Somehow, it gave me confidence. I felt like I was funny, and suddenly I had opinions on things I'd never even thought about. It seemed so innocent at the time, four girls watching movies and drinking cocktails together. And it was, I suppose. But for me, it changed things. It changed how I dealt with situations. They drank for fun, and I drank because I needed it." She looked at Ava for a moment before she continued. "I didn't see that at the time, of course. To me, alcohol was like a magic elixir that made me social and even popular. I studied aviation engineering and I partied a lot, unable to deal with the sudden freedom that came with being away from my parents' supervision. It really affected my grades, but I was too scared to miss out, or maybe too desperate to fit in. I wanted to be a pilot, or an aeroplane engineer at that point, but the way my exams were going at the end of my second year, it didn't seem like that was an option anymore. I told one of my new friends, and she offered some kind of pill to help me concentrate, so I could stay up for weeks on end to study and get my grades back to where they were. I'm still not sure what it was exactly, probably Modafinil or whatever the equivalent was at the time. I didn't think it was a big deal. They were easy to get hold of, especially at Uni, and everyone took them once in a while. It worked. My grades went back up, and I started taking more and more of them, even after I collapsed one time. I hadn't slept properly for days, and I'd forgotten to eat too. I was so skinny back then. In the meantime, I still went out most nights, wasting away my student loan just to be popular. I had girlfriends from time to time, but each and every one of them broke up with me, saying I was absent and not 'all there', that I couldn't give them what they needed. They were right. I couldn't even hold a good conversation when I was sober, because all I could think of back then was when I could have my first drink of the day." Mia turned her head to face Ava. "In my third year – I was twenty at the time - I did an internship with a national airline. I drank even more at night to make up for the long days without alcohol. I took uppers in the morning to wake me up. I was a total mess and the funny thing was, nobody knew it. And although I didn't want anyone to know, somehow being alone in the mess that I'd created made it even worse. I have no idea why I was so self-destructive. It's not like I had a bad childhood or suffered trauma." Mia shrugged. "It was the loneliest time in my life, even though I went out at least four times a week." She swallowed hard, taking her time. Ava didn't interrupt her. She took her hand and listened quietly.

"I went home one weekend to visit my parents," Mia continued. "It was a Saturday afternoon and I had finally agreed to have dinner with them and my younger sister after having avoided them for weeks. I was anxious about seeing them, scared they could sense I had a problem. On top of that, I was about to tell them that I'd been kicked out of university, as my attendance had been poor, my grades weren't good enough to pass and I was barely able to function, let alone, graduate. By then, I'd become an expert at getting hold of prescription drugs, so I took two tramadol to calm myself down and drank half a bottle of wine in the car, topping up the bottle I'd already drank at home. I was driving fast. Way too fast, with music blaring through the speakers in an attempt to sober myself up just before I arrived." Mia shook her head. "I guess I was too hazy to see my little sister run out of the driveway to greet me. She was only five years old then, a sweet little girl. My mother always called her a happy accident. She was totally surprised when she found out she was pregnant again at the age of forty. Anyway, Ami ran out of the driveway just as I pulled in. I turned the wheel in an attempt to avoid her, but I hit her anyway before driving into a tree. I didn't have my seatbelt on, so I smashed my head against the window." Ava squeezed Mia's hand when a tear ran down her cheek. "I heard Ami scream in agony before I passed out, and all I could think for those few lucid seconds was: 'Oh my God, she's going to die. I killed Ami'. It was horrible." She paused. "The next thing I remember is waking up in hospital. I'd been out for seven hours. The doctors told me I had a brain injury and later, after performing several tests on me, they concluded I'd lost most of my hearing in my left ear. The hearing never came back."

"That's why you couldn't sign up to apply for your pilot's license." Ava said in a whisper.

"Yeah. But by then, I didn't care anymore, I felt as if I didn't deserve it. Hell, I didn't deserve it, Ami could have been dead." Mia cried. "She was in a coma for three days, but they wouldn't let me see her because I was under investigation. She'd broken her arm in three places, and she had two broken ribs amongst other injuries. I remember thinking about ways of taking my own life if Ami didn't wake up. My parents couldn't even look at me. They had smelled the alcohol on my breath that day, in the ambulance, and the results of my blood tests showed the alcohol and tramadol in my system." Mia sighed. "Thank God, Ami woke up, and her brain was functioning fine. It was a complicated case, because it was an accident, involving my own sister. My parents didn't press charges against me as I was their daughter but the court gave me a big fine, suspended my driver's license for two years, and gave me a referral order for a rehab centre. I didn't resist, of course." She sighed. "I spent two months there. By the time I was out, Ami was walking again, but she couldn't play or do anything fun for months. And she was just a little kid." Ava wiped a tear from Mia's face.

"Does she remember what happened?"

Mia shook her head. "No, she doesn't remember anything. There are still small scars on her arm, and a tiny one on her skull, where the hair doesn't grow, but my parents never told her what really happened. I think the story is that she fell down the stairs or something, I don't even remember. They asked me to keep it quiet too, and so I did. After that, I decided to stay clean for the rest of my life, but the cravings have never left me. I trained to be a flight attendant hoping a responsible job would help me stay on the right path. And it helps, of course it does. It gives me an excuse around people. The crew think I'm some kind of saint, being 'miss perfect' in my job. If only they knew..." Ava didn't comment. Instead, she raised Mia's hand up to her mouth and kissed it.

"Did you relapse a lot, before your last time, on holiday?"

Mia shrugged. "Four times before that. Most of the relapses were just plain stupid. The time before my last relapse, I think it might have been the bottle of free Champagne they gave me with my room upgrade that drove me to drink again. The day was no different from any other day. I'd been working, and I was in my hotel room. I wasn't upset, or anxious or anything like that. Anyway, I couldn't resist. I thought one more time wouldn't hurt. Maybe I wanted to see if I was okay, if I could have a glass without downing the whole bottle and more. That was so stupid. I should have known better. After two hours, I'd drunk everything in my minibar and was passed out on the bathroom floor. Luckily, I wasn't due to fly the next day, so I slept it off." Mia paused. "And then it was like starting all over again, even if it was just one night. The cravings got worse after that, so I went to the AA meetings more often. And it helps a little, you know? Makes me feel less alone." She bit her lip and looked into Ava's eyes. "Until this day, you're the only one who knows about my problem. Apart from the people I see in AA, of course. My parents think binge drinking was just some reckless thing I did when I was young and stupid, but it's still here." She balled her hand into a fist and held it against her chest. "It's like there's a demon inside of me, fighting to get out, testing me every single day."

"I know how it feels to have a relapse," Ava said. "You get so angry and disappointed with yourself, and you're convinced that you're a lost cause. But don't forget how many days you've resisted the urge to drink. Count the good days instead of the bad days. It's a never-ending battle, but you're stronger than you think, Mia."

"Thank you." Mia managed a smile and wiped her cheeks. "It feels good to tell someone. Especially about my sister. I've never talked about it and it keeps haunting me, when I'm alone. There's the guilt, of course..." She paused. "It's always there, and sometimes I feel like I'm just waiting to be punished for what I did."

"Hey, that's nonsense, and you must know that deep down. Your sister is fine now, right?"

Mia nodded. "She is."

"Have you thought of telling her about what happened?"

"I've thought of it, yes. I was hoping it might take a little bit of the guilt away. You know, the eighth step of AA... make amends, ask for forgiveness. But my parents begged me not to tell her, ever. They were afraid it might cause friction between us, later on in life." She shrugged. "And now it feels like it's too late."

"It's never too late." Ava gave her a sweet smile. "But more importantly, I think you need to stop blaming yourself. It was a long time ago, and your sister is fine now, so why can't you forgive yourself? You'll need to let it go at some point, you know just as well as me that there is no way to move forward if you don't. It's the first step."

"I know." Mia looked up at her, and Ava felt her heart sink when she saw the pain in her eyes. "I almost killed her, Ava. How can I ever forgive myself for that?"

"Your sister is a fantastic swimmer, and on her way to becoming a physiotherapist. That's quite something. Be proud of her. Cherish her, don't ignore her."

"I am proud of her. But I can't seem to shake the guilt off, and I feel terrible for lying to her all these years."

Ava folded her hands over Mia's. "It was a long time ago. We're here in the present now. And family is family. You need to talk to her, Mia. Tell her how you feel. You might not see the point of it now, but it's really important that you do. I'll be there if you want..."

"I know. Maybe one day. Maybe soon." Mia smiled back. "But enough about my problems. I want to hear your story now, if that's alright. You've been sober for a long time. What made you drink?"

Ava was silent as she thought about it. "I don't know. What made me drink initially was rebellion, I guess? I was always the bad girl anyway, what with being gay and all." She locked her eyes with Mia's. "As I told you, my parents moved from Jordan to London when I was young. We were a happy family most of the time, but although my parents were very liberal, being gay was not one of the things they could accept from me initially. My father always said he had no problem with gay people, as long as his own children weren't one of them. After I told them I was attracted to girls, when I was about sixteen, their reaction wasn't exactly what I hoped it would be. I couldn't understand how my parents could love me, yet not accept me for who I was. They tried everything in their power to change me, and for a while, even I felt bad about who I was, even though there was nothing I could do about it. And so, I drank to escape, and drank to make myself feel a little better. But it never made me feel better. The only thing it did was make me crave more, to numb myself so I wouldn't have to think and worry." She smiled sadly. "I guess alcohol doesn't agree with me the way it does with most people. I always hoped to become that person who could have a glass of wine with dinner and the occasional brandy before bed. But I've found out the hard way that that's not an option. I drank in secret for years, almost every night that I spent on my own. The night before I was supposed to start my first job as a second officer, I looked at the bottle of vodka in front of me and panicked. I knew I couldn't carry on like that, especially not if I was going to be responsible for all those lives up in the air, so I took myself to the nearest meeting instead." Ava looked relieved after telling her, Mia thought. Even her body language had opened up, as if a barrier had been lifted between them.

"It was the best decision I ever made," Ava continued. "I wasn't too keen on the spiritual angle when I first started going. The first place I went to was leaning that way, and so I assumed all meetings were like that. But it really helped me, and now I don't care anymore."

"I'm glad you went." Mia smiled. "Otherwise I doubt I'd be in bed with you right now." She shifted a little, running her hand through Ava's hair. "So, what happened six years ago? Were you in New York?" She hesitated. "You said you'd been sober for six years and seven months. Was that the first time you fell off the wagon?"

Ava moved closer, pulling Mia against her. "No. It was the third time, and the worst if I may add, caused by my only other weakness besides alcohol."

"What's that?" Mia asked. "Drugs?"

Ava shook her head and rolled her eyes. "No. Women."

"Right." Mia chuckled. "Why am I not surprised?"

"Well, this particular woman happened to be my best friend's girlfriend. She encouraged me to drink, just like your ex did with you. Not her fault though, I take full responsibility, of course. Anyway, I ended up kissing her right in front of him."

"Ouch."

"I don't think 'ouch' even begins to cover it." She winced. "I hit him too, that night. I haven't spoken to him since. He still lives in New York apparently, in the same neighbourhood where we used to share an apartment."

"Maybe you should pay him a visit next time you're there." Mia twirled a loose strand of Ava's hair around her finger. "He might have forgiven you by now."

"Maybe." Ava sighed and rolled herself on top of Mia, drawing a soft moan from her mouth. She grinned, tracing the side of Mia's breast, down to her waist, before taking a hold of her bottom and squeezing it. She was clearly done talking. "I'd like to stall this conversation and continue to screw your brains out until we have to leave this room. Do you agree that's a good idea, Miss Donoghue?"

Mia giggled when Ava started kissing her way down over her breasts, softly biting into her nipple. She kissed her belly, her thighs, and moved back up, sliding her tongue through Mia's folds until she started to moan underneath her.

Mia groaned at the arousal that stirred inside of her again. Ava was really, really good at this.

"I think that's a great idea," she whispered through ragged breaths.

36

DUBAI, UAE

"Thank you for last night." Mia sat on the edge of Ava's bed. She had dressed and packed her bag, and now they'd moved to Ava's room, so she could get ready.

Ava grinned, ironing her white shirt. "Oh, believe me, you don't need to thank me for that. I think I should be thanking you instead. You're..." She hesitated. "God, you're something else, Mia."

Mia laughed. "I mean, thank you for everything. It was good to talk besides all the mind-blowing pleasure you gave me." She picked up Ava's pilot's cap from her pillow and put it on. It didn't fit right, and was hanging off her topknot, but she smiled as she looked in the mirror anyway, and decided it looked good on her.

"Yeah. It was nice. Really nice." Ava switched off the iron and sat down next to Mia, eyeing her cap.

"It suits you."

"Oh yeah?"

"Yeah." She hesitated for a moment as her face turned more serious. "I really like you, Mia."

"I really like you too." Mia knew she meant it. Ava wasn't a player, she was honest, sweet, wonderful, all the things Mia had been hoping for her whole life. And Mia didn't want to say goodbye. "So, what do we do now?"

"What do you want to do?"

Mia pondered over what to say. At last, she decided to be honest. She'd been nothing but honest so far, after all. It felt good to finally have someone to talk to. Besides that, Ava was about as close as she'd ever get to her ultimate fantasy, and she'd be damned if she'd let her go.

"I'd like to do this again," she said. "I mean, I'd like to go on another date and spend more time with you." Her cheeks turned rosy. "Not just one. Lots of dates and lots of... nights. I feel like we have a connection." She made sure she steered away from words like 'relationship' and 'commitment', it was way too early for that. People got funny about that sometimes, although if it was up to Mia, Ava would be hers, and only hers.

Ava lifted her chin, gazing into her eyes. "I know what you mean with connection. And I'd love to see more of you too." She looked genuinely happy when she kissed Mia softly, trying to hold back because she had to get dressed. But, as had happened so many times before, it proved impossible to stop once she had her mouth on Mia's.

"Let's check our schedules," she said after tearing herself away from the kiss that got deeper and more intense than she'd intended. "I'm taking you out next time. Wherever we may be. And you've got my number, and I've got yours."

"I'm looking forward to it." Mia hesitated. "Ava?"

"Yes?"

Mia gave her a soft smile. "Let's keep this quiet, okay?"

Ava nodded as she slipped into her shirt. "Yeah. You're right. I don't want to get a reputation for sleeping around with the cabin crew in the first months of my job, and I haven't even read the company policy guidelines yet." She laughed. "Are we even allowed to do this? I couldn't bring myself to read the six hundred pages of legalities, but technically, I'm your superior on flights."

"I think we're good." Mia laughed too. "It happens all the time and they tend to turn a blind eye unless there's a serious conflict. But just for now, I'd like to keep it to ourselves. I've got fourteen people reporting to me on most flights, and I don't want them to start talking behind my back." Mia was glad they saw eye to eye on this, and although the connection she felt with Ava was stronger than she'd ever imagined was possible, she had no idea how Ava really felt about her. Besides that, she wanted it to be her secret for just a little bit longer. It was nice to have a secret that was positive, for once.

37

LONDON, UK

"Mia? Is that you, sis?" Ami's voice sounded worried. "You never call me. Are you okay?"

"Yes, I'm fine." Mia smiled. It had been a long time since she'd heard Ami's voice. She was only forty-five minutes away on the tube, but Mia had used up every single excuse by now not to get in touch with her. Seeing Ami was always difficult, so she usually avoided meeting up. It brought back memories she'd fought hard to suppress, and with the memories came the cravings. So she'd opted for a phone call instead, after looking at her mobile for hours. Finally, she'd dialled Ami's number, hoping furiously she wouldn't pick up. "Mum told me you were up for selection for Team GB, and I realised I hadn't spoken to you in a really long time. I just wanted to wish you luck. It's amazing, I had no idea you were such a good swimmer."

"Thanks, Mia." Ami cleared her throat. "I've gotten a lot better over the past two years. Even my left arm is in great shape now. But I'm nervous as hell. I'm not the best, but I'm in the top twelve, so it depends on how I do in the coming month."

"Don't be nervous. You're going to do fine." Mia felt a stab at the mention of Ami's arm. *That was me. I did that.* "How's Uni?" she asked, changing the subject.

"It's great." Ami sighed. "It's quite hard to combine with my training, but I'm just about managing. My coach is beside himself with excitement, so he's making me get up at five every morning to get my training in before I go to Uni, and then I have to do another hour of weight training in the evenings, six days a week. I spend a lot of time on the tube, back and forth."

"Wow, that sounds like a lot. So, no partying for you, then?"

"Nope." Ami chuckled. "Although I allow myself to let my hair down a little two nights a month." She paused. "I miss you, Mia. Mum hasn't seen you in months and I... well it must have been over a year since I last saw you. I know you're busy and always away with your job, but I'd really like to see you."

Mia closed her eyes and took a deep breath. It meant the world to her that Ami still wanted to see her, even though she'd been a terrible big sister, ignoring her phone calls and avoiding family get-togethers.

"I miss you too, Ami." She hesitated, excuses flying through her mind. *Enough. You've done this for too long now and it's time.* Ava was right. She would have to talk to Ami at some point, or she'd never be able to deal with the guilt. "Let's meet up soon," she finally said. "I could come and visit you? Take you out for dinner?"

"Really? That would be great." Ami sounded excited now. "If you come on a Saturday, I can have a glass of wine and maybe even some cheese at the same time." She laughed. "I've had just about enough of eggs, chicken breasts and whole wheat pasta."

"Sure." Mia flinched. Ami's enthusiasm was heartbreaking. "I'll buy you a big, fat cheesy pizza and we can catch up over dinner. I'm away a lot over the next two weeks, but I've got some holiday booked after that, so let me know when you're free and I'll make it work." She wanted to confess, tell Ami everything. And if her parents had a problem with that, she'd deal with them later.

38

CAMBRIDGE, UK

"And what's happening in your life, Ava?" Ava's mother asked, putting the food on the table. "I don't want to talk about moving away anymore, it only causes fights." They'd been discussing her wish to move back to Jordan, but Zaid had suggested to change the subject because their father was starting to get upset.

"Nothing much." Ava took the plate with lamb stew that her mother handed her and helped herself to rice and salad. "I've done my flat up, as you know. It looks great now. Even the kitchen fits into the new colour scheme."

"Good." Her mother shot her an approving look. "I'm glad you finally came around to doing that. Would you like me to ask your auntie to buy you some pillows, or some tapestries? She can send them together with my package. I've ordered some spices."

Ava frantically shook her head. If she let her aunt in Jordan help her with the interior of her flat, the place would look like a bazaar in no time. "Thanks Mum, but I'm fine. I'm happy with the way it looks."

"You look happy," her father noticed.

"Yes, you do." Her mother studied her face. "Anything else you'd like to share?"

Zaid elbowed her under the table. "Is it a bird, Sis?"

"How about you mind your own business, Zaid?" Ava shot him a warning look.

"It is!" Zaid threw his hands up in the air. "Look at her face, she's turning red. Oh my God, my lezzer sister finally got laid." He couldn't stop laughing. "I'm a psychologist Ava, you can't fool me."

Ava found it hard to believe sometimes that her brother was a grown man with a very grown-up career. Because at home, he was still the same kid that used to hide dog turds in her shoes and superglued her fingers together while she was sleeping.

"Watch your language, Zaid!" Their mother turned to Ava. "And that goes for you too. No L-words or F-words at the dinner table, you can do that in your own time."

"The L-word isn't a swearword, Mum," Zaid protested.

"Well, it is when you say it like that." Noor's expression softened. "Now, please tell us about this..." she hesitated, "woman." Her eyes went from Ava to Zaid and back. "Because Zaid is right. You do look a little bit flushed, and I'm getting awfully curious now."

Ava didn't think she could possibly feel more uncomfortable. She'd never discussed a girlfriend with her parents. There had never been anyone serious enough to mention to them. But she knew they'd been waiting, mentally preparing themselves for the day she would tell them she was seeing someone. A woman. She'd given them plenty of time to get used to the idea. Twenty-one years. Still, she was surprised at the casual tone in her mother's voice when she asked the question.

"It's nothing," Ava stammered.

Her father was staring at her now too, and so was Natasha, who was wise enough to stay out of it, but still clearly fascinated with the family dynamics over the topic.

"Come on, Ava. Don't be shy." Her mother straightened her back, indicating she would not give up until Ava had spilled the beans.

Ava chewed her food slowly in an attempt to buy time. She could get up and run out of the door, but she was thirty-seven years old, and that wasn't really an option anymore. Finally, she swallowed and sighed.

"I've been on a couple of dates with someone from work."

Zaid gave her a big grin. Her parents smiled too. God, how she was dying to leave the table. She felt like a trapped animal, waiting for a herd of predators to pick her apart. She cast a fleeting glance at Zaid, whom she wanted to strangle for putting her in this awkward position.

"That's wonderful," her mother said, lowering her cutlery. She folded her arms in front of her and leaned in over the table. Ava noticed sweat marks on her red silk blouse. Her mother never had sweat marks. "Are you going to tell us about her? What's her name?" She paused. "I assume it's a woman?"

Ava couldn't help but roll her eyes. "Of course it's a woman. I'm gay, Mum. Her name is Mia," she said eventually. "She's a senior purser for the airline. But it's only been going on for a little while and I don't know if it's going to work out, so I'd rather not talk about it."

"Alright." Her mother seemed to understand. "But you know we would love to meet her, right? If you two keep dating." Sweat was pearling on her forehead now too.

Despite the awkwardness, Ava was touched by how hard

they were trying. Even Zaid was quiet now, thankfully. She looked at her father, who gave her a nod.

"Yes, you must bring her over, so we can meet this lucky lady."

"Okay." Ava said, diverting her gaze back to her plate. "I might bring her over some day. But for now, can we please drop the subject? I can't eat when you're all looking at me." She sighed in relief when no one protested, glad the conversation was over. She was nervous enough as it was and the butterflies in her stomach hadn't left her all day. Tomorrow she would fly to Kuala Lumpur, and Mia would be there too.

39

LONDON, UK

"How do you feel about the whole uniform thing?" Mia was topping up her make-up in the staff room, just before the briefing.

"I don't know. Doesn't bother me in general, apart from this ill-fitting waistcoat," Farik said, pulling at the navy fabric. "Why, do you have a problem with it?"

"Actually, I do," Mia said sharply. "A shirt and a hat are one thing, I can live with that." She sighed, struggling to get her eyeliner straight. "But the high heels, the skirt, the hair, the nails and the make-up... I think it's sexist. I mean, think about it. In most industries, uniforms have evolved for women since the fifties. In fact, in a lot of places, workwear is so androgynous now that men and women can choose to wear the same." She turned to Farik and continued. "With the exception of aviation. It's the most backwards industry when it comes to women's rights. We're basically dressed up as lust objects, what with the red lipstick, the eyeliner and the French manicure."

"I like it," Farik said. He was the only man on their crew who insisted on wearing eyeliner, even though he wasn't technically allowed to. Mia had never given him a warning, because their passengers didn't seem to mind. They never commented on it anyway. "I wish I could wear a bit of lippie too. Nothing too obvious, just a touch of gloss." He pouted his lips. "But that might be pushing it." He nudged Mia away from the mirror and ran a hand through his hair. "But I suppose I can see where you're coming from. You do look like a high-end hooker."

"Fuck off, Farik." Mia huffed. "I know for a fact that I do not look like a hooker."

Farik laughed. "Okay, okay. I get your point about the heels and the make-up." He smiled at his reflection, clearly pleased with how he looked. "So, what are you going to do about it? I mean, if you're planning on fighting for equal treatment, I'm in, as long as I get to fight for my lipstick too. Can't we go to the Union?"

"One step at a time, Farik. We'll never get out of our heels if we start with your make-up demands." Mia gave him an apologetic look. "I'm sorry, it's nothing personal. Lynn and I have already spoken to the union representative about our concerns." She put her make-up bag on top of her case and secured her hair with generous amounts of hairspray. "Not that Lynn really cares." She chuckled. "But she likes drama, and she likes to feel important, so I recruited her to the cause with the promise of giving her all the credit. And apparently, many others have done the same, following other airlines that have managed to change their dress policy over the past years. In fact, enquiries on the topic have been so overwhelming lately that they're going to organise a petition next year on relaxing the skirt and shoe policy. It doesn't help with all this crap," she said, pointing to her face. "But at least it's a start."

"Well done you." Farik grabbed Mia's make-up bag and searched for the eyeliner. "Just don't forget about me."

Mia smiled. "If you're willing to put the time in, I'll help you," she said. "As soon as you and I are allowed to wear the same uniform. Why don't you come to the next meeting with us? You might joke about it, but I know it's important to you."

Farik's smirk dropped and he gave Mia's arm a quick squeeze. "Thank you. That might be the nicest thing you've ever said to me." He turned when Ava walked in and helped herself to a coffee from the machine.

"Hi Captain."

"Hey guys. Don't mind me. I'm just going to grab a cup of this terrible coffee. We were early today and the machine didn't work in our briefing room."

Mia couldn't stop staring at Ava, as flashes of their recent night surfaced in her mind. She was getting turned on just at the sight of her, and now wasn't a good time, as her crew had started to arrive. Ava met her gaze while the she filled up her cup and smiled.

"Hey Mia."

"Hi," was all Mia could manage to say.

"We were just talking about women's rights and how ridiculous we're made to look in our jobs," Farik said, interrupting their moment. "Apart from you, I guess." He looked Ava up and down. "You look like you were born to wear that uniform."

Mia had to agree with him. There was nothing sexier than Ava in her uniform. She oozed confidence and charm, pulling off the look way better than her male colleagues. Mia turned back to her suitcase before Farik could notice the chemistry between them, and slid the make-up pouch into the front compartment. *God, now I'm being the sexist one.*

40

KUALA LUMPUR, MALAYSIA

"Are you still coming out for dinner tonight?" Lynn asked as they made their way to their hotel in Kuala Lumpur. They were driving past gleaming skyscrapers, metal and glass structures and luxury shopping malls interspersed with colonial architecture. It never failed to amaze Mia how clean everything was, as if even the roads were polished on a regular basis. "Jack, myself and some of the others are going to the street-food market tonight," Lynn continued.

Mia shook her head. "Sorry, I'm tired. Think I might get room service." She didn't care if her friend thought she was flaky. It had been seven very long nights since she'd last shared a bed with Ava, and she wanted her all to herself. Ava was sitting in front of her, next to Jack. They were also discussing their plans for the evening.

"I have to make some phone calls and catch up on some much-needed sleep," she heard her say.

Mia smiled. She could smell Ava's shampoo, and was dying to touch her, but she told herself it would be worth the wait.

The bus turned onto a side road, heading towards a row of luxury hotels surrounded by large gardens.

"First stop is The Golden Lily," their driver yelled, pulling up in front of a modern skyscraper. The tech crew made their way out of the bus and waved goodbye to the cabin crew.

Farik, who was sitting in the back of the bus, gasped. "The Golden Lily? What the fuck is that all about? Since when does the tech crew get to stay in five-star resorts?"

"So long suckers," Jack teased. "I'm going to have a swim in the rooftop infinity pool before I meet you for dinner." He grinned. "After I've had my glass of complimentary Champagne." He stuck his head back in the bus and looked at Farik pointedly. "And I'm going to take a little nap on one of the pool loungers with memory foam mattresses. I'll see you guys at eight."

"Great!" Lynn yelled back. "If you're such a big shot, you won't mind paying for us tonight, then?"

Jack gave her a middle finger as he walked around the bus to get his case from the boot.

"Fuckers." Lynn rolled her eyes. "We work much harder than they do and what's our reward? A measly three-star shithole with a freezing cold pool?"

"It's a four-star actually," Mia corrected her. She was in a way too good of a mood to let the rest of the crew wind her up. "And if you're willing to get yourself into a ten-year long debt and a rigid training programme to get your pilot's license and carry the responsibility for five hundred people, you can have that too."

"What happened to you, traitor?" Farik sneered. "You're supposed to be on our side. Fight for our rights, remember?"

Mia laughed. "Chill out, Farik. It's only a hotel. Besides, don't you have some sugar daddy to stay with? How did it go with the other one in Abu Dhabi anyway?"

"It was fabulous, thank you very much." He looked out of the window and was quiet for the rest of the journey.

MIA HAD A LONG SHOWER, shaved her legs, applied generous amounts of coconut lotion to her skin and blow-dried her hair. She grinned at the fact that she hadn't paid that much attention to her appearance in years. It felt exciting, to get all dolled up before heading to another hotel for a booty call, even liberating, in a way. She had her favourite playlist on and sang along as she ironed an oversized cotton shirtdress, a white one with blue stripes this time. She'd seen the way Ava had looked at her when she'd worn her white one in New York, and although the nights were steaming hot in Kuala Lumpur, the fabric was light, and she could always roll up her sleeves and open up the three top buttons. Or four when the heat became unbearable. The sexual tension and anticipation that oozed through her body was terribly distracting as she tried to concentrate on what to pack. Was she going to go back to her own hotel room tonight? Or would she stay over? If she did, she'd have to leave early tomorrow, so the other crew members wouldn't see her. Just in case, she decided on a toothbrush and underwear only. Ava would have the rest. She looked at her watch. Quarter past eight. Her colleagues would be gone by now, the ones that were heading into town anyway. She went to the lobby and asked the bellboy for a cab to The Golden Lily.

"HEY CAPTAIN." Mia took on her flirty tone again as she joined Ava on the sofa in the lobby of The Golden Lily. "Nice hotel. I can see now why Farik got so worked up." The marbled lobby was so polished that she could see her own reflection in the floor and the reception desks. A long row of glass elevators reached up to the forty-second floor, moving up and down like a game of Tetris. The air around them smelled of lilies.

"Hey gorgeous. You look amazing." Ava kept her voice down in the busy hotel lobby but couldn't manage to suppress a smile. "How was your shift?"

"It was okay." Mia shifted a little closer, touching Ava's hand in between them. "There was a woman who had failed to mention until check-in that she had a severe peanut allergy, so we had to remove all peanuts from the plane before take-off and find replacement snacks within thirty minutes. Not that that's anything new, it happens at least once a week and frankly, I don't get why the catering department still offers peanuts as an option." She counted on her fingers. "Then there was a man who was snoring really loudly, leading to complaints from nearly all the passengers around him." She shrugged. "What could I do? I woke him up three times. In the end, I handed out earplugs, which everyone already had, just so it looked like I was doing something about it." She sighed. "And one of the new crew members spilt a drink over someone's expensive coat, so I had to talk the passenger out of putting in a complaint. What about you?"

"Not nearly as eventful," Ava said. "But I managed a smooth landing, and that's always good, right?" She turned to Mia, holding her gaze. "You'll tell me if you're tired? I know how hard you guys work, and if you need your rest then..."

"No." Mia's eyes widened as she shook her head frantically. "No, I'm absolutely fine." There was nothing that could keep her away from a night with Ava. Not after having missed her for a week. She looked so good in her black skinny trousers and her white sleeveless top, showing off her arms and just enough cleavage to fire up Mia's imagination.

"Okay, great." Ava gave Mia's hand a quick squeeze, sending a spark through Mia's core. "Because I'm taking you out for dinner and we're going somewhere special."

AFTER A FIFTEEN-MINUTE TAXI RIDE, they arrived at the restaurant where Ava had made reservations.

"I hope you like it," she said, walking up to the hostess.

"What's not to like?" Mia was pleasantly surprised by the ground floor entrance, as most restaurants were located in the many high-rise buildings in town. The restaurant and its garden were surrounded by ivy-covered stone walls, and Mia could hear the soothing sound of running water and crickets chirping as they waited to be led through.

"Follow me please," the hostess said after checking their reservation.

Mia was stunned when they entered the oasis, shielded from the noise and chaos of the city. The jungle of tropical plants and trees was broken up by wooden platforms with tables on them. The garden was only dimly lit by candlelight, casting a romantic glow over the tables. The restaurant's kitchen was hidden away in a traditional looking wooden building at the edge of the premises, from where a path led to the tables, allowing the waiters to bring out the dishes on trolleys. The food smelled delicious.

"Oh my God Ava, this is perfect," Mia said, admiring the

waterlilies in the pond next to their table. A frog hopped from one big leaf to another, before it disappeared under water.

"I'm glad you like it. It's my favourite restaurant here." Ava smiled as she pulled out Mia's chair for her.

"Wow." Mia sat back and studied Ava's face. She looked beautiful in the candlelight. "You're quite the charmer, aren't you?"

"Only for you, Mia." Ava opened the drinks list and turned to the waitress, who had just approached their table and handed them the menus. "I'll have the tarik. Hot please."

"Is that the black tea with condensed milk?" Mia asked, looking up at the waitress.

"Yes, it is. We serve it hot and iced."

"Great. I'll have the same but iced please." Mia realised she was still grinning as she scanned the menu. "And a big bowl of laksa," she added after a couple of seconds.

"It's very, very good here," the waitress said as she jotted down her order. "Great choice."

Ava laughed. "My God, Mia. You're quick with your ordering." She handed her menu back to the waitress. "I'll have the same. And we'll also have some some roti canai to start with, if that's possible."

"Of course." The waitress smiled. "Would you like some water with that? We have bottled water, or water from our spring?" She giggled when Mia turned towards the pond. "Don't worry, it's bottled in the kitchen, so there won't be any algae or frogs in your jug."

"Okay. In that case, spring water sounds wonderful," Mia said, relaxing in blissful happiness. She was sitting in a tropical garden, about to eat her favourite food, and there was the most stunning woman opposite her, with a look in her eyes that told her she'd be up all night for all the right reasons.

"I know I've already told you, but you look great tonight." Ava looked her up and down, resting her gaze on Mia's cleavage.

"So do you." Mia couldn't keep her eyes off Ava. "It's been a long week, and I've been looking forward to tonight." She surprised herself by being completely honest. "I've missed you."

Ava grinned. "Have you now?" She shifted in her chair, leaning in over the table. "I've missed you too. And I've thought about you a lot." She paused. "I don't understand how this thing works or how it happened, but I'm happy to surrender to it."

"How what works?" Mia leaned in too.

"Well, you know, you meet someone, and you think they're hot. And then they turn out to be funny, intelligent and kind too. And then on top of that, there seems to be some kind of vibe where you just understand each other on all levels. You don't need to explain yourself or make excuses." Ava paused. "And don't get me started on the chemistry or the sex, because that's just way beyond..."

"Shhh..." Mia giggled. "That last part can't be a topic of conversation tonight, since I'm doing everything in my power not to kiss you right now." She skimmed the premises. "I don't think the staff would appreciate it, and neither would the local police." Her face became more serious. "But yes, you're right. It's strange how it just works. Makes me wonder what the hell I did to deserve sitting here with you."

"Maybe the universe has decided to give us both a

break," Ava said. "We've both struggled for years. Maybe this is the point where it gets easier." She shrugged. "You're the best distraction from alcohol I've ever had, that's for sure. Not that that's the reason I'm here with you, don't get me wrong," she hastily added, "but I feel really happy right now, and I'm calm... I forgot how it felt to be calm." There was a silence. "Am I being too full-on? Please tell me if I am and I'll shut up. I don't want to put you off."

"No, you're not." Mia sighed and smiled. "You could never put me off."

They both leaned back when the waitress arrived with their drinks and a plate of egg filled roti with dahl.

Mia broke off a piece of the fluffy flatbread that was fried crispy on the outside and scooped it through the lentil soup. She moaned in delight as she took a bite.

"So good."

"Yeah, right?" Ava took a bite too and nodded. "So, have you looked at our schedules?"

"Of course I have." Mia swallowed before continuing. "And it's not looking great, is it?"

"Four weeks until our next flight together."

"At least it's Dubai." Mia said. "Two nights this time. Better than one, I suppose." She took another bite of the roti. "I've got a holiday booked in in two weeks' time. That's why I'm not on the schedule for the second half of the month. I had so many days left, they practically forced me to book them a while back."

"Yeah. I saw that too." Ava cocked her head. "Are you going somewhere nice?"

"I haven't booked anything yet. My parents want me to come home for a couple of days, but I was thinking about checking myself into a yoga resort instead. Not that I'm a huge yoga fan." She chuckled. "I'm not very good at it either, but yoga resorts seem to agree with me. Green juices, lots of exercise, like-minded sober people, for different reasons, but still..."

"Sounds good." Ava smiled. "I tried one in India once, but it was too hippie-happy for me. They made me chant for an hour each morning and I had no idea what I was doing."

Mia laughed. "I've never had to participate in anything like that, but then I usually stay in Europe. I do enough long-haul flights as it is, so I try to avoid jet lags when I'm off." She looked up at Ava. "Where do you go when you have time off work?"

"Nowhere specific. I tend to stay with my parents for a couple of days. It's been a while since I went on holiday. I was in Jordan four years ago, and my last holiday was three years ago, when I went to Ibiza."

"Ibiza?" Mia gave her an amused look. "Why is it that I can't picture you there?"

"Wasn't my idea. I was having an affair at the time and Danielle – that was her name - begged me to come with her. She and her husband had a really nice place there on the coast, and he was away for a couple of weeks, so I went."

"Right." Mia tried to hide the stab of jealousy she felt at the mention of someone else who had been a part of Ava's life. She knew that was crazy, but she couldn't help it. "Did you love her?"

"No." Ava shook her head. "It was more convenience, to be honest with you. For both of us I think. Danielle was so terrified of getting caught that we couldn't go anywhere. I don't think her husband ever found out. She's still with him."

"Do you still speak to her? If you know she's still with him, then you must..."

Ava laughed. "I saw her on the cover of a tabloid in the

briefing room. Her husband's a football player, so she's a bit of a socialite. But please don't tell anyone. I promised to take her super gay secret to my grave."

Mia frowned, mentally digging through recent gossip magazines she'd read. Then she gasped. "Danielle Hunter? It's not her, is it?"

"Yeah. It's her." Ava winced, regretting bringing up Danielle on their date. "But as I said, it's over. It was over three years ago, and I haven't spoken to her since. She kept trying to contact me, so I changed my number."

"But..." Mia paused to think. "She's absolutely stunning. She's been on my flights a couple of times. I've served her. And I hate to say it, but she's lovely."

"She's nowhere near as stunning as you." Ava's eyes sparkled as she delivered the compliment.

Mia rolled her eyes. "Yeah, right." She threw her hands up in despair. "How am I supposed to compete with her, Ava?"

"Come on, Mia. You're not competing. You beat her the moment you walked into the cockpit the day we first met."

"Smooth." Mia shot her a sarcastic grin. "You've got a knack for saying all the right things, don't you, Captain?"

"Just being honest," Ava said.

"Curry laksa." They were interrupted by the waitress, who cleared the table and put two large bowls filled with spicy coconut soup, rice vermicelli, tofu puffs, prawns and beansprouts in front of them.

Mia inhaled the aroma with a delighted grin on her face. "Okay, topic of hot footballer's wife is now officially closed. Let's talk about this instead." She tried a spoonful and smiled. "Mmm. How good is this?!"

"Come on, I want to show you something." Ava reached out her hand for Mia's after their taxi had dropped them off at The Golden Lily. Mia took it, entwining her fingers with Ava's as she followed her around the back of the hotel. It was dark, apart from the dimly lit footpaths around the pool area and the Palm Garden, where loved-up couples were enjoying the last hours of the evening around a big fountain that danced to the classical music playing from the speakers that were hidden in the trees.

"Where are we going?" Mia arched an eyebrow. "I can't see where I'm walking. Are you sure there's anything back there? Look, it's fenced off."

"Just wait," Ava said, lowering her voice. "Let's see if we're lucky tonight." She climbed over the low, wooden fence and Mia followed her. Although the footpath was overgrown now, it was still clearly visible, circling around a tree and a couple of big bushes. Mia's eyes were slowly getting used to the dark. She could make out the remains of a recreational area, with tree trunk benches and an old barbeque, overgrown with moss. Ava, who was walking in front of her, seemed to know exactly where she was going.

"Almost there," she said, leading Mia around another big bush. "Careful, there's a pond here."

Mia's jaw dropped when she was suddenly confronted with hundreds of tiny lights, flickering around her. They moved in random directions, some of them blinking on and off.

"Wow." She squeezed Ava's hand. "Are those fireflies? I've never seen fireflies before." She jumped back as one of them flew towards her, skimming her forehead.

"Yeah. It's great, isn't it?" Ava put an arm around her and pulled her closer. "I've stayed in this hotel before, when I flew for my old airline. One of my colleagues told me about it, back then. They're not always here, so we're in luck tonight." Two fireflies landed on a tree-trunk right in front of them and turned off their lights.

"Are they okay?" Mia leaned forward to study the tiny insects. They were almost invisible now.

"I think they want some privacy," Ava said softly. "Fireflies blink to attract the opposite sex, then switch off their lights when they've found their mating partner."

"That's sweet," Mia said, kneeling down to find them on top of each other. Waves of twinkling lights lit up the grass surrounding the pond and the air around them, bathing Ava's face in a shimmer that made her look angelic. The night was warm and humid, and there was a sweet, tropical scent in the air. Mia felt calm and happy, almost spiritual. She stood up and rested her head on Ava's shoulder. "It's breathtaking." She reached out her hand in an attempt to touch one of the fireflies, but it was too fast. It flew around them before landing on the back of Ava's hand. Ava slowly brought her hand up, in between them. The little insect flickered several times before it flew away.

"I feel so lucky. I wouldn't have missed this for the world."

Ava smiled and planted a tender kiss on her cheek. "I love spending time with you."

"Me too." Mia looked up at her. "This thing we've got going on..." She looked down again when she realised she was about to ask a very serious question. "What does it mean to you? I mean, I really like you and I think about you all the time." She paused. "I know it's too early to ask because we've only been on three dates, but I need to know that you won't..."

"Won't what?" Ava frowned.

"That you won't sleep around if we're going to continue to see each other. I got so jealous tonight when you told me about Danielle, and I know it's ridiculous, but I just need to know where I stand."

"Seriously?" Ava shot her a flirty glance, sending a flash of heat through Mia's core. "Are you telling me you don't know where you stand? Look at me." She pointed at her face. "Do I look like I don't care to you? Jesus, I can't stop smiling when you're around."

Mia smiled too. "Okay, that makes me feel better." She paused to collect herself, then asked the question she'd been dwelling on all evening. "Does that mean we're exclusive?" She felt her face burn and shook her head in embarrassment.

Ava looked at her with a mixture of amusement and tenderness. Then she leaned in and kissed her. Softly at first, then deeper as she parted her lips, taking Mia's face into her hands. Mia's head started spinning as she sank into Ava's warm mouth, grabbing onto her arm. The kiss turned wilder as their hands started leading a life of their own, searching for bare skin underneath each other's clothes. Mia felt Ava's hands on her ass, pulling her closer towards her. They both knew it was time to stop, or there would be no going back.

Ava pulled out of the kiss and pressed her forehead against Mia's. "I would very much like that." She chuckled before she pressed another kiss against Mia's mouth. "And I'd already made that assumption, I hope you don't mind."

"Not at all." Mia was grinning from ear to ear. She cocked her head and batted her eyelashes. "Then it won't be presumptuous of me to assume you'll want to spend the night with me?"

"No. I'd love to spend the night with you." Ava kissed her

one more time before they both turned back to the firefly display in front of them. "And by the way, you never have to ask me that ever again."

KUALA LUMPUR, MALAYSIA

"Would you like a coffee of something?" Ava asked when they got to her room on the thirty-fifth floor.

Mia opened the curtains and looked out over the sea of light. The city was still very much awake. Way down, in between the skyscrapers, she saw tiny cars, buses, and crowds of people. To her left were the iconic Petronas Twin Towers, a short distance away. The noise from earlier that day seemed so far away now, after their tranquil dinner and their walk to the pond. She turned back to Ava, who was holding up the kettle in the swanky little kitchen unit opposite the bathroom. The room was tastefully decorated, with a traditional wooden four-poster bed and a cosy seating area by the window.

"No, I think I'm good," she said, picking up Ava's uniform tie that was hanging over a chair as she walked towards her. She tied it around her neck. "How does it look on me?"

Ava stared at her and put down the kettle. "It will look

better without that dress, that's for sure." She grinned. "No offence to your dress."

"Oh yeah? You think so?" Mia crossed her arms and removed her dress in one swift move, standing in front of Ava in only a white lingerie set and the navy tie. The look in Ava's eyes turned her on, and she knew Ava wanted her. She reached behind her back and unclipped her bra. Ava walked up to her, removed it and let it drop onto the floor. Then she pulled down Mia's knickers. Mia stepped out of them.

"I know where it would look even better," Ava said, removing the tie from Mia's neck.

Mia held her breath, staring up at her in anticipation. "Oh yeah? Where?"

Ava nodded towards the bed. "Lie down."

Mia walked to the bed with shaky legs. She was wet and aching to be touched. She dropped down and propped her head on the pillow, stretching one leg in front of her, the other, slightly bent inwards as Ava approached her with the tie. Mia expected to be blindfolded, but instead, Ava took her wrists and lifted her arms over her head, smiling as she tied them together.

"What are you doing, Captain?" Mia giggled. Ava was sexy when she took charge.

"I'm going to tie you to the bedpost, Mia." Ava bent down and gave her a longing kiss until Mia moaned softly. She looked down at her. "Are you okay with that?"

Mia nodded slowly. "Whatever you want," she said, almost whispering.

Ava took her wrists and moved them over to the corner of the bed, where she tied them to the post, securing the knot with a final hard pull. Then she looked Mia up and down, unable to keep the smirk off of her face. "You have no idea how sexy you look, Mia." She stood up and turned to the door. "I'll be right back. Don't go anywhere."

Mia lay there, waiting for Ava to come back. Not that she had a choice. She wriggled her wrists. There was no movement in the knots, but she couldn't deny that she kind of liked being tied up. There was something incredibly exciting about being submissive to Ava. Where were they taking this new game they were playing? She'd never done anything like this before, but with Ava, it seemed like the best idea in the world.

A couple of minutes later, Ava came back with an icebucket. She stood next to the bed for a moment, watching Mia. "You're hot," she said, taking an ice cube out of the bucket. She dimmed the lights before climbing on to the bed, straddling Mia. "Way too hot. I think I might have to cool you down a bit. Tell me to stop when you want me to," she said in a soft voice. She put the ice cube in her mouth, leaving a wet trail on her lips, and lowered herself over Mia, sliding the ice-cube over her nipple.

Mia let out a moan as soon as the cold sensation hit her breast. Her initial reaction was to use her hands to push Ava away, but she couldn't, and it turned her on, more than she'd expected. Much more. Ava looked at Mia while she shifted her mouth over to her other breast. She repeated the movement, caressing her with cold sensation before pushing the ice cube into her cheek. Then she placed her cold mouth around Mia's nipple, biting it softly at first, then harder.

"Fuck!" Mia cried out as a mixture of pain and pleasure shot through her, sending a warm glow between her legs.

Ava looked up. "Are you okay?"

"Yeah." Mia nodded. "I'm more than okay."

Ava looked at her intently, a small smile playing around her mouth. Then she moved further down, caressing Mia's ribcage and her belly with the ice cube that had now almost melted. Mia wiggled and moaned as Ava's mouth went lower and lower, her cold tongue sliding over her skin after swallowing the last bit of ice. Ava took another ice cube out of the bucket next to the bed and kneeled in between Mia's legs. She slowly spread them apart, still looking up at Mia. She was breathing fast, her breasts rising and falling rapidly.

"Do it," Mia begged, slamming her head back against the pillow. She needed it.

Ava placed the ice cube between her lips and slowly traced her centre, leaving a tingling feeling on Mia's over-sensitive skin.

"Yes. Fuck, yes." Mia panted through ragged breathing. The ice-cold sensation between her legs turned into a warm glow but came back again tenfold when Ava moved up, rubbing the ice cube over her clit. She held Mia's legs in place with her hands, so she couldn't move, but kept a close eye on her to make sure she was enjoying their play.

Mia closed her eyes in ecstatic bliss, bucking her hips when Ava made circling motions with her mouth, causing an agonizing tingle that felt painful and delightful at the same time. Ava then swallowed the rest of the second ice-cube and let her cold tongue run over Mia's centre before sucking her clit into her mouth.

"Oh God," Mia groaned, surprised by the force of her orgasm. She clenched her thighs around Ava's head, holding her mouth in place while she arched her hips, riding out the waves that shot through her like lightning. When she relaxed her legs and opened her eyes again, Ava's chin was resting on her belly, and she had a huge grin on her face. She looked pleased with herself, although the darkness had not left her eyes.

"Jesus, Ava. You really know what you're doing." Mia was still trying to catch her breath, wondering what the hell had just happened. "Come here," she whispered. "Untie me. I want to pleasure you."

Ava moved up to kiss her. Her mouth was cold when her tongue skimmed Mia's lips. She untied Mia's hands, lifted them towards her mouth and kissed them.

"You just have." She bit her lip, a small smile playing around her mouth.

"I understand." Mia did. She could sense the pleasure Ava got from being in control, from making her feel good. "But I want to touch you."

Ava hesitated.

"Come here," Mia said again. She took the bottom of Ava's top and pulled it over her head. Then she unbuttoned her trousers. "Please take these off."

Ava stood up and took them off, leaving her in her bra and her briefs. She looked vulnerable.

"You're so beautiful." Mia let her eyes wander over Ava's body as she stood there, next to the bed. She patted the mattress. "Lie next to me. Please."

"I'm not used to women touching me like that," Ava said as she got back on the bed. She turned on her side, facing Mia. "I find it hard to let go."

"I'd be honoured to be the first." Mia smiled as she went in for another kiss, slowly draping herself over Ava. Ava kissed her back, but it felt different, as if she wasn't entirely there. Mia could sense her internal struggle.

"I'm sorry, I just can't." Ava took Mia's wrists again and rolled them over, so she was on top. "Not yet."

"That's okay." Mia said in a sweet voice. "It's fine."

"I'm sorry, it's just that..."

"Don't apologize, Ava. We have all the time in the world

and I'm not going anywhere." She let out a chuckle. "I wouldn't even be able to if I wanted, the way you're pinning me down right now."

"Does it bother you?" Ava nestled her thigh between Mia's legs.

Mia took in a quick breath as she felt another stir of arousal. "Do I look bothered?" She grinned.

"Not exactly."

"Well then…" There was a silence. "Have me. I can't deny that I like it, the way you take control. I guess it's something I never knew about myself." Mia lifted her head to kiss her, but Ava lifted her head too in a teasing manner. "As long as you kiss me right now because I'm starting to get impatient."

42

KUALA LUMPUR, MALAYSIA

"Until next time," Mia said reluctantly. The moment she left Ava's room and got a taxi back to her hotel, this thing they had, that was making her so happy would cease to exist, at least in the presence of their colleagues. There would be no more kissing, no more touching, and no more sweet words. Mia would get on the bus with the rest of the cabin crew and pretend she hadn't seen Ava over the course of their stay. Then they would pick up the tech crew and Ava would greet her and talk to her like she talked to the rest of her colleagues. Mia hated that part, but she couldn't deny that it was exciting in a way, having this sexy secret that her colleagues were oblivious to.

"Next time seems a long time from now." Ava ran a hand through her hair.

"Why don't we meet up in London?" Mia asked, looking at Ava. "If you want to. I mean, dating usually starts close to home, right?" She chuckled. "I suppose we've done it the other way around. I know almost everything about you, but I haven't even seen where you live."

"I would love that." Ava hesitated. "But we've only got

one overlapping day off next week and I promised my parents I'd come over for dinner. They're very passionate about our weekly dinners and I already cancelled once this month because I had the decorators over." She shuffled on the spot, contemplating. "Unless…"

"Unless what?" Mia asked when Ava went silent, a blush forming on her cheeks. Any 'unless' was good as far as Mia was concerned, as long as she got to see her.

"Unless you'd like to come with me?" Ava shook her head. "I'm sorry. Forget I ever said that. It's a bit too early to ask you to meet my parents."

"I'll come if you want me to." Mia lingered by the door, her hand still on the handle. Ava's proposal sounded like music to her ears, but she didn't want to come across as overly keen.

"Really? You'd like to come?" Ava looked perplexed.

"Yeah. I would. I mean, I can play along if you just want to introduce me as a friend. I'd love to meet your parents. Your stories have made me curious."

Ava chuckled. "I don't know how to say this, but I've already told them I've been on a couple of dates with you, so I don't think they'd believe me if I told them you were just a friend." She held up a hand. "I wasn't planning on telling them, it was my brother's fault, he's always on to me. Oh God, I haven't freaked you out now, have I?"

"No, of course not." Mia gave her a reassuring smile. "I'd love to come with you." She felt warm and fuzzy just at the thought of getting a little bit closer to Ava and seeing the part of her she didn't yet know. They were just standing there, grinning at each other sheepishly.

"Okay. That's a date then." Ava stepped towards her, lingering in front of Mia's face, their lips almost touching. "I need to warn you about my brother though. He's a pain in the ass."

"I'm sure I can handle your brother."

"I'm sure you can." Ava took Mia's full bottom lip between her own lips, bit down gently and tugged. Mia let go of the door handle and wrapped her arms around Ava's neck, sinking into another long kiss.

"I really need to go now," she mumbled, taking a step back. Ava followed her, unable to let go. She grabbed Mia's ass and pressed her against the door, stealing another minute of Mia's heavenly mouth.

"I'm sorry," she said after letting go of Mia. Their eyes locked in a hungry gaze. "I can't seem to stop myself."

Mia took a deep breath in an attempt to collect herself. She wanted Ava to rip her clothes off, and go back to where they'd left off, but the clock was ticking. She forced herself to open the door and stepped outside, giving herself some space so she wouldn't throw herself at Ava again.

"I'll see you soon," she whispered, before disappearing down the hallway.

43

KUALA LUMPUR, MALAYSIA TO LONDON, UK

"Hey, Mia. Are you awake?" Lynn nudged Mia, waking her up from her blissful hour-long nap in the only available first-class cabin. When in need of a rest, she preferred the passengers' seats to the crew rest, which bore more resemblance to a coffin than to a bed. She blinked and looked at her phone.

"I am now. What is it, Lynn? I've got ten minutes left. My alarm hasn't even buzzed yet."

"The captain's asking for you," Lynn continued, standing back up. "I mean Ava. If you're too tired I can tell her that…"

"No." Mia shot up at the sound of Ava's name. "Wait. I'm coming. What's up?"

Lynn shrugged. "No idea. She was just asking if you had time to come into the cockpit for five minutes. There's no emergency."

"Sure." Mia straightened her uniform, put her shoes back on and fixed her hair. "How do I look?"

"Very fuckable." Lynn gave her a wink. "Just don't distract her too much. I'd love her to land us all safely."

Mia buzzed before opening the door to the cockpit,

turning her face to the camera. Ava pointed at Jack, who was asleep in his chair, and put her index finger in front of her mouth. Hassan, today's second officer, wasn't there. Mia guessed he'd gone for his two-hour break in the crew rest. Ava beckoned her to come closer and stand behind her seat and pointed at the view in front of them. Mia stared ahead as she leaned over Ava's seat, her eyes falling on the most colourful horizon she'd ever seen.

"Not bad, huh?" Ava whispered, looking up at her. "A sunrise over the Indian Ocean at thirty-five thousand feet. Even with the sun behind us, it doesn't get any better than this."

"It's breathtaking," Mia said in a low voice. She put a hand on Ava's shoulder and Ava covered it with her own as they watched the morning unfold. The first slivers of light were bright red, before the sky turned orange, creating a halo around the few lonely clouds in front of them. It was quiet on the flight deck, and it almost felt as if they were watching a silent movie, waiting for the plot to reveal itself. Mia took a deep breath and marvelled at the sight, knowing this would be a moment she'd never, ever forget.

"That's Oman," Ava said, pointing to a patch of yellow in the distance. "It's an astonishing sight when we get closer, the desert blending in with the colours in the sky." She looked up at Mia, whose gaze was fixed on the spreading light. Up in the air, dawn didn't last long, and the full daylight came much faster than on the ground. "I just thought you'd like to see it."

"Thank you." Mia smiled and squeezed her hand. "Thank you for thinking of me." She nodded towards Jack. "He's not supposed to be asleep, is he?"

Ava shook her head. "I told him it was fine as we've got a smooth flight ahead." She leaned her cheek against Mia's hand on her shoulder and closed her eyes for a brief moment. "Can you stay for another ten minutes? It only gets better from here."

"`I'm sure Lynn can manage without me for a little while longer." Mia felt a beautiful sense of calm as they watched the sky theatre slowly changing its backdrop, shifting in colour again, and it dawned on her that she was finally truly happy.

44

CAMBRIDGE, UK

"Nervous?" Ava looked at Mia sideways as she was about to press the doorbell.

"Not really." Mia laughed. "But you look like you are."

"I guess I am. I've never brought anyone home." Ava rolled her eyes. "And my parents have never seen me together with a woman, even though they've known I was gay for over twenty years."

"I thought you said it wasn't a big deal?"

"I didn't think it was a big deal at the time. I'm thirty-seven years old. Bringing a date home hardly seemed like something big." Ava pulled a grin. "Until now. Not it seems like the biggest fucking deal in the whole world."

"I can leave if you're uncomfortable?" Mia offered. "I wouldn't mind. I'll take an early train back and..."

The door opened before she had the chance to finish her sentence, and Ava's mother appeared in the doorway.

"What are you two standing here for? There's a doorbell, you know." Ava's mother gave Mia a curious once-over, then held out her hand and smiled. "I'm Noor. And you must be Mia?"

"I am. It's lovely to meet you, Noor." Mia studied the elegant woman who had the same piercing green eyes as Ava. It was almost intimidating, being face to face with an older version of the woman she was dating. "You look just like Ava."

Noor took a step back and chuckled. "Thank you, I'll take that as a compliment. Please come in, dinner is almost ready and everyone is dying to meet you, Mia."

Mia followed Ava into the living room. It was bathed in a cosy glow from the red tapestry and the pillows, lit up by the many ornate globe lanterns placed around the room.

"You have a beautiful home," she said, stopping to look at some of Ava's childhood pictures on the wall.

"Thank you, Mia. I try my best to make it as homely as possible." Noor ushered them to go into the dining room, where Zaid, Natasha and Ava's father were already sitting at the table.

Mia felt three pairs of eyes staring at her as she approached them. "Okay, now I'm nervous," she whispered. To her surprise, Ava took her hand and gave it a quick squeeze as she led her to the table.

"Guys, this is Mia. Mia, this is my father Ahmad, my brother Zaid, and his girlfriend, Natasha."

"Welcome to our humble abode," Ava's father said. He stood up to greet Mia with a hug and two kisses. "We never thought this day would come." He placed his hands on Mia's shoulders and took a good look at her. "But here you are. I'm Ahmad. Please, sit down and join us."

Mia sat down next to Natasha and introduced herself before turning to Zaid. "And you're Zaid." She smiled, extending her hand. "It's great to meet you. I've watched some of your shows, you're good."

"Thank you, I try," Zaid stammered, shaking Mia's hand over the table. Ava was amused to see that for once, Zaid was lost for words. She sat down next to her brother, opposite Mia, and gave him a sharp warning look, just in case.

"Hey Sis." He looked at her with an approving grin that almost bordered on admiration, but he didn't comment.

Ava relaxed a little now that the formalities were out of the way, and smiled at Mia in an attempt to put her at ease. But Mia didn't seem to need the support. She was already talking to Natasha, laughing at something she'd said.

"Would you like some tea, Mia?" Noor held up a tea pot. "Or do you prefer wine with dinner? We're not big drinkers in this family but we always have a couple of bottles in the cellar, and Natasha likes a glass from time to time."

"Tea would be lovely, thank you." Mia handed Noor the small glass. "Thank you so much for inviting me. It's lovely to meet you all."

"Likewise." Noor cast Mia a warm smile. "Ava has never brought anyone home, so it's a big thing for us."

"Please Mum, don't..."

"No, Ava," her mother interrupted her while filling the other glasses. "I need to say this." She turned to Mia. "We weren't very supportive of Ava when she was younger. In her sexuality, I mean." She looked flustered. "Although we grew up fairly liberal in Jordan, Ava's father and I come from a different world, and it took us a while to get used to the idea. But we've been living in the UK for half our lives now, so things have changed. I talked to one of my students who is also gay about it, as Ava understandably had no desire anymore to discuss such things with me. She opened my eyes." Noor paused. "I was worried that our behaviour when she first came out was stopping Ava from bringing people home, because she never, ever did. She never spoke about people she was seeing either, until she finally admitted she was dating you. I just want you to know that we are so excited to meet you, Mia. Ava has been... well, she's been smiling a lot lately, and that's a joy for any mother to see." She put a hand on Ava's shoulder and squeezed it.

"Thanks Mum." Ava blushed, torn between embarrassment and pure happiness. It was the first time her mother had admitted to her mistakes openly, something she'd never expected to hear, especially not in Mia's company.

"That's very sweet of you to say." Mia blushed a little too. "Ava is an amazing woman. I feel lucky to have met her."

"Enough with the soppiness now," Zaid said, sensing his sister and her girlfriend were starting to feel slightly uncomfortable being the centre of attention. "Let's eat. Mum, would you like me to put the food in the serving bowls?"

"Yes please, Zaid. That would be lovely. I'll finish the bread, it will just take five minutes."

Ava looked at him as he stood up. "Thank you," she mouthed.

"He's not all bad, huh?" Natasha said after Zaid and Noor had disappeared into the kitchen.

"Not today." Ava chuckled. "Come on, Natasha. Doesn't he get on your nerves sometimes, with his practical jokes?"

Natasha laughed. "What you don't know about me," she said, "is that I beat him at his own game all the time. Last time he got home late from the pub, I heard him fumbling with the lock and waited in the hallway with my hand on the light switch. I'm sure you can imagine how that went down. Two different neighbours came over to check on us."

Ava laughed. "Sounds like he's found his match in you."

Natasha nodded with a grin. "Looks like you have found your match too."

"So tell me, Mia," Ava's father interrupted them from the head of the table. "How long have you two been seeing each other? As Noor mentioned, Ava doesn't share very much." He took a sip of his tea, winking at Ava.

"I'm not sure." Mia frowned. "Ten weeks, maybe?"

"Something like that," Ava said. "We don't see each other that much because we're often on different flights."

"Well, I'm glad it hasn't stopped you. Our daughter is always on the go, that's for sure. But at least you can relate to each other's lives, right? Noor and I were lucky to work in the same field for most of our lives too. It's nice to have something to discuss together when you get home, and that there's always someone who understands your highs and lows when it comes to your job." He chuckled. "It's not the same anymore since I retired. Noor treats me like a senile pensioner sometimes." He held up a finger. "But you should hear me play the trumpet. I've really improved since I've had more time to practice."

"I'd love to hear you play," Mia said. "Do you perform?" She turned to Ava and Natasha. "Have you guys ever heard him play?"

Ahmad leaned in over the table and lowered his voice. "Now that's an interesting question, Mia. I've invited them to come to a concert a couple of times, but none of them seem very excited at the idea. Whenever we perform, they're all very busy suddenly. Even my wife, who encouraged me to take it up in the first place."

"That's not true," Ava interrupted him. "I would have come but I was genuinely working the last time you were doing a gig at the..." She frowned. "Where was it again? Oh yes, it was at the crochet and knitting festival in Grantchester, wasn't it? I was absolutely gutted I missed it."

They heard laughter coming from the kitchen as Zaid came out with a bowl of steaming hot rice and a plate of freshly baked bread.

"I'd watch that sarcastic tone if I were you, young lady." Ava's father shot his daughter a half amused, half- annoyed look before he looked up at Zaid. "And you too, boy."

"But I didn't say anything," Zaid defended himself.

"It's not what you said, it's what you're about to say. I can tell by that smirk on your face." He turned to Mia. "You see what I have to put up with?"

"Stop the fighting everyone," Noor interrupted them as she put a bowl of stew on the table. "It's time to eat. Zaid, will you get the salads please? Let's not scare Mia away."

45

CAMBRIDGE, UK TO LONDON, UK

"Your family is lovely." Mia had made herself comfortable next to Ava on the train back to London. It was late, and the carriage was quiet. "They made me feel so welcome and your mother's cooking is out of this world."

"Yeah, it's pretty good." Ava kissed her temple. "They really liked you too, I could tell." She grinned. "Thank you for coming with me. I almost had a stroke just before we went in, but it turned out to be a good night, actually."

"The pleasure was all mine." Mia stared up at her and bit her lip, hesitating. "Would you like to come back to my place? Or we could go to yours, if you prefer?"

"Yeah." Ava's eyes darkened. "I have to get up at six, but I wasn't planning on spending the night apart from you, that's for sure." She brushed her lips against Mia's and shivered when Mia ran a hand up her thigh.

"Good. Me neither." Mia couldn't deny that she was nervous, bringing Ava into her home. So far, their nights together had been spent in hotel rooms, where they were on neutral grounds. "I can't remember the last time I had a woman in my home." She rolled her eyes. "Apart from my ex, of course. Since Marsha, it's just been me in my bed."

"As you know, I don't make a habit of bringing women home to meet my parents either," Ava retorted. "I guess we'll both have to get used to this."

"SORRY FOR THE CLIMB," Mia whispered when she opened the door to her flat, just after midnight. The three flights of stairs were steep and narrow, but they didn't seem to bother Ava. She switched on the lights in the kitchen. "Welcome to my home."

"It's nice," Ava said, looking around. "It's got character."

"Yeah, well it's old. It's still got most of the original Victorian features, except for the modern kitchen and bathroom. I haven't done much to it yet." Mia chuckled. "And I probably never will." She opened the fridge. "Would you like a soda, or a water?"

Ava walked up behind her and closed the fridge door. "No." She stripped Mia's cardigan off her shoulders, threw it on the floor and kissed the back of her neck. "I want you to take this top off." She lifted Mia's silk top over her head and tossed it on top of the cardigan. Mia could hear by the sound of her voice what was coming and right now, she wanted it more than anything. She shivered when Ava's mouth returned to her ear, spreading hot breath across her neck as she gently bit down on her earlobe. "And this," Ava continued, unbuttoning Mia's trousers. Mia let her pull them down and stepped out of them, her breath fast and ragged with anticipation. Ava's hands traced her spine upwards, reaching between her shoulder blades. "And the rest," she whispered, unhooking Mia's black bra. Mia gasped when Ava removed her bra and pushed her against the cold fridge door, squeezing her ass hard before pulling down her briefs. "And then," she continued in a seductive tone, "I want you to put both hands next to each other on the fridge and stand very still." She pulled Mia's hair, forcing her head back slowly while she softly bit her neck. Mia heard something clinking behind her. When she looked over her shoulder, she saw that Ava had brought along a pair of fluffy white handcuffs. Ava turned her head back to face the fridge and kissed her neck, before bringing her mouth to Mia's ear. "I've got a little present for you."

46

LONDON, UK

Mia studied herself in the bathroom mirror as she pulled down the collar of her shirt. There was still a love bite on the base of her neck, just above her right collarbone, a reminder of her passionate night with Ava. She shivered when she thought back to their love making, arousal stirring inside her as the memories flooded back. Ava was a very good at making her do things she'd never tried before. Not only had Mia surrendered willingly, she'd begged Ava to bite her and to suck her neck so hard that she had left small purple bruises. She smiled at her reflection, feeling a little different today. Good different. She'd discovered a side to her sexuality she didn't know she had. It had all felt so natural with Ava, as their relationship developed. She wanted her, and more than anything, she trusted her. Ava still wouldn't let Mia go very far with her, but Mia knew she would trust her eventually. It was only a matter of time, she told herself. She'd introduced her to her parents after all, and that was a pretty intimate thing to do. Ava had left early yesterday morning and since then, Mia had mostly been lying in bed, daydreaming.

Having never been the type to lounge in bed while awake, today she had spent hours on end doing just that, replaying every second of her night with Ava again and again. She had eventually gotten up, showered and dressed, and was now starting to feel hungry. She was just about to head out to the supermarket to stock her empty fridge up before they closed, when her doorbell rang.

"Hey, Mia."

Mia was taken aback when she saw Ami at her front door. "Ami!" She took her younger sister into her arms and closed her eyes while she held her. "What are you doing here? You're lucky to find me home, I'm not here very often. I thought we weren't meeting until next Saturday? Shouldn't you be in bed by now? I thought you always got up at..." She stopped mid-sentence when she sensed something was wrong.

"I was hoping you'd be home." Ami sniffed. "I was upset and the only place I could think of to go was here."

Mia could tell she'd been both crying and drinking. Her eyes were red-rimmed, and her breath smelled of alcohol. It was a shock, seeing her baby sister like this, and it felt like she was staring at herself at that age. But she knew better than to comment on the fact that Ami was drunk.

"Oh my God, come in, Ami. Can I get you anything? There's not much food in the house I'm afraid, but I have some cheese and crackers if you're hungry." Her voice was unsteady, as a deep feeling of unease was creeping up on her.

Ami sighed. "Do you have wine? Vodka? A beer? I need another drink."

"I'm sorry, I don't have any alcohol in the house." Mia gave her an apologetic smile. "But we can go to a pub if you like? There's one around the corner." She couldn't remember the last time she'd set foot into a pub, but it was better than getting Ami a bottle from the off-licence and having her drink it right in front of her, in her own flat.

"No, it's fine. I just remembered I've got some right here." Ami staggered into the living room, produced a bottle of vodka from her backpack and took a long slug before she let herself fall on the couch. "I've had a really, really, really shitty day."

Mia looked at the almost full bottle of vodka on her table and forced herself to focus on making herself a cup of tea, as she switched on the kettle with a trembling hand. Her little sister was drunk, just like she herself used to be. And if that wasn't bad enough, she wanted to talk. Ami never wanted to talk. *This is the moment I've been dreading half my life and it's happening, right now.*

"Everyone is lying to me, Mia," Amy said out of nowhere, slurring her words a little. "Mum, Dad, Grandma..." She looked at Mia, who put her mug on the table and sat down next to her. "I need to know the truth."

Mia chewed her cheek, unsure of what to say.

"My left arm," Ami continued when Mia didn't speak. "It's been years since I've had that strange pain, but it's been playing up again. I thought I'd hurt myself during the training, so I went to a physiotherapist. It was a bit better after that, but it started hurting again last week and I just couldn't swim fast enough." She started sobbing again, burying her face in her hands. Mia sat down next to her and put an arm around her. She felt sick, nauseated. "I didn't make it through selection, Mia."

"I'm so sorry to hear that." Mia squeezed Ami's shoulder. "I know it won't make you feel any better right now, but you could try again next year."

"That's not everything." Ami fell silent for a moment. "I

had my arm x-rayed at the hospital this morning, just to be sure that there was nothing strange there, and apparently, I have an old injury, Mia. It must have happened when I was young and it's healed really well over the years, but it's clear that something very serious happened to me that no one's ever told me about." She sniffed. "And now it's ruining my future."

Mia felt her own tears stream down her face. She would lose Ami. After tonight, she would lose her forever. She'd always kept her distance because she knew this day would come, and she'd hoped that somehow it would be easier if they weren't that close. But it wasn't easier. Ami was her own flesh and blood and she loved her more than anything.

"I did it," she whispered. "I did that to you. I fucked up your arm and your head and your ribs and I put you in a coma for three days. It's all my fault."

Ami lifted her head and looked up at her slowly, her eyes wide. "You?"

"Yes." Mia started shaking uncontrollably, sobbing as she tried to continue. "I was twenty when I hit you with my car. I tore onto Mum and Dad's driveway, speeding like an idiot. You were only five then." She tried to catch her breath, gasping for air. "I was drunk and high on opiates. I'm so, so sorry, Ami. You couldn't remember anything when you woke up in the hospital. Mum and Dad told me it was better if you didn't know. They were afraid we'd grow apart." She waited for Ami to speak, but there was only silence. "That's why I don't drink. I've been fighting my addiction ever since." She shrugged. "Well, I've tried to. I'm dealing with it every single day but mostly, I'm sober. I go to AA, it helps a little."

Ami continued to stare at her through hazy, bloodshot eyes. She swiped a lock of dark hair away from her forehead.

"How could you not tell me? And how could you think I'd never find out? I'm studying physiotherapy for God's sake!"

"I'm so sorry," Mia pleaded again. "I was scared of losing you. But now I just regret not spending more time with you. I love you, Ami. You're my little sister. Please don't hate me." Mia reached out for Ami's hand, but Ami moved away from her. Her eyes were cold and sharp now, as if the truth had suddenly sobered her up.

"Please don't go, Ami," Mia begged again. "Can we please talk about this?"

Ami turned and looked away, avoiding Mia's pleading eyes. Then she stood up, picked up her bag and walked out of the door without saying a word.

MIA STAYED THERE and watched her leave. She knew that there was nothing she could do or say to make her come back, to make it better. What good was an apology, now that Ami's dream was ruined? *I'm sorry I fucked up your life? I'm sorry I lied to you for thirteen years? I'm sorry I kept my distance because I couldn't look at you?*

The open half-full bottle of vodka was still on the table, only inches away from her trembling hand. *It's not going to solve anything.* She reached out for it, picked it up and closed her eyes as she inhaled the sterile scent of misery.

47

LONDON, UK

"Ava?"

"Mia?" Ava frowned as she heard Mia's unsteady voice over the phone. "I've just landed." She hesitated. "Are you okay?"

"No." Mia sniffed. "No, I'm not okay." She paused. "Ami... she found out about the accident. Her arm... it's playing up again and she didn't make the team..." She cried quietly. "I ruined her life, Ava. And now she knows that, and she hates me."

"Mia?" Ava walked out of the airport terminal, hailing a cab. "Are you drunk? Please tell me you haven't been drinking." She could hear Mia swallow.

"There's nothing left. The vodka that Ami left behind... it's all gone. I drank it and there's nothing left."

"That's okay. You don't need any more, I'm on my way, Mia." Ava slipped into a cab and gave the driver Mia's address before she turned her attention back to Mia. "I'm coming and I'm going to make you a coffee and we're going to talk about this, alright?" She sighed when Mia didn't answer. "You're not in this alone, Mia. You've got me."

"No, Ava. Stay away from me. I'm poison. I'll ruin you, just like I ruined my sister and myself." There was a silence. "I need another drink."

"Please don't drink anymore," Ava pleaded. She closed her eyes and clenched her phone in her hand. "Go and sit on the balcony and clear your head. Drink water and coffee, try to sober up." She could hear Mia breathing heavily on the other end of the line.

"That's easy for you to say. You're the strong one, Ava. You're not weak, like me."

"You're not weak, Mia. Do you hear me?" Ava raised her voice when Mia didn't answer. "You've been almost ten months sober now for God's sake. And longer before that. You're strong!"

"Like that even matters. And what's ten months anyway? It's not like it's an achievement, it hardly counts," Mia said through sobs. "Besides, it's not going to help my sister. Maybe this is my punishment. Maybe I'm meant to be an alcoholic, maybe this is my way of paying for what I did to Ami. I sure as hell deserve it."

"That's bullshit, and you know it. Your sister is going to be okay. She may not become an Olympic swimmer, but she can still make a life for herself in any other career. She's smart and still very young. She'll find other passions. And even if she doesn't..." Ava swallowed hard. "She loves you and she needs you. She might be angry right now, but she'll come around. And I need you too, Mia. I need you to be sober, so we can be there for each other."

"You need me?" Mia fell silent.

"Yes, I need you. I think you're amazing and funny and attractive and strong. This, what you're doing right now, it's nothing. It's not the end of the world. You can start over again, tomorrow. You don't need alcohol to fuel your sadness. Just try to calm down, okay?" Ava was getting really worried now. "Stay where you are and I'll be there in half an hour." She tried to keep her head clear as the cab driver manoeuvred them through the busy traffic. A relapse was a serious thing. *I just hope she can get past this.*

THERE WAS no answer when Ava rang the doorbell. She rang again, then tried the door handle. The door wasn't locked, so she let herself in. Mia was fast asleep, curled up on the couch. Her cheeks were red from crying. She stirred a little when Ava ran a hand through her hair, but she didn't wake up. Ava felt a lump in her throat at the sight of Mia. She looked so vulnerable, and so sad. The empty bottle of vodka was next to her on the floor, on its side. Ava winced when she picked it up. She threw it in the bin, took the bag out and tied it so Mia wouldn't have to look at it in the morning. Then she washed her hands thoroughly, walked back to the couch and put an arm around Mia's waist in an attempt to lift her.

"What are you doing?" Mia mumbled, stirring awake.

"Just trying to get you on your feet, okay? I'm taking you to bed." Ava held her up while Mia staggered towards the bedroom.

"Go away. I don't want you to see me like this." Mia turned away from her.

"I'm not going anywhere, Mia." Ava opened the door to Mia's bedroom and supported her as they made their way to the bed. Mia fell down and went back to sleep, turning her back to Ava. Ava stood next to the bed, looking down at her. Even now, Mia was beautiful. Even now, at her lowest. She took off Mia's shoes and her cardigan and got into bed next to her. It would be better if she were here tomorrow. Mia would need all the support she could get when she realised she'd been drinking, and that she'd undone ten months of hard work. And if anyone understood how that felt, it was Ava. *Oh Mia, what have you done?* She wrapped an arm around Mia and held her, listening to her heavy breathing until she fell asleep.

AVA JERKED HALF-AWAKE at four in the morning and was hit with the smell of alcohol. She sat straight up, balancing on the verge of panic. *Oh God, have I been drinking?* Then she saw Mia, sleeping next to her, and she sighed in relief at the realisation that it wasn't her. She'd been so preoccupied with Mia's wellbeing that she hadn't noticed it before, but now, lying next to her in a dark, silent room, there was no escaping the alcoholic fumes that penetrated her nostrils. She lifted her chin and sniffed, like a rat drawn to poison. Her stomach turned, and suddenly she felt sick and disgusted. *I have to get out of here.* Ava stood up and grabbed her phone to order an Uber. She hesitated for a moment, looking down at Mia. She knew it would be better if she was here tomorrow. But she had too many thoughts running through her mind. Bad thoughts. And above all, it hurt her seeing Mia like this. She had no idea how much she cared for Mia until now, and it was scary how difficult it was being around her, in this state. Ava turned to take a final look at Mia before closing the door behind her, walking into the first light of dawn.

48

LONDON, UK

The room was dark, but the thin strip of light fighting its way through a gap in the curtains indicated that the sun was already high. *What time is it?* Mia picked up her phone on the nightstand and noted it was midday. *Am I late for work?* She thought long and hard, but her brain didn't seem to want to function, so she checked her calendar and sighed in relief. She was off today. Mia blinked a couple of times, trying to remember what had happened, and where the feeling of dread deep in her stomach was coming from. Then it clicked, and her world came crashing down like a ton of bricks. She turned on her stomach and buried her face in her pillow. *No. Please no.* She recognized the symptoms she'd hoped never to feel again. A headache, a sore neck from sleeping in the same position for hours, a dry mouth, the smell of vodka in the room... *Vodka. Oh God, Ami. She knows.* The memories came back now, faster than she could handle. She remembered Ami's shock and disbelief, and she remembered her walking out without a word. She also vaguely remembered Ava carrying her to bed. *Is she still here?*

"Ava?" she called. There was no answer. Mia sat up and raised her voice. "Ava, are you there?" Silence. She felt her heart pounding in her chest. *She's gone. Why?* A knot tightened in her stomach. She felt worse than she ever had after a relapse. Ava had come and left. Maybe she couldn't handle the fact that she'd been drinking, not while she had her own sobriety to deal with. Mia wasn't sure what made her feel worse: her relapse, or the fact that Ava had seen her drunk. She felt ashamed and dirty as she tried to sit up, slowly. A feeling of nausea made its way up from her stomach. She put a hand in front of her mouth, gagging as she ran to the toilet, throwing herself over the edge of the seat.

MIA FORCED herself to look in the mirror as she turned on the shower. Her eyes were bloodshot and puffy, and there were red streaks on her cheeks, from crying. Her skin was pale, and the healthy blush was gone from her face.

"You did this to yourself," she said. "You did this." Anger arose in her as she faced herself. Without thinking, she slammed her fist against the mirror, cracking it. A shard fell in the basin but most of it stayed in place, deforming her reflection. There was blood trickling down her wrist, but she didn't care. She picked up the marble toothbrush holder and attacked the mirror again, with even more force this time. Shards flew around her and fell on the floor. She slammed it over and over again until there was nothing left but the backing, dangling off a single screw.

Mia felt helpless as she undressed and got in the steaming shower, with barely enough energy to stand up. *Here we go again.* She lifted a finger and wrote on the glass divider:

'Day 1.'

Then she sunk down on the floor and pulled her knees up, resting her forehead on them as she cried. The blood from her hand mixed with her tears and ran down the drain in a light pink stream of gloominess. *Blood, sweat and tears. All for nothing.*

49

LONDON, UK

shouldn't have left. Ava hadn't been able to sleep after she got back to her flat. She'd been awake for hours, trying to justify her behaviour. But the truth was, there was no way of justifying running off in Mia's hour of need. What if she'd woken up and started drinking again? Ava knew all too well that there wouldn't be anyone there to stop her. Mia was a loner, like her. And although her problem was something only Mia could deal with, she still should have been there for her. *Why did I run?* She could, and did, come up with multiple excuses, all relating to her own problems. But she knew those were only excuses. There was also something else, something that had already made her leave that very first night, outside Mia's hotel room in New York. She knew even then, that Mia was different to other women, that she might very well be the one. And that was frightening, because Ava hadn't felt this close to anyone since she'd stopped drinking. *No. That's not true. I've never felt this close to anyone.* The instant connection they'd had on the day they met was more powerful than she'd ever felt before. And yes, it was risky, spending her time with someone who fought the same demons she did, especially when Mia was more likely to relapse. But it was also a blessing, knowing that Mia knew exactly how she felt. They got each other on all levels. After hours and hours of tossing and turning, Ava got up, put on her running tights and headed outside. She wasn't getting anywhere by staying in bed and feeling bad about herself. As she ran, she noticed she was going a different route today. She was heading towards Mia's flat.

"HEY." Ava bent over, steadying her hands on her knees as she looked up at Mia, standing in the doorway. She felt exhausted but was exhilarated to see that Mia was sober. She looked tired and worn-out though, with dark circles under her eyes. She was wearing a black silk kimono and her hair was still wet from a recent shower.

"Hey," Mia replied with little enthusiasm. She opened the door and led the way into the kitchen. "Coffee?" she asked.

"Water please," Ava said, still trying to catch her breath.

Mia poured her a pint of water and put it on the breakfast bar between them.

"How are you feeling?" Ava asked. She felt silly for asking a question to which she knew the answer but had no idea how else to start the conversation.

"Crap," Mia mumbled, pouring milk into her coffee.

Ava noticed a bandage on her right hand. Blood had seeped through the dressing above her knuckles. "What's that?" she asked, reaching out to examine Mia's hand. "Did you hurt yourself?"

Mia pulled away. "It's nothing. I was angry."

Ava nodded. "I know." She hesitated. "I'm sorry I left last night. I…"

"You don't need to apologise," Mia interrupted her. "I understand, believe me. I'm no good for you, Ava. You've done so well, staying sober for almost seven years. Being around me right now isn't going to work for either of us because quite frankly, I'm a mess. Look at me." She raised both hands, pointing down at herself. "I'll be a bad influence on you and you know it." Her voice broke as she started to cry. "I can't be with you. It's not fair on you, Ava."

Ava reached over the bar and took Mia's face in her hands. "A bad influence? Do you even realise what you're saying? You're my light, Mia. You're the one who completes me." Ava was shaking, balancing on the edge of panic. She couldn't lose Mia. She was the best thing that had happened to her in a long time. "I'm sorry I left you last night. I should have stayed with you, made sure you were okay, and I'll never forgive myself for leaving. And yes, I'm not going to lie, I'm scared of what being with you might do to me after your relapse. I don't know what I'll be like with you because you make me feel so many things again. And feeling things means there's a chance I might get hurt, and that's something I won't be able to control." She shook her head. "But you know what? I don't care anymore. It's about time I let myself feel things, that I let you in. As long as I have you for as long as you'll have me, I'll cope, because I need you."

Mia shook her head. "I don't blame you for leaving, Ava. It's not that." She closed her eyes and took a deep breath. "I can't do this. Can't you see? I'm clearly not relationship material at this point. I'm the worst thing that could possibly happen to you right now. You're doing so well, I don't want to ruin it for you."

"Mia, don't say that." Ava walked around the bar and attempted to take her hands, but Mia took a step back.

"We shouldn't have been dating in the first place." Mia winced as she took a sip of her coffee. "Not in the first year of sobriety, they say. There's a reason for that. You're okay but I'm not. I think we've established that." She put her mug down, walked over to the front door and opened it, waiting for Ava to leave.

"Don't do this, Mia." Ava could see the pain in Mia's eyes, and she wanted to take her in her arms, hold her. But Mia looked guarded, and her body language told her not to. "I can help you," Ava tried again. "You don't see it now, because you're upset and disappointed in yourself. But I believe in you. And yes, I know it's advisable not to date in the first year, but you can't plan who you meet, and you can't plan life. It's unpredictable. And we're so lucky to have met. Don't throw that away, please. If you hadn't had the fight with your sister, you would have been fine. You can get over this. We can, together."

Mia was silent as she opened the door further, staring down at her feet. "Please leave."

Ava knew there was no point trying. Mia had made up her mind. She walked out with a lump in her throat, unable to look back as the door closed behind her.

50

TUNIS, TUNISIA

The cold water made Ava gasp when she dove into the pool of her hotel in Tunisia and raced to the other end in front crawl. *One.* She counted internally as she tapped the edge and turned under water. Her shoulders were still aching from her swim that morning, but exercise was the only thing she could think of to keep her mind off Mia. Not that it worked. *Two.* The empty feeling inside reminded her of what was missing in her life, and it hurt like no pain she'd ever experienced. She'd been counting the days without Mia. Ten days now. Ten very long and anxious days, and ten very long and sleepless nights. It wasn't just her own misery that kept her up at night. She was worried about Mia, mostly. She hoped Mia was managing to stay sober, but she knew the first weeks after a relapse were the hardest, and Mia wasn't in a good place. *Three.* The thought of not having her in her life anymore felt unbearable. Not being able to send her a message, or to call her. She'd tried, of course, but Mia had ignored her every time she'd reached out. There was no chance she would see her at work anytime soon either. Their schedules hadn't crossed since they'd last seen each other, and Mia's two-week holiday was starting today. She could either use that time to get herself back in a better place, or she could drink her misery away at home, without anyone knowing, and Ava knew the latter was not out of the question. *Four.* She missed Mia's smile and she missed the feeling of Mia's hand in hers. She missed talking to her, kissing her, falling asleep with her and waking up with her. She missed her all the time, but most of all, she wanted Mia to be happy. If that meant she'd have to step back and let her be, then maybe that was for the best. *Five.* Ava swam faster now, ignoring the pain in her muscles. *No. I'm not going to let her go.* Anger and frustration arose in her, making her speed up even more. *I can't let her go.* She lost count after a while and only stopped when she realised she was struggling to breathe. She pulled herself up by the stairs and tore off her goggles, panting heavily as she held on to the big, square pot of a palm tree next to the pool.

"Are you okay?" a woman who'd just entered the pool area asked.

"I'm fine," Ava said through short breaths. "Thank you." She kept her eyes fixed on her feet as tears started running down her face. They mixed with the chlorinated water, dripping from her hair and stinging her eyes. She didn't care. She was in pain, and it felt good to finally cry and let go of control. Her safe place was gone. The one person who really understood her, the one person she trusted, was gone from her life and there was nothing she could do about it. Despair spread through her body like a shot of cheap whisky when it finally hit her that this might be the end. She straightened her back and returned to her deckchair where she'd left her towel and her phone, keeping her eyes away from the pool bar. She'd spotted the bottles on the top shelf earlier, seducing her to drown her sorrows, promising to make her feel better, even if just for a little while. *It's not the solution. You're stronger than that. Control, Ava.* Her head turned back to the bar for a split second, where the bottles of white and brown liquor were glistening in the evening sun. A party of five were drinking cocktails in their swimwear. They looked happy. *Why can't I be like them?* But Ava knew she never could. One drink would not turn into two or three, but into days and nights of one drink after another, and after that, she'd fall into a dark, dirty well, so deep that it seemed almost impossible to climb out of it. And that was where Mia was right now, in the bottom of the well. Ava just hoped she could see a glimmer of light through the cracks in the cover. *Control, Ava.* Ava took a deep breath and dropped down on her pool lounger, not feeling any less helpless than before her swim. Her mind was full of contradicting thoughts. Mia needed time, and she needed to do this on her own, Ava knew that. But she missed her, and she wanted to be by her side, supporting her through her dark journey. Even if they were just friends, for now. *I'm not letting her go.*

51

LONDON, UK

Only twelve pm and already on her fourth coffee, Mia closed her notebook and put away her *Arabic for beginners* course, fed up with studying when she wasn't taking in a single thing. Distraction had been her plan of action, a sour attempt to numb the gloom she felt each time she took a minute to herself. So far, she'd cried a lot, devastated by another failed attempt to never drink again. She'd managed to stay sober after that night with Ami, and although she was miserable, she felt a little stronger every morning. She'd gone back to work, and her flight to Egypt last week had been a blessing. But now two long weeks of holiday stretched in front of her like a long, eerie tunnel she'd rather avoid. She was only one day in and had already started to panic. *What the hell am I going to do?* Mia didn't have many friends – she'd made sure of that, declining every single social invitation that had crossed her path for the majority of her adult life – and spending time with her family wasn't an option either. She called Ami every day, but Ami never picked up or returned her calls.

Mia wasn't surprised. She'd seen the hurt in Ami's eyes, and she didn't expect to ever hear from her again.

And then there was Ava... Letting go of her had been heartbreaking, but it had also been the right decision. Although she missed her like crazy, Mia didn't want Ava to see her like this. It wasn't fair on her. Ava needed to surround herself with positive people, not some weak and depressed mess like herself. But being without her had been much harder than Mia had anticipated. She was constantly on her mind, and it distracted her from staying focussed on her goal: staying sober and being happy. It was easier said than done. Mourning the loss of a sister who wasn't even dead, and terrified of speaking to her parents, she was far from happy. Yesterday, she'd woken up and gone back to sleep, unable to think of a single reason to get out of bed. But the thing was, she'd been happy. Ava had made her truly happy for the first time in years. Talking to her had felt like a confession, relieving her from her sins, just a little. And that little spark of hope was enough to make Mia feel a big change was about to happen in her life. *For as long as it lasted.* She'd fucked it up again. She'd fucked it all up years ago, when she almost killed her sister, and now she'd fucked up her sobriety for the sixth time and sent away the one person who'd made her happy. *Stop it, Mia.* Mia needed somewhere to go. Somewhere without alcohol and as far away as possible from Ava and her own flat, where she'd let herself down only a week ago. Mia grabbed her iPad and stepped out on her balcony, determined to find a last-minute holiday.

"Hey Mia." Tuesday leaned over the balustrade as soon as she sat down.

"Hey there, Tuesday." Mia managed a smile, although her greeting didn't sound genuine. Company was the last thing she wanted. In fact, she felt like screaming at her neighbour, telling her to fuck off and leave her alone because right now, any outlet for her anger would be a relief. If Tuesday had picked up on her mood, she didn't let it show.

"I've been meaning to thank you for dinner the other night. I really enjoyed it, and I was wondering if you'd like to come over here later so I can return the favour. I'm cooking a tagine." She laughed. "No, let me rephrase that. I'm attempting to cook a tagine."

"That's really nice of you but I don't think tonight is a good night. I'm not feeling great at the moment," Mia said, looking up from her iPad briefly.

"Care to share?" Tuesday asked. "Sometimes it helps to talk, even when you don't feel like it." She leaned in further and lowered her voice. "The walls are thin in these old flats, and when the balcony doors are open the sound-proofing is non-existent. I'm sure you're aware of that. Even if you try, you can't escape from what's going on next door. Don't pretend you haven't heard me when I've had Wally over."

"Wally? Wally from the deli? Is he your regular Saturday night visitor?" Mia pointed down to the floor below them. Despite her mood, she couldn't help but giggle.

"He is." Tuesday grinned. "Anyway, what I was trying to say is that I know you're going through a hard time." She paused. "And I'm here for you if you need me. That's what neighbours are for, right?"

"What do you mean?" Mia asked, suddenly guarded.

"I'm a recovering alcoholic too, you know." Tuesday's face was serious now.

Mia frowned, failing to hide her surprise. "You?"

"Twenty years sober." Tuesday held up a hand. "And

from what I gather, you could do with some support right now."

Mia wanted to say something, but she had no idea what. Her eyes shifted from Tuesday to her balcony door and back, trying to decide whether to escape or not. *My very own neighbour?*

"There are more of us than you might think," Tuesday said casually, as if she was talking about the weather. "So, are you coming over or what?"

"I…" Mia swallowed hard, her eyes fixed on Tuesday. "I don't know… Okay then." She stood up, still wondering how her neighbour, who she'd only had dinner with once, had managed to get her out of her chair in her current state. She shook her head as she put her iPad on the table, put a chair next to the railing and climbed over it.

"So, how are you doing today?" Tuesday asked, once they'd started eating an hour later. Tuesday's tagine was surprisingly good, and Mia hadn't realised how hungry she was until she took the first bite. She hadn't eaten a proper meal in days.

"Not great." Mia took another bite, trying not to stare into Tuesday's living room. It was like nothing she'd ever seen. Purple velvet sofas stood against a blue wall with some kind of Greek-looking mural painted on it. There were fluffy pillows in all the colours of the rainbows on the couch and on the floor, and pink fairy lights were attached across the length of the living room ceiling. But for some reason she couldn't explain, she felt comfortable here, and she decided to be honest. "I feel like I've spent months trying to put a ten-thousand-piece puzzle together and someone's just messed it up right in front of me."

"And that someone was you." Tuesday looked at Mia intently.

"Yes, that someone was me. And now I have to start from zero again."

"Yes, you do." Tuesday refilled their water from a pink, rhinestone covered jug. Any other day, Mia would have laughed at an attempt to turn such a mundane object into something precious, but today, she understood. Tuesday was doing everything in her power to elevate the simple act of drinking water into something important, and the rhinestones suited her. "But it's not the end, you know," Tuesday continued. "It's a new beginning, and new beginnings are always hard. I know it's difficult, but try not to think about your failures. Think about how well you did before this happened and how you could do it again, but better this time. Maybe make it last this time, because that's your goal. That's what we all strive for."

Mia leaned back and let her shoulders hang. "I know. But it's hard right now."

"It is, sweetie. I know it is. Do you have a sponsor?"

"No. I've never had one."

"Why not?" Tuesday looked shocked.

"I don't know." Mia reflected. "I suppose I never got close to people in AA. And I was just fine, managing on my own." She hesitated. "Or I thought I was..." She didn't bother to finish her sentence. It wasn't like Tuesday hadn't heard it all before.

"Until what?" Tuesday gave her a cynical look. "Until you got yourself into a difficult situation? Until you felt shit about yourself? That's what sponsors are for, you know." Her expression softened, and she sighed, placing a hand on Mia's. "Call them sponsors, call them support, call them anything you like, but you need at least one person in your life who understands, and who you can call on anytime, day or night, when shit hits the fan." She tightened her grip. "I live right next door. I've seen a lot and I've been through a lot. I can relate, so let me help you."

Mia raised her head, her eyes red-rimmed and tired. "Thank you." She tried to swallow away her tears. "I think I might need your help, Tuesday."

"I know, sweetie."

LONDON, UK

The audience at the modest South London theatre gave Zaid Alfarsi a standing ovation, which he graciously accepted, thanking them over and over again. Ava was sitting in the front row, looking up at her little brother whom the people present here tonight clearly adored. She had to admit that she was incredibly proud of him, and that the whole positive thinking idea, which she had always looked down on as a cliché, was kind of inspiring. She felt good despite her nerves about the meeting they were about to have. Ava had called him earlier that day and admitted that she needed advice. By now, she had no idea what to do about her situation with Mia. She had left her alone because Mia had asked her to, but something deep inside her told her that Mia needed her more than anything right now, and she was pretty sure that she had no one else to turn to. Not even Lynn knew about her issues.

"There she is," Zaid said when Ava met him back stage a little later.

"Here I am." Ava hugged him and looked him up and down. "Sharp suit." She ruffled a hand through his hair, before he had a chance to duck away. "But you need to take it easy on the hair gel next time. Your head is as shiny as a new penny under that light." Ava smiled at him. "Seriously though. You were great up there, and I can't believe I've never been to one of your sessions before. I'm so proud of you, Zaid."

"You are?"

Ava nodded. "You've very, very good with people and by the looks of it, all of them have left with a smile on their face. You seem to have done wonders for that woman with social phobia that you called onto the stage first. I just saw her in the toilets, and she looked transformed. She was chatting away with another woman waiting in there, and she didn't seem uncomfortable at all."

"Feeling inspired and motivated can do a lot for a person," Zaid said. "The energy she got from tonight might not stick with her forever, but for now, she'll crawl out of her shell little by little and realise how good it feels to be a part of the world. Because that's all she wants." He put an arm around Ava's shoulder and led them through the back door, into the night. "And if I can help that woman make one friend, or even just join a book club or something, then my work is done. The rest is up to her." He pointed at Ava's suit jacket. "I see you decided to wear a suit for the occasion too? Very fancy."

Ava took off her jacket and hung it over her arm, leaving her in a pair of black trousers and a white, sleeveless blouse. It was too warm for a blazer, really. "Well, it's a theatre. I couldn't exactly rock up in jeans and a t-shirt now, could I?"

They crossed Trafalgar Square which was, even at this time of night, still heaving with tourists. They were taking pictures, sitting on one of the four lions guarding Nelson's Column, or posing in front of the statues and the historical buildings. Others were hanging out on and around the stone steps, taking a rest from their long walks or bathing their sore feet in the fountain when the police officers were out of sight.

"Embankment?" Zaid asked, as they crossed the road, heading towards the riverside.

"How about the Vietnamese place on Northumberland Road instead?" Ava suggested. "That one will still be open for food." She had, in fact, never been for a drink or a meal with her brother before. They always met up at their parents' house, and outside that they both had their own lives. Zaid had no idea that Ava avoided pubs like the plague.

"Sure. I don't know which one you mean, but I'm starving. Vietnamese sounds good." He looked at Ava sideways. "Care to tell me what's bothering you? Is it Mum and Dad?" He cocked his head and frowned. "Do you need money?"

Ava couldn't help but laugh. She'd never seen him this serious. Clearly, he was enjoying the fact that she'd asked him to help her. "No, it's not about Mum and Dad, and I don't need money either. And even if I did, I wouldn't ask my baby brother for it." She opened the door to the Vietnamese restaurant and sat down at a small table by the window. "It's about me," she continued. "I'm in a bit of a difficult situation and I'm not sure what to do. And I hate to admit it, but I thought you might be able to help me, with you being good with people and all..." She picked up the menu, avoiding his surprised stare.

"Shoot," Zaid said.

"I need to know that I can trust you first." Ava looked up now, making sure Zaid knew that she meant it.

"Of course you can trust me, I'm your brother. Or we could treat this as a consultation, so that client confidentiality applies, if that makes you feel any better?" He sighed. "Look, I know I'm always messing with you, but that doesn't mean I can't be serious when I have to. Besides, I'm good at helping people. It's what I do."

"Okay." Ava nodded slowly. "Shall we get some of those rice flower pancakes?" She asked, buying herself more time. Ste was starting to get cold feet. "And some shrimp spring rolls, and maybe a portion of chicken sate?" She was far from hungry, but at least it would give her some distraction if she needed it. "And a sparkling water for me." She ticked the boxes on the menu with a pencil she found in the cutlery pot. "What do you want to drink?"

"I'll have an Asahi beer."

Ava ticked that one too, before waving the slip at the waitress. She took a deep breath, feeling sick with nerves.

"I have a problem," she started carefully. "But that's not really the issue here. I mean, I've got everything under control."

"You're not sick, are you?" Zaid looked worried now.

"No." Ava paused. There was no easy way to tell her brother, so she decided to just come out with it. "I'm a recovering alcoholic, Zaid. I've been sober for fourteen years now, with three relapses in between. The last time I had a drink was over six years ago, so I'm doing alright." There. She'd said it.

"You?" Zaid leaned in. He looked shocked to his core. "How could I not have seen that? I thought you just didn't care for alcohol, like Mum. Jesus, Ava. How long has this been going on?"

"Since I was sixteen." Ava leaned back and met his gaze. The worst part was over, and somehow, she felt relief, instead of panic.

Zaid sat back, processing the information. "You were an alcoholic at the age of sixteen?"

"Maybe not an alcoholic," Ava said. "But that's when I started using alcohol as a coping mechanism. I was going through a hard time with Mum and Dad. They treated me differently after I told them I was gay." She held up a hand. "And I'm by no means blaming them for my drinking, I need you to know that. Things are good between us now, and I'd like to keep it that way. But yeah, that's when it started. I was upset, and I couldn't sleep at night, so I always had a small bottle of whisky under my pillow. I smoked a lot of weed too. It helped me get rid of my anxiety a little."

"Ava..." Zaid took her hand. "I knew you were hanging with the wrong crowd and all. That's why Mum sent you to Jordan, right? To live with Auntie Hala."

"Yeah. And that was a good thing, all in all. I got my shit together there. Thought about my future, decided I wanted to become a pilot." Ava shrugged. "But when I came back and started my training, I couldn't stop using alcohol as a crutch, each time I had an exam, or even just at social events. I've learned to deal with my anxiety over the years, but it was hard for me back then to spend time with new people sober. I'd always been shy, and alcohol helped me come out of my shell more, so I slowly started drinking again. I was never, ever drunk on flights, but during ground training I would always have a bottle of vodka somewhere in my bag, or in my pocket. People never noticed as I would never drink quite enough until I got home at night." Her eyes met Zaid's. Although he tried to hide it, she could tell he was shocked.

"I need you to know, Zaid, that I've never had a drink before a flight, and I never will. Even back then. It was just about the only boundary I didn't overstep. I stopped drinking on the day I started my first job as a second officer. I was twenty-three then." She paused. "I had my first relapse when I was twenty-six. Some girl broke up with me. I wasn't even that upset, I think I just saw it as an excuse to allow myself to drink my so-called sorrows away. I had to take a week off work after that, called in sick and pulled myself together. It was hard, that first time. I thought of giving up my job. Didn't think I'd ever be able to maintain a career as a pilot. But the AA meetings helped. They made me believe in myself again."

"What happened after that?" Zaid's voice was calm and kind, not in the least accusing.

"I had another relapse when I was twenty-nine. Nothing really happened that time to trigger it. Willpower can work in mysterious ways. Sometimes it's there and sometimes..." She shrugged. "Anyway, I walked past a pub with one of my colleagues after a hectic week at work and I just really felt like a cold pint, you know? I looked at the people standing around the tables outside, and I thought: 'Surely I'd be able to only have one by now? Or even two, just like everyone else on a Friday night.' My colleague asked me if I wanted to go in. I think I fancied her a little, so I didn't want to waste the opportunity to spend time with her. I should have said no, but I didn't. She left after two drinks, when I was already pretty tipsy. It doesn't take much when you never drink. I don't know what time I came home that night, but I carried on the next day, thinking that I might as well now that I'd already messed up." She paused. "It didn't feel good, but I still did it. That's the part of it I'll never understand."

"Yeah. It's hard to know why we do what we do sometimes." Zaid frowned. "Was that the reason you moved to New York?"

Ava nodded. It felt good to share her story with her

brother. "I applied for a transfer the following week, after I'd sobered up. Starting with a clean slate seemed like the easiest way to move forward. And it was, in a way. I told everyone I didn't drink for religious reasons, and people respected that. No questions were ever asked, and no drinks were ever offered to me. And then I messed up again, and messed up big, one night. I kissed my best friend's girlfriend right in front of him"

"And then you moved back to London," Zaid said after doing the math. "Are you okay now? Do you still have urges? Is that why you wanted to talk?" He stared at the beer the waitress had just brought him. "Fuck." He looked up at the young Vietnamese woman. "I'm sorry. I mean, can I please change my order? I'll pay for it, of course."

The waitress gave him a confused stare. "You want one more?"

"No!" Zaid waved his hands, pointing at the bottle and gesturing for her to take it away.

"It's okay." Ava chuckled. "I'm fine. Your drink doesn't bother me."

"Doesn't matter. I wouldn't be a good brother if I drank this in front of you." He took the bottle and put it back on the service bar before helping himself to a can of Coke from the fridge behind the counter. He held it up for the waitress to see.

"I'll pay for both," he said, reassuring her. "Sorry about that." His expression turned serious again as he sat back down. "So, you said earlier that you attend AA meetings. Are you seeing a psychologist too?"

"Yes. Not a psychologist. I've been going to the meetings for around fourteen years and I try to go once a week, if there are any in the country I'm in. I had a sponsor a while back, but we hadn't spoken to each other for a long time. I recently caught up with her when I was in New York. We're both doing well now, so I think we'll just stick to the friendship with a silent understanding that we can always call each other if things get difficult."

Zaid gave her a small smile. "Good. That's good."

"Zaid," Ava continued, "What I actually wanted to talk to you about is Mia." She swallowed hard. "Do you promise you'll keep this to yourself? Doctor-patient confidentiality?"

"Of course."

"Okay, well, Mia is in the program too..."

ZAID WAS silent after Ava had finished talking. He nodded, looking down at his hands that were resting calmly on the table. "Listen," he finally said, lifting a hand to scratch his head. "What we discussed just now goes no further, obviously. But I don't want to give you advice from a professional point of view. I want to give you advice as your brother because I can tell that you really care about Mia, and I want you to have your shot at happiness too, even, as you mentioned, if you're just friends for now. I've seen how happy she makes you." He smiled. "It's sweet. Besides, you seem like you've got your own house pretty much in order, so I'm not going to tell you that it's a bad idea to date an unstable recovering alcoholic if you're struggling with recovery yourself. Because that's what any psychologist would tell you."

Ava nodded.

"Good. That's good. Because Mia needs help and support, I agree with you on that." He thought for another moment. "The drinking is something Mia will have to deal with alone. It's her decision to stay sober, and only hers. There's nothing you can do to influence that if she can't find the strength. You must know that better than anyone. But what you can do is help her in other ways. Help her deal with the reason for her anxiety at this very moment. She needs to either make peace with the fact that she'll never see her sister again, or somehow find forgiveness, or at least a mutual understanding between herself and her parents. And if possible, between herself and her sister. From what I understand, that's what's been bothering her most of her life and it's most likely the source of her pain, her frustration and her restlessness. Do you know her sister?"

"No. I know *of* her. I can probably track her down."

Zaid winced. "It's the worst advice I could possibly give you, especially coming from a psychologist, but as I said, I'm only speaking as your brother right now, and maybe it's worth a shot."

Ava leaned back when the waitress put down their dishes in between them. "Are you saying I should talk to her sister?"

Zaid shrugged. "I don't know. That's up to you to decide." He hesitated. "I'd say there's no harm in trying."

53

LONDON, UK

"You were looking for me? Who are you?" A younger and shorter version of Mia stood in the doorway of her student flat and curiously looked up at Ava as she opened the door a little further. Ava was still in her work uniform, and that had been a conscious decision. Uniforms tended to inspire trust in people, and right now she needed every little bit of help she could get. Ava studied the girl and felt a stab when she immediately thought of Mia. It was scary how much alike they were. Although Ami had broader shoulders, most likely from swimming, Ava guessed, their faces were almost identical.

"I'm Ava." Ava held out her hand. "I'm a friend of Mia." She shook her head. "We're more than friends, I suppose. At least we were. But I haven't seen Mia in a while and I'm worried about her." There was music and laughter coming from the flat.

Ami shook her hand hesitantly. "Is she okay?"

"I'm not sure to be honest. She's not in a good place, I know that." Ava's eyes fixed on Ami's. "And I know you aren't either right now. I know what's been going on, but I'd still really appreciate it if we could talk." She paused and leaned against the doorpost. "Mia doesn't know I'm here."

Ami lingered on the spot and Ava could almost hear her thinking frantically. She chewed her cheek the same way Mia did, and fiddled with a lock of her hair, before she took a step back.

"Okay," she said. "Come in." She gave Ava a good glance-over, resting her gaze on her pilot's cap. "More than friends, did you say?" She frowned. "I didn't even know Mia was gay."

Ava wasn't sure how to reply to that, so she ignored the comment as she stepped into the messy hallway, relieved that she was at least being given the chance to talk.

"I'm really sorry if this is a bad time," Ava said, gesturing to the party in the living room. The door was open, and she could see people dancing. She noticed the pungent smell of alcohol, that had no doubt soaked into the stained crème-coloured carpet over the years. Despite the festivities, Ami seemed sober. She looked tired, if anything. She also had the same look Mia sometimes had after a long shift, and it was hard, being face to face with a woman who looked so much like Mia.

"It's my flatmate's birthday," Ami explained. "But it's okay. I wasn't really in the mood to celebrate anyway." She led the way up the stairs. "Let's go to my room. It's a mess, but I suppose that doesn't really matter right now."

Ava took in Ami's bedroom and remembered when she herself used to live like this, with all her belongings crammed into a small space. There were books and paper-work everywhere. Clothes were strewn across the floor and on the desk chair. The desk was barely visible underneath the heaps of make-up, accessories and shoe boxes, and there were empty beer bottles on the shelves above it, next to a couple of standing frames with family pictures and an impressive collection of swimming medals, dangling from the nails in the wall. Ami cleared the chair and threw the clothes into a corner.

"Here," she said, patting the back rest, before taking a seat on the single bed opposite Ava. "Talk to me."

54

LONDON, UK

I t had been a bad day. Mia had found a couple of yoga retreats online, but she couldn't bring herself to book any of them, let alone pack a bag and drag herself to the airport. She wanted to, even if it was just to get away, but she had no energy left after crying throughout the night. She'd finally fallen asleep when the sun came up, exhausted and on an all-time low. She hadn't expected it to be any different. It wasn't the first time she'd been through a relapse. This time however, she also had to deal with the fact that she'd lost her sister, and Ava, who was constantly on her mind. Tuesday had been a welcome distraction, and even a great support, but as soon as Mia got into bed and was alone with her thoughts the despair washed over her as if it had been lurking in a dark corner of her room, waiting for her return. Miserable didn't even begin to describe her mood. She stirred the pot of ready-made pasta sauce aimlessly, having no desire to eat it. Its white substance was lumpy, and just the sight of it made her feel sick. She turned off the gas and pushed it aside, just as someone knocked on her door. Mia ignored it, resting her forehead on her arms, folded in front of her on the kitchen counter as she leaned forward and groaned.

"Mia?" There was another knock.

Mia froze, recognizing her sister's voice. *Ami?* She sprinted to the door and opened it, unsure whether she'd imagined it or not.

"Ami?" Mia was lost for words when she saw Ami standing in front of her. "Ami," she said again, tears welling up. "You're here." Mia swallowed hard. "You're here," she repeated in disbelief.

Ami produced a small smile. "Yes, I'm here," she said in a soft voice. "Can I come in?"

"Of course, I'm sorry." Mia opened the door wider, letting Ami in. She followed her sister into the living room and sat down next to her on the couch, just like she had, just over two weeks ago. "I'm so glad you're here." Mia covered her mouth with a hand, still in shock at Ami's unexpected visit. She was crying again, but this time in relief. Tears ran down her face and her shoulders shook as she looked up at Ami. "I can't believe you're here," she said through sniffs.

Ami put a hand on Mia's shoulder and gave her a squeeze. When Mia started crying even harder, she took her into her arms and hugged her tight. Mia laughed through her tears.

"I'm sorry, I'm a mess."

"Don't apologize." Ami gave Mia a kiss on her temple and leaned against the backrest of the couch, folding a leg under her thigh. "I was too harsh on you. I blamed you because I needed someone to blame and that was unfair of me."

"It wasn't unfair," Mia said. "It was my fault, entirely. It was all me, Ami, I..."

"Wait, let me speak." Ami held up a hand. "I know it was

an accident, and that you've been paying for it all these years. The guilt you must have felt..." She paused. "I know everything. I know how you've struggled and I know how low you've felt. How you've been avoiding going home, and how you've been avoiding me. It all makes sense now."

"You know?" Mia frowned. "How?"

"Ava," Ami continued. "She came to see me, and she told me you weren't in a good place. She told me everything." Ami gave Mia a pleading look. "But please don't be mad at her. Ava is a great woman, she didn't know what else to do. She really cares about you, Mia." She chuckled awkwardly. "I didn't even know you were into women. Isn't that crazy? How little I know about your life? I mean, do Mum and Dad even know you're gay?"

"I told them." Mia paused. "When I was fifteen. But we haven't spoken much since the accident. I felt Mum and Dad still blamed me. Which I deserved, of course. You should have seen their faces... They couldn't look at me when I got back from rehab, and after that, well, we never talked about it. Or about anything important for that matter. We just went on with our lives and buried it so deep that sometimes it almost seemed like it never happened."

"You shouldn't have stayed away because of me." Ami was crying too now. "I'm so sorry that what happened made you feel this way. All I ever wanted was to hang out with my big sister, to be friends. I've missed having you around, Mia. And Mum and Dad miss you too. Mum's upset that she hasn't seen you or spoken to you in a while, so please believe me when I say that they don't blame you anymore." Mia handed her a tissue to blow her nose and took one for herself.

"Really?"

"Yeah. You know what they're like. They love to talk

about the weather and the neighbours and all sorts, anything but difficult conversations. They've been avoiding the subject, sure. But that doesn't mean they don't want to see you."

Mia stared ahead, processing what Ami had just told her. "It feels so good to finally talk to you, Ami, and to say what's important." She hesitated. "Can you ever forgive me?" There was finally a tiny glimpse of hope that she could get on with her life and focus on her future, without having to worry about her past.

"It was an accident," Ami said. "You didn't run me over on purpose."

"But I was drunk and medicated," Mia admitted.

"Yes, you were. But I'm just glad you're still around, that you didn't kill yourself that day." Ami reached out to touch the scar on Mia's forehead and traced a finger down to her ear. "And your hearing. How come I didn't know about that either?"

"Mum and Dad are good at keeping secrets," Mia said. "They were afraid we'd grow apart if you knew that I was the one who'd caused you probable permanent damage. It's ironic, isn't it?" She sniffed. "We were surprised you made it so far in swimming, since you could barely use your left arm for years when you were younger."

Ami raised her left arm and gave Mia a wave. "Well, my left arm works just fine now. Maybe not Olympic Gold fine, but that's something even the most perfect arms won't achieve either." Her expression became more serious. "Hey, I want you to know that I'm glad you stopped drinking and that you've got your urges under control now. And yes, I forgive you, if that's what you need to hear." She smiled. "I love you, Mia."

"I love you too." Mia felt light as a feather. The enormity

of what she'd done had been weighing her down since that day, thirteen years ago. She'd been chained to her guilt, and now, that chain was crumbling. "But what about your swimming career? You must be so upset..."

Ami nodded. "I was. I am. But I've thought long and hard about this, and I don't see the point in holding a grudge. Sure, I was disappointed that I didn't get through, but it's not like it had been my lifelong dream. It was a hobby, and I guess I've been lucky to become very good at it. It doesn't mean I'm going to stop swimming now. I love it and it's a part of me. But so is my dream of becoming a physiotherapist." She smiled. "I'm re-evaluating my life and it's not as hopeless as it seemed when I first got the news. In fact, I'm looking forward to having a bit of time to myself." She shot Mia a grin. "And fried food. Tons of fried food and heaps of cheese."

Mia laughed. "It's about time I ordered that pizza I promised you, then."

"Pizza sounds great." Ami put a hand on her knee. "By the way, Ava is great. You're lucky to have her."

"Yeah. I know." Mia smiled. "And I'm glad you met her, even if it was under these circumstances." She shook her head. "After my relapse, I told her we needed to stop seeing each other. I don't want to drag her down with me. I know it's the right thing to do, but it doesn't feel that way."

"I don't think you need to worry about that, Sis. She seems to be crazy about you and she'll wait until you're ready. You just need to let her know how you feel about her." Ami shuffled a little closer to Mia and raised an eyebrow. "Hey, you want to know something?"

"What?"

"I'm dating someone too."

"Really? Tell me about him." Mia frowned. "I assume it's a *him*?"

"Yes, it's a *him*." Ami chuckled. "Although I do date girls too, from time to time."

"Okay..." Mia leaned back, finally relaxing her body a bit. "I had no idea about that either. Mum and Dad certainly never told me about it."

"No, you didn't know that, did you? We've got a lot to learn about each other." Ami gave Mia a wry smile. "Mum and Dad only hear what they want to hear, no matter what you tell them. And to be honest, I don't care if they live their lives as ostriches if that's what makes them happy, as long as you and I don't."

Mia studied her sister. She looked a lot like her. They had the same dark hair, although Ami's was shorter, the same full eyebrows and the same smile, pulling slightly to the left. "You've grown up a lot, Ami. You're very bright, way brighter than I was at your age." She smiled. "Now tell me about this man you're dating..."

Ava grabbed her bag from the luggage rack and got out of the bus in front of her New York hotel. She checked her phone once more but there were no messages. Another flight and another night had passed, and still no word from Mia. The excitement that she usually felt when she came here was missing. Right now, she just wanted to sleep away the hours and try not to think about Mia. She was with Raf and Mohammed, the first officer she'd only just met, and was seriously hoping they wouldn't try to persuade her to go for lunch.

"Thank you," she mumbled when a bellboy opened the door for her. Raf and Mohammed were already at the check-in desk. She lingered by the entrance, pretending to admire the lobby she'd seen many times on her previous trips, until they finally went up to their rooms.

"Ava," a voice called from the seating area. Ava turned to see who was calling her, although she'd recognized the voice immediately. She couldn't believe it. There was Mia, and she looked more beautiful than ever. Casually dressed in jeans and a yellow silk top, she waved at Ava from the couch as she stood up. She looked nervous, fiddling with the hem of her top, but blended in with the modern lobby's yellow and white interior as if she were on a photoshoot. Her long, dark hair was straightened, and hung around her face and her shoulders like a silk curtain. She smiled as she walked towards Ava and hugged her.

"Mia." Ava held Mia tight and buried her face in her neck. Her smell felt like coming home and she sighed as a wonderful warmth spread through her. "What are you doing here?" she whispered.

"I needed to see you." Mia let go, took a step back but grabbed both of Ava's hands. She held her gaze as her their eyes locked, and smiled. "I've missed you."

"I've missed you too." Ava swallowed away the lump in her throat. "You're okay. Thank God, you're okay."

"I'm getting there." Mia stroked Ava's cheek, her smile widening. "It's so good to see you, Ava. I hope you don't mind that I came? I was driving myself crazy at home and I realised the only place that could give me some kind of peace was wherever you were."

Ava squeezed her hand. "I'm so glad you came. I've missed you so much, Mia." She studied Mia. "You look well. I mean, you look amazing," she corrected herself.

"Thank you." Mia giggled. "So do you." Her face turned more serious. "Listen, I'm sorry for just turning up like this but I had to." She paused. "And I don't know what I can give you right now but maybe we could just talk and... I don't know."

"Hey, it's fine, I get it," Ava said, lowering her voice. People around them waiting in line for check-in were looking at them. "I know you're not in that place right now. I know you can't just flip a switch and throw yourself back into a relationship. But I'm really happy you're here, and I'd love to talk." Ava meant it. She felt a warmth that she couldn't quite comprehend at the mere sight of Mia. It felt comforting and familiar, but exciting at the same time. "I don't need anything from you right now. I just want to be there for you when you need me."

"Thank you." Mia's vision blurred with tears as she sighed in relief. "Thank you for understanding." She smiled. "And thank you for talking to my sister. I have a lot to tell you."

Ava raised an eyebrow. "You spoke to Ami?"

"I did." Mia squeezed her arm, leading them towards the check-in queue. "Thanks to you." She shook her head at Ava's apprehensive expression. "Don't worry. I'm not mad at you for reaching out to her, Ava. I'm grateful."

"That's a relief," Ava said. "She promised me my visit would stay between us, but she's clearly not as good at keeping secrets as you are. Also, I'm really sorry that I told her we'd been seeing each other. I just assumed she knew you were gay."

"It's okay." Mia gave her a reassuring look. "I know as much about my sister as you do now. I'm completely out, it's just that we don't talk much in our family. But I'm looking forward to getting to know Ami better. We're having lunch next week."

"Oh yeah? That's wonderful, Mia."

"It is." Mia fell silent for a moment. "I feel good, Ava. I mean, I'm not totally there, of course not, but I feel positive and hopeful, like I know deep inside that it's going to be different this time. That I can stay sober for good."

Ava put an arm around Mia's waist and pulled her against her. "You have no idea how happy that makes me. And you're doing so well already." She ran a hand through

Mia's hair. "Don't worry about the days to come, just enjoy today, with me."

"You're right." Mia leaned her head on Ava's shoulder. "I booked my own room. I guess... It just seemed like the right thing to do, even though I really want to be with you."

"Of course. I understand. But that doesn't mean I can't take you out for a coffee, right?" Ava asked.

"That would be nice. I'm staying for two nights, and I saw on your schedule that you're not flying back until late tomorrow. We could do some fun stuff together, unless you have plans?"

Ava chuckled and looked at her watch. "Even if I did have plans, they'd be cancelled right about now." Her expression fell sombre. "Thank you for coming, Mia. I was so worried about you."

"I know." Mia's eyes met Ava's. "But I'm okay now, and seeing you has really made my day." She hesitated. "Hey, there's a meeting at that place in Brooklyn I'd like to go to first. Do you want to come with me? We could go for a coffee afterwards?"

Ava smiled. "I'd follow you anywhere."

56

NEW YORK, USA

"I have a surprise for you," Mia said, as they walked through Cobble Hill on their way back from the AA meeting. "You might not like it but, as you interfered in my business with my sister, I figured you couldn't blame me for doing this."

"For doing what?" Ava followed Mia down the street where she used to live, surprised to see that they were heading towards Imani's coffee shop. "How do you know about this place? I used to come here all the time."

"Just trust me on this one and don't get mad, okay?" Mia opened the heavy door and stepped into the cosy aroma of freshly roasted coffee beans. "Nice place," she said.

Imani was behind the counter, serving a customer. She let out a shriek when she saw Ava, immediately dropping what she was doing. She ran around the counter to greet her.

"There's my girl!" She hugged Ava, and then her gaze shifted to Mia. "And who's this pretty lady?"

"This is Mia." Ava blushed, suddenly unsure of how to introduce Mia. "My friend."

"Oh, my goodness. Did you just say the word *friend* and blush at the same time? And look at *you*." Imani turned to Mia and gave her a hug too. "Welcome, Ava's *friend*." She articulated the word in a mocking tone and laughed louder than Mia had ever heard anyone laugh.

"It's great to meet you," Mia said, almost choking in Imani's tight embrace.

"Likewise." Imani took a step back and looked her up and down.

Mia liked this Imani. She didn't expect one of Ava's old friends to be so outgoing, but it was refreshing to meet someone who didn't hold back. Imani was clearly herself at all times. As she tried to pretend to be engaged in Ava and Imani's conversation, her eyes shifted to a man by the window. *That's him.* She recognized him from the pictures on his social media page. It hadn't been hard to track him down. In fact, it had only taken her ten minutes on her phone during one of her breaks at work. She had his first name, the airline he'd flown for, and she'd guessed he might still live in Brooklynn. Apparently, that was all you needed nowadays to find someone.

"I'd better go back to my customers, it's really busy right now," Imani said. "Don't want them to leave bad reviews." She stroked Ava's arm. "We'll catch up later, okay? I assume you're here to see Pedro?" She gave Ava's arm one last squeeze. "I'm proud of you for doing that. He's right over there, by the window."

Ava froze at the mention of Pedro's name. "What?" She looked around and her eyes widened when she saw her old friend. "Did you...?" She turned to Mia.

Mia winced. "I'm sorry, but I'm doing this for you." She took a step back. "I'm going for a walk now. Call me when you're done, okay?" She was gone before Ava could get another word in.

Ava shuffled nervously on the spot, glancing at the door. But Pedro had already seen her and waved her over. She braced herself, waved back and walked over to his table.

"Pedro." She could hardly believe he was sitting here, waiting for her as if nothing had happened. Pedro stood up and gave her a long hug. Ava closed her eyes and squeezed him tighter against her. She'd missed him.

"I can't believe it's really you, Ava." Pedro took her by the shoulders and gave her a genuine smile. "And you're still as smoking hot as you were six years ago. Or is it seven now?" He shrugged. "I stopped counting after two years, figured I'd never see you again." Pedro gestured towards the table for her to join him. "I've missed you."

Ava smiled, curiously looking him up and down. "I've missed you too." She sat down, speechless for a moment. "I can't believe you're here," she finally said. "That you're here and that you want to speak to me." She made a point of looking him in the eyes as she lowered her voice. "What I did to you was unforgivable."

Pedro shrugged. "Hey, it was a long time ago. I've moved on. You've moved on."

"Yeah, but she was your girlfriend and..." Ava looked down at the table.

"She was promiscuous as fuck. Cheated on me five more times after that. All with women, I may add. I called it a day way too late, but you know how crazy I was about her. I just didn't want to see the truth."

"I'm so sorry," was all Ava could manage to say.

"I know you, Ava. And that wasn't you, that night. Whatever made you do what you did, was big enough to make you quit your job and leave the next day." Pedro paused. "That was the worst thing for me. That you just left without saying goodbye, without explanation. We did everything together back then. We worked together, lived together, hung out together..."

"Exactly." Ava took a deep breath. "I was ashamed of what I'd done. I figured you wouldn't want to speak to me ever again, so I packed up and moved back to London."

"You shouldn't have done that."

"I know."

"Two double espressos on the house." Imani put the cups in front of them with a beaming smile. "It sure is good seeing you both here again."

"Thanks Imani. You're an angel." Pedro gave her a wink before turning back to Ava.

"Look, whatever happened, I'm not holding a grudge, if that's what you were afraid of. I'm not angry anymore, I'd just love to have you back in my life."

Ava tried to suppress the tears that were welling up now. She'd imagined seeing Pedro again many times, but the scene had always involved anger and rage. There was none of that today. Pedro was his old self, calm and sweet, like he always used to be.

"I'm a recovering alcoholic," she suddenly heard herself say. "I was back then too." She couldn't believe she'd just told him. Apart from Mia and her brother, Imani was the only one in her circle of friends and family who knew this about her.

Pedro's eyes widened. "But... I always thought you didn't drink for religious reasons."

"No." Ava shrugged. "I'm hardly religious." She hesitated. "And every time I said I was going to the mosque... well, I was going to AA meetings. That's my church, I guess."

"Right." Pedro let the information sink in.

"Look, it's not an excuse, Pedro. I'd never use being drunk as an excuse. It was awful of me, and I'm ashamed of myself. But I wouldn't have kissed your girlfriend that night if I hadn't been drinking. That's just not me. I'm not me when I'm drunk. I turn into this selfish, nasty person who doesn't give a shit about anyone but herself." She swallowed hard. "But you were my friend, my best friend. I need you to know that."

Pedro sat back and studied Ava. "I had no idea," he said. "Why didn't you tell me you had a problem?"

"It's not exactly something I'm proud of." Ava took a sip of her coffee. "And besides, I prefer dealing with it on my own, I always have. Nobody but me can help me. And I've been doing okay. Haven't had a drink since that night."

"That's great." Pedro took her hand over the table. "So, you're doing well? And that lovely woman who messaged me, are you seeing her?"

"Yeah, I'm good, and Mia is amazing." Ava paused. "We're not exactly seeing each other. It's a delicate situation at the moment but... I think I'm falling in love with her." Again, she'd spoken the words before thinking them through. She hadn't told Mia yet and hell, she hadn't even realised it herself until this very moment when she'd said it out loud. But she knew it was true.

"Love?" Pedro shot her a teasing smile. "Damn, I never thought I'd hear the L word coming from your mouth."

"I didn't either." Ava blushed, hoping the truth virus, that had apparently nestled itself in her blood today, wouldn't make her say more things she wholeheartedly meant but hadn't thought through. "Life can surprise us sometimes. And you? Imani told me you've been seeing someone for a while now. Pretty, dark-haired girl, she says."

"You've been talking about me?"

"Maybe a little. I wanted to know you were okay." Ava said hesitantly.

"I'm more than okay." Pedro picked up his phone from the table and scrolled through his pictures. "This is Valerie," he said, handing his phone to Ava. "We're getting married next year."

"You are? Congratulations. I'm so happy for you." Ava took a closer look. "She's gorgeous."

"Don't you get any ideas now." Pedro grinned. "Just kidding." The smile dropped from his face as he looked back at her. "It's good to have you back, Ava."

"Yeah. It's really good to see you again," Ava said. "It's been so long... your accent has changed. You sound so American now."

"That's what you get from living here. If you can't beat them, join them, right?"

Ava laughed. "So true." She looked up at him, nervously playing with the sugar bowl in between them on the table. "Do you think maybe we could meet up again sometime? I'm in New York about once a month, and I'd love to see you next time. Unless you'd rather leave it with this? I'll understand if you do."

Pedro shook his head, pointing a finger at her. "Don't you dare bail on me again, Ava. Hey, I have a better idea. Why don't you and Mia join myself and Valerie for dinner tonight? We could go somewhere low key, maybe that little pizza place on Moore Street? It's still there."

Ava nodded, smiling from ear to ear. "That would be great." She got her phone out. "First of all, let me get your number." She handed Pedro her phone to save his number. "And Pedro?"

"Yeah?" He said.

"Do you happen to know anyone who rents out private planes around here?"

57

NEW YORK, USA

"I had fun last night." Mia put a hand on Ava's thigh as she was driving towards their mystery destination on Long Island. "Pedro and Valerie are lovely people. I wouldn't mind seeing more of them."

"Yeah. They're great." Ava couldn't stop smiling. "Thank you, Mia. I really appreciate what you did. I don't think I'd have ever spoken to him again if you hadn't lured me there yesterday."

"I'm glad it worked out." Mia sighed. "I'm mostly just relieved you didn't want to kill me after I set you up. You didn't look too pleased when you realised why you were there."

"Maybe I need to listen to you more often."

Mia laughed. "If you're planning on listening to me right now, I'm going to take this opportunity to say that you seriously need to learn how to drive. I can't believe you don't have a driver's license."

Ava shrugged. "It was never one of my priorities." She covered Mia's hand with her own. "Besides, you look sexy behind the wheel."

Mia shot her a flirty glance before shifting her eyes back on the road ahead. "I'm glad my driving floats your boat and I love this flashy rental car. But what I really want to know is, where the hell am I going?"

"I told you, it's a surprise." Ava chuckled. "Don't worry, I think you'll like it." She pointed to an exit. "Take the 110 here."

Mia took the exit onto a smaller and quieter road. They passed through small towns and farmland towards Farmingdale. "You know Farmingdale's not exactly a tourist destination, right?" Mia said.

"I know." Ava pointed again. "Take a left here."

Mia did as she was told and burst out into laughter. "Walmart? Is that where you're taking me? Is that why we needed a car? For all the shopping?" Then she spotted the sign for Republic Airport. "Unless we're..." Her eyes widened as she looked at Ava. "We're not going to fly, are we?" She steered the car onto a smaller road, in between two large fields. The heat of the afternoon sun was creating a mirage over the ground in front of them, forming ripples shimmering on the road ahead.

"No." Ava smiled. "You're going to fly. You said you always wanted to, so here we are."

Mia's eyes widened. "You can't be serious. I can't fly."

"I am serious. I'll teach you. I'm qualified, and I'll be sitting right next to you, with equal control over the plane, so you don't have to worry about a thing."

Mia was silent, processing the information. "Are you sure?"

"Yeah. In here." Ava nodded towards a big car park, with only five occupied spaces. "Come on, we're late."

"CAN YOU HEAR ME?" Ava asked, after she'd done her inspection and given Mia a thorough briefing, explaining the controls and instruments in the cockpit. After that, they'd listened in on ATIS, which informed them about the airport weather conditions. She adjusted Mia's headset after putting on her own.

"Loud and clear, Captain." Mia replied.

"Good." Ava chuckled. "But you're the captain today, so you can call me officer. Are you ready?"

"No." Mia laughed nervously, looking down at her shaking hands. The two-seater propelled aircraft was tiny, and she didn't exactly feel safe, even with Ava sitting right next to her.

"Hey, it's okay if you want to back out." Ava put a hand on Mia's shoulder. "You never asked for this."

"No, I want to." Mia took a deep breath. "I really want to."

"Okay then." Ava gave her a reassuring smile. "I'm right here and I'm going to make sure we're safe. I won't give you control until we're up there, so for now just try to relax." She turned on the master switch and pulled out the control wheels, performing several tests she'd explained earlier. In her nervous state Mia had already forgotten about half of them, but she kept telling herself she was in safe hands with Ava.

Ava pushed in the mixture ridge, flipped the switch to the fuel pump, checked the fuel flow and reversed the process. "Okay, beacon switch is on. Can you tell me what that's for, Mia?"

Mia chuckled at Ava's schoolteacher tone of voice. "It's so others can see we're about to take off."

"Very good." Ava looked both ways to make sure there

was nothing in the way. "Clear," she yelled, making sure anyone in close proximity of the aircraft could hear her. Then she turned back to Mia.

"Okay, first, we're going to start the engine. It takes a little while to warm up." Ava turned the key next to her control wheel, explaining out loud what she was doing while checking the oil pressure and listening in to ATIS again. The propeller started spinning and the engine was roaring so loudly that Mia had trouble hearing her for the first couple of seconds, even with her headset on. Ava spoke to ground control and read out the number of their aircraft, their location and the direction they were heading, awaiting clearance. The complex jargon in the response sounded like Russian to Mia. "We're going to line up at runway number two," Ava continued. "Apparently, taxying is just like driving a car, but I wouldn't know as I've never driven one before," she joked. She released the brakes and immediately applied them again to make sure they were working and steered the aircraft towards the runway with her feet. That surprised Mia. She always thought the control wheel steered the plane on the ground, not some pedals operated by the pilot's feet. She was also amazed at the complications of getting such a small aircraft off the ground, and suddenly found she had a whole new respect for pilots. Ava seemed completely at ease as they headed towards the runway, staying in the middle of the yellow line on the asphalt.

"Now we just need to perform a couple more checks," Ava said as they came to a halt on the runway. She pointed at the cockpit display systems, repeating out loud what they were once more. "Turn coordinator, heading indicator, airspeed, altitude, vertical speed, altimeter. Everything is working fine." She ran final checks on the engine, before running through another full checklist in her hand, explaining to Mia into detail what she was doing. Then she spoke to ground control again, informing them they were clear for take-off. They taxied and picked up speed on the short runway. Mia held her breath as they lifted off the ground in one smooth motion. Although she'd spent a big part of her life up in the air, it was a whole new experience, sitting in the cockpit when taking off. The speed felt different, now that she could see everything in front of her. Beside her, Ava continued to communicate with ground control as they climbed. Walmart became smaller and smaller, and the cars on the road below them turned into tiny coloured dots as they reached their altitude.

"This is amazing." Mia sighed once they were flying over the Long Island coastline. Her nerves were now gone as she gazed down at the narrow, sandy islands, peninsulas jutting out, separated from the mainland by shallow bays. The water looked a vivid blue from above, and the sand much whiter than she'd imagined. "It's actually really beautiful from up here."

"Long Island is beautiful," Ava said. "But the thing is, everything looks better from above. You don't see the rubbish on the beaches, or the grumpy looks on people's faces. It's the bigger picture that captures you. It makes everything look simple and that's why flying feels magical." She chuckled. "God, I'm having so much fun. I haven't flown a small plane in years."

"Aren't they all the same? You know what you're doing, right?" Mia's eyebrows raised in alarm.

"Of course I know what I'm doing." Ava gave Mia a reassuring smile. "Think of aircrafts like cars; driving an old timer is not the same as driving a brand-new automatic. The principle is the same, but the tools are different, and to me it's great, flying something else for a change." She put a hand on Mia's knee. "But as much as I'm enjoying this, we're not here for me so I'm handing over to you now."

Mia looked down at the control stick in front of her and gulped.

"It's okay," Ava said. "Take it. I've explained how it works, now just move it a little, just to get a feel for it."

Mia carefully moved the control stick to the right and the aircraft titled slightly.

"That's good. Now try the other side. Careful, not too much." Ava said.

Mia did as she was told and smiled when they tilted to the left and started turning slightly.

"Great." Ava checked if Mia was okay before she continued. "You're going to follow the coastline, right to the very tip of Long Island and then you're going to turn back. Are you comfortable with that?"

"I think I can do that." Mia was grinning now as she turned them towards the Atlantic coast again and followed the thin strip of beach underneath them. "Oh my God, I'm flying!" she yelled. "Look at me, I'm flying!"

"THANK YOU," Mia said wholeheartedly when she stepped out of the plane. Her legs were still shaky from excitement, and her voice had a squeaky edge to it, but she felt on top of the world. "I felt so powerful up there." She sighed. "Wow. Can we do this again sometime?"

Ava laughed. "I'm glad it didn't freak you out. We can go anytime our schedules permit, just name the date."

"Isn't it really expensive?" Mia asked, biting her lip. "I've got some savings but I'm not sure if I can afford..."

"Don't worry about it." Ava took her hand as they

headed back to the airport building to hand back the keys and paperwork. "It's not as much as you think. Pedro's friend gave me a good deal and it's not like I've got anything else to spend my money on."

"But I can't..." Mia hesitated. "As much as I'd love to, we can't date right now. I'm going to do it right this time, and I..."

"I can give you lessons as a friend, can't I? Listen, I know you need time, and I understand that more than anyone." Ava hesitated and squeezed Mia's hand. "I'll wait for you, Mia. I promise. Even if it takes months, or years. I just want to have you in my life. If that means only having the occasional coffee together, or a weekly phone call, I'm fine with that. And I know I've already said it, but I need you to know that I'm grateful, for what you've done for me. It means so much to me to have Pedro back in my life and I don't know if I would have had the courage to contact him if you hadn't stepped in. I really care about you, Mia. You're special and..." She fell silent for a moment. "Well... maybe you're the one. I want to keep you close, and if you change your mind I'll respect that, I promise."

Mia almost choked with emotion at hearing her words. Her eyes welled up as she squeezed Ava's hand back.

"I care about you so much," she said softly. "I wish I could spend every waking hour with you, but I don't want to throw myself into anything before I know I'm ready and stable. Especially not with you. I don't want to jeopardize your sobriety, or our potential future together." She looked up at Ava. "You're all I ever dreamed of, Ava. You're all I've ever wanted and it's so fucking hard not to kiss you, or to do what feels natural."

Ava took Mia in her arms and hugged her tight. The

word 'future' had her choked up too now, and she smiled through her tears, knowing they were going to be okay. "Hey, don't cry. It's going to be fine. Everything's going to be fine. And in the meantime, I'll be here waiting."

58

LONDON, UK

Mia's phone beeped. She picked it up and smiled, trying to multitask as she stirred her mushroom sauce and chopped her salad at the same time. It was Ami.

'Sorry I'm late. Looking for parking.'

Ami's visit was a welcome distraction. Only ten weeks had passed since her relapse, but they had felt like years. Mia had spent most of her time looking at her phone, waiting for Ava to be available so they could have long conversations about nothing in particular. Just gossip and updates on where they were in the world and what they'd done. Hearing her voice was always the highlight of her day, and every time Ava told her she missed her, it gave Mia strength to stay sober. Mia was doing better now, much better, and she felt stronger and calmer every day. On the rare occasions when Ava and she were on a flight together, they'd go out for dinner, but Ava would never try anything other than to hug her before she said goodbye and went back to her hotel. She wouldn't flirt with her like she used to, but she would make sure that Mia always knew she was the most important person in her life. Mia appreciated her support more than anything, but she missed their flirty banter. The chemistry was still there. That much was obvious from the fleeting looks Ava gave her and the light touches that felt more like electric shocks to Mia sometimes. But they'd managed to steer away from anything more than what they were desperately trying to be right now: just friends. She poured the sauce into a bowl and gathered cutlery just as the doorbell rang.

"Ami!" She smiled, welcoming her sister.

Ami hugged her and stuck her nose up in the air. "What's that amazing smell, Sis? Are you seriously cooking? I thought you only ever got food from that place downstairs?"

Mia laughed, pointing at her kitchen. "I'm glad you think it smells nice because I have no idea what I'm doing. Wally from the deli is on holiday with my neighbour Tuesday. It's really cute. I think they're in love."

"How sweet." Ami walked over to the kitchen, dipped a finger in the sauce and tasted it. "This is really good, Mia. Where did you learn to cook like this?"

Mia laughed. "YouTube." She turned her laptop towards Ami, showcasing a steak and mushroom sauce 'how-to' video. "They make it look really easy but it's not, believe me, and I apologize in advance if the steak is dry." She studied Ami. "You look good."

"Thanks." Ami beamed. "I feel good, I guess."

"Is it this man you've been seeing?" Mia asked.

"Nah. We broke up a couple of weeks ago." Ami grimaced. "Actually, I broke up with him. I didn't really see it going anywhere, so I thought it best to put a stop to it before we both got too invested."

"Oh. Sorry to hear that." Mia moved the chopped ingredients of her salad into another bowl. "Are you okay?"

"Yeah, I'm fine," Ami said, not sounding remotely bothered. "I guess we don't know each other that well yet. I go through relationships faster than lapses in the pool. You need to know that about me." She laughed. "It's not like there's anything fundamentally wrong with me, but I like to explore my options before I commit, if you know what I mean. Plus, I tend to fall head over heels and then change my mind once I get to know the person. It's not ideal, but it seems to be a pattern with me."

Mia laughed too. "At least you know yourself well enough to say that."

"Yeah." Ami nodded with a smile. "If only I could apply my knowledge in a practical way and stop wasting time with people I'm never going to end up with, that would be great." She pointed at the two steaks, resting on a plate. "Need help?"

"Only with eating it." Mia said, handing the salad bowl to her sister. "Could you put this on the table please? Oh, and the salt and pepper and olive oil, they're right over there." She pointed to a basket on a shelf over the kitchen counter. "I'll take the rest." It was an amazing feeling, having Ami back in her life. They talked about everything and there hadn't been a single awkward moment since they'd started to hang out together. Ami was fun, unpredictable and full of surprises, that much she'd gathered by now, and she really enjoyed her company. They hadn't met up often; only three times since they'd rekindled their relationship. But those times had turned into long nights, catching up on every aspect of each other's lives, resulting in Ami falling asleep on the couch way after midnight every time.

"So, how's it going with Ava?" Ami asked after they were seated.

Mia cut her steak and smiled at the mention of Ava's name. "She's amazing. Not a day goes by that we don't speak, and I miss her constantly. I miss the intimacy, you know?"

"But you haven't gone there yet?" Ami asked. "After your relapse?"

"No." Mia sighed. "I don't know if I'm ready. I want to get things right this time."

"But you miss her, right? And you want to be with her?" Ami pointed her fork at Mia.

"Of course I want to be with her. My whole body is craving her, every minute of the day. I just don't want to fuck it up." Mia's eyes blazed with passion.

"So, you're waiting?" There was a challenging undertone to Ami's voice.

"Yes, I suppose so. I'm waiting for the right moment."

Ami scrunched her face. "You're waiting until you're ready?"

"Yeah." Mia frowned. "What's wrong with that?"

"Nothing," Ami said, scooping some salad onto her plate. "It's just that..."

"What?" Mia asked sharply.

Ami winced. "I'm not sure I want to have this conversation. I don't want to get into a debate. Can we just forget that I ever said anything?" She took a bite of her steak. "Wow, this is really good."

"No, we can't." Mia gave her sister an awkward smile. "You're doing this thing with your eyes and I don't know you well enough to know what it means, so I think you should just say what's on your mind. Spill it."

"Okay. Well... what I was wondering about is, how do you know when you're ready?"

Mia looked at her sister. That was a good question, because she had no idea herself. She'd been waiting for the AHA-moment, but nothing had changed, apart from the fact that she felt a little stronger every day, and that she missed Ava's touch more and more as time passed. Ava had been nothing but gentle and patient, and Mia knew she would continue to be just that until she initiated the change in their status. But it didn't make it any easier being around her, because Ava was her ultimate fantasy and so much more.

"Doesn't the pain of missing her physically weigh you down when you're doing this by yourself?" Ami shrugged. "I mean, wouldn't you be so much happier if you two could just fuck every now and then?"

Mia chuckled at Ami's directness. "I guess so." She turned serious. "But it's not that simple. I don't want to jeopardize Ava's sobriety."

"Ava seems fine." Ami said. "I'm no expert, but she seems pretty stable to me, and I think you're scared because she's so fucking perfect." She straightened herself and looked Mia in the eye. "I think you're more scared of messing up yourself than you are of messing up Ava. You're feeling insecure right now, and that's understandable. You're afraid to make mistakes but you also want to be happy, right? Isn't that everyone's endgame?"

"I guess," Mia answered, unsure of where her sister was going.

"So, why don't you just go for it? See where it takes you? Why waste precious time thinking about things when you could be doing them?" Ami was on a roll now, and she wasn't holding back. "Why wait for the right moment when

Ava makes you feel amazing right now?" She leaned in over the table. "Listen, you might think I'm too young and impulsive to say this, but I know what I'm talking about. Life can take funny turns sometimes, and you might have to re-evaluate what's important every now and then. But waiting for things to improve is not going to change anything. Just do what makes you happy, Mia. And if it goes wrong, so be it. Relationships go wrong all the time, anything can happen. So, seize the moment and enjoy what you have while it's still there." She took Mia's hand. "Look, I know the rules are there for a reason. I've read just about everything about AA that there is to read by now, and most of it makes perfect sense to me. But every situation is different, and in your case, I think you'd be in a much better place if you just did what made you happy, because she's good for you, and you're good for her. And most of all... I think she loves you."

"You do?" Mia sat back, silenced by Ami's proclamation.

"I really think she does."

"I love her too," Mia whispered. "I've thought about what you've just said, about just going for it. And you might be right. But then what if you're not? What if we get back together and I relapse again? What if I drag her down with me?"

"From what I can see right now, how determined you are and how strong, that seems unlikely. It's possible, of course, but unlikely. I mean, what if your plane crashes tomorrow? What if Ava gets run over by a car?" Ami knocked on the table. "Wouldn't you have wished you'd spent every free moment with her, no matter what the circumstances were?"

Mia gave Ami a sad smile. "Of course. But I still want to do this right." She fell silent for a moment. "I think she might be the one."

59

KUALA LUMPUR, MALAYSIA

I t was dark by the time Mia got back from her shopping trip in Kuala Lumpur. She threw her bags onto the bed and kicked off her leather sandals, swapping them for a pair of white Havaianas. Her bags were mainly filled with presents for Ava. A coffee mug, a t-shirt, five pouches of curry paste, a box of novelty balcony lights, and a silly water jug that looked like an aquarium, with glittery fish and plants sandwiched in between the double glass exterior. It was just another excuse to see her when she got back, Mia knew that. It was her way of showing Ava that she cared, and that she thought of her every second of the day. She walked onto her balcony, welcoming the breeze as she searched for her phone in her bag. She was contemplating whether to join her colleagues for dinner when her eyes caught a glimpse of the city, shimmering behind the trees of the hotel garden. The lights reminded her of the fireflies she'd seen with Ava. But then everything reminded her of Ava, all the time. The longing to be close to her was always there, and now it was all that she wanted. She stared through the trees for a moment, before she unconsciously picked up her bag and made her way downstairs towards the reception desk. She lingered there, feeling like she was sleepwalking, like she had no control over where she was going next.

"Could you please get me a taxi to The Golden Lily?" she heard herself say.

MIA FOUND THE FENCE, and the footpath Ava had showed her, and worked her way through the undergrowth, barely able to see in the dark.

There they are. The fireflies were back. Or maybe they'd never left. Mia stood breathless for a moment, staring up at the beautiful display of blinking lights as she replayed the vivid memory of that wonderful night with Ava. She remembered what Ava had told her. *Fireflies blink to attract mates of the same species, then switch of their lights when they've found their mating partner.* Goosebumps appeared on her arms as she watched two of the little insects settle down on the ground in front of her. They blinked for a little while longer before they became invisible in the dark.

"You're a match," she whispered, missing Ava like crazy. She sat down on a tree trunk and watched the fireflies. Time went by and the darkness became thicker and richer. It wasn't the most comfortable spot, and she felt the occasional sting from a mosquito bite, but there was something very soothing and almost meditative about just sitting there in the heat, the faraway sound of the hotel's classical music nearly drowned out by the tropical noises of frogs and other animals she couldn't identify. Her mind kept going back to what Ami had said a few weeks ago. *Maybe she's right. Why wait to feel happy and ready when I've never felt better than when I'm with Ava?* It didn't make any sense, when she put it like that. And Ami had a good point about Ava. Ava was stable, and she would be fine. Mia's hand navigated towards her phone in her lap. However, as if by telepathic communication, it buzzed, Ava's name appearing on the screen. A couple of fireflies moved towards her, curiously checking out the new source of light. Mia let it ring a couple of times to see if they would come any closer, but they didn't seem attracted enough to land on it. She smiled as she picked up the phone, a jolt of joy shooting through her.

"Hey, Ava. I was just thinking about you."

"Good thoughts, I hope?"

"Always." Mia smiled and closed her eyes at Ava's warm voice, the sound giving rise to butterflies in her stomach each and every time she heard it.

"How's KL?" Ava asked.

"It's nice. I've been shopping today." Mia stretched out her legs in front of her, trying to get into a more comfortable position. "And studying. I think I'm ready to practice my conversational skills with you now."

"Really? I can't wait." Ava paused. "I'm still home for another two nights if you're not too tired when you get back."

Mia could picture Ava smiling on the phone. She sounded cheerful. "That would be great. How's London?"

"Rainy. I miss you."

"I miss you too." Mia fell silent for a moment. "The fireflies are still here. I'm looking at them right now. They're beautiful."

Ava sighed. "Yeah? Did you sneak into the Golden Lily? I wish I was there with you."

Mia felt a lump in her throat, and she swallowed away her tears. Ava was so sweet and patient, perfect in every way, and she'd give anything to have her beside her right now.

She made a decision there and then. "Ava... I've been thinking a lot, and I'm not sure what I'm waiting for anymore. I feel good, but I just don't feel complete without you. I want us to go back to the way we were... I'm ready."

"Are you sure?" Ava's voice was soft.

Mia watched the fireflies twinkle. "Yes, I'm sure. It's all I can think of right now, how much I want you... I'm happy when I'm with you. How can that not be a good thing? You're good for me. And I'm pretty sure I can be good for you too."

"You are good for me." Ava let out a sigh of relief at hearing the words. "Mia, you have no idea how happy I am right now." She hesitated. "I hope you know that you're the one for me. Whatever happens, we'll get through this together. You and me, okay?"

"I know." Mia began to cry. Silent tears of joy fell into her lap. "You and me." She smiled. "I want to see you. Can I come over to your place, when I'm back? I'm dying to see where you live."

"Of course," Ava said. "I would have invited you over sooner, but I didn't think it would be the smartest idea for us to be in my flat together. It's hard when we're alone. Boundaries blur, and it's impossible to peel my eyes off you. You know what I mean."

"I do." Mia looked up at the sky. "Believe me, I've struggled just as much as you have... I can't wait to kiss you."

Ava chuckled. "I'm so excited, I can't even think straight right now. And I'm going over to my parents for dinner in a couple of hours. What are they going to think when I'm sitting there with that goofy grin on my face all evening?"

Mia laughed too. "You'll be fine. Say hi to your parents from me, will you?"

"I will. Sweet dreams, Mia. I'll see you soon."

"Yeah. I'll see you soon."

MIA STROLLED BACK to the hotel, taking in the world. It seemed perfect, as if everything had fallen into its place. There were so many stars tonight, and the scent of rain was still in the air from a thunderstorm that had passed over earlier that morning. She walked through the hotel gardens and past the lovers' fountain, where the same classical tune played over and over again. It was quiet now, and she sat down on the edge of the fountain, took off her flip-flops and hiked up the hem of her white thin-strapped summer dress before she lowered her feet into the water. The lights under the water feature turned from red to orange, making her skin glow as tiny droplets splashed onto her face and arms. For the first time in her life, Mia thought about her past and her future with a complete inner calm. Thoughts and memories, both painful and happy, came and went, but none of them upset her. Everything was simply the way it was meant to be and finally accepting that felt like taking a long, warm bath. *Everything is going to be okay.*

60

CAMBRIDGE, UK

Ava put her phone down and sank back into her couch with a cup of tea in her hand. She smiled as she looked out of the window. Rain tended to make her feel a bit sad usually, but right now, she was on top of the world. *Mia.* Every time she thought of her the world seemed better and brighter, and she got this warm feeling she couldn't quite explain. Their conversation had changed everything. It was a promise of a new start, maybe a long future together. She took a sip of her tea and folded her legs underneath her. The soft robe engulfed her while she relaxed into doing nothing at all. Ava had never been one to contemplate her future. She was simply content with the present, but now that they had both been more than clear on what they wanted, she couldn't help but fantasize about the possibilities that a future with Mia entailed. The thought of waking up next to her as often as they could felt exhilarating, and the thought of having a life together, sharing everything and making new memories made her heart sing with joy. She couldn't wait to see her.

"WHAT HAVE you all been up to?" Noor asked when the whole family was seated around the table.

"We're going on holiday," Zaid said, referring to himself and Natasha.

Natasha shook her head. "Zaid means *he's* going on holiday. I'll be working. I've been booked in for a photoshoot in Dubai in a couple of weeks' time. It's for a French swimwear brand." She put a hand on Zaid's. "But I'm sure we'll have more than enough time to explore the city together in the evenings, and I've got a full day off before we start so I won't look tired on the first day of the shoot."

"That sounds exciting," Noor said, filling her plate. She handed the plate back to Natasha, then turned to Ava. "Ava?"

"What?" Ava looked around the table when she heard her name. She'd been distracted, to say the least.

"Your plate?" Noor studied her daughter. "What a shame Mia couldn't come. We haven't seen her in such a long time. Is she coming over again soon?"

Ava smiled. "Sure Mum. She's just been away with work a lot. I'll bring her over next week, or the week after."

Zaid's eyes met Ava's over the table, and he raised a questioning eyebrow. Ava gave him a small nod, her smile broadening. He grinned back and winked at her.

"What are you two conspiring about?" Noor looked from Ava to Zaid and back.

"Actually Ava," Zaid said, stirring his stew, "I was going to ask you, if you could arrange a ticket for me. To Dubai. Natasha's got her flights through her agent but I haven't booked mine yet, and it just occurred to me that you might be able to get me a discount or something."

"Sure," Ava said immediately. She was more than happy to help him out. After confiding in him, she felt closer to

Zaid than ever, and she wanted to do something nice for him. "It'll be free, if I put you on the stand-by list. I'll try to get you into business class, but you might have to be a bit more flexible regarding the times and dates. Give me the dates that Natasha is there, and I'll work something out around that."

"Thank you, Sis." Zaid grinned and nudged Natasha. "See? That's how easy it is with a sister who's a bad-ass Captain."

Their father looked at them with suspicion. "Why are you two being nice to each other all of the sudden?"

Zaid shrugged. "Why not?"

"Isn't that what you always wanted, Dad?" Ava asked.

"Of course it is, darling," her mother intervened. "But I agree with your father, it is unusual. You're never nice to each other."

"Well, maybe now's the time to start." Ava stood up. "Excuse me, I need to use the bathroom." She lifted a leg to step around the chair and tripped when her foot struck the wood. She fell towards the empty chair next to her and only just managed to grab on to it, stopping herself from falling. When she tried to straighten herself, she tripped again. She looked at Zaid, who was crying with laughter opposite her, then down at her shoelaces that had, of course, been tied together under the table. She stepped out of her shoes and gave Zaid a warning look as she walked away from the table.

"Asshole."

61

LONDON, UK

"Hey." Mia said softly.

Ava opened the door further and stared at her for a moment, before she remembered to greet her back.

"Hey. Come in." Mia looked radiant and beautiful and sexy in a little navy dress and navy suede flats under a trench-style raincoat. Her hair was loose and wet from the rain, her face makeup-free, and her skin had a healthy glow. They studied each other for a while, unsure whether to kiss or not. Ava closed the door behind Mia and smiled as her gaze dropped down from Mia's eyes to her lips. Mia's mouth pulled into a small smile too, as she took a step towards Ava, wrapping her arms around her neck, and kissing her. Ava moaned softly as she felt Mia's tongue playing with hers, and she deepened the kiss while she ran one hand through Mia's hair, the other drifting over her back, before coming to rest on her ass. It felt amazing to have Mia in her arms again. She felt a shiver when Mia pulled out of the kiss and looked up at her.

"Wow. Nothing's changed, huh?" Ava whispered.

"No." Mia giggled quietly, her eyes dark with desire. "It doesn't feel like it."

"It's so good to see you again." Ava took Mia's raincoat and hung it on the coat rack by the door.

"It's good to see you too." Mai looked Ava up and down. "You look..." She shook her head, lost for words. Ava was wearing jeans, and a white tank top underneath a blue checked shirt that she wore open. *No bra.* Mia swallowed, fighting to pull her eyes away from Ava's breasts. "You look hot."

"Thank you." Ava ran a finger over Mia's cheek. "And you look cute and sexy, as always." She held her gaze for a moment, then took a step back. "I'm sorry, let me get you a towel."

"No need, I'm fine." Mia smiled, biting her lip. "It's just my hair and it's just rain." She kicked off her shoes and walked past Ava into the flat.

"I didn't take you for a farm-house kitchen kind of woman," Mia said as she entered Ava's open kitchen and dining room. "But now I'm here, I guess it suits you."

"It was already here when I bought it." Ava switched on her Nespresso machine. "But I don't mind it now. Makes me feel domestic from time to time." She held up a cup. "Coffee?"

"Sure." Mia crossed the dining room and opened the doors to the small balcony facing the street, letting the London noise in. It was raining even harder now, but the wind was blowing away from them, leaving the small seating area dry. "Nice view," she said, leaning over the balustrade. Ava joined her on the balcony and handed Mia a mug, looking out over the leafy residential street. There was music coming from one of the pubs around the corner, and black cabs were lined up before the traffic lights, waiting to drop off already drunk Londoners at the many hotspots in the area.

"You have a really nice place," Mia said. "It's not what I expected at all, it feels homelier."

"Thank you. I've only recently started appreciating it myself." Ava made a point of pulling out one of the wooden chairs from underneath the square table for Mia. "My lady." She then lit the three candles that were placed on a piece of slate in the middle.

"Thank you." Mia giggled. "You're so gallant, Captain."

Ava grinned. "You're gorgeous, did you know that?" She leaned against the door, staring at Mia. "Oh, I almost forgot." Ava went inside and came back with a plate full of homemade cakes and sweets. "My mother made these. I had to promise her I'd make you try at least one of each. I know there's enough for at least six people, but she'd kill me if I didn't offer them to you." She sat down next to Mia and sipped her coffee.

Mia took one of the sugary treats and moaned as she ate it. "Your mother's sweets are amazing," she said after swallowing it. "But I already knew that." She held the plate out for Ava, but she waved a hand.

"No thank you. I've got about ten bags of those in my freezer. She always insists on me taking some home after dinner. That's usually after she's lectured me on my non-existent bad eating habits." She chuckled. "Not sure how she manages to justify these sugary calorie bombs as acceptable, but anyway, feel free to take as many as you want when you leave. Do you think your parents might want some? They'll be fine for years, as long as they're in the freezer."

Mia laughed. "My parents are food barbarians. Anything sweet that doesn't look like a chocolate bar or custard is off the menu." She tried another one. "I, however, would be eternally grateful to have these in my freezer. So I'll take a bag, thank you very much." They were silent for a while, staring into the night as they drank their coffees.

"I have food," Ava finally said. "It's ready to heat up if you're hungry. I wasn't sure if you'd want anything after your flight, and I know it's late." She looked at her watch. It was almost eleven. "There's some food I brought home from my parents, and I've also got a Jamaican takeaway, just in case you prefer something different. But please don't feel like you have to eat it just because I ordered it." Ava wondered why she was suddenly blabbing on as if she was nervous. Was she really nervous?

"You're so sweet." Mia put a hand on Ava's thigh. "But I'm good." She pointed at the plate in front of her. "This is perfect. I'm not really hungry right now. It's seeing you again, it makes my stomach do funny things... but in a good way," she added with a grin.

"I think mine's doing the same," Ava said, looking down at the mug in her trembling

hands. "And it's worse than ever."

"I don't think that's a bad thing." Mia said, lowering her voice. "Hey, I've been thinking... I want you to meet my parents, Ava."

Ava turned to her, surprised at the sudden change in conversation. "Okay... I would love to meet your parents."

Mia looked shocked, as if the words had left her mouth without permission. "I mean, it's time, isn't it?" She didn't sound too convinced now she had voiced her idea, but she carried on. "They're not like your parents, not educated and sophisticated. In fact, they're quite basic in their conversation, but maybe now is the right time for me to open up to them a bit, you know? Now that Ami and I are okay, and I don't need to think about the lies and the..."

"Stop worrying so much, Mia," Ava interrupted her. "It would be an honour to meet your parents. They made you after all." She put a hand on Mia's. "Hey, it's going to be fine. You've taken the first step and the rest will be easier. And I'll be there with you."

Mia nodded, terrified about the fact that they were even having this conversation. She took a deep breath and decided to be completely honest.

"I don't know how to have a relationship with my parents. I don't know how to communicate with them. It's been too long... Too many lies, too many excuses, I guess."

"And tomorrow you can take the first step towards repairing that relationship," Ava said in a soft tone. "There's never a right time, so you might as well do it sooner rather than later. Don't think about what's broken, think about how to mend it. They love you and they want to see you. That's the best start you could possibly have." She paused to think. "Listen, your parents have made mistakes, and they know that. They should have told your sister what happened, they shouldn't have asked you to lie, and they shouldn't have stuck their heads in the sand when it came to your drinking problems. But they didn't mean to cause you any harm, they were just dealing with it the way they thought was best." She took Mia's hand. "You can change everything for the better, Mia. If the relationship with your parents is based on lies, be completely honest with them. Tell them how you feel about the fact that they made you lie to your sister your whole life. Tell them you're a recovering alcoholic but that you're doing just fine. But don't forget to tell them that you love them too, because that's the most important thing. You need to be honest. Completely honest."

"Like you're being honest with your parents?" Mia asked. Her tone wasn't sarcastic, just questioning.

Ava sighed. "I'll do the same. I think it's time for me too."

"Okay." Mia seemed to think about that, before she looked back up at Ava. "Would you really do that?"

"I think we both need to." Ava's gaze met Mia's. She gave her a smile and squeezed her hand. "What have we got to lose? We've got each other."

Mia smiled back at her. "Yes, we do." She moved a little closer, summoning up the courage to say what she'd been wanting to say for a while now.

"I think I love you, Ava." She shook her head. "No, that didn't sound right." A nervous chuckle escaped her mouth. "I know I love you. That's what I was trying to say." She paused. "And you don't need to say it back, I just want you to know that I think you're amazing, and that I love you."

Ava sat back, silently processing what Mia had just told her. The happiness she felt at those three words pulled her face into a big grin. Her eyes locked with Mia's and teared up.

"I love you too," she said for the first time in her life. It felt right, and she meant it. Mia was everything to her. She was her friend, her lover, her rock and now so much more.

62

LONDON, UK

"This is it." Ava opened the door to her bedroom and turned on the light to reveal an immaculately styled, spacious room. Mia stepped inside and looked around. There was a sense of calm, accentuated by the use of white and light grey colours. The bed looked luxurious and inviting, and there was no clutter. The lighting was soft, as if Ava had gone to great lengths to perfect the atmosphere in there, bathing the bed in a cosy glow.

Mia chuckled as her gaze fixed on the bed-end. "Why am I not surprised you've got handcuffs attached to your bed?" She tried to supress a pang of jealousy.

"It's not like that," Ava was quick to reply. "I haven't used them in years. I lost the keys a long time ago, so I just left them there." She smiled as she opened the top drawer to her nightstand and produced another pair. "But I've got a spare pair if you fancy trying them out."

Mia looked at the handcuffs that were dangling off Ava's fingers. She hesitated for a moment, took them, then put them back in the drawer and closed it. She then pushed Ava onto the bed and crawled on top of her, straddling her thighs. Ava's first reaction was to throw Mia off of her and turn them around, so that she was on top, but Mia refused to move when Ava's hands tugged at her waist.

"No," she said. "I love it when you're all bossy in bed. You know that, and we can play that game anytime you want. But tonight, if we're going to make this work, I need you to let go. I need you to trust me." Ava looked at her and smiled, but Mia could sense the hesitation in her eyes. "It's okay. It's just me." She stroked Ava's cheek gently, then traced her fingers down and let them linger on the neckline of her tank top.

Ava nodded and swallowed hard. "I know." She paused. "And I'll try. It's just been a very long time since anyone..." She stopped halfway through her sentence, her eyes lingering on Mia's. Mia could feel Ava's internal conflict as she tried to relax. She bent forward and kissed her softly, drawing a moan from Ava's mouth.

"See? It's just me," Mia repeated before claiming her mouth again. Ava closed her eyes as she deepened the tender kiss that was now turning more passionate when Mia draped herself over Ava, pushing a thigh between her legs. Ava gasped at the contact.

"I want you to give yourself to me," Mia whispered. "I need you to surrender, Ava. I want you to be mine tonight, and I want us to be together. Really together and equal. No boundaries, no inhibitions and no games. Can you try?"

Ava took in a quick breath as Mia kissed down her neck and opened her shirt. She lay still, staring up at Mia, her heart beating fast. There was anticipation and desire in her eyes, but also something else, something Mia hadn't seen before.

"Don't be scared," Mia whispered. She slid Ava's shirt

over her shoulders and waited for her to take it off, before she pulled the tank top over Ava's head, exposing her small breasts. She placed her warm hands on them and felt Ava's chest heaving up and down, with either excitement or fear, she wasn't sure. "It's okay," she whispered again. She bent forward and placed a trail of kisses over both Ava's breasts, before softly taking a nipple into her mouth. A smile crept on Mia's face when she heard Ava sigh in pleasure, and she moved on to her other nipple, biting down gently as she let her tongue twirl around it. Ava moaned again, a little louder this time. Mia continued to kiss her breasts and her neck until she felt Ava relax, and her breathing steadying. Then she raised herself, pulled her dress over her head and tossed it on the floor, next to the bed, before she started unbuttoning Ava's jeans. She bit her lip as her eyes locked with Ava's, desperately trying to read her mind. Ava was hesitant, but helped Mia pull them off and allowed her to take off her briefs too. Mia let her gaze wander over the gorgeous naked body in front of her for a moment, her lips parting in a mixture of desire and awe.

"You're beautiful," she said in a soft voice. She reached around to unhook her bra at the back and threw it on the floor before she crawled forward and slowly lay down on top of Ava.

Ava gasped at the contact. "You feel incredible," she whispered, as she traced the sides of Mia's breasts down to her waistline. She ran her hands back up, weaving them through Mia's hair as they kissed, softly at first, then hungrier as they started grinding into one another. Each time Ava reached for Mia's wrists, Mia took her hands instead, tenderly reminding her of what she wanted, what she needed from her.

Mia pulled out of the kiss when she heard Ava moan

again, her breathing ragged and her eyes full of longing. She kissed her way down Ava's neck again, towards her breasts.

Ava found herself caught in a delicious conflict as she lay there, now fully surrendering to Mia. Her mind told her to stop what was going on, and to take back control, but her body seemed to be enjoying the attention as a warm sensation spread between her legs. She felt Mia's hands caressing her breasts, her tongue on her nipples, and her mouth on her stomach as she kissed her way down. It felt good.

"Are you okay?" Mia asked, looking up at her.

Ava nodded, unable to keep her eyes off Mia when she let her tongue slide down towards the patch of dark hair between her legs. She'd never experienced the need to be pleasured by someone else, never liked the idea of giving up her dominance, and in the past, she usually hadn't even wanted to take off her clothes in bed. But there was something about Mia that made the agonizing feeling of letting go pleasurable, and Ava felt herself relax and start to crave more now. She trusted Mia, longed for her. And when Mia's tongue slipped between her legs, she couldn't help but cry out. Instinctively, she covered her mouth, not used to letting go like this. Her other hand was in Mia's, their fingers entwined. The warm tongue on her centre, licking her up and down in a teasingly slow manner was driving her wild. Mia looked incredibly sexy, the way she moved her hips while bringing Ava towards a growing orgasm. Ava buckled when she felt lightning was about to strike. She didn't want it to end yet. It was too soon. It felt really, really good, and she wanted to share the moment. To be together, like Mia had begged her to. She ran her hand through Mia's hair and pulled her up.

"Wait," she whispered. "Please come here." She kissed Mia, marvelling in the strange sensation of tasting herself.

Mia lifted her gaze to meet Ava's and she gave her a small smile. Her eyes were darker than Ava had ever seen them. She lowered herself on top of Ava, covering her, as if she wanted to possess every inch of her. Her hand moved between Ava's legs, making Ava gasp and close her eyes when she explored her again with her fingers. Ava slid her own hand in between them and did the same. Mia moaned when she felt Ava's fingers on her sex, and she started to ride her hand in a slow rhythm, her hips moving in the most sensual way while she entered Ava with two fingers.

Ava's vision blurred when she felt Mia inside her, penetrating her slowly. "Yes," she groaned, not sure if the words were coming from her own mouth. "Don't stop, Mia." She wrapped her arm around Mia's shoulders and held her tight, while her other hand continued to thrust, now covered in Mia's warm wetness. She felt free and complete, as she adjusted to Mia's rhythm, listening to the beautiful sounds she was making as she entered her. They moved as one, and when Ava stopped thinking, she understood what Mia had meant. They were together.

Mia lifted her head, searching for Ava's eyes. "Look at me, Ava."

"I'm here," Ava whispered, her eyes meeting Mia's. She felt a wonderful heat building up inside of her and was unable to hold back any longer. She finally let her orgasm wash over her, forcing herself to keep her eyes open and look at Mia. There was no yesterday, no tomorrow, no thoughts and no holding back. There was only now, right now, with Mia. Her muscles tensed and relaxed, giving her waves of pleasure each time Mia moved into her. Ava was helpless, in the mercy of the beautiful woman on top of her, and she didn't care anymore. She stroked Mia's hair and traced her cheek while she rode out the last waves. Mia was close now, and Ava smiled when Mia moaned, her face pulling into an expression of complete ecstasy, before she fell over Ava and buried her face in her neck, shaking.

The togetherness and the closeness, was something Ava hadn't experienced before. She closed her eyes and pulled Mia tighter against her. She felt her, really felt her. Their breathing was synced, and their hearts were beating as one, hard and fast. In that moment, she realised that she needed to be loved. A tear trickled down her cheek as she held on to the only person she wanted to be with. She cried quietly. Mia looked up, took her face into her hands and kissed her tears.

"I love you so much," Ava whispered, again.

63

GRAZELEY, UK

"Hi Mum, Dad." Mia gave both her parents a hug. "This is Ava."

Mia's mother seemed timid as she shook Ava's hand. "It's very nice to meet you Ava."

Ava gave her a warm smile in an attempt to put her at ease. "It's very nice to meet you too, Mrs. Donoghue."

"Please don't call me that." The woman, who bore no resemblance to Mia whatsoever, let out a chuckle. "My name is Dot."

"Okay, Dot it is." Ava watched Dot retract her trembling hand. She was about Mia's height, but slightly heavier. She had blue eyes and a short, bleached coupe, carefully styled with generous amounts of hair gel. She was wearing a black sleeveless dress with a floral print that looked a bit too tight for her, and black pumps. Her round face was normally friendly, Ava guessed by looking at the crow's feet around her eyes, but right now she looked nervous as hell, as she fiddled with her long, painted nails. "Thank you for having me."

"It's no bother dear. It's exciting to have you both over.

We haven't seen Mia in a while and she certainly never brings..." Dot hesitated, cracking her brain over what word to use. "Friends home," she finally said. "I mean, women." Dot continued to concentrate on her red nails until she suddenly remembered they were in the middle of introductions. "Oh, and this is my husband, Ron."

Mia's father, a tall slender man with dark eyes, shook Ava's hand and mumbled something Ava couldn't understand. He seemed in a worse state than his wife, but at least he had his big beard to hide behind.

Mia watched her parents struggle and felt sorry for them. It wasn't their fault that she'd never brought anybody home. She'd kept that part of herself away from them, and so they'd never been given the chance to get used to the fact that she dated women.

"Shall we go into the living room?" She suggested, saving them all from a painful silence.

"Mia!" Ami came out of the bathroom as they crossed the hallway and gave Mia a hug before turning to Ava. To Ava's surprise, she got a hug too. "Good to see you again, Ava. I'm glad you're here."

"Have you two met?" Dot asked, mystified.

"Yes." Ami squeezed Ava's arm. "We met a little while ago." She left it at that as she walked ahead into the living room where the table was already laid out for Sunday lunch.

"It smells great, Mum," Mia said in an attempt to clear the awkwardness. "What are we having?"

"Chicken and roast potatoes with carrots, peas and gravy," Dot said, nodding towards the kitchen. "And bread and butter pudding for desert. It's almost done." She turned to Ava again and looked her in the eyes this time. "Do you eat meat, Ava? I completely forgot to ask, but then again Mia didn't mention anything about..."

"Don't worry, Dot." Ava put a hand on Dot's arm. "I'll eat just about anything and right now, I can't think of anything better than a roast. Do you need help in the kitchen?"

Dot's eyes widened, as if Ava had just proposed something absurd. "No thank you, dear. I'm quite alright. Just sit down and enjoy yourself."

"I'll give you a hand, Dot," Mia's father said, slipping out of the living room. Judging from the surprised look on his wife's face, Ava wondered if he'd ever set a foot in the kitchen, let alone offered to help.

"Oh my God, they're so awkward," Ami whispered after both their parents were out of sight.

"What did you expect?" Mia said. She would have laughed about the situation if it wasn't for the talk they were about to have. "They've never seen me with a woman before and they have no idea how to behave."

"Why can't they just try to behave normally? Dad's eyes look like they're about to pop out." Ami laughed.

"Give them a break," Ava said. "This is hard for them and it's not going to get any easier today." She took Mia's hand under the table. "Are you okay?"

Mia nodded. "I think so. I just want to get it over with."

"Don't worry, they'll loosen up," Ami whispered. "They always do, after a couple of drinks." She smiled at Ava. "Dad likes a beer with his Sunday lunch and Mum drinks this disgusting sweet wine that..." She put a hand in front of her mouth, her eyes widening as she realised her mistake. "I'm so sorry, I completely forgot." She winced, looking at the bottle of wine on the table in front of them. "You're both..." She picked up the bottle. "Shall I take this away?"

"No, it's fine." Mia waved it off. "We're okay."

Ami grimaced. "Are you sure? Because I don't want either of you to feel uncomfortable."

"I serve alcohol to people in my job every day," Mia reassured her. "Believe me, I'm fine."

"Me too," Ava chipped in. She sat back and tried her best to look relaxed. Ami's presence helped – Ava felt comfortable around her, and she liked Mia's younger, cheeky sister. "So, how have you been, Ami?" she asked. "After the news I mean, about the team selection."

"I'm okay," Ami said, chewing on a fingernail. "I've been less exhausted, that's for sure. I have more energy to study now, and I met up with friends last weekend. It was fun." She turned to Mia, who looked mortified. "Mia you have to let it go. How many times do I have to tell you?"

"I'm trying." Mia managed a smile. "I'm really trying."

"Good," Ami continued. "Because I really need you to stop beating yourself up over this. It was a long time ago and I'm just happy to have you back in my life again." She sighed. "I'm going to try for the team again next year by the way, but I'll make sure I keep my life balanced, so I don't overdo it on all fronts. If I don't make it then, I'm going to give up and just swim for fun. I've realised that life can be quite nice when you have time to enjoy it."

"I CAN'T REMEMBER the last time you were here for Sunday lunch, Mia," Dot said as she put down the chicken for her husband to carve.

"I don't think I do either," Mia said, hesitantly. "I'm sorry I haven't been around much."

"Don't apologize, dear. I know you're always away, and I know how much you love your job. We're happy for you, aren't we, Ron?" She sat down and turned her attention to Ava, a little more prepared this time.

"So, Ava," she said, clearing her throat. "I hear you two met at work. Mia tells me you're a captain."

"I am." Ava handed her plate to Dot. "We work for the same airline, although our shifts don't overlap that often."

"That must be hard, flying a plane," Ron mumbled in an attempt to join the conversation. He held up a bottle. "Would you like a beer Ava, or do you prefer wine? My wife has an excellent white if you'd like to try it. Nice and sweet, she says. Never tried it myself, I don't like wine."

"No thank you, I don't drink." Ava gave him a polite smile.

"Okay. More for me, then." Ron poured a beer for himself. "Do you mind if I ask why? Is it something to do with your religion?"

"No, it's nothing like that," Ava said. "I'm in the program. The AA." She exhaled slowly. It was terrifying, saying it out loud. But she was here to support Mia, no matter what.

"Oh." Ron paused to think for a moment. He stopped pouring the beer into his glass and put the bottle back down. Dot stared at Ava, almost scooping the potatoes onto the table. "Does that mean you're..." He hesitated. "Eh... an alcoholic?"

"I'm a recovering alcoholic," Ava answered, "That's why I don't drink anymore."

"Right." Ron looked to his wife for help, but Dot avoided his gaze. "And the airline lets you fly, like this?"

"Dad, she's still got her arms and legs, of course she can fly." Ami rolled her eyes. "You guys sometimes..."

"No, it's fine, Ron. It's a question I get asked a lot," Ava lied. No one had ever asked her the question before, because no one knew. "I don't drink anymore, so I'm absolutely fine to fly. I'm not unstable. I've been sober for a long time now, and I've learned to deal with difficult situations." She gestured to his beer. "It's okay," she said with a chuckle. "You can drink that beer in front of me. I'm not going to be tempted or upset."

Dot concentrated on the carrots now, plating as slow as she possibly could, trying to delay the moment she would have to join the conversation. Finally, she stopped topping up Ava's plate, its contents enough to feed a whole family. She passed Ava the plate.

"Thank you, Dot. I'm not sure if I can finish all of this but it looks delicious." Ava managed a smile as she stared at the tower of food in front of her and then turned to Mia, encouraging her to say something.

Mia winced at her and shrugged. She looked terrified, and Ava felt sorry for her.

"Are you seeing a psychiatrist, Ava?" Ron asked.

Ava tried not to laugh, despite the serious subject matter. "If you mean a psychologist, Ron, then no, I'm not seeing one. The AA meetings are enough for me. I go once a week, wherever I am in the world. They keep me focussed."

"Maybe we should talk about something else, Ron," Dot said, desperately trying to steer the conversation in a less controversial direction. "How about your parents, Ava? What do they do?"

"Actually, Mum, I think we should stick to the current subject." Mia looked at both her parents, gathering every ounce of strength she had in her. "I'm a recovering alcoholic too. That's what I wanted to tell you both."

As expected, there was a silence at the table. Her mother looked confused at first, then her face pulled into a horrified grimace. She put the serving spoon back into the bowl with the carrots and sat down. Her father just stared at her, expressionless.

"I'm telling you this," she continued, "because I want to be honest with you both. I don't want to avoid coming home on weekends anymore and continue making up excuses, lying to you about why I don't drink. I want us to be able to talk about things."

"You're not an alcoholic, Mia," her mother said in a thin voice. "Look at you. You're a beautiful functioning young woman with a steady job. Sure, you might have had some problems when you were younger, but we've dealt with that. It was erratic, adolescent behaviour. You know better now."

"If you mean that you dealt with my problems at the time by sending me to rehab for two months, sure," Mia said, ignoring her mother's warning looks. "But that was only because I had to undergo some form of treatment under the terms of the court order. And when I returned, you automatically assumed that everything had been magically solved and you made me stick my head in the sand, made me pretend nothing had ever happened. That awful moment was never talked about again, ever. As long as no one knew, nothing had ever happened. You thought the problem had been buried."

"Mia, we are not going to go there, do you hear me?" Dot's eyes widened, indicating that the discussion was over.

"Your mother is right. You're not an alcoholic," her father said. "I never worry about you, you're always busy and away, out and about. We've never have to lend you money or help you out. You're stable. How could you possibly be an alcoholic?"

"Oh, so just because you can't see it, you refuse to recognise it's there?" Mia raised her voice. "What about Ava? She's a pilot, for God's sake. You might not be able to see it, but the struggle is real. Every single day. I'm trying to be open with the both of you, you don't seem to realise how many sleepless nights I've had over this. I've been nervous all week worrying over how to tell you and now that I've finally found the courage, you're trying to brush it under the carpet as usual. How do you think that makes me feel? Did you not wonder why I never come home on weekends? Or why I dodge birthdays and celebrations? Or why I move around all the time? Why I don't have many friends? Why I never go out? Or why you haven't had dinner with me in a restaurant since my seventeenth birthday?" She paused. "I'm very good at hiding my addiction because I learned from the best."

There was a silence. Her parents exchanged glances, both looking more than uncomfortable now.

Mia looked at Ami, who gave her an encouraging nod. "I told Ami what happened," she continued. "I told her that I almost killed her. She knows everything now."

Dot blinked a couple of times before the tears came. She looked from Mia to Ami and back, panic written all over her face.

"Why didn't you tell me, Mum?" Ami shifted her gaze. "Dad?" She paused. "I asked you last month, when I realised my arm was playing up again. We had a conversation and I asked you if you could think of any reason my arm should be weaker on that side, no matter how hard I trained. And you told me you didn't have a clue. Why keep it quiet? And why did you tell Mia to keep it to herself? She's been carrying this secret with her for years, avoiding me because she couldn't face me." Ami had tears in her eyes now too. "I understand you were trying to protect us, and that you wanted us to have a good relationship, but your strategy sure as hell backfired. I'm only just getting to know Mia now, and you have no idea how great that feels." She started crying. "To finally have a sister who wants to spend time with me."

"Please, Ami." Mia stood up and took Ami into a hug. It felt so good to be able to hold her and to comfort her. "It's not their fault. They were just doing what they thought was best for us. This is a conversation, not a fight. We need to talk."

"It wasn't our intention for you to grow apart," Dot sobbed. "The doctors said there might be permanent damage to your arm and we didn't want you to blame Mia. But then you grew up to be so strong and healthy, so we didn't feel the need to tell you about it at all."

Mia's father cleared his throat. "We were trying to protect you both," he said in an unsteady voice. "And Mia, we saved your future don't you see that? Who would have hired you knowing you had a drinking problem, and was also a drug addict who almost killed her sister? You'd already been kicked out of university, and had been banned from driving for two years, so your chances of a decent future were already slim. Then there was the village, what would the people here think of you if they knew?"

"I know you did that for me," Mia said. "And I am grateful that you are both amazing parents who always had my best interests at heart." She stopped, fighting the tears as she bit down on her trembling lip. "But what I really need to know is that you've forgiven me for what I did to Ami. Because I'm in this great place right now, with Ava and Ami, and with my job, but I can't move forward unless we talk about this. There's always been this shadow hanging over me..." She swallowed hard, trying not to cry. "I've always had this fear that you hated me for what I did, even though you've always been kind to me."

"How could we hate you?" Dot looked hurt. "We love

you more than anything, Mia. Both of you." She looked Mia in the eyes, then down at her plate before she burst into tears again. "We only wanted the best for you," she sobbed. "And now you're an alcoholic because of us."

"No Mum, that's not true," Mia said, raising her voice. "My drinking problems have nothing to do with you and Dad. It started long before the accident. I mean, it's the whole reason *why* it happened. There's no one to blame for my problem but me. I'm just one of those people." She hesitated for a moment, stood up and walked around the table to give her mother a warm hug from the back. It had been years since she'd done that. Dot took Mia's forearms and pulled them closer against her chest. Her whole body was shaking.

"I'm so sorry. I should have seen you were struggling, and I should have helped you." Dot sniffled.

"You don't need to apologize." Mia kissed her mother on the top of her head. "I just need to know that you've forgiven me."

"Of course we've forgiven you," Dot said in a thin voice, the sobbing subsiding a little. "It was an accident. We were angry with you, sure. But we also saw your pain, and how you suffered while Ami was in hospital." She shook her head. "But I'm not going to lie, Mia. I felt relieved when the court sent you to rehab. We had enough on our plate with Ami, and we didn't have the energy to deal with you on top of that. I know we should have talked about it, but we just wanted everything to go back to normal. I'm sorry for that." Dot tightened her grip on Mia's arms. "But we forgave you a long time ago."

Mia felt relief wash over her, and she pressed her cheek against her mother's. "Thank you," she said in a soft voice. "I love you, Mum." Then she walked over to her father, whose eyes were filled with tears too. She'd never seen him emotional like that.

"Come here, Mia," he said as he stood up, holding out his arms. Mia walked into the embrace. "And you too, Ami." Ami joined them in an awkward three-way hug. "We love you both so much. And we're so proud of you." Mia smiled as they let go of each other. In those ten minutes more had been said than in the past thirteen years, and it felt as if a wall had lifted between them.

"Are you okay, Mum?" she asked when she'd sat back down next to Ava.

Dot nodded and wiped her face. "I'm okay, sweetie. I'm glad we've talked about this, and that you and Ami are fine." She sniffed again. "But you've also just told me you're an alcoholic, and that breaks my heart." Her lip started to tremble.

"I'm a *recovering* alcoholic, Mum, like Ava. And we're doing well, both of us." Mia took her mother's hand over the table. "There is an open meeting in two weeks' time, in a church in Chatham, and I'd like you both to come with me."

"You go to church?" Dot asked in surprise.

Mia shook her head. "No, but the meeting is in a church, and it's open to friends and family." She paused. "Listen, I just want this out in the open, that's all. I don't want you to worry about me, and I don't want you to be ashamed of me. All I want is for you both to join me, just once, so you know how it works. After that we can leave this behind us and move on, because it doesn't define who I am. But it is a big part of me that I've always kept to myself, and I want to be honest with you now. I'm not going to tell anyone else, and I don't want anyone else to know. The only other people who know this about me are Ava, Ami and my neighbour Tuesday."

"I'm going to invite my parents too," Ava said in an attempt to help Mia. "They don't know about my situation either, but I'm going to tell them." Dot and Ron both looked up at her.

"Aren't you afraid it will upset them?" Dot asked.

Ava shrugged. "Of course. Just like Mia was afraid before she came here today. But I've got the feeling they'll be okay. The fear is mainly mine, I think. It's really scary to tell people who are close to you. My brother knows and is very supportive. And Mia will be there too, of course." She squeezed Mia's hand under the table.

"Ava's brother is Zaid Alfarsi," Mia said in an attempt to lighten the mood.

"Nooooooooooo! The hot motivational speaker?" Ami's eyes widened to the size of golf balls. "Is that true, Ava?"

Ava laughed. "Yes, Zaid is my brother."

"Will he be there too, at the meeting? Because if he's coming, I want to come too. Is he single?" Ami asked.

"He has a girlfriend," Ava said, grinning. "And no, he won't be coming. I don't want to attract unnecessary attention to myself or to Mia. His presence tends to do that. But I'm sure I can introduce you at some point, if you'd really like to meet him."

"Really? I'd love that! So, what's he like in real life?" Ami continued her interrogation. Mia was grateful for Ami's enthusiasm, now that the hardest part of the conversation was over. She looked around the table as Ava talked to Ami, feeling emotionally exhausted, but also very blessed to have so many people in her life who cared about her. Her parents were shocked and upset, but they were finally opening up and, more importantly, she knew they'd forgiven her. Her mother was listening in on Ami and Ava's conversation, clearly intrigued by the idea of having a celebrity in their midst, but too drained to join in. Her father was sitting back, sipping his beer, engrossed in his own thoughts. And her sister was there by her side, and Mia knew she would always be there for Ami, no matter what. She watched Ava smile and her heart lit up. She was so beautiful that Mia sometimes found it hard to look at her without losing herself. Despite the relief she was feeling now that she'd come clean to her parents, Mia couldn't wait to get home. They still had a lot to discuss, but now wasn't the time. Her parents would need to talk to each other, and to Ami. Everything needed to be processed and that was fine. Soon, she and Ava would take the train back to London and go to Ava's place to spend another amazing night together before they would fly to their separate destinations in the morning, and Mia wanted to make the most of it. She put a hand on Ava's thigh, a sign that she was ready to leave soon, and Ava covered it with her own, letting her know that she had received the hint.

EPILOGUE –KUALA LUMPUR, MALAYSIA

The Golden Lily in Kuala Lumpur was busy. Although the tourist season was now over, there was a big manufacturing conference in town and most of the hotels were full to the brim with businessmen, suffering from the heat in their suits and ties. It was late, and Mia was lying on one of the benches in the Palm Garden, resting her head on Ava's lap, after a fun dinner with some of their colleagues.

"I'm starting to get used to this place," she said, listening to the hotel's playlist that never changed its selection of classical tunes. She hummed along to the melody.

"I'm starting to get used to you," Ava replied, bending forward and planting a soft kiss on her lips. She looked around to make sure no one had noticed and grinned. "That was an insightful conversation tonight. I had no idea everyone knew about us."

"I guess they put two and two together." Mia chuckled. "I keep requesting the same flights as you, and I'm always coming out of your hotel in the morning. I don't think it was that hard to figure out." She pulled Ava's face down into another kiss. "I suppose it doesn't help that I'm unable to take my eyes off you either." She stared up into Ava's green eyes.

Ava's mouth pulled into a smile when their eyes locked. "Same here. At least it's out in the open now, no point hiding it anymore." She sighed. "Anyway, I was getting tired of sneaking around. I'm proud to have you as my girlfriend and I'm also proud that everyone knows I'm with the most gorgeous woman in the world."

"You're such a charmer." Mia pulled a strand of hair away from Ava's face and twirled it around her finger. "But you have Farik to thank for that." Farik had brought it up during dinner at a shabby karaoke restaurant that he'd chosen for his own selfish reasons. Still on a high from getting a big round of applause after singing a Disney ballad, he'd pointed to Mia and Ava and said: "And now it's time for you two lovebirds to do a song." Not that there was much space left for them to do a performance – Farik had put his name down seventeen times, pissing off the locals who'd had to wait for Farik to finish each time they wanted to have a go. After his comment eight pairs of eyes had stared at them, delighted that the long-standing gossip had been confirmed, as neither of them had denied it. Mia had given Ava a kiss on her cheek and Ava had grinned sheepishly.

Mia's phone beeped, and she picked it up to check who was messaging her. She laughed when she opened the picture Lynn had sent her, and handed her phone to Ava.

"Really? Are they still together?" Ava pulled the phone closer and winced at the picture of Lynn in a bikini and Captain Bob Slender in his swim trunks with his arm around her on a beach, sipping cocktails with the sun setting in the background, with the caption: *Greetings from*

Barbados. "I gave them a week, but it's been what... a year now?"

"Something like that," Mia said. "Lynn likes to keep me updated on her longest relationship ever. They seem happy together though, don't you think?"

"I'd be happy, if I was him," Ava joked. "But I'm not sure what's in it for Lynn, or how his grown-up kids feel about their new step-mum." She took another look at the picture, studying their faces, ignoring Bob's hand resting on Lynn's breast. "But yeah, I suppose you're right, they do look happy." Mia's phone beeped again. "It's your Mum," Ava said, handing Mia her phone back.

"Fuck. Don't open it then, she'll know that I've read her message." Mia locked her phone and put it back in her bag. "She probably just wants pictures." She sighed. "Mum wants to be involved in everything since you set up that group chat with us and our parents. That was by far your worst idea ever, by the way."

"I know." Ava grinned. "I have to keep my phone on silent now, because the messaging never stops. Even my Dad is constantly on it. Did you see that trumpet video he sent today?"

"I'm afraid I did," Mia said playfully. "My eardrums are still hurting. I'm glad you suggested we'd all go out for dinner after that open AA meeting though. It's crazy how well our parents get along now, isn't it, considering they're different species entirely. My Mum even attempted to cook some of your mother's family recipes last week, but she couldn't find half of the ingredients in their village, so she substituted them for whatever she had in her cupboard with the same colour. I can tell you, Ami and I had a rough time getting through that meal."

Ava laughed. "All I can say is, I'm glad I wasn't there."

She stroked Mia's hair, the way she knew Mia liked it. "But joking aside, I'm glad it all went so well. If an overload of texts is our biggest problem, then I'd say we're pretty lucky."

"You're right." Mia stared up at Ava lovingly. "I feel lucky. I had no idea how truly amazing it would be, waking up in your arms most mornings, knowing that everything is just the way it's supposed to be." She fell silent for a moment. "I can't begin to tell you how much you mean to me."

Ava placed a tender kiss on her forehead. "You don't need to tell me, Mia. I know." She held her gaze for a moment, before turning her head and staring into the garden. "Hey, do you want to go for that walk you promised me? See our little friends, if they're still there? They tend to disappear towards the end of the year, when it gets colder."

"Okay." Mia stood up and rolled her shoulders. "I'm sure they'll be there. It's still really warm and humid."

Ava walked over to the fountain and splashed some cold water on her face. "Warm is an understatement. It feels like high summer."

"It does." Mia handed Ava a tissue from her bag to dry her hands, but she'd already used the scarce fabric of her cotton khaki-coloured shorts to do that. "But I'm not complaining." Mia used the tissue to dab her forehead instead. "I like seeing you in tiny outfits."

"Oh yeah?" Ava shot her a cheeky grin. "Well I happen to like seeing you in that short white dress you're wearing. You want to know why?"

"I think I know why." Mia jumped up and giggled when Ava reached under the hem of her dress and grabbed her ass as they walked towards the back of the garden.

They sat down on a pile of leaves they'd gathered on the damp ground and switched on the torches of their phones.

It was a ritual they'd developed over the many times they'd been here together. As soon as the lights were on, the fireflies came towards them, curiously checking out the mystery light source. The insects circled them and came a little closer when Ava started switching her torch on and off. Mia held her hand out over her phone until one of them settled on the back of her hand, still blinking.

"I think he likes you," Ava said. "He's certainly trying to impress you."

"It looks like it." Mia brought her face closer, marvelling at the brightness of the light the tiny insect produced. "Hey little man, do you want to be my friend?" The firefly blinked one more time before flying off.

"I guess not." Mia chuckled.

"Don't worry, here's another little shimmering guy, all by himself." Ava bent forward, pretending to pick up a firefly from the forest floor. When she straightened herself and opened her palms, it wasn't a firefly that was shimmering in her hands. Mia narrowed her eyes as she studied the object. Suddenly, her face pulled into a mixture of surprise and delight.

"It's a ring," she gasped. "Is that for me?" She teared up and swallowed down the lump in her throat, overwhelmed by the unexpected gesture.

"If you'll accept it," Ava said in a soft voice. She held the ring up as their eyes locked and took a deep breath. "I love you, Mia," she said. "You're my light. You're the one for me. I feel strong every day, because you give my life meaning. You make me happy, and you give me a reason to stay sober and to be the best person I can be." She swallowed hard, fighting her emotions. She wanted to say it, needed to say it all. "You've been sober for fourteen months now and I want you to know that I'm so proud of you. But I also want you to know that I'll continue to support you whatever happens, just as I know that you'll always be there for me." Her voice broke. "Because who knows? Life is long, right, if we're lucky. And anything can happen. But as long as we have each other, I know we'll be okay." A tear rolled down her cheek. Mia took Ava's face in her hands and kissed it away. She smiled, her vision blurred by her own tears.

"Are you asking me what I think you're asking me?" she whispered.

"I'm sorry," Ava continued, shaking her head with a smile. "I almost forgot the most important part." She took a hold of Mia's hand and lifted it. "Mia, beautiful Mia... will you please marry me?"

Mia was silent for a moment, still processing what was happening. Then she nodded, grinning from ear to ear. "Yes," she said. "Of course I'll marry you. It's all I've ever wanted."

"You have no idea how happy that makes me." Ava slid the diamond ring on Mia's finger. "Thank you."

"It's beautiful," Mia said, admiring the ring, before leaning into Ava. "I can't believe this is happening." She brushed her lips over Ava's. "I love you so much."

Ava couldn't stop smiling. "And I can't believe you're going to be my wife." She weaved her hands through Mia's hair as she kissed her, quietly moaning when Mia straddled her lap and deepened the kiss. She traced Mia's arms and felt goose bumps appear on her skin as they sank into each other in the dim lights of their phones and the flickering fireflies. Mia shivered when she pulled away from Ava's mouth and looked into her green eyes that had turned dark now. She knew that look all too well and it did things to her she couldn't even begin to describe. Nothing had changed, and before she knew it, the familiar stir of arousal began to settle in her core, making her ache for more.

Ava traced Mia's cheek and her jaw, skimming her fingers down to the pool of her cleavage, where she let them rest for a moment, before tugging her closer by the neckline of her dress. "Do you want to go up to my room?"

"Yeah. I really, really do, Captain," Mia said through ragged breathing. A smile played around her mouth as she admired her ring again. They stood up and cast one last glance at the fireflies, before they picked up their phones and turned off the lights.

ACKNOWLEDGMENTS

First and foremost, I'd like to give a huge thanks to Claire Jarrett, my editor. I'm sorry you had to suffer from my lack of organisation but I want you to know how much your patience and time are appreciated. I love working with you and your involvement and input have made the writing process a whole lot more enjoyable. I'm learning from you every day.

Laure Dherbécourt, my beta reader, thank you for being so flexible and thorough, for making me laugh through your notes, and for teaching me basic facts about nature and the compass rose :)

My friend, Captain Brooke Castillo (and in case you are wondering, yes, she is a badass, hot, female captain:)), you've been super helpful by giving me insights into the mysterious world of the cockpit. I still owe you a karaoke session!

My friend, Elle Simmons, you've kept me hugely entertained with your extensive insider knowledge of airline procedures and juicy cabin stories we passengers are not supposed to know about. Let's keep up with the Skype-and-wine!

Zainab Nassir, thank you for educating me about life in Jordan. It's the first country I've written about that I haven't visited but now I'm intrigued and I want to go there!

And most of all, I'd like to thank Emilie Bruff and all the other wonderful people I've spoken to who are struggling with alcoholism for being so open and honest with me and enabling me to build a picture of what it's like to be a recovering alcoholic. Our conversations have been invaluable, and I was touched by your stories. I wish you all the strength and love in the world.

ABOUT THE AUTHOR

Lise Gold is an author of lesbian fiction. Her romantic attitude, enthusiasm for travel and love for feel good stories form the heartland of her writing. Lise's novels are the result of a quest for a new passion, after spending fourteen years working as a designer. Lise lives in the UK with her wife.

ALSO BY LISE GOLD

Lily's Fire

Beyond the Skyline

The Cruise

French Summer

30533167R00224

Made in the USA
Lexington, KY
10 February 2019